Geniuses

NEIL W. FLANZRAICH

authorHOUSE®

AuthorHouse™ LLC
1663 Liberty Drive
Bloomington, IN 47403
www.authorhouse.com
Phone: 1-800-839-8640

Front cover illustration by Joshua Allen.

Published by AuthorHouse 08/01/2014

ISBN: 978-1-4918-4952-1 (sc)
ISBN: 978-1-4918-4953-8 (hc)
ISBN: 978-1-4918-4954-5 (e)

Library of Congress Control Number: 2014900260

This book is dedicated to my love, Kirochka.

Contents

The Past Is Prologue

A heavy mist rose from the bog, all but blotting out the night sky and allowing the full moon to illuminate the marsh with an eerie yellow glow. The old man trod carefully along the muddy path. A dog howled somewhere off in the distance. Behind him, flames engulfed a castle, yet another sign of terrible defeat. His lungs fought the fog and smoke for what little oxygen the dense air offered.

The cold night chilled him to the marrow of his ancient bones. One hand grasped the walking stick that he used to support his uncertain steps; the other pulled his heavy woolen cloak and hood tighter around his tall body. He felt the familiar ping and knew he was getting nearer. Finally, he reached the cave. He bent low to pass through the small opening, his long white beard dragging along the ground.

Once inside, he could stand again. From a pocket inside his cloak he drew forth a torch, which he lighted with a single thought. The cave was instantly illuminated. The light of the torch shone on the thick golden hair of his old friend, who lay wounded and dying not twenty feet in front of him. On the ground next to his pierced body were a sword and golden shield, the latter emblazoned with the man's coat of arms and his signature double *R* crest. He hurried to his friend's side and, with difficulty, knelt beside him.

"Sir Reginald, I received your cry for help from a far off part of the kingdom. What has happened to you, my dear friend?"

"Thank God you're here," his wounded friend said. "I'm dying. I will not last the night. How goes the battle?"

"Before I speak of the tragic end to our noble dream," the old man said sadly, "tell me what befell you, Sir Reginald."

"If the great King Arthur's kingdom is lost, I have no more claim on knighthood," Reginald said. "I am but a defeated and lost man, stripped of all but his last breath."

"Nay, old friend. For me, you will always be a great knight, Sir Reginald Reynolds, trusted friend to our liege lord, Arthur the King."

The bearded man looked upon his friend with sorrow, afraid to speak the terrible question that he knew he had to ask. "Your castle is ablaze. What has happened to you and your family?"

Sir Reginald could barely breathe through his terrible grief and the pain of approaching death.

"My beloved wife Rowena and my sweet young daughter Rachel were brutally murdered. The fiend who killed them also mortally wounded me. He left me for dead. With the last of my strength I escaped the castle and crawled to this ignoble grave."

By the light of the torch, the white-bearded man could see blood in his friend's ears. A huge red stain covered his chest. His golden eyebrows arched over blue eyes clouded with the specter of death.

"Sir Reginald, who did this great villainy?"

"He is one of our breed," Reginald replied. "He came from another land. I felt the ping. He asked me for help, which I gave freely. I trusted him and shared all that we had and all that I knew of our kind. I treated him as a friend, as part of my family."

After pausing to catch his breath, the knight continued, "Over time I came to learn that he was far older and far more powerful than I had realized. He seemed to share our chivalry. He claimed to hate tyranny as much as we. But when the fighting began, instead of siding with us to preserve freedom and protect the Ordinaries, he joined the traitor Mordred and the evil ones fighting with him. He turned on us without warning. He killed my family and has ended my life. He wants to destroy all we stand for."

Reginald paused to draw upon the last of his strength. "My only solace is that this beast does not know of my young son, Richard, who left home two years ago to seek his fortune."

With the last of his strength, Reginald grasped the old man's arm and looked deeply into his eyes. "Tell me, dear friend, will Richard, will my line, the Reynolds line, continue? Use your powers to look into the future and tell me what you see. Will my family be avenged? Will Camelot be restored?"

Reginald coughed violently, spitting blood. "Tell me, old friend, before I join my ancestors, will justice be done?"

His friend's pain and imminent end weighed upon the old man like the heavy cloak of death.

"Brave knight, I cannot say whether my words will comfort you, but I will look into the dim mists of the future and tell you what I see."

He clasped Reginald's right hand, held it tight, closed his eyes, and trembled before his vision.

"Merlin, do you see anything?" Reginald asked as death raced toward him like a hungry wolf.

"Yes, Sir Reginald. The distant future opens to me. This is what I see."

Chapter 1
First Day of School— The Fair

On a cold afternoon in early September, with the sky gray, and sullen, Jason Phillips stood on a grassy rise that overlooked the athletic field that served as the site for the Laurel Glen High School fair.

Phillips, a new teacher at the school, was six feet tall and handsome, with piercing brown eyes, a square jaw, and a lean, athletic frame. Anyone guessing his age would have placed him in his early forties, and indeed his dark brown hair was free of gray and his face largely unlined. He wore a brown tweed jacket, a pale blue shirt and tie, dark brown slacks, and matching wingtips. On his left wrist was an antique Rolex watch, with a round pale yellow face and brown leather band.

Phillips's outfit was appropriate for an ordinary day in September, but this day was anything but ordinary. A cold wind ripped loose anything that wasn't tied down and colored the faces of those who were outdoors, including Phillips's. His cheeks and nose, ordinarily on the pale side, were ruddy and raw.

Laurel Glen was a private high school located in Golden Gables, Maryland, an affluent suburb of Washington, DC. One hundred and twenty five years old, it had an excellent reputation as a college preparatory school. The campus was dominated by the ivy-covered Laurel building. Built in the Victorian Gothic style, it was named for the school's benefactor, Rutherford Laurel, who made a fortune in shipping and banking. Most classes were held in the Laurel building and its two modern wings, which had been added to the nineteenth century structure.

Some seventy-five yards in front of the Laurel building was a small, man-made lake. To the right of the lake was a three-story red-brick building where the library, cafeteria, and student center were located. The building, known simply as the student center, was accented on the right-front corner by an octagonal glass turret that served as a large sunroom and café. To the left of the lake was a modern gymnasium, and behind the gym was another old gray Gothic building that served as the dormitory for the residential students.

At the front of the campus stood a large Victorian house. Known throughout the campus community as the Betsy Building, or simply the Betsy, it was named for Laurel's wife. Once the home of Rutherford and his family, the Betsy now housed the school's administration. The Laurel building and the Betsy served as the two poles of the campus, with the Betsy standing at the north end of the campus and the Laurel at the south. The athletic field, which that day was covered with booths and tables for the annual school fair, was located to the south of the Laurel building.

Thanks to the school's irregular topography, the main campus stood above the playing fields. In order to get from the campus to the fields below, one had to walk down a winding cobblestone path. Near the bottom of the path was a grassy rise, which was where Phillips stood.

It was the first day of the school year. The purpose of the fair was to introduce students to the wide variety of extracurricular activities the school offered and to allow the clubs to recruit new members. More than fifty tables and booths stood in a large rectangle. All the school clubs were represented, including those for math, chess, glee, debate, hiking, drama, and languages. Not to be outdone, the basketball, soccer, lacrosse, track, volleyball, and tennis teams had set up booths as well, though their presence served more as a reminder to the students that they were still the most important organizations at the school. The fair also gave students the chance to get to know one another and to meet their teachers in an informal setting.

"Hello, Dr. Phillips," Dorothy Van Doren called out, striding toward Phillips with an energetic, military gait. She was in her mid-fifties, of average height and well proportioned, if slightly cylindrical. Her hair was brown and, thanks to a recent visit to her stylist, free of gray. Her eyes were small and bright, her mouth turned up slightly at the edges, her face well-lined but firm. Dorothy Van Doren was the school's assistant headmistress, a post she had held for five years, as well as the school's primary teacher of European and American literature. She had taught those courses for twenty years. She was the key figure on the committee that had brought Phillips to Laurel Glen. She and her fellow committee members had interviewed him three times and felt certain of their choice, but Dorothy did acknowledge privately that he had an enigmatic bearing and was still very much a mystery.

Phillips was well qualified, to be sure. He had two PhDs, one in political science and another in the Greek classics. He had been teaching at Montgomery Community College in Rockville, Maryland, a suburb of Washington, DC, but said he had grown tired of teaching adult education and wanted to reach younger students.

As she approached him on the knoll, with occasional gusts of wind whipping his hair, she saw again his solitary and cautious nature, and felt the intimation of secrets in his deep-set eyes.

Involuntarily, a memory came to mind of her telephone call to one of the people Phillips had offered as a reference—Dr. William Clifford, a legendary professor of comparative religions at George Washington University. Clifford had been at George Washington for thirty years and was widely regarded as one of the preeminent religious scholars in America. He was also a moral force in academia, having been a leader in numerous causes, and was often invited to speak at conferences that featured the likes of the Dalai Lama, Elie Wiesel, and Thich Nhat Hanh. Dorothy was herself a graduate of George Washington University, and as an active alumna had known of Dr. Clifford for many years. She had even attended public lectures by the renowned professor.

The appearance of Dr. Clifford's name on Phillips's resume had caught Dorothy's eye during her cursory perusal of a tall stack of applications, causing her to pause. "Hello," she'd said out loud, though no one was in her office at the time. "Now who is this Mr. Phillips who has the temerity to invoke one of the academic gods as a reference?" She looked more carefully at Phillips's resume and then corrected herself. "Oh, I see, *Doctor* Phillips. *Double* Doctor Phillips. Hmmm."

She picked up the phone, called George Washington University, and was put through to Dr. William Clifford, who, much to her surprise, actually picked up the telephone.

She introduced herself and told Clifford the purpose of her call. Instantly, the great man became enthusiastic.

"He's absolutely one of the most brilliant people I have ever met. Don't be put off by his private nature, Mrs. Van Doren. If you manage to land him, he'll be the best hire you'll ever make in your life."

"How do you know him, Dr. Clifford?" she asked.

"It's a rather curious story. He wrote a lengthy and brilliant critique of one of my books, *The Goddess and the Origins of Religion*. Now mind you, I get letters from colleagues and critics from all over the world. Most of them are potshots or chest thumping, if you want to know the truth of it. But what Jason Phillips wrote was beyond any doubt the most illuminating and inspiring piece of writing I had ever read on a subject that, to be honest, I know a thing or two about. With little effort, his letter could have been published as a major article in any relevant professional journal, including the *Harvard Theological Review*. But rather than publish his piece, which I dare say might have challenged me with its insight and erudition, he offered the piece to me 'with the hope that it might make some small contribution to your thinking.' That's a direct quote from his letter to me.

"Well, I had to meet this man," Clifford continued. "So I wrote him back immediately and asked him if he wouldn't like to meet and have a chat. He was at Montgomery Community College, just a thirty-minute drive from me. We met for dinner one night and had the most remarkable conversation. I'm too old to mince words, my dear, so I'll speak frankly.

4

His knowledge of religion is vast—and I'm not exaggerating. He'd cite references to support a point, and he did it with such ease that it was as if he were reading them off his napkin. Also, he was able to relate religious subjects to physics, art, and archeology, as well as contemporary works of literature. You'd think that such a person would be arrogant and rather impossible to bear, but he was immensely humble, even understated, as if he was acknowledging that I already knew everything he was saying.

"We started meeting periodically over the course of about eighteen months. I showed him some of my work, which I was flattered to learn he had already read. I must admit that I picked his brain and he contributed generously to my thoughts on all kinds of subjects within my field."

Dr. Clifford's voice suddenly shifted from enthusiasm to intimacy, as if he were about to let Dorothy in on a secret.

"One thing I came to realize, Mrs. Van Doren. Jason never spoke about his personal life. Not a word. Nothing about a wife, children, parents, or where he might have grown up. Nothing. A couple of times, I tried to make gentle forays into his background, but he very politely put me off. I couldn't even get him to tell me how he had come to such a great knowledge of this field. Don't get me wrong, he went to good schools, but a man of his knowledge should be at the top of academic circles. I should have heard of him! No, no, he told me. The study of religion was just a hobby with him. He liked the subject, found it fascinating. I tried to get him to apply for a position at GW, but he wouldn't have it.

"Anyway, if you get him at your school, you've done a sight better than I did," Clifford said. "Believe me, you've got a real talent there."

Dorothy hung up the phone and released a long exhalation. "Wow," she said aloud. "That's about the highest praise I have ever heard, and from one of the preeminent figures in the world."

And so far, Clifford seemed right about everything, including the matter of privacy. Dorothy had done a thorough background check on Jason Phillips and found nothing but glowing reports everywhere he had worked or lived. He had no criminal record, not even a traffic ticket. His former employers sang his praises. He also had a history of volunteer work at community kitchens, homeless shelters, and as a tutor to adult students at the local community college.

During one of the hiring committee's interviews with Phillips, Dorothy asked him if he had ever been married. His curriculum vitae listed his marital status as single.

"Yes, quite a while ago," he said. His voice took on a lower note. "My wife died after a long struggle with cancer. We had no children and I decided afterwards that I was better off a bachelor."

"I'm sorry to hear that, Dr. Phillips," Dorothy said, and then returned to professional matters.

Now she was standing next to him on the grassy rise, with the wind gusting periodically like a hovering hawk.

"Thinking about making a foray into the mouth of hell?" she asked him, smiling.

Phillips returned the smile. "Oh, I've already charged the Cossacks, Mrs. Van Doren," he said, obviously catching her reference to Tennyson's "The Charge of the Light Brigade." "Just taking it all in from another perspective."

"Call me Dorothy," she replied, charmed by his response. "I think you'll find that we're an informal bunch around here...at least most of us."

"Okay," Phillips said. "Then Jason, if you will."

"It's too bad about the weather," she said. "It's unseasonably cold this year. I've never seen anything like it, to be honest."

Phillips seemed pensive for a moment, as if the comment might mean more to him than Dorothy expected or intended.

"Yes," he said. "It is strange, no doubt about it."

They took a minute to survey the seven hundred or so students milling about the field below them. Students wandered from booth to booth or gathered in cliques. Despite the heavier jackets and scarves demanded by the weather, each group was instantly recognizable. The cheerleaders and jocks—all of them blessed by nature with obvious beauty—occupied the center of the field, with the wannabes and the hangers-on orbiting the stars. The techno-geeks, spastic in their movements and ridiculous in their sudden outbursts of laughter, gathered around the table for the computer science and technology club. The intellectuals, many of them dressed as if they were ready for dinner at the Princeton club, raised their chins and spoke in rapid, breathy cadences, or stuffed their hands in their coat pockets and spoke through their scarves in faint imitation of Dylan and James Dean. Over near the trees were the Goths and vamps who, having rejected the entire scene, dressed in ripped jeans, layers of black tops, oversized coats, and black boots and found their inspiration in Edward Cullen and Bella of the *Twilight* series. And then there was the saddest group of all—the boys and girls who had no clique and no real home among the students. They wandered the grounds trying desperately to be invisible, and yet were conspicuous in their loneliness.

"They're a good bunch on the whole," Dorothy said. "Still, when I think about what's really going on down there, inside their hearts, I cannot help but feel terribly sympathetic for all the suffering at this age. High school is pure hell. All those cliques. Who's in this week, who's out the next. And then the suffering of those who are outcasts … Well, it's Dante's nine circles, Dr. Phillips. Dante's nine circles."

She was curious if he would get that literary reference as well.

"Perhaps," he said. "But I hope it's not that bad. After all, we do not have 'Lasciate ogni speranza, voi ch'entrate' on the sign by the gate into our school."

Dorothy could not help but laugh. As a lover of Dante's "Inferno" she knew that that Italian sentence was the last line on the inscription over the entrance to Hell, and it meant "Abandon all hope, ye who enter here".

But then Phillips turned to her and said, "But I agree there's certainly a lot of raging hormones and carnal fantasizing going on down there, Dorothy."

"So I see you've noticed Ronnie Urlacher too," she replied.

"The red-haired kid with the braces?" Phillips nodded in the direction of Urlacher.

"Yes, the one who is drooling over Mary Jane Wilson," Dorothy said. "She's a beautiful girl, but she hasn't got much self-esteem, and she dresses a little provocatively."

"Maybe I should go down there and save Ronnie from Dante's second circle," Phillips said.

Dorothy knew that in the *Inferno*, Dante wrote that that circle of hell was reserved for people whose lives were governed by lust. So Phillips was two for two. Maybe he really was as good as Dr. Clifford said.

She laughed as Phillips started toward the fairgrounds and the ogling Ronnie Urlacher. "You are an angel of mercy, Jason," she called jokingly after him.

But her amusement suddenly turned to concern. Phillips was no more than thirty yards away when she saw his face become creased with pain. He placed his right hand on his forehead as if to massage a searing headache. Dorothy almost ran after him to ask if he was all right, but remembered his private nature and thought better of it. Just as suddenly as it had arisen, the pain seemed to pass. Phillips clearly relaxed and resumed his walk toward the booths.

"How's our new man doing?" a voice said in Dorothy's ear.

She turned to see Carl Brimley, the school librarian, standing next to her. She hadn't even heard him approach.

"Oh, Carl, I didn't notice you there."

"Yes, I saw that you were very attentive to our new social studies teacher," Brimley said.

Carl Brimley was in his early sixties. He was round, short, and bald, with a profusion of curly salt-and-pepper hair that grew in ringlets along the sides of his head. "Oh, he's quite something, Carl," Dorothy said.

"What's he doing?" Carl asked.

"He's saving Ronnie Urlacher's soul."

"That's going to take a lot of doing," Carl said as he watched Urlacher gawk at Mary Jane Wilson.

Ronnie had taken a position some twenty feet behind Mary Jane Wilson and was ogling her as she filled out a form on the drama club table. Ronnie's thick red hair was standing up, thanks to the blustery wind, and his braces were fairly chattering from the cold.

He decided that a different vantage would give him a better angle from which to take in more of Mary Jane's beauty, so he walked over to the adjoining booth—which belonged to the Debating Club—and stationed himself at its far side. He took the club's sign-up sheet from under the rock that was serving as a paperweight. He held the sheet in front of his face, as he looked over the top of the sheet.

"Interested in debating, Ronnie?" a man asked him.

The words blindsided Ronnie, flustering him. He recognized the man standing beside him as the new teacher, Jason Phillips.

"Uh, yeah, as a matter of fact I am," he said, regaining his bravado.

"Then sign the sheet and move along."

"I'm still thinking about it," Ronnie said, certain that his cover was intact.

"You're not fooling anyone," Phillips said. "Now sign the sheet or move along. Since the school isn't handing out credits for gawking, I'd say that the practice will not help you one bit this semester."

Ronnie wilted, suddenly aware that he had been made. He put the sign-up sheet down, turned his back on Mary Jane, and walked away.

From the grassy knoll, Dorothy and Carl Brimley watched the scene play out.

"Well, mission accomplished," Brimley said. "Now, if we could get Mary Jane Wilson to dress a little more conservatively, we'd have one less problem."

She and Brimley watched Phillips walk toward a stand of pine trees at the far edge of the field.

"What's he doing now?" Carl said.

Both watched as Phillips pulled a cell phone from his jacket pocket. For a moment he stared at it, but then apparently decided against making a call. He put the phone back in his pocket, rubbed his forehead again, and headed off in the direction of the mathematics club booth.

"Well, that's enough checking out our new colleague for today," Brimley said with a smile. "But we will keep an eye on our mysterious friend, won't we, Dorothy? And get him to do something about this damned weather, if you can. This cold and wind! It's September, for crying out loud. Don't the weather gods know that?"

Dorothy laughed. "I'll keep an eye on him, Carl. But who will keep an eye on you?"

A large group of students had gathered at the booth for the math club and Phillips headed over to investigate. With the consent of the administration, the club was offering a contest: guess the number of jelly beans in a large glass jar and win a get-out-of-detention-free card. The gimmick was working far beyond anyone's expectations. Everyone wanted to register a guess, even those who never expected to get detention or were not the least bit interested in the math club.

Phillips looked up at the sky as if to assess the weather, and then checked his watch and walked in the direction of the chess club booth. Up ahead, he saw four tall lacrosse players intimidating a couple of smaller boys. Before he could get there, another boy—no bigger than the two who were being bullied—attempted to intervene.

"Bug off," he told the lacrosse players. "No one asked you over here, and these guys weren't bothering you."

One of the lacrosse players reared back and punched the third boy in the stomach and then threw him to the ground.

Phillips raced over to the melee and grabbed the lacrosse player by the back of his shirt. "What are you doing?" he asked. "What's wrong with you?"

The athlete said nothing.

"What's your name?" Phillips asked.

"Stan Brown," the boy said.

"Well, Stanley, you've got detention," Phillips told Brown. He whipped out a yellow pad from his pocket, wrote Stan Brown's name on the top sheet, and handed it to him.

"Report to the headmistress's office after school today. Don't even think about skipping because my last stop this afternoon will be that office and I'll be looking for you. As we both know, you're on the bubble here, and any more incidents like this one will be enough to send you packing. Now get out of here."

Phillips then turned to the boy who had been punched and thrown to the ground. The boy was on his feet and brushing the dirt from his clothing.

"Are you all right?" Phillips asked.

"I'm fine, sir. No problem," the boy answered.

"What's your name?"

"Grinsky. Paul Grinsky."

Phillips looked closely at Grinsky and took in the boy's measure. He was perhaps five feet seven inches tall, with dark brown hair and bright round eyes. Despite his short stature, he wasn't a frail kid. On the contrary, he was solid and well proportioned. Phillips knew that Paul was a first-generation American, his parents having emigrated from Slavistan some twenty years before. Slavistanis were tough people, and Paul was no exception to his heritage.

Paul turned to the two boys who had been bullied by the lacrosse players and looked them over. The two nodded as if to say, Fine.

"Okay, Paul," Phillips said. "Stay out of trouble, all right?"

"Yes, sir, I plan to," Paul said.

"Right now I'd like you to go over to the nurse's office and get yourself checked out, okay?" Phillips said.

"I will, sir, but I'm sure I'm okay."

"You're probably right, but I'd like you to do that nonetheless."

Paul nodded and headed toward the student center, where the nurse's office was located.

Phillips turned his attention away from Paul Grinsky and strode purposefully toward a booth on the other side of the fairgrounds, where a small group of girls had gathered in front of a table.

Diane Barkowsky, the school's lead cheerleader, was serving up her special brand of poison with the support of a couple of her cheerleader friends, Susannah Arnold, a tall, lanky blond, and Linda Saunders, a short, buxom brunette. The target of Diane's bile was the classmate she hated the most, Roxanne Reynolds.

Roxanne sat behind the table for her Community Outreach Club. She was flanked by two friends and coworkers, Sarah Doherty and Lyla Ann Bell.

"So, Lady Duh Duh," Diane said, "what are you doing with this club anyway? Are you on some kind of mission? I mean, are you like Mother Teresa or something?"

Susannah and Linda let out a burst of theatrical laughter.

"Are you like saving the world, Roxanne?" Diane continued.

Roxanne pushed a strand of her golden hair behind her ear. As she stared back at Diane, Diane realized Roxanne was not the least bit threatened by her, which momentarily confused the cheerleader.

At five foot five, with dark brown hair and a tight, shapely body, Diane knew she was pretty. But she also knew her prettiness paled in comparison to Roxanne's beauty. Roxanne had the luminescent features and beautiful figure of Grace Kelly, a movie actress Diane had once seen in an old, classic movie.

Diane hated her for that. She also refused to believe that any girl who looked like Roxanne would be involved in the Community Outreach Club. What was community outreach anyway? Some kind of do-gooder thing that brought food and clothing to the town losers? That Roxanne had actually created the club and turned it into a thriving operation in the two years she had been at the school was impossible for Diane to fathom. Roxanne was just a dumb blonde, for crying out loud. She didn't get a single answer right in any of her classes. She was a loser herself.

Ah! It suddenly hit Diane. Maybe that's what attracted her to the losers she was involved with.

"No, we're not saving the world, Diane," Roxanne said, "but we are trying to make a few people's lives a little easier. Is that so hard to understand? Why don't you help us? We need volunteers for our club and it would be great if you joined us."

Sarah and Lyla had listened to Diane's rant like a couple of thoroughbred race horses chafing at the bit. The two teenagers had a lot in common, though one was of Irish decent and the other African-American. Both were smart, attractive girls in uniquely ethnic ways—Sarah with her Irish girl-next-door beauty; and Lyla, an African-American princess, with high cheekbones and a gorgeous light-up-the-room smile. They were also from tough communities not far from Golden Gables. And both had very short tempers.

"Join you?" Diane laughed through her words. "Join you for what? So we can run over to Martin Luther King Boulevard and hand out turkeys to the junkies?"

Susannah and Linda laughed again, which fueled Diane's glib vitriol "I mean, do free needles and condoms come with the food you give away? You know, I read that they take donated food and sell it for drugs. Did you know that, Lady Duh Duh? That's what you're really doing, you know. Funding their habits. Lady Duh Duh, junkie queen."

That was all Sarah could take. "Well, Diane, I've got news for you," she said. "Because of the generosity of this community—something you wouldn't know a thing about—we provided two hundred meals and complete Thanksgiving and Christmas dinners to more than fifty families last year. We also provided clothing and Christmas presents to those families. And we screened them all carefully and all of the families ate the food we provided."

"Yeah," Lyla interjected. "And we don't need your skinny little ass helping us, either."

Lyla Ann had been born in the projects in Arlington, Virginia, and raised in a tough section of Silver Spring, Maryland, not far from Golden Gables. Her mother, Corina, was a licensed practical nurse. Her father had left them when Lyla was born, but Corina married Howard Bell, who adopted Lyla as his own. Howard worked for Amtrak and, together with Corina, provided Lyla with the means to attend Laurel Glen. That raised the odds considerably for Lyla getting into a great university. She wanted to be a doctor.

"Look here, Diane," Lyla said, "you nasty little tramp, what gives you the right to come over here and get down on us like this? You know, if we wanted to, we could jump over this table and woop your sorry little ass from here to the Betsy. Why don't you take your little band of hos back to that dark place where all you devils come from and get out of our faces?"

Roxanne sprang from her chair and was about to bring an end to the fighting when she was stopped by the sound of a warning ping inside her head. She looked beyond Diane and her cheerleaders and saw the new teacher, Jason Phillips, approaching. Both locked onto each other's eyes, watching the other attentively as Phillips kept walking toward the booth.

The five other girls were busy screaming at each other, but then Diane realized Roxanne was ignoring them. She looked around and saw the connection between Roxanne and Phillips. Baffled, she interpreted the moment in the only way she knew how—Phillips and Roxanne were flirting with each other. Anyone who gave Roxanne attention was instantly more attractive to Diane, and at the same time the enemy.

Susannah, Linda, Sarah, and Lyla also noticed Roxanne's attentive look at Phillips and stopped fighting as well.

"Well, what's going on here?" Diane said, her voice heavy with innuendo.

Phillips arrived and said, "My name is Jason Phillips and I'm a new teacher here. Is there a problem?"

"No, no," Roxanne said. "We're just trying to recruit some new members."

Diane let out a small, cynical laugh and then gave Jason Phillips a sly smile and a long temptress look.

Phillips ignored her.

"Okay, girls," she said, miffed, "let's leave these three nuns so they can go back to playing with the lepers. So long, losers."

Phillips watched the cheerleaders leave and then turned his attention to the three students behind the desk.

"I'd say you girls have about eight minutes before it starts pouring," he said. "Maybe you should wrap things up."

"Yes," Roxanne said.

"I'll see all three of you in some of my classes," he added. He already knew that this semester Roxanne was in his social studies class and that Sarah and Lyla were in his English class.

"Yes, we'll see you tomorrow," Roxanne said. Sarah and Lyla also bid Phillips good-bye.

From a distance, Diane called to Roxanne, "Is that how you get your donors, Lady Duh Duh? Don't forget to give him the turkey."

Roxanne had taken all she could. She considered immediate retaliation, but rejected the idea. Still, her anger boiled.

"We'd better get our stuff and get out of here," she said to Sarah and Lyla. "School's over anyway. Do you guys have rides home?"

"Yes," Sarah said. "We're both taking the bus."

"Okay, well, I'll see you tomorrow. I've got something I want to do right now."

She gathered up her papers and marched over to the math booth. The sky was about to burst open and all of those who had been waiting in line to guess the number of jelly beans were gone.

Two boys were still manning the booth. Seeing Roxanne headed their way was akin to watching a goddess approach. Both were suddenly alert and fixing their hair.

"Can we help you, Roxanne?" one asked.

"Please give me a slip of paper to write down my guess," Roxanne said.

"Sure, sure, Roxanne. We would love to have your entry for the jelly-bean contest. Your guess is as good as any, right?"

"We'll see," Roxanne said, still fuming at Diane.

She wrote down her name and the number of jelly beans, handed in the paper, and then turned and marched away.

"The drawing is next week, Roxanne," one of the boys called after her. "We'll let you know if you won."

"I already know," Roxanne said under her breath.

With that, the sky opened, the rain fell in torrents, and Roxanne hurried for shelter, the wind and rain whipping everything in sight.

Chapter 2
Ten Days Later

Roxanne and Sarah Doherty stood in front of their hallway lockers in the Laurel building like a couple of happy conspirators. Huddled close to each other, they continued a conversation they had had the night before over the telephone, talking about their respective crushes.

Roxanne had confessed to liking George Jackson, captain of the Laurel Glen basketball team and the most desirable boy in the school. Jackson was well more than six feet tall, with dark hair, large blue eyes, and a smile that radiated self-awareness and confidence. Like many natural athletes, but especially basketball players, he walked with a graceful lope that suggested low gear in a race car that could suddenly explode with speed and power. He was being recruited by Division 1 college basketball programs and expected to go to a good university on a basketball scholarship.

"Oh my God, Roxanne," Sarah had said when Roxanne told her about George. "He's got such a thing for you."

"Do you really think so?" Roxanne asked, overcome with excitement.

"Absolutely!" Sarah's voice dropped into a conspiratorial tone. "Sally Heitzman was standing next to George on Monday—their lockers are next to each other—and she overheard him tell Jimmy Taylor that he thought you were the hottest girl on earth. Sally played dumb, like she didn't hear a thing, but she told Lyla and Lyla told me. Oh my God, that's so great," Sarah continued. "You guys would make such an incredible couple. You've got to get him to ask you out, Roxanne. That's your mission, girl."

"I know, I know," Roxanne said. "I don't know how I'm going to do it, but I'll think of something."

"Don't worry," Sarah said. "Just keep giving him that look I saw you give him yesterday and he'll come running."

Both girls laughed.

"Okay, I told you who I like," Roxanne said. "Now it's your turn. Who is he?"

Sarah paused, and Roxanne could envision her friend's face coloring. "Paul Grinsky!" she said abruptly. "I think he is the most incredible, sweetest boy in the school. He is so hot. He's smart, too, and really good looking." Sarah sighed.

The conversation continued like that for another thirty minutes before they said goodnight.

Now it was Thursday morning—8:20, ten minutes before first period—and both girls were still excited by the possibilities of love.

The school year was ten days old and people had settled into their routines. Students flowed up and down the hallway on their way to their first period classes. Classroom doors were open on either side of the hallway, the walls between the classrooms embedded with student lockers. The marble floors gleamed with fresh polish. Lamps hung on long brass chains from the high white ceiling. The building combined the atmosphere of the nineteenth century along with the obvious care of a well-endowed modern institution.

"Roxanne, I'm so excited for you," Sarah said as students passed by, clearly within earshot. "You and George make such a great couple."

Sarah had large blue eyes and light brown hair that fell to her shoulders. Faint freckles dotted the bridge of her small nose, which crinkled whenever she smiled. She was small boned and thin, shorter than Roxanne, but bursting with energy and enthusiasm for life.

"Sarah, you nut. Someone is going to hear you," Roxanne said.

"That's the point, Roxanne. How else is George going to find out you like him? Boys need to know that before they ask you out. I read that somewhere…something about feeling safe or something."

Roxanne's voice dropped to whisper. "I don't know what you read, but I'm sure there are lots of ways to get the message across without announcing it in the hallway."

Apparently Sarah didn't agree. Her face reddening, she closed her eyes tight and said in a voice meant to carry, "I think Paul Grinsky is really hot, Roxanne."

Roxanne rolled her eyes. "Well, that should do it, Sarah."

Sarah smiled conspiratorially. "I hope so."

"But just in case the gossip mill doesn't work, maybe I can help. You know that Paul's a really good friend of mine. He's always trying to help me with my homework and stuff. What if I said something to him about you, how great you are. You know, just matter-of-factly, like totally random? Would that be okay with you? Then I could tell you what he said."

"Would you do that, Roxanne? That would be so great."

"Of course I would. For you, anything, you know that." Roxanne looked at her watch. "Oh my God, we've got to get to our classes."

Sarah said, "Okay, but don't forget your promise."

"Don't worry, he's as good as yours, sister," Roxanne said.

They each grabbed their books from their lockers, slammed the doors shut, and ran off. Roxanne had gone only two or three steps when she felt the ping go off in her head. Shifting to high alert, she looked up and down the hallway, which was still filled with students hurrying in both directions. Dr. Phillips was nowhere to be seen, so it wasn't his presence she felt. Who was it then?

She had felt the ping go off periodically over the last week or so, usually while she was in a crowded hallway. At first, she'd attributed it to the presence of Dr. Phillips, but the strength of the ping meant the person was close by and sometimes Dr. Phillips was nowhere to be found. Someone else was setting off her neurological alarm.

She put the mystery aside for now and hurried off to room 110.

Most of the students were in their seats when Roxanne entered the classroom and walked to her desk on the far side of the room, near the windows. She felt the ping, indicating the presence of Jason Phillips. Meanwhile, everyone else took notice of Roxanne.

She wore a pink cashmere sweater, a white skirt, and light brown leather boots with a low heel. When she entered the room, a thrill went through the air, especially among the boys who stared at her as if she were some kind of movie star. Boys nudged one another, some making comments under their breath.

Not everyone was pleased to see Roxanne, nor with the reaction she caused whenever she entered a room. Diane Barkowsky pretended not to notice, but nonetheless followed Roxanne's every step with narrowed eyes.

Roxanne sat down next to Paul Grinsky, who had been her friend since the two met at Laurel Glen in ninth grade. Now both were juniors, and Paul was among the few male friends Roxanne could count on. One of the reasons their friendship was possible was that Paul seemed immune to the effects of Roxanne's beauty and instead was attuned to her vulnerability and her heart. His friendship was sincere and, if truth be told, he felt protective of her.

"So, how'd you do with the homework assignment?" he asked.

"Gosh, Paul, I hope I read the right assignment," she retorted.

"It was on Manifest Destiny. I should have texted you last night. Sorry."

"Oh, don't worry. I'll just lay low today."

The words had no sooner left her mouth when Dr. Phillips started the class by saying, "So, Roxanne, why don't you tell us what Manifest Destiny is, and some of your thoughts on the subject?"

Roxanne paused to gather her thoughts, and as she did, she noticed Diane Barkowsky casting a gleeful glance her way. Diane had obviously overheard Roxanne's comment to Paul and was anticipating Roxanne's embarrassment.

Roxanne took a breath and let out a long exhalation.

"Well, Dr. Phillips, the reading was utterly childish and false, in the way that half-truths can be used to paint a false picture. It's the kind of propaganda that is fed to young students in order to keep us from knowing the true effects our arrogant, nationalistic ambitions have had on the less powerful.

"The notion of Manifest Destiny, a term originally coined in 1845 by a newspaper man named John O'Sullivan, refers to the belief that Americans—that is, white Anglo-Saxons—are inherently superior to the rest of the world and that they have a divinely inspired duty to spread democracy and the American way of life by any means necessary.

"The assigned reading failed to discuss the impact of Manifest Destiny on Native American populations, especially the grabbing of their lands and the destruction of their way of life.

"Though Manifest Destiny was a distinct part of American policy, it actually revealed primitive ambitions that have long driven leaders all over the world. The belief in their racial superiority led Europeans to colonize India and Africa and to perpetuate the institution of slavery.

"Might I make a suggestion, Dr. Phillips? Rather than have us derive all our information from a single history book—and a bad one at that—perhaps you could assign additional reading that might help us develop a larger and more enlightened point of view."

Jason Phillips was smiling with more than a little kindness in his eyes. He knew Roxanne's frustrations. The rest of the class was awestruck. They looked at Roxanne with eyes as wide as saucers, mouths hanging open. The only person whose expression revealed more than surprise was Diane. Her suspicions had just been confirmed. Yes, this was the real Roxanne. So many of Diane's fears were now realized: Roxanne was not the dumb blonde she made herself out to be, but a brilliant and beautiful young woman, someone Diane had no chance of competing with. Diane's world came crashing down all around her.

The moment seemed suspended in time, and Roxanne knew it wouldn't do. She had had her fun, or at the very least had let off some steam. And Dr. Phillips was clearly sympathetic. But things had to be put right, and she decided not to wait. In the vernacular of the playground, she needed a do-over.

Closing her eyes and leaning her head back ever so slightly, she attuned her mind to the nervous system of every student in the room. Once she was linked with them, she released an electro-magnetic pulse that changed the brain chemistry of everyone in the classroom…everyone except for Dr. Phillips. He was immune to her powers. But every student in the class suddenly froze and entered a momentary state of suspended animation.

If the students' brain activities were being monitored, the tests would have revealed an array of biochemical changes, including a precipitous drop in acetylcholine levels, causing the immediate loss of memory for the two minutes that Roxanne had been speaking. Roxanne's comments were completely erased from the minds of every student in the classroom.

She looked around to confirm the effects of her actions and realized that, yes, everyone was still waiting for her to answer Dr. Phillips's question. Dr. Phillips, of course, was aware of what she had just done and acquiesced to her judgment.

"Could you please repeat the question, Dr. Phillips?" she said in a light, airy voice, assuming her standard persona of the dumb blonde.

Dr. Phillips played along. "Yes, Roxanne, please tell us your thoughts on Manifest Destiny."

"I'm so sorry, Dr. Phillips, but I totally read the wrong chapter last night." Smiling brightly, she threw back her blond mane and looked around the room, as if waiting for people to acknowledge what a brilliant answer she had just given to a complex question.

Jimmy Schmidt, the class cutup, shook his head in disbelief and smacked himself hard on his forehead. Diane, glorying in having more ammunition to use against Roxanne, laughed out loud and then covered her mouth, pretending she couldn't keep her laughter contained. Ronnie Urlacher pulled at his red hair and said to Henry Moore, the boy seated directly behind him, "Who cares if she's dumb? She's the hottest thing on two feet."

"Okay, Roxanne," Dr. Phillips said. "But please go over that material tonight. Paul, why don't you tell us about Manifest Destiny."

Paul answered the question quickly and efficiently, and the discussion of US domestic policy during the pre-Civil War period continued. When the bell rang, Dr. Phillips announced that there would be a test at the end of the week and that everyone had better be prepared.

Paul turned to Roxanne. "Why don't we study together tonight? We can Skype, have our books out, send some questions and answers back and forth. You know, drill a little bit? Sound good?"

"That would be great, Paul. How's eight o'clock."

"Eight it is."

A perfect opportunity to talk to Paul about Sarah, Roxanne told herself.

Out in the hallway, Diane was surrounded by some of her cheerleader friends and waiting to pounce on Roxanne. "So, Lady Duh Duh, another duh-duh day. What some of us were wondering was how exactly did you get out of junior high. No, how did you get out of third grade?"

Roxanne hurried down the hallway on her way to her math class. Diane and her cohort followed, speaking to Roxanne's back but loudly enough so that everyone in the immediate vicinity could hear.

"Did you, like, pay someone off? And what did you pay them with, Lady Duh Duh? I know your family doesn't have any real money, that's for sure. I'll bet you gave somebody one of your naked turkeys. Is that what you did, Lady Duh Duh? Inquiring minds want to know."

The cheerleaders all laughed loudly.

Roxanne whirled around and faced Diane, who was momentarily taken aback. "Diane, don't look now, but I think your zipper is down and your panties are showing. Are you trying to get a little extra attention today, Diane? Are you, you know, advertising something?"

Shocked, Diane looked down and saw that the top button of her jeans was undone and her zipper was down to its nadir, revealing light blue panties. Her face reddened as she pulled up her zipper and buttoned her pants. She looked around the hallway, hoping no one else had noticed the faux pas.

A small crowd of boys were looking at her.

"Nice panties, Diane," Ronnie Urlacher said.

Fortunately, the bell rang and they all scurried off to their respective classes.

At lunch, Roxanne and Sarah sat together in the cafeteria and Roxanne revealed her plan to speak to Paul that night over Skype.

"As soon as you get off, text me," Sarah said.

Any further conversation was interrupted by the sound of someone tapping a spoon against a water glass. Everyone in the cafeteria turned toward the sound. The dean of students, Sean Murphy, stood in the middle aisle of the cafeteria, tapping a spoon against a glass.

"Your attention, please," he said. "Please give me your attention. I have an announcement to make."

The din faded until the only sounds were the clashing of plates being loaded into the dishwasher and the voices of a few students who refused to stop talking.

"I wanted you all to know that we have a winner to the math club's jelly-bean contest. In fact, we have two winners. The names are posted outside my office, but I'll save you the trouble of having to make a special trip. The winners of the contest are Roxanne Reynolds and Andor Lysenko. Ms. Reynolds and Mr. Lysenko should come to my office at the close of school today to receive their get-out-of-detention passes. Okay, congratulations to our winners. Let's have a big round of applause for Roxanne Reynolds and Andor Lysenko."

Raucous applause sounded, most students clapping and cheering for no other reason than to seize the opportunity to make noise. Here and there, students made bemused comments such as, "Roxanne Reynolds guessed the jelly bean contest? Are you kidding me?" Or "Andor Lysenko, who's he?" But the high school attention span being what it was, they all quickly moved on to weightier matters, such as someone's latest crush or the blouse so-and-so was wearing that day.

After the last class ended, Roxanne went to Dean Murphy's office, which was located on the third floor of the Laurel building. Most of the administration offices were in the Betsy, including the headmaster's office. Dean Murphy insisted on being close to the students and therefore made his perch on the top floor of the gray-stoned Laurel.

Roxanne had reached the third floor when she felt the ping. Surges of caution and excitement rose within her as she reached the door to the dean's outer office. Turning the knob, she entered the lair of the dean's secretary, Mrs. Julia Flanagan.

In her mid-fifties and overweight, Julia Flanagan was the perpetual mother. "Oh, Roxanne, wonderful to see you," she said. "And congratulations! What a guess! And right on the money. How is it possible, dear? Small miracles, Roxanne. I always say that these small miracles are just God's way of letting us know that he's always watching over us."

Roxanne barely registered Mrs. Flanagan's words or her big motherly smile. The ping was coming from the inner office, she realized.

"I'm sure you're right, Mrs. Flanagan," she said.

"Dean Murphy and Mr. Lysenko are already inside waiting for you," Mrs. Flanagan said.

Roxanne knocked on the dean's door and entered when he called for her to come in. The dean sat behind his large desk, facing the door. He was short—five foot five at best—thin and spry, with light-colored hair.

Behind the dean was a credenza, upon which stood stacks of papers. Beyond the credenza was a large, arched window. Seated on the other side of the dean's desk with his back to Roxanne was a boy Roxanne didn't recognize—and the source of the ping.

The boy got up from his chair as she entered the office and turned to look at her. Instantly, their eyes locked and an electric charge flew through Roxanne's body.

"Please, sit down, both of you," Dean Murphy said. "I don't know if the two of you have met. Roxanne, this is Andor Lysenko. Andor, this is Roxanne Reynolds."

The two nodded at each other and shook hands as they sat down. Again, Roxanne felt an unmistakable heat.

Andor was tall and athletically built, with dark brown hair, dark eyes, wide Slavic cheekbones, and a strong jaw. He was handsome and radiated a quiet, purposeful aura.

"Roxanne," the dean said, "Andor just arrived in the US earlier this month from Slavistan. He's a senior. Roxanne's a junior, Andor. She's doing wonderful work with her Community Outreach Club. How many people did you provide meals for last school year, Roxanne?"

"About two hundred," Roxanne said.

"Oh, that's wonderful," Dean Murphy said. He prattled on about the long history of community service performed by students at Laurel Glen.

Both Roxanne and Andor faced Dean Murphy, who fully believed he had the attention of both students, but something else was occurring of which the dean had absolutely no knowledge. Andor and Roxanne were communicating with each other telepathically.

"I didn't know that there was another student here of our kind," Roxanne said to Andor.

"Like the dean said, I just arrived a couple of weeks ago," Andor replied silently. "I saw you a couple of times and wanted to introduce myself, but I always seemed to be late for class or some appointment. I'm still trying to find my way around."

"Have you met Dr. Phillips? He's one of us."

"Yes, I met him on the first day I came to the school. He seems like a nice man."

"Yes, he really is. I like him."

Dean Murphy had concluded his homily on community service and decided it was time to speak about what really perplexed him. He smiled broadly and opened his hands as if to draw Roxanne and Andor closer to him.

"So we have a bit of a mystery here, don't we?" he said. "How the dickens did the two of you guess the right number of jelly beans in that jar? There were 10,488 jelly beans and that was no little jar. It took five teams of students to count five individual groups of jelly beans. Each team knew the amount they'd counted, but no one knew the number for the other groups, so no one but me knew the total number of jelly beans.

"I dare say that unless you caught me talking in my sleep—and mind you, my wife has complained about that for years—I don't think you could have known the number of jelly beans in that container."

Dean Murphy raised his eyebrows and smiled as an opening for Roxanne or Andor to speak, if they had something to say. Neither did.

"Anyway, before the contest opened, I told the Math Club that anyone who got within five hundred jelly beans of the number would be the winner. So imagine my surprise when not just one person guessed the exact number, but two people go it right. That must be some kind of miracle, I told myself, though for the life of me, I cannot discern its meaning. Anyway, it's amazing, wouldn't you say? Hmmm? What are the chances?"

Andor kept looking at Dean Murphy, but directed a thought to Roxanne. "With our kind, the chances are exactly 100 percent."

Roxanne smiled and looked down at her hands, folded in her lap.

"I think we just made lucky guesses, Dean Murphy," Andor said.

Roxanne noted that his words revealed a faint accent, hardly noticeable, but there on the edges of the words.

"Maybe I got the number in a dream or something," Roxanne said, trying to be helpful and very blond. "I just felt I knew. That's all I can tell you."

"Of course, Roxanne," the dean said. "And please don't get me wrong, no one is accusing either of you of any wrongdoing. As I say, the only way you could have cheated was to read my mind. Neither of you can do that, right?"

Andor smiled at the dean. Roxanne looked slightly embarrassed. Neither said a word.

"We didn't get the number by reading your mind," Andor said finally.

Again, Roxanne noted the trace of the Slavistani accent and heard in Andor's voice a deep and unmistakable strength.

"Yes, of course," Dean Murphy said. "Anyway, I am prattling on like this because I'm just astounded, that's all. I know that everything is on the up and up. No doubt about it. So please forgive me if I intimated anything but pure amazement at the both of you. Anyway, this isn't much of a prize, especially since I don't expect either of you to ever get detention, but here they are: one get-out-of-detention pass for each of you. Congratulations."

"Thank you, Dean," Roxanne said.

"Thank you, Dean," Andor said.

"Okay, I'm expecting good things from both of you this year," Dean Murphy said. "I'm going to be cheering both of you on. So off with you now, and good luck."

He smiled warmly and shook hands with Roxanne and Andor. Both then left the dean's office and found themselves standing awkwardly together in the hallway. They walked down the stairs in silence, both blocking their thoughts from the other. Neither knew what to say. Finally, they found themselves outside the Laurel.

Andor decided to speak out loud to Roxanne, in case anyone was watching them. "Would it be possible for us to talk sometime? You know, about how you get along here and what this place is like?"

"Oh, I'm sure you will pick up things quickly," she replied. "But we can talk sometime, sure."

"Okay, see you around," Andor said, feeling slightly rejected and angry at himself for being at such a loss for words.

"Yes, see you around," Roxanne said.

With that, Roxanne hurried off to her car, parked in a small student parking lot next to the Betsy.

Roxanne arrived at the Tudor-style home where she lived with her parents. Though the house was modest, it sat on about two acres of land, much of it wooded in the backyard. She entered the living room and called out to her mother

"I'm in the kitchen, dear," Rebecca answered. "Come on in. You can help me finish dinner."

Roxanne hung up her coat and went into the kitchen.

"Smells good, Mom." She peered into the pot on the stove and saw two pieces of sole cooking in a sauce of basil, garlic, tomatoes, and leeks. On the counter was a serving bowl that already contained roasted potatoes.

"Why don't you take out some kale from the refrigerator?" Roxanne's mother suggested. "Clean it and chop it up, and we'll steam it."

Appearing to be about thirty-five years old, Rebecca Rogers stood five feet nine, like her daughter, and was strikingly beautiful. Her wavy light brown hair fell to her shoulders. Her eyes were large and also light brown. Her figure was that of a dancer, long legged and lean. Unselfconscious and completely without artifice, she carried herself with a certain strength and dignity. She knew who she was—a strong woman with her own life, interests, and freedom, who had committed herself out of love to her husband and only child.

Rebecca and Roxanne communicated telepathically, because it was most comfortable for them. It was more intimate as well, though both could shield any thoughts from the other and thus have complete privacy. Rebecca was exceedingly powerful and could penetrate her daughter's shield if she desired, but such a forceful intrusion into her daughter's thoughts was something she would never consider doing. Nevertheless, the love between mother and daughter was so strong that Rebecca could feel anything untoward or vexing that Roxanne experienced.

"So, how was your day?" she asked Roxanne, already knowing many of the day's highs and lows. "Those girls are bothering you again, aren't they?"

"Diane hates me," Roxanne replied.

"We both know why," Rebecca said. Though she sympathized with her daughter for what she had to go through, she did not approve of Roxanne's revenge. "I know it's hard, sweetheart, but taking retribution is a slippery slope. Today it's giving her a small embarrassment. Tomorrow it's hurting her physically. And what then?"

"Mom, do you really think that what they're doing to me is fair?" Roxanne asked.

"No, it's not fair. Life isn't fair a lot of the time. But you're dealing with children. If you're not careful, you could hurt her badly. And that could happen in an instant if you don't control your emotions. Your father and I have told you this many times: we grow stronger through ethical restraint. Our energy isn't wasted on petty disputes, vindictive acts, and unrestrained dark emotions. Those states weaken us and lead us down paths of chaos. Believe it or not, Diane Barkowsky is here to help you learn how to use your abilities. She's one of the most important lessons you will learn at Laurel Glen. And besides that, it's part of our kind's Code of Ethics. We don't interfere in the lives of Ordinaries unless we can help them in a matter of life and death, and even then we are urged to act with restraint. And right now, I'm worried about how you are handling the situation with this girl."

"Mom, do you think it's easy playing the dumb blonde every minute of every school day?" Roxanne asked, nearing tears. "I am humiliated every day by those cretins."

Rebecca softened. She put down the large spoon she was holding, turned off the burner on the stove, and hugged her daughter. "Let's sit for a minute." The two went into the living room and sat on the sofa.

"You are so good," Rebecca told Roxanne. "I don't blame you one bit for giving Diane a little bit of her own medicine. She deserves a lot worse, I know. But part of our learning is to understand how delicate life is, especially the lives of Ordinaries. It's so easy to make a mistake, and a mistake for us could mean permanent injury to one of them."

Rebecca paused, kissing her daughter on the forehead. "I am so proud of you. And I have complete faith in you. I know you will be careful."

"Okay," Roxanne said, her voice softer. The two held each other. "Don't worry. I'll be careful with Diane, believe me. Though I have to tell you, sometimes I want to do to her what Jim Carrey did to the Steve Carell character in that movie *Bruce Almighty*. Do you remember that funny scene when Steve Carell is doing the newscast on television and Jim Carrey turns him into a blithering idiot in front of thousands of people? Wasn't that funny? Sometimes, that's what I'd like to do to Diane in front of the whole school."

"I know, I know, dear. That scene was hilarious. And you could do it too," Rebecca said. "But who would you be after you'd done something like that, and where would your life be heading?"

"Life is hard when you have to be the one who does the right thing, especially when others don't care."

"It's not whether or not others care. You should care, and I know you do." Rebecca kissed her daughter's forehead again. "Okay, why don't you check your e-mail while I finish making dinner?"

Rebecca walked toward the kitchen, but suddenly remembered something. "Your father wants to talk to you tonight."

"Oh no," Roxanne said, "not another lecture from afar about protecting Ordinaries."

"No, something else," Rebecca said. "He wants to talk to you about the boy you met today—Andor Lysenko. He's not at Laurel Glen to study, that's for sure."

Chapter 3
Roger Reynolds in Westminster Abbey

Westminster Abbey, located in central London and across the street from the Houses of Parliament and Big Ben, is the Church of England's crown jewel. Entering the abbey through its western entrance, below its twin Gothic towers and enormous stained glass windows, a visitor is at once awed and humbled. Along either side of the main corridor, or nave, tall gray columns stand like sentinels that reach toward the dizzying heights of the abbey's arched ceiling. Directly in the center of the nave is the dais of the high altar, bathed in golden light, and beyond it is St. Edward's Chapel. To the left of the altar is the North Transept, whose outer wall houses an enormous, circular stained-glass window. To the right of the altar is the Poet's Corner, where the tombs of some of England's greatest figures are located, among them Geoffrey Chaucer, Robert Browning, Alfred Lord Tennyson, and Charles Dickens. The Abbey is a memorial site for other great Englishmen, including William Shakespeare, Samuel Johnson, Oliver Goldsmith, and Sir Isaac Newton, and the place where British monarchs are crowned, including the current queen, Elizabeth II.

Finally, it is the office of Roger Reynolds and his team of a dozen unusual men and women. Behind the Poet's Corner and above the Pyx Chamber and the museum is an array of modern offices that are entirely unknown and invisible to the world of ordinary men and women.

A hidden elevator located in the South Wing provides access to the workplace where Roger Reynolds and his team conduct their secret business every day.

The presence of Reynolds's offices is hidden by a combination of highly advanced stealth technology, known only to Genius scientists, and by the far more advanced mental powers of those who work in them. Reynolds and colleagues have hidden their lair behind an illusion of tall trees, empty space, and a blanket of forgetfulness that dulls and disorients the mind of anyone who ventures near. And they have done it for a very long time.

This is but a small fraction of their powers. They refer to themselves as Geniuses—not in the common use of the word, as for those with IQs between 150 and 180, but the kind that the early Romans conceived of when they originally coined the word. The original Latin meaning described a guardian spirit or demon, meaning a guide who possesses or is capable of bestowing extraordinary abilities and oracle-like intelligence. For the Romans, a genius was someone who had divine powers, and certainly this is an apt description of the kinds of talents possessed by Roger Reynolds and his like. For starters, they have IQs of a thousand or more. Because of their advanced understanding of health and medicine, they live exceedingly long lives, in some cases many centuries. They communicate telepathically and read the minds of ordinary people at will. Their nervous systems are capable of generating enormous amounts of energy and directing it like a laser beam at a given target, which can destroy a person or object. A minority of them has the power of telekinesis; a much smaller fraction of them can levitate. These are but a few of the abilities with which nature has blessed them.

Despite these extraordinary gifts, Geniuses are distinctly human. Nature shuffles the genetic deck in all of us. For a very tiny minority, a mere few hundred of the seven billion people on the planet, the results are especially propitious, offering up characteristics and capabilities that are beyond the wildest imaginings of the rest of us.

Historically, Geniuses have kept themselves hidden from the world, largely for their own protection. Only rarely did individual Geniuses emerge as leaders or public figures. Instead, most chose to withdraw from the world or to serve as advisers or teachers to leading political figures, scientists, inventors, philosophers, religious leaders, artists, and musicians. In that role they came to be known as muses or spiritual guides, which no doubt inspired the original meaning of the word genius. Only later did the word fall into common usage and take on the definition that we associate with it today, meaning someone with above-average intelligence.

By some mysterious but irrevocable decree from nature, Geniuses found themselves divided into two large families—those of the West, of which Roger Reynolds and his collaborators are a part, and those of the East. This East-West divide extends far beyond mere geography. It represents distinctly different ideologies and approaches to life, especially to Ordinaries. In that regard the two sides can be considered polar opposites, yin and yang. The Western Geniuses took a yin or relatively passive approach to those they referred to as "Ordinaries". As they saw it, Western Geniuses were benign, extending their hands in service when they deemed it appropriate, especially in times of crisis, such as during war or economic chaos. Eastern Geniuses, on the other hand, are more yang, an aggressive form of Geniuses, seeking to control Ordinaries whenever they considered it necessary. As far as the Western Geniuses were concerned, the Geniuses of the East use Ordinaries for their own purposes. They see Ordinaries as inferior beings who need *shepherding*, a word they often use to disguise their underlying intentions to dominate, control, and direct the fate of whole societies. To Western Geniuses, the Eastern Geniuses are bent on autocratic worldwide rule. At the same time, they are forced to keep their abilities and intentions hidden. Both Eastern and Western Geniuses have realized since the beginning of civilization that their numbers are too few, and that if Ordinaries ever found out that such extraordinary men and women existed, they would see them as a threat. They might gather in large numbers, and their armies could marshal enormous arsenals that could overwhelm and destroy the Geniuses.

On this point, both Eastern and Western Geniuses have agreed since the beginning of civilization. Geniuses are the hidden dimension within humanity, the most powerful people alive, who paradoxically are forced to keep their natures secret, despite their awesome powers.

Roger Reynolds is among the most powerful Geniuses in the world, and therefore one of the most powerful people. But on this day, he was feeling anything but powerful.

Roger's office, with its wide windows and grand views, looked out upon Parliament and Big Ben to the southwest. To his immediate south lay Parliament Square, a little patch of green that on this day, like so many others, provided a site for demonstrators of one stripe or another to gather and hurl slogans and epithets at their ministers as they went to work. The demonstrators' enthusiasm for rancor was not the least bit inhibited by the rain that fell in steady sheets.

Roger sat behind his desk and gazed out the window at the traffic flowing on Parliament Street and across Westminster Bridge, which passed over the Thames. A tall man, considerably over six feet tall, he was lean and fit, with thick golden hair and bright blue eyes. His nose was arched and long, with wide nostrils. His mouth was well-contoured, wide, and normally tightly closed. On this day he wore a dark blue suit, yellow shirt, and blue and yellow tie. Anyone looking at him would guess him to be in his early forties. In fact, he was far older, specifically 170 years old.

Roger had occupied his current offices for more than one hundred years, but Geniuses had conducted their secret work in Westminster Abbey for as long as the Abbey had existed, some thousand years.

On any other day, Roger was a decisive man who thrived on challenge. Even on this day he appeared calm and relaxed. In fact, he was in turmoil. As he sat in his high-backed leather chair, motionless, his mind was accessing vast streams of mental and electronic communications to better understand what was going on in Slavistan, and what his most dread adversaries, a set of twin brothers, Karl and Klaus Kleper, two of the most powerful Geniuses of the East, were doing

The Klepers sat atop a vast pyramid of power. Presidents and ministers; armies of generals, admirals, and lieutenants; bankers and business people; scientists, engineers, and foot soldiers answered to their command, though only a handful knew their names and none knew the extent of their power. The brothers, and their circle, were unknown to the world, yet they controlled the governments of much of Eastern Europe and Central Asia, including the largest and richest country, Slavistan.

Roger and his cohort had been battling the Klepers for more than a century, always facing each other through their respective intermediaries: the Ordinaries who made up the ranks of government leaders, diplomats, soldiers, revolutionaries, and industrial and technological leaders in the Western and Eastern Hemispheres.

Roger and the Klepers first met on the strategic battlefield during the Spanish American War of 1898. Since then, they and their kind had been involved in both world wars, the Korean Conflict, the Vietnam War, the Cold War, the destruction of the World Trade Center, and the Iraq war. They were the competing forces behind the Great Depression and its recovery. They were on opposite sides in the liberation of India from British rule, the creation of Israel, the Cuban missile crisis, the Civil Rights movement, the Islamic Revolution of Iran, the collapse of the Soviet Union, and the fall of the Berlin Wall and the reunification of Germany. They and the Ordinaries they guided were the primary sources for the mind-boggling advances in medicine and computer technologies that drive modern life.

Despite their adversarial relationship, both sides observed one tacit agreement: the battle was waged between the combatants, the powerful men and women of their kind who were directly involved in whatever were the latest struggles for supremacy. The fight was not carried to innocent members of family and loved ones. Only those who pulled the strings and moved the chess pieces were fair game and thus open to attack.

That had been the rule since the reign of King Arthur, which was the last time the code was breached by treachery. But with the arrival of Andor Lysenko at Laurel Glen, the Klepers had changed the rules of engagement. It was apparent to Roger that the Klepers had targeted the Reynolds family, specifically Roxanne. Moreover, they wanted Roger to know they were coming for his daughter, his wife, and eventually for him. No doubt they meant to neutralize him in order to accomplish some larger strike against the US capital. By targeting his family this early in the war—and he had no illusions, this was indeed war—the Klepers were hoping to distract and weaken him, to occupy his mind so thoroughly that he would make mistakes. And Roger had to concede the point; the strategy was working already. The more preoccupied he became about his wife and daughter, the less attention he would give to the larger plot of the Eastern Council of Geniuses.

The fact that they had breached the code and put Roger's family at risk could mean only one thing: the Klepers were risking everything to achieve global domination. Two men stood in their way. Roger Reynolds and his boss, Alexander Astrakhan, the leader of the Western Council of Geniuses and considered the most powerful Genius in the world. If they could take Roger out and find a way to destroy Astrakhan, they could take control of the world's primary power centers, including governments, military, and banking.

Roger already felt more vulnerable than he had felt since childhood. Rebecca and Roxanne were more important to him than his own life. They occupied his heart completely, but in very different ways.

Rebecca was his wife, lover, confidant, collaborator, and best friend. No one had ever been closer to him than she. But Rebecca was powerful, brilliant, and tough. She had already withstood many of life's bitter assaults, disappointments, and failures. She had been tested and tempered in war with the Geniuses of the East. And by marrying Roger, she'd known what she was getting into.

Roxanne was another matter. She was still an innocent—he couldn't see her any other way—which meant that her purity, hope, and idealism remained intact. Roxanne still saw all people, Ordinaries and Geniuses alike, and all of life as good. She still believed. And her belief was among the most precious intangibles in his life, because he still believed that human nature was essentially good.

Roxanne embodied all that was beautiful about life, all that had to be preserved in order to make life worth living. This was what drove him in his work—the fundamental belief that he and his team could stop the Eastern Geniuses from interfering in the unfolding goodness of people everywhere, whether Ordinaries or Geniuses..

The problem for Roger was that doing his work was the only way he knew how to show his daughter he loved her. Too often, he was all thumbs around her. What could he do with such a pure and beautiful child? He had asked himself when she was still very young. Yes, he had played softball and basketball with her when he'd had the time and she was still interested in sports. But he didn't have the time anymore and Roxanne's interest in sports waned when she was ten. They did share books, went to the movies and the theater as a family. They went on trips together, and he and Roxanne talked about subjects in which she was interested, such as mathematics. But he had to admit the problem was deeper than having time or mutual interests. He just couldn't relate well to a daughter, and he knew it.

How could he express his love for her? He didn't dare tell her about himself and his past. His childhood was too filled with trauma and loss to share with a girl who was being raised with the sort of love and support he had not known during his own youth. Why spoil her childhood by telling her of his struggles and pain? That would only make her feel guilty about her life. It might even evoke maternal instincts in her toward him. The thought of that repulsed him. But what could he tell her? That he was driven to protect her and the world from men and women who were inherently corrupt and evil, and whose great powers made them extremely dangerous? Oh, sure, tell her that and ruin her innocent view of the world. She was a child—she was entitled to her innocence for as long as it lasted. Besides, what were parents for but to protect the innocence and purity of youth, and to allow their children to make their own decisions about life in order to discover what they were good at and what they truly loved? Youth was fleeting, gone too soon. In any case, the world needed children in order for humankind to be reminded of the existence of such purity. This was what civilization and the rule of law were meant to preserve—that no matter what anyone's age, they were all still innocent and vulnerable children in their hearts.

This knowledge drove him in his work. Ironically, what he did every day had also led him to a single, blinding conclusion: he was the problem in his family. He carried the battles and the horrors of the world in his tissues, in his nervous system, in the great brain that he possessed. In the end, he was a warrior. There was no escaping that fact. His life had already been shaped and corrupted by too many battles and their horrors.

When he was just a boy, evil men had killed his parents. That memory, and all that followed, drove his life's purpose. But it was yet another form of darkness that he feared about himself.

Was this his fate? To suffer terrible loss in childhood and be placed on a warrior's path, only to be consumed by the battles he had waged and carried in his soul, thus becoming a carrier of the very darkness from which he tried to protect his family? The war he had been waging had now drawn near to his home and threatened those he loved the most.

What bitter irony, he thought again as he sat motionless in his office and stared at the great edifices of Parliament. In the process of doing what he believed to be right, he made those he loved a target of evil people.

Abruptly, Roger broke off his reverie. He shifted his thoughts in order to communicate directly with his colleague, Denise Parker, who was busy in her office down the hall.

"Yes, Chief, what can I do for you?"

"I need you to find out everything you can about Andor Lysenko. Born in Slavistan; he's in his late teens. He just arrived at my daughter's school. I'm concerned he's an agent of the Klepers."

"I'll get right on it," she replied.

"Let's round up the entire team in two hours."

"I'll take care of it."

It was already 9 p.m. London time, five hours later than on the east coast of the United States.

Roger next directed his thoughts to a second colleague, Stephen Elliot, who was in his late twenties and the youngest of Roger's protégés.

"Stephen, sorry to interrupt like this, but I have an assignment for you that has to take precedence."

"All ears, Chief," Stephen replied.

"I need you to get me everything you can of communications between the Klepers and any Ordinaries for, say, the last six months. Many of their orders will be sent through Ordinaries' computers, which will be no trouble for you. Please ask Denise for any help you may need. We'll be meeting in two hours and I'll brief you then on the reason for my request."

"Sure thing," Stephen said. "I'll bring along what I've got by then."

Roger then directed his thoughts to a senior colleague, Simone Laurent. Simone had been with Roger throughout the entire twentieth century. They had fought in two world wars together, and had been engaged in every other major conflict and virtually all diplomatic initiatives, and many of the major technological advances of the century. Roger loved her like the sister he'd never had.

"Simone, the Klepers are on the move," he said. "They've targeted my daughter, and very likely Washington, DC. I need you to work with Denise to monitor the mind of Andor Lysenko, the Klepers' agent, and find out anything you can about what they're telling him to do. Also, I need you to monitor any communication between our kind in the Klepers' camp and anyone in the US, especially of our kind who are in the DC area. Needless to say, we're keeping all of this quiet, Simone. We're meeting in two hours."

"*Bien sur, mon chef,*" Simone said. After a pause, she added, "Roger, we'll protect Rebecca and Roxanne."

"Thank you, Simone."

Roger sat back in his chair and focused his thoughts on two old friends who were not part of his London team—Freddy and Ellis Davies, Genius brothers, former soldiers, and now security specialists extraordinaire.

Freddy and Ellis were rock climbing the Nose at El Capitan in Yosemite Valley when Roger tuned into their thoughts. They were two days into their climb and cursing each other for various mistakes they claimed the other had made along the way.

"Hi, guys," Roger interrupted.

"Hiya, Chief," Ellis came back. "What's cookin'?"

"Whatever it is," Freddy said, "it's got to be better than what we ate last night… year-old beef jerky and water. Great planning, bro."

"Hey, beef jerky's always been fine by me. What do you want, filet mignon on a rock?"

"I want something I can actually chew and eat, not the stuff they make shoes from, Ellis."

Roger broke in, smiling. "Listen, guys, how far are you from the top?"

"Another two days," Freddy said. "What's going on?"

"The Klepers are on the loose and I need your help." Roger hesitated, but decided to tell them how important his request was. "It's personal this time."

"We're already on our way down, Chief," Freddy said. "We'll be at the bottom in two hours. Let's talk then."

"Thanks, guys. Contact me as soon as you're safely on the ground."

"Will do," Ellis said.

Roger closed off communication and then settled into his chair to link his mind with Rebecca's. The process was like perceiving an opening in the veil we refer to as reality and stepping through to another dimension where distance does not exist. The heart and mind of a loved one became as close and intimate as one's own breath.

"I miss you," Roger began. "How are you today?"

"Fine, dear. All's well here. We miss you too. How are you?"

"We're fine. Lots to do. Let's talk after I've had a chance to speak to Roxanne."

"Sure. We have a lot to share with you too."

"Let's bring in Roxanne then."

Roger and Rebecca opened to their daughter, who sat on the sofa opposite Rebecca in their living room.

Roxanne greeted her father in the same way she had been doing since she was a child. "Hi, Dad," she called out mentally in a falsetto. It was her way of saying that she was still his little girl. Roger felt his heart open and so much sadness rush in.

"Hiya, sweetheart. How's it going?"

"Pretty well, Dad. How are you?"

"We're fine here. Very busy. You met someone important today, didn't you?"

"Do you mean Andor Lysenko? Is he important?"

"Well, I think it's important when you meet someone of your own kind, someone who is different in ways that you are different. Isn't that important to you?"

"Yes, I suppose it is," Roxanne replied.

He could tell she was growing cautious with the direction of the conversation. "Listen, honey, I'm not telling you what to do—"

Roxanne cut her father off. "That's good, Dad, because you know that gets us into trouble."

"What I wanted to ask you is simply to be cautious with Andor," Roger said in the most balanced way he could. "He's Slavistani, and as you know they're at war."

"I know, Dad. I read the newspaper too."

"I know, I know. What I meant to say is he's also from the Eastern Council of Geniuses, which means he has a distinct point of view when it comes to how the world should be ordered and how our kind should interact with Ordinaries."

"Dad, what are you trying to tell me? That he's an eighteen-year-old psychopathic dictator bent on world domination?"

"No, honey, I'm not telling you that," Roger said, even though that was exactly what he meant. "What I am asking you is simply to be cautious with him. Please do not reveal anything about the family, or even your schedule for any single day, or week, or month. Be circumspect, okay? It's possible that his arrival has a greater significance than simply a teenage boy wanting to go to school in the US. The United States and its allies still don't know how to respond to Slavistan's aggression. And Andor could affect US leadership."

"I think Dad is open but cautious, sweetheart," Rebecca added. "He's just trying to protect you."

Roxanne was not backing down. "Dad, do I have to remind you that I'm seventeen years old?"

In her reply, Roger heard Roxanne's anger at him for being gone so much. She was not letting him off the hook, and he knew it.

"Must we see everything in geopolitical stratagems?" she said. "Do I have to see every social encounter like some kind of Disraeli?"

"All I am asking you to do is be careful around him, and be circumspect," Roger replied. "That is, until we are certain of his intentions. Once we know he's in the US purely for an education, I will back off."

"Okay," Roxanne said. "I'll be careful, whatever that means. But it's my life. Once I graduate from high school and am off to college, I will make my own choices. Don't expect me to choose a boyfriend on the basis of how it will affect the world, okay?"

With that, Roxanne closed her mind and walked out of the living room. She entered her bedroom and slammed her door shut.

Rebecca and Roger sighed simultaneously. "Sorry," Roger said.

"It'll be okay," Rebecca replied.

"As much as I sympathize with Roxanne's feelings, the threat is real."

"You're under stress, darling. I can feel it."

"Yes, I suppose I am. I'm concerned for her." Roger refrained from revealing how deeply concerned he really was.

"It will be okay," Rebecca said. "It always is. And we know that you will do all you need to do to make it okay."

Roger wanted to go to her immediately, hold her in his arms, and make love to her.

"What do you think about you and Roxanne visiting Alex for a little talk?" he asked.

"Can't hurt," Rebecca said. "Maybe he can serve as a soothing, objective voice in the emotional storm."

"Yes. Alexander to the rescue, saving me again."

Both laughed and then were silent, allowing their feelings for each other to fill the void between them.

Chapter 4

Roxanne and Rebecca Visit Western Council Headquarters

With Roxanne in the passenger seat, Rebecca drove her Volvo station wagon south on Rocky Creek and Potomac Parkway, on their way to the southwest section of Washington and a meeting with Alexander Astrakhan. It was late Saturday morning and traffic was light. The weather had finally cleared. The sky was a faraway blue, and the autumn sun bathed the day in a crystalline yellow light. Earlier, while the two ate breakfast, Rebecca had asked Roxanne if it would be okay with her if they visited their old family friend Alexander at the Western Council of Geniuses headquarters and then do some shopping in Georgetown.

"From time to time," Rebecca said, "your father and I have turned to Alexander for help on important matters. He's a very wise old friend. I know that on some level this is an intrusion into your personal life, but your father and I just want you to be safe. If Alexander can add something of value, we'll hear it and take it into account. If not, we'll let it pass. And we all know that, in the end, you must make your own choices. Would it be okay with you if we talked to Alexander? It would mean a lot to your dad and me."

Roxanne thought for a moment and then replied, "Okay, Mom, but let's make it a short visit. I'd love to get out and enjoy the sun."

"You bet, sweetheart. Let's clean up breakfast and go."

Rock Creek and Potomac Parkway passed through a long, forested park that was named for Rock Creek, a ribbon of water that ran through the park and emptied into the Potomac River. The park was a favorite place for runners who loped along the trail, as cars hurried north and south on the narrow and curving strip of highway.

Rebecca and Roxanne enjoyed the air and the sun and the wooded park, each allowing their thoughts to drift. Neither one intruded on the other's privacy. Finally Roxanne silently asked her mother a question.

"Why is Alexander Astrakhan so important to the family?"

"He was instrumental in shaping your father's life. He even saved his life once."

"Really?" Roxanne said. "How?"

"As you know, your father was born just before the American Civil War. His parents lived in Vermont and were strongly opposed to slavery. They were heavily involved in the Underground Railroad, which shuttled slaves to safe havens in the North. Just before the war ended, a horde of riders stormed your grandparents' house and killed both of your dad's parents."

Roxanne recoiled in horror. "Mom, that's terrible. I never knew that. Murdered? That must have had a huge impact on Dad!"

"It did. He never told you the story because he's always trying to protect you from some of the harsher realities of life—including his own life. Anyway, no one knows how the group managed to catch your grandparents by surprise. Somehow, their defenses were down, which very likely means they were in the company of someone they trusted. It's possible one of our kind was involved, but we don't know. Your father, who was only five years old at the time, happened to be at a neighbor's house when the raid occurred. He sensed something terrible had happened and insisted that the neighbor take him home. When they arrived, both his parents were dead, their horses and livestock stolen, and their home burned to the ground. He saw their charred bodies lying on the ground, along with his destroyed home, and it traumatized him. He says he's never fully gotten over it.

"To this day, we do not know who was involved. We suspect the Eastern Geniuses had a hand in the murders, but we have no proof.

"In any case, with his parents dead, your father could easily have been shipped off to an orphanage run by Ordinaries, which would have been tragic. He never would have been understood, and his abilities would have been suppressed. Fortunately, Alexander got word of your grandparents' deaths and intervened.

"Alexander was two centuries old then and he knew many of the Geniuses around the world, including your grandparents. He arranged for your father to be raised by people of our kind. Alexander also had your father sent to special schools for Geniuses, right up through his university training. He's been your father's benefactor throughout life."

"You said he saved Dad's life," Roxanne said. "How did he do that?"

"During the Vietnam War, the United Nations sent an international team of diplomats and Red Cross personnel to assess the war and see what could be done to bring the conflict to an end. Your father and Alexander were part of that team. They went there to see for themselves what the situation was and to determine if the Western Council of Geniuses should intervene in ending the war. In fact, the Eastern Council was doing all it could to prolong the war and drain the Americans of every drop of blood, will, and treasure. Roger and Alexander were traveling through the back country to a small village where they were to meet Ho Chi Minh. When they arrived, the village was heavily bombed. They later found out that there was a military target nearby where weapons were stored. In any case, a few of the bombs fell on the village. One of them landed just one hundred feet from your father and blew him backward. He was flying directly toward an open booby trap. A pit with sharpened bamboo stakes that were meant to impale any outsider who invaded the village. Alexander saw your father was going to land in the open pit. Alexander is an extremely powerful Genius, maybe the most powerful Genius in the world today. Using his mind and his power of telekinesis, he literally pushed your father's body aside so that your father landed on soft earth. The two got to safety and made their way to another village, where they met Ho Chi Minh. The war ended shortly after that."

Roxanne was awestruck. "Wow, it's no wonder Dad reveres him."

The two continued the drive in silence. Soon, the highway took them out of the park and along the edge of town known as Foggy Bottom, where they passed well-known buildings, including the Watergate complex, George Washington University, and the Kennedy Center for the Performing Arts.

Rebecca telepathically said to Roxanne, "Alexander, of course, is your father's mentor, but he has done so much good for Ordinaries that your father looks at him as a kind of paragon, an ideal for all of us to attain.

"It was Alexander who planted the idea in the minds of scientists to combine drugs as they searched for a treatment for AIDS. The AIDS virus mutates very quickly in the face of any single treatment. A single drug might be useful in reducing the overall viral load, but its effectiveness is overcome when the mutating virus shuffles its genes and no longer responds to treatment. Alexander inspired scientists to use three or four anti-viral drugs simultaneously. He also *suggested* they regularly change the drugs in order to thwart the virus's mutating capacity. Every time it changed its genetic makeup, a drug was waiting in the system to corner the illness and fight it. And it worked. Many thousands of people are alive today because of that idea."

Roxanne had always respected Alexander, and liked him too, but now her respect was tinged with intimidation. Rebecca read her thoughts and assured her that Alexander always wanted to be treated like a favored uncle.

"He won't like it if you're too shy with him today," Rebecca said. "So let's go on treating him like a member of our extended family, okay?"

"Okay, Mom."

Rebecca got off Rocky Creek Parkway and joined Independence Avenue. From there, she turned south and soon pulled up in front of an enormous construction site. Instantly, their nervous systems were impacted by a symphony of pings. Reflexively, Roxanne turned to look at the construction site in order to ascertain the source of all that energy.

It was hard to make out the actual building through all the scaffolding and plywood ramparts, though the entire site looked like any other large building project. In fact, it was anything but. It was all an illusion created by advanced technology and powerful minds, which kept the actual enormous and beautiful building hidden.

Rebecca led Roxanne along a plywood walkway laid over dirt and littered on both sides by construction debris. The walkway led to an enclosed plywood portico. Several yards farther, a pair of plywood doors hung loosely on make-shift hinges. The doors were the entrance to the main building, which to an Ordinary's eye seemed in the early stages of construction. Once Rebecca and Roxanne opened the plywood doors, they entered a large glass-enclosed atrium that was flooded with sunlight and color. The atrium, which was twenty stories high, served as a great hall to a building that was an ultra-modern marvel. An amazing variety of plants lined the periphery of the atrium, including tall flower-bearing trees, bushes, and great vines that seemed to call out for attention. Birds flew freely and lighted on the branches of the trees. Crystalline glass refracted the sunlight and threw rainbows of color in all directions. The fragrance of flowers heightened the experience, so that it was like stepping into a heavenly realm.

Roxanne stood for a while and looked up in awe. She had not been there since she was a child, but even her photographic memory had not prepared her for this wondrous place.

Beyond the atrium, hallways opened to grand rooms that were also bathed in sunlight. Some of the hallway walls appeared to be made of marble while others were thick, clear glass. Within the glass walls, elevators whisked people to the upper floors and back down again. A dozen large monitors were embedded in the marble walls, all showing recordings of actual events from thousands of years ago. The documentaries revealed epic-making inventions or great leaps forward in human thought. Thanks to their advanced technology, Geniuses had been recording events for several millennia. One monitor ran footage of the Parthenon being constructed. A team of Geniuses were on site, directing the construction. Another monitor depicted a series of inventions in the ancient world.

Roxanne recognized Archimedes's pump, which he had designed twenty-two-hundred years earlier for King Hiero of Syracuse in order to pull water out of the bottom of ships. Archimedes himself described on the video how he invented the pump. Roxanne moved on to the monitor telling the story of Leonardo Da Vinci and his many inventions. As in the others, Leonardo himself was interviewed, though he had been unaware the conversation was being recorded. As she looked around, she saw the creation of the Roman abacus, humankind's first computer; Hans Lippershey and the invention of the telescope; the Wright Brothers and their biplane; and Steve Jobs and the Apple computer.

A monitor along one wall showed footage of Moses in the Sinai; on the monitor beside it, Jesus was teaching on a hillside outside of Jerusalem. Roxanne was dizzy with sensory overload.

"All of this is a lot to take in at once," Rebecca said, smiling at Roxanne. "We'll come back soon and spend a day. For now, let's go take in one of the exhibits inside."

They walked down a hallway, past the elevators, and into another enormous room, this one also flooded with sunlight and color. Scattered throughout the room were small daises.

Rebecca directed Roxanne to a dais near the great windows. "Go ahead, tell the exhibit that you are ready for it to begin."

Roxanne sent a thought into the air above the dais and immediately a famous entrepreneur appeared on the dais as a holographic image. Roxanne gasped in surprise and pleasure.

"Hello, Rebecca and Roxanne," the man said. "Welcome to the Headquarters of the Western Geniuses. This is an introductory presentation on our kind, a sort of précis on a few of our uncommon abilities, and some of our many contributions throughout the centuries."

Roxanne took her mother's arm and said with delight, "I didn't know he was one of us."

Rebecca smiled. "Oh, yes. You'd be surprised by the number of entrepreneurs, actors, and inventors who are Geniuses,"

"It's no wonder I've always liked him," Roxanne said.

The famous man in the holographic presentation continued. "Our kind, in fact, is a tiny minority among the seven billion people alive on the planet today. Our number ebbs and flows between about four hundred and six hundred in the entire world. How did we come to be? The simple answer is that nature gives rise to anomalies. We are a certain kind of anomaly.

"Ninety-nine percent of humans fall in the middle of a bell-shaped curve of human intelligence. These people have IQs between seventy and one hundred and thirty. They are the majority and therefore considered normal. But there are also people outside the norm, at both ends of the bell curve. The farther out you go at each end, the smaller the population and the greater the anomaly.

"At the lower end of the curve, IQs can be twenty and lower. These people have special needs and require a great deal of care throughout their lives. At the other end we find ourselves, those whom we refer to as Geniuses, people with IQs of one thousand or greater. Like our brethren at the lower end of the curve, we, too, represent an extremely small portion of humanity.

"Our advanced nervous systems and high IQs give us special abilities. For one thing, we experience life much more intensely. For example, our capacity for taste and smell are highly advanced, even more advanced than some animals. We also compute more rapidly than any computer that Ordinary scientists have yet invented. We are many times more creative than Ordinary minds. We command vast stores of knowledge, which we can retrieve in an instant.

"We have the power to send and receive thoughts as bundles of electromagnetic energy."

The images within the hologram changed. A man and a woman appeared, facing each other. Discernible ripples, waves of electromagnetic energy, flowed between them. The waves, which seemed soft, viscous, and powerful, were attached to what appeared to be tiny golden dots. The man and woman absorbed the waves and dots they were sending to each other. As they did, they became increasingly relaxed, open, and happy. They smiled lovingly at each other.

"What you are seeing, Rebecca and Roxanne, are actual thoughts passing between two people. In this case, the thoughts are those of love."

The two people disappeared and the narrator returned.

"Our ability to generate enormous amounts of energy within our nervous systems is the source of the warning signal, or ping, that we experience when we approach another of our kind.

"Our talent for sending and receiving thoughts give us a variety of capabilities. For one, we can communicate telepathically with each other. We can implant ideas in other people's minds. We can increase the intensity of the energy in these thought bundles to alter their biochemistry. We can use this energy to heal or injure. The energy we send can become so powerful, we can literally destroy a person's nervous system and thus cause his death. This, of course, gives us enormous responsibility in how we deal with people, especially Ordinaries.

"Our telepathic abilities allow us to communicate with animals, and this has given us a unique relationship with the animal kingdom."

Again, the hologram changed to show a variety of animals—a squirrel, a rabbit, a wolf, and a family of whales. Roxanne and Rebecca sent the animals telepathic greetings, and they could telepathically receive the animal's warm reactions.

"We also have the ability to block the thoughts of others and to protect our own thoughts. This barrier, or shield as we call it, can be amplified considerably. It can become so powerful that it can change the flight of objects that might be thrown or fired at us.

"We age more slowly than the common population. Because of our intellectual capabilities, we have made advances in nutrition, mind-body healing, and medicine that contribute even further to our longevity. We also have immense healing energy and can cure illnesses and heal wounds with a single touch.

"Some of us have even more advanced abilities. A minority of us can move objects with our minds. Some can suspend themselves in midair. Others can see the future. Some can turn energy into matter and matter into energy. The legends of alchemists being able to turn lead into gold are, in fact, true stories about Geniuses with that very special gift.

"The displays that you saw in the atrium represent great strides forward in human development. In these and many other cases, people of our kind, whom we refer to as the Old Ones, gave highly intelligent members of the ordinary population the ideas for these inventions."

The holographic image changed to the pyramids being built. The image expanded and enveloped Roxanne and Rebecca so that they were standing in the Valley of Giza as ancient Egyptians constructed the Great Pyramid. Near them, Pharaoh Khufu stood next to two men whom Roxanne realized were two of the Old Ones the narrator had mentioned.

"The images you see right now are actual holographic recordings taken during the construction of the pyramids. Our elders provided the technology that was needed to build the pyramids. Contrary to what many ordinary scientists maintain today, the pyramids were not mere burial sites, but structures specifically designed to channel vast amounts of electromagnetic energy from the cosmos into the earth in order to enrich the fertility of the soil and provide an abundance of food to the Egyptian population. These solar and cosmic rays were also used in religious ceremonies in order to enhance human consciousness, which led to periods of peace and greater harmony among peoples.

"The Old Ones served as guides and teachers to Ordinaries. They helped Ordinaries build not only the Egyptian pyramids, but many of the great temples and megaliths of the ancient world, including those at Machu Picchu in Peru, Tiwanaku in Bolivia, Stonehenge, and the Moai statues on Easter Island. Ordinaries have long noted certain similarities among these sites. That commonality arose because they were all constructed with the guidance of the Old Ones. You'll find other exhibits that explain the meanings of these and other ancient sites.

We also served as advisers and supporters of many of the great spiritual teachers of the ancient world. You'll find exhibits on the great masters of spiritual thought and life in adjoining rooms.

"Time and the evolution of thought have affected our kind, as well. As you know, the Geniuses of the East and West have developed very different ideologies over the millennia. The Geniuses of the East see

Ordinaries as inferior beings who must be controlled and directed according to the wishes of the Eastern Council of Geniuses.

"The Eastern Geniuses have been careful to impart knowledge only when it serves their purposes. This is one of the reasons why, in recent centuries, far more invention, creativity, and philosophical development have taken place in the West than in the East.

"We of the Council of Western Geniuses—the governing body of our kind in the West—have developed a set of principles that guide us in our relationship with Ordinaries. We see all human beings, Ordinaries and Geniuses alike, as a single people whose destinies are united. Respect for human life and dignity is the core principle in our dealings with all of humanity. We are committed to liberty, self-determination, freedom, and democratic principles for all. In support of these principles, we have followed the model established long ago by the Old Ones who kept our presence hidden from the world. As a general rule, the Old Ones counseled nonintervention. When we do intervene, we do so only in secret. They taught us to provide support only when Ordinaries are ready, and to act from our core principles.

"On the other hand, we are constantly vigilant in our efforts to check the aggression of the Council of Eastern Geniuses, whose primary goal has been world domination and autocratic rule."

"I can quickly give you an early illustration of how our kind has intervened over the millennia to prevent the Eastern Council from dominating humanity. In 490 B.C., under the influence of Eastern Geniuses, the Persian emperor King Darius I sent an invasion force of more than 40,000 of Persia's dreaded warriors against the Greek city-state of Athens. With the strategic help of our ancestors, the vastly outnumbered Athenian army defeated the Persian army on the plain of Marathon, and drove the Persians into the sea."

As the narrator spoke images appeared of the Greek victory at the Battle of Marathon and of the Greek solider, Phaedippas, who ran 25 miles back to Athens, uttered the word *victory* and then died.

"Athens was the birthplace of Western democracy and of much of early Western culture. Had the despotic Persian empire conquered

Athens, the course of history and Western civilization would have been very different."

The narrator continued, "Eastern Geniuses have supported many other tyrants since then." At that point, an image of Eastern Geniuses appeared standing behind an array of tyrants, including Genghis Khan, Adolf Hitler, and Joseph Stalin.

"Well, that's our short presentation, Rebecca and Roxanne. It's been a pleasure talking to you both. There are many other exhibits you can take in, either as holographic presentations or as lectures in the auditoriums throughout the building."

The narrator leaned toward Rebecca and Roxanne and adopted a conspiratorial tone. "But let me make a suggestion to you both. Check out the talks on religion, religious leaders, Atlantis, Lemuria, and UFOs. I think they would be of more interest to you at this time than some of the others."

"Thank you for the suggestion," Roxanne said, completely charmed.

"It's getting close to our appointment time," Rebecca said to Roxanne. "Let's go meet Alexander."

Rebecca led the way to an elevator whose doors opened immediately and welcomed the two inside. "Eighteenth floor, please," Rebecca told the computerized elevator. The doors were in the process of closing when a voice called out, "Hold the doors please, computer."

The doors instantly reversed direction, opening for a spry old man who hurried inside the elevator and told the computer, "Seventeenth floor, please." He looked at Rebecca and Roxanne and his face instantly came alive.

"Well, if it isn't Rebecca Reynolds, and I dare say …. This must be … No, it couldn't be. Roxanne?"

Rebecca smiled warmly and said, "Cecil Pasternak, what a pleasure. You look wonderful. How long has it been since we have seen you?"

Cecil Pasternak was a small man, perhaps five feet four inches tall, and lean. He wore dark pants, a white shirt, suspenders, and a colorful bow tie. His hair was white and thin, his eyes soft and round, his face well-lined but still youthful. His smile was full of warmth and good humor.

"Rebecca, you look more beautiful every time I see you," he said. "And yes, it has been a little while. Three years this coming Halloween. We saw each other at the costume party here at HQ. You were dressed as a cat, which made every man in the building crazy. They all wanted to pull on your tail." Cecil gave a sly smile and a wink.

"You devil," Rebecca said, her smile equally sly. "You're still full of vinegar and sweetness, aren't you?"

"Not sure about the sweetness, but yes, I can be a touch sour now and then, but never in your presence. And what about this young beauty with you? Oh, my goodness. You are going to set the world on fire, my young princess. How old are you now, Roxanne?"

"Seventeen, Dr. Pasternak," Roxanne said. "And I'm afraid it's been more than three years since I've seen you. I was too young to go to that Halloween Party, as I recall." Roxanne turned her mouth down in mock disappointment. "I believe I met you last when I was ten."

The computer announced that they had arrived at the seventeenth floor. The doors opened and remained open while the three continued talking.

"How do you do it, Cecil?" Rebecca asked. "How do you stay so young and full of energy? You don't look a day older than sixty-five."

"Well, truth be told, my dear, I'm 428. Don't tell anybody though. I don't want the expectations of others to slow me down."

"What's your secret?" Rebecca asked.

"Well, since no one else is in this elevator, I'm going to tell you: I focus on the present – not on the centuries I've lived through – and I take a daily nap of twenty minutes. Can't live without it. It's like a prescription—I never miss it. I lie down on my couch at precisely 12:45 and sleep for twenty minutes. That's all I need. I'm up at 1:05 and I feel great."

"Why don't you visit me sometime, both of you?" he continued. "I'm still running the central computer. Come by and meet the great Oracle. The thing is a marvel, though I dare not say that out loud. She's very caught up with herself…incorrigible. Demands we call her Delphi. Otherwise she acts up." Resuming his smile, Cecil said, "Well, wonderful to see you both." He waved and left the elevator.

The elevator doors closed again and whisked Rebecca and Roxanne to the eighteenth floor and the office of Alexander Astrakhan. They exited the elevator and walked along a curved hallway that was lined with floor to ceiling windows that offered stunning views of Washington.

Roxanne was excited to see Alexander. She had seen him many times at their home and at other places, but had never visited him at his office. She was looking forward to meeting him in his own environment.

As they approached Alexander's door, Jason Phillips walked out of an adjoining office and came toward them. Upon seeing them, his expression changed dramatically, suddenly becoming darkly suspicious. Roxanne felt his defenses go up and become firmly reinforced, as if he had just encountered an enemy and was about to be attacked.

"Hello, Dr. Phillips," Rebecca said in a friendly tone.

He nodded. "Rebecca, Roxanne," he said, but he kept walking, defenses still up, suspicions still strong.

Mother and daughter looked at each other in puzzlement, both acknowledging the chill and the impressions that had flowed to them. Rebecca shrugged as if to suggest Phillips's reaction had nothing to do with them.

"He's probably not feeling well," she said. Nevertheless, she took her daughter's arm in an instinctive gesture of protection.

A few steps later, they had reached Alexander Astrakhan's outer office and they entered.

Chapter 5
Alexander Astrakhan

Rebecca and Roxanne entered Alexander's outer office and were immediately confronted by a woman Rebecca knew well, his diminutive and unwelcoming secretary, Elizabeth Braumau. The walls of Ms. Braumau's office were covered in an ancient Asian garden scene at sunrise, rendered in shades of gray, gold, and black. The floor was covered with an expensive carpet the color of charcoal. Elizabeth Braumau's desk, which was placed directly opposite the door to the hall, had a glass surface set on a pedestal the shape of an hourglass. An oversized computer screen stood on top of the desk. Otherwise the desk was clear except for a small framed photograph of Ms. Braumau and Alexander Astrakhan in Graz, Austria, right before World War I.

To Ms. Braumau's right was the ornately paneled redwood door to Alexander Astrakhan's office. To her left was another door that led to a small kitchen and even smaller restroom.

The secretary herself seemed to live in a permanent state of annoyance. Though she appeared to be in her mid-fifties, Ms. Braumau was a century older. Her small eyes, tightly closed mouth, and small-boned frame conveyed exactly what she embodied—discipline, order, and machine-like efficiency. Her standard uniform was a black skirt, dark stockings, black shoes, and a black jacket with a Nehru collar that was buttoned at the neck. On her best days, she was curt and to the point. Rebecca well knew that if you said too much, she would cut you off with an icy stare and a sharp remark. Her four most commonly spoken sentences were:

56

"Sit down. He'll be with you when he's ready," and "No, he cannot speak to you today. He's too busy."

Her family was from Simbach am Inn, Germany, located on the German-Austrian border. Ms. Braumau immigrated to Austria at the turn of the century, where she met Alexander Astrakhan and began her long career as his assistant. She had now been serving him for more than a century. It was her singular purpose in life. Alexander Astrakhan was the chief administrative officer of the Council of Western Geniuses, the highest ranking Western Genius, and as far as Ms. Braumau was concerned, the most important man alive. Indeed, Alexander reported only to the Council of Western Geniuses' board of directors, and even then, his judgment was so respected that he was considered nearly infallible.

Alexander himself was a bachelor and acted toward Ms. Braumau as if she were an intimate family member.

"Elizabeth, why don't you get us both a cup?" he often suggested telepathically to her at around 4 p.m., his usual hour for afternoon tea. The thought was communicated more out of habit than out of any need to remind her. She would already be preparing his beautiful Austrian tea set, complete with ornate teapot, creamer, sugar bowl, and serving tray, all made of bone china and trimmed in gold.

It was the moment of the day she loved the most. She would arrange the teapot, cups, bowls, and an assortment of his favorite biscuits on the tray and then carry the entire ensemble into his enormous office, the proud servant offering sustenance to her lord. The two would then sit together, if time allowed, and have a little chat about the day's developments, all of it communicated telepathically and diligently protected from anyone who might try eavesdropping. Alexander was Ms. Braumau's raison d'être. If he had announced one day that it would help him if she would launch herself from the top of the building, she would not have hesitated. She had the loyalty and protective instincts of a Doberman pinscher, and everyone knew she would not hesitate to kill a visitor if Alexander suggested it.

Rebecca had encountered Ms. Braumau many times before and always treated her with light-hearted respect. Most of the people who worked at the Council of Geniuses headquarters were intimidated by her, but Rebecca felt a certain compassion for a woman who had no husband, no children, no friends, and absolutely no access to her heart—save, of course, for the one person she loved but who would forever remain out of reach, Alexander Astrakhan. She was a tragic figure as far as Rebecca was concerned, a prisoner of her own disappointment and isolation. All of which made her a woman to be pitied, not feared. Rebecca suspected that at some point, Ms. Braumau's concrete facade would collapse into a rubble of regret—regret for missing all the warmth, tenderness, kindness, and love that life had offered her but she had refused. Ironically, the crisis that might precipitate the collapse of her angry facade was her only hope for a real life. Only then might she finally open up to the tenderness that existed behind her imposing walls.

Before Rebecca could announce the purpose of their visit, Ms. Braumau said, "He's waiting for you. Go in."

Roxanne followed her mother through the ornate redwood door into Alexander's inner office and immediately marveled at the palatial surroundings. Alexander enjoyed nice things and it showed. The office was huge, about the size of four of Roxanne's bedrooms put together. To the far left two Louis XIV sofas and a Queen Anne wingback chair were placed around a large fireplace. Small tables and bookshelves were arrayed tastefully along the periphery of the office. In a far corner of the room sat an ancient Greek krater, or vase, easily four feet tall, once used for mixing water and wine. Some of the shelves held ornate vases, crystal ware, and small works of art. Roxanne saw a female figurine that, knowing Alexander, was surely an authentic goddess figure from prehistoric times. On other tables, she recognized a bowl from ancient Greece, a vessel from Mesopotamia, and a ceramic work by Jean Cocteau. Displayed on the walls were early works of great artists that would have made any museum proud—a Cubist piece by Picasso hung over the fireplace; a mystical forest scene by Cezanne occupied part of the south wall. Next to it was a large rendering of the Hudson River Valley by

Thomas Cole, and next to it was another large work, this one by Jackson Pollock. Smaller works appeared throughout the room, including a framed pencil drawing by da Vinci.

Unable to resist, Roxanne walked closer to look at several letters that were framed and hanging. They were all from famous leaders. "My dear friend, Alexander," was how a letter from Maximilien de Robespierre began. Other letters were from the Duke of Wellington, Woodrow Wilson, and Theodore Roosevelt.

She also couldn't help but notice one other theme that was present in Alexander's office—guns, most of them handguns, from various historical periods. Among them were the Paterson revolver, favored by the early American Army; several versions of the nineteenth century Colt single action revolver, including the famed Colt .45, the so-called peacemaker; and the Luger, a German gun which was one of the first semi-automatic pistols. A Winchester rifle hung on the north wall as well.

On the far side of the room was Alexander's ornate Louis XIV desk, which was very much the desk of a great king. On top of it sat a multi-screened computer, which Roxanne realized was linked to the central computer on the seventeenth floor, the most powerful computer on earth.

When she was done gazing in wonder at all the treasures in the office, Roxanne's attention was grabbed by the amazing view of Washington DC.

Behind Alexander's large desk and high-backed leather chair, an enormous window ran from floor to ceiling and wall to wall. The view of the city was stunning. And before the window stood the great man himself, Alexander Astrakhan.

Tall and lean, looking every bit a man of power and taste, he was dressed in an obviously expensive gray suit, with a white shirt, red tie, and matching handkerchief in the left breast pocket. His hair was thin on top and fell just over the edges of his large ears. He wore a small beard at his chin, a Van Dyke. His face was thin, his cheeks lined. His small gray eyes were alert and charged with energy. He held a highly polished black walking stick, tipped in gold, in his right hand, but he didn't lean on the stick. Indeed, his body exuded a strength and vitality that suggested a man in his fifties.

Roxanne and Alexander embraced briefly and Roxanne placed a small kiss on his cheek.

"How are you, Uncle?" she asked.

"I'm fine, my dear, fine." He turned to his window and lifted his walking stick, pointing north. "Indulge me as I orient you to the view. Of course, straight ahead is the Washington Monument. Beyond that, the Ellipse, and even farther, the White House."

"Oh, yes," Roxanne said. "It's so beautiful."

"That long park running east west is, of course, the National Mall." As he spoke, he moved the stick left and right, indicating the mall. "If you look to your far left, you can see the Lincoln Memorial."

"The view is awesome, Uncle Alexander. I've always loved the Lincoln Memorial. You can almost feel his presence in the concrete."

"You're right, my dear. But as wonderful as that memorial is, it's a small tribute to a great man." Alexander smiled at Roxanne. "Did you know I knew him?"

Roxanne gaped at Alexander. "You're kidding me."

"No, no, I really did know him, and quite well. At the time, I was the editor of the Illinois *Sentinel*, which meant I had the inside track on Lincoln from the very start. I reported the Lincoln-Douglas debates all across Illinois, and I was at Cooper Union in New York City when he gave his famous speech against slavery. I wrote laudatory articles about him and he courted me during his campaign. He knew how to use the press, let me tell you. Later, during the war years, I continued to see him occasionally at the White House.

"Truth is, he was one of the greatest men I have ever met. Doesn't matter that he was an Ordinary. He was a giant—not so much for his intelligence but for his character. People refer to him as Honest Abe and talk about his remarkable tolerance. Both are true, of course. He was supremely tolerant, almost to a fault." Alexander gave Roxanne a wry smile. "But what made him great, at least in my opinion, was that he was singularly focused, absolutely determined, and when it was necessary, completely ruthless."

Alexander became pensive and quiet, and at that moment Rebecca jumped in.

"Roxanne," she said, "Uncle Alexander was the one who urged President Lincoln to choose General Grant as the central commander for the Union Army."

Roxanne was even more amazed, realizing that that recommendation changed the course of the Civil War. "That's amazing," she said. "Please tell me what you told the president."

"Well, Lincoln would have come around to the same choice eventually on his own," Alexander said. "As a rule, I follow the advice of the Old Ones. We make gentle suggestions and let Ordinaries decide for themselves. But yes, I did recommend Grant to him early on.

"He needed Grant, that's for sure. You know all about Lincoln's generals. For example, McClellan hesitated constantly and treated Lincoln with disrespect, called him a gorilla and all of that. An arrogant man, I always detested him. Once when I was in the White House, the President wanted my thoughts on McClellan. I didn't hold back. 'He doesn't want to get his hands dirty, sir,' I said. 'More show than substance.' That's when I made the recommendation. I said, 'If I may, Mr. President, have you considered General Grant? He would make a fine replacement for McClellan.'

"'Grant? Who is he?' Lincoln asked. He hadn't even heard of Grant at the time.

"I told him Grant was a major general and had commanded the troops in the Mexican-American War. 'He just captured Kentucky and Tennessee at Shiloh,' I told the president. 'Absolutely routed the confederates, even though he was outnumbered.'

"Lincoln seemed to consider my suggestion, but he said, 'It's a grave act, replacing the army's central commander. But I'll consider it.'

"Of course, he had to go through Halleck, Burnside, and Meade before he realized all four of them—including McClellan—were weak men, more aristocrats than warriors. It was Lincoln who pushed them to do their duty. Finally, he studied Grant and realized that here was a man who matched his own enormous will and ruthless determination to save the union.

"Grant was the most brutal general alive. The only reason Lee surrendered at Appomattox was because he knew he was up against Grant, who would kill every living thing between him and victory. Grant was Lincoln's man. Those two knew how to take history by the fist."

Alexander was looking inward now, but turned his gaze back toward the memorial.

"I sometimes stand here," he said, not attempting to hide his fatigue, "and look at the Lincoln Memorial when I am feeling beleaguered and in need of solace. I dare say old Abe and I have had many a chat over the past ninety-two years, since they built the memorial."

Rousing himself out of his brooding, he looked at Roxanne with kind eyes and a gentle smile. Roxanne's heart warmed. She felt the gravity of this man and the weight of responsibility on his shoulders.

"Enough of the silly musings from an old man," he said. "Let's have a look at you, my dear." After looking deeply into Roxanne's eyes, he said, "You, Roxanne, are becoming a great beauty." He turned to Rebecca. "This truly is your daughter, with her father's amazing golden hair. The two of you light up this room."

Rebecca gave him a hug and a kiss on the check. Alexander gestured toward the sitting area by the fireplace. "Let's sit and have a cup, shall we?"

With that, Ms. Braumau entered, carrying the tea set. She set it down on the coffee table between the two sofas. An array of sweet delicacies had already been laid out on the table.

"Why don't you sit on this sofa?" Alexander said, gesturing to the sofa on the left. "That way you can look out over the city when you get tired of looking at this old face." He sat on the Queen Anne chair and directed their attention to the tea and desserts on the table.

"Allow me to give you both the grand tour of what we have on the table," he said, obviously relishing the role of host and tour guide. "These beautiful orange pastries are from the Philippines and they're called ginataang pinipig. They're made from coconut cream mixed with sweet potatoes and banana. They're wonderful. You must try one. Over here, we have a variety of almond cookies. These are from Portugal and those over there are from Syria. You know, people think marzipan cookies originated on the Iberian Peninsula, but in fact they came from the Middle East, where the almonds are especially delicious."

He gestured to another part of the table. "These flakey Italian pastries are from Naples and they just arrived today. I love them. These are Belgian chocolates, and over here we have Austrian chocolates, all filled with various surprises. They say that Belgian chocolate is the best, but Austrian chocolate is my favorite, though I must confess a certain bias for my homeland. In any case, both varieties are made daily." He smiled and winked. "And I have them flown in daily."

Suddenly, he became introspective and spoke as if to himself. "Unlike Ordinaries with their limited capacity for taste and smell, I cannot bear day-old fare."

He turned to Ms. Braumau. "If you please, Elizabeth," he said, and she poured the tea. Once all the cups were filled, she left the room. "*Danke*, Elizabeth," Alexander said, sending the thought to his faithful assistant.

After they had enjoyed their tea in silence for a minute, Alexander asked them how they liked it.

"I love it," Roxanne said. "It's oolong, right? But I've never tasted an oolong like this. Where is it from?"

"Right you are, my dear. It is indeed oolong." Alexander held his cup at the level of his diaphragm and looked down into it, as if he were holding a chalice. "This oolong is very special. The tea leaves are grown high up in the Wuyi Mountains of Fujian province. The tea is actually grown on cliffs. I've watched the growers cure the tea. They put kilos of tea leaves in great big sheets and roll them around by hand, gradually crushing the leaves until the mass becomes as small as a basketball. As the tea leaves are crushed, they release their oils and that starts the oxidation process. It's very sweet, right? Naturally so. The reason is that it's not as oxidized as many common teas. The longer the oxidation, the darker a tea gets. Notice how light this tea is. It's known as the blue-green variety. Very little oxidation, but rich in flavor. That's no little trick. The tea makers in the Wuyi Mountains spend their lives perfecting the art of tea."

Rebecca winked at her daughter and sent her a little thought over the telepathic airwaves. "Isn't this fun?" Roxanne smiled back at her mother.

Alexander turned to Rebecca. "May I say as an old man—old enough to be your father many times over—that you become more radiant every time I see you, Rebecca." As she smiled at the compliment, he abruptly switched gears. "How is Roger? I mean, really, how's he doing? He's all business with me, as you know. You're probably the only person on earth who really knows him."

"He's fine, Alex," she said. "He's got his hands full, as you know. He's very busy. I think he wants to come home soon. He misses us."

"Of course. Who could blame him?"

Turning to Roxanne, Alexander said, "Let me tell you something, Roxanne. Your father's name will not appear in any historical account written by Ordinaries, but he's done more to shape the last century than any ten of the most famous Ordinaries of the last one hundred years. I'm happy to tell you that we did a lot of it together. But he deserves most of the credit, and I say that as a fact, not out of any false modesty."

"Well, if you ask Roger," Rebecca said, "he'll tell you that that is not quite the way he'd phrase it. To quote one of his favorite aphorisms: 'At a hundred crucial moments in history, Alexander turned the tide in favor of freedom.' That's what Roger witnessed."

"We turned the tide together," Alexander said, clearly embarrassed. He turned to Roxanne. "Your father is a great man, never forget that."

"Thank you, Uncle Alex," Roxanne replied. "I wish he were home more often, though."

"Of course, you do. And he wants that too. Believe me. He doesn't share much with me, but he shares that. He loves you more than you could ever know."

The three sat in silence while they sipped their tea. Roxanne tried the ginataang pinipig. "Wow, this is delicious," she said to Alexander. He smiled appreciatively.

"Tell me about school," he said to her. "No, no, tell me about this new boy, Andor Lysenko. Is that his name?"

Roxanne was momentarily taken aback. She had been thoroughly enjoying Alexander's hospitality and felt blindsided by his question.

"Just a second," Alexander said, "may we invite your father to join us? I would like him to be part of this conversation, if it's okay with the both of you."

"Yes, please," Rebecca said. "I would like that too."

Roxanne, conscious of being outnumbered by the adults and wary that the conversation was about to become too parental, nonetheless said, "Okay. Sure."

All three closed their eyes and looked within, passing through that veil of reality to the other dimension where distances do not exist. Because she was young and still developing her abilities, Roxanne's telepathy could not reach London on its own. Roger could reach her, of course, and thus communication between them was easy.

Still at his desk in London, Roger felt a tingling sensation in the back of his neck that brought his attention to the series of directed thoughts being sent to him from Rebecca and Alexander Astrakhan. He opened his mind and was immediately in communication with them in Washington. He knew Roxanne was also with them.

"How are you, Rebecca?" he asked. "And Roxanne, how do you like Alexander's office? First time, right?"

"I love it, Dad. But we wish you were here."

"Me too, sweetheart. I'm coming home soon."

Alexander spoke. "What do you think the British position will be on the hostilities in Slavistan, Roger?"

"It's wait and see here in England, much like the US position. A significant minority fear that the hostilities will spread beyond the neighboring countries and into Western Europe. The prime minister and Parliament aren't sure what to do right now."

"And what do you make of this young Genius from the East coming to a suburb of Washington?"

"We don't know yet," Roger replied. "Certainly it's troubling, but we have very little knowledge of what he may be up to, if anything."

Roxanne jumped in. "Daddy, why can't he be just another foreign student? Happens all the time. I don't understand why this has to be such a big deal."

"You may be right, Roxanne," Roger said. "We just don't know. The truth is, Andor could influence the actions of the US government, especially if he manages to get close to one or more leading government officials."

"Roxanne," Alexander said, "we believe that the Eastern Council is controlling the leader of Slavistan, Victor Grozny. Grozny is a murderer and a megalomaniac, and he would be trouble even if left to his own devices. But he's being manipulated to start a border war with his neighbors, Bulgaristan, Czeckostan, and Cossackia, countries which are not yet under the Eastern Council's control. Grozny has sent teams of thugs into these three countries to stir up trouble. They murder men, women, and children, rape young girls, and burn farms. At the same time, the Eastern Council has created counterterrorist squads, but in fact they are Slavistani terrorists masquerading as Bulgaristanis, Czeckostanis, and Cossackians to make it seem as if both sides are fighting. These so-called counterterrorist teams cross into Slavistan and commit the same kinds of atrocities against their own people. All of this is done to create the appearance of a grassroots war that lends legitimacy to Victor Grozny's true ambitions, which are a military takeover and annexation of these bordering nations.

"The Eastern Council is committed to autocratic rule, starting in individual countries such as Slavistan and hoping to spread throughout Asia and Eastern Europe. Eventually, they hope to achieve a worldwide government that is dominated by Eastern Geniuses. A stronger and more aggressive Slavistan would be the centerpiece for further aggression.

"While all of this is going on, it's important for the Eastern Council to control public opinion in the West, especially in the United States. We are concerned that Andor Lysenko may have some part to play in all of this. You are right, though. We don't know for sure if he is a part of the Eastern Council's plan. He could be an innocent young man who has escaped the Eastern Council and wants to make a life in the United States. Please believe me. We all want that to be true. But until we know for sure, we must ferret out the truth. Can you understand?"

Roxanne considered what Alexander had said. "Yes, I suppose I do understand," she said after a moment.

"Did you have any impressions when you met him?" Alexander asked.

"No, none. I only spent thirty minutes in his company, and most of it concerned a jelly-bean contest at our school."

Alexander smiled. "Ah yes, the jelly-bean contest."

Roxanne immediately felt a hint of guilt. She knew her parents and Alexander did not approve of any Genius flaunting his or her abilities. Alexander, though, didn't embarrass her by pushing the point.

"Did you talk at all to young Andor?" he asked.

"Yes, a little. He asked to see me again so that I could tell him what it's like for our kind at Laurel Glen, but the request seemed innocent and understandable."

"Of course, my dear, of course. Do the two of you share any classes at school?"

"No. He's a senior and I'm a junior."

"Roxanne, could you excuse me for a moment while I speak to your parents privately?"

"Of course, Uncle," Roxanne replied.

Shielding his thoughts from Roxanne, Alexander communicated directly with Rebecca and Roger. "If you both agree, I would like to ask Roxanne to let us know if Andor says anything that might reveal his purpose for being in the US or any plans he might have for being here. Of course, that is up to both of you."

"I'm a little uncomfortable with that request," Rebecca said. "What are the parameters? We're not asking her to spy for the Western Council, are we?"

"I have the same concerns, Alex," Roger said.

"Quite right," Alexander answered. "First, I am sure that Andor will seek out Roxanne, if only to speak to someone of his own kind. He's in a foreign country, he may have no one here of our kind to offer support, and certainly no one like Roxanne at his school. It would be natural for him to seek her out, even if he is exactly what he says he is.

"So when Andor seeks out Roxanne and the two of them talk, would it be all right to ask her to share any insights she has with the two of you? If they are meaningful, I would ask you to pass them on to us here at the council. That is all I am asking."

Rebecca and Roger conferred privately, and then Rebecca said that the request was acceptable to both of them, as long as Roxanne was not asked to do anything that went beyond the limited request he'd described.

"Thank you," Alexander said. He opened to include Roxanne again.

"Roxanne, Andor could be entirely innocent of any connection to the Eastern Council, just as you say. And we are proceeding on that premise. But we must also proceed cautiously, which means we must be alert.

"Would it be asking too much of you to simply tell your parents if anything in your conversations with Andor make you suspicious about his intentions, or reveal any connection to the Eastern Council?"

"I guess I could do that," Roxanne said, though the idea made her apprehensive.

"We're not asking you to do anything out of the ordinary," Alexander said. "Conduct yourself as you would with any other school friend. But we're asking you to be alert with Andor and to tell us if anything untoward turns up."

Roger jumped into the conversation. "We do not want you to do anything that would put you at any risk, Roxanne. That means, you do not seek him out or try to invade his thoughts."

Rebecca concurred. "If you feel you'd simply like to stay away from Andor, then that's what you do, honey. And we definitely are not asking you to spy. If the two of you happen to talk and you feel something is wrong, you tell us. Otherwise, we assume Andor is exactly what he says he is—a young man who wants to have an education in the West. Is that okay with you?"

"I guess so," Roxanne said.

Alexander again sealed Roxanne from his thoughts.

"Roger, I'd like to take some security measures to protect Roxanne, if that meets with your approval. Lionel Clearwater could assign one of our security specialists to her. She'd never actually see the man, but he could monitor any interactions between Roxanne and Andor and take protective measures in the event Andor did something aggressive. Would that be all right with you?"

Lionel Clearwater was the chief of security at the Council of Western Geniuses headquarters. He and his officers monitored all crimes and misdemeanors associated with Geniuses throughout the West.

"Yes, Alexander," Roger replied. "Rebecca and I would appreciate that very much. Thank you."

"We have to be on our toes here," Alexander said. "You and I know the dangers, and we are not going to let anything happen to this beautiful child of yours."

"Once you and Lionel have a man in place, please let me know who he is," Roger said. "Also, please circulate his reports to me."

"I will indeed," Alexander said. "We will keep you informed of his every action and impression."

Alexander exhaled and reopened the communication to Roxanne. "Well, thank you both for coming. And Roger, thank you for all that you are doing and for being present with us this afternoon. Now, if all three of you will excuse me, I will get back to my duties. Thank you, Roger. We will speak soon." With that, Alexander smiled at Rebecca and Roxanne and embraced each of them.

"Let's all be in touch again soon. Is that agreeable to the two of you?" he asked. "Our visits are too infrequent and I want to know how the two of you are doing. Besides, you both bring such beauty and joy to this lonely old man's life."

Rebecca and Roxanne smiled and agreed to see Alexander soon.

"Now," Rebecca said, "Roxanne and I have some shopping to do." She took her daughter's arm and led her out of Alexander's office. When they entered the outer office, Ms. Braumau stood by the open door to the corridor, arms folded and a scowl on her face, waiting for the two visitors to hurry along.

Rebecca and Roxanne were back in their car and driving to Georgetown when Roxanne finally said, "Why do I feel so uncomfortable with what just happened?"

Chapter 6
Roxanne's Evening Phone Calls

B y evening, the weather had turned unseasonably foul again. A wind-driven rain had people hurrying from their cars to their homes, or into stores, or other ports of shelter. That night, as the rain whipped the windows of her house, Roxanne ensconced herself in her room.

The room was bathed in soft light, thanks to a floor lamp in the corner of her room near the window. The room was alive with color—the walls were lime green, yellow, and white. A bedspread of pink and white covered her double bed. Opposite the bed was a poster of Mark Rothko's *Violet, Green and Red*. Next to it was a large picture of Einstein with the quote, "Gravitation is not responsible for people falling in love." Also on her walls was a poster of a large field of flowers, another of Johnny Depp, and still another of an R.E.M. album cover, which consisted of the words Part Lies, Part Heart, Part Truth, Part Garbage written in white on a black background. To the left of her bed was her desk with her computer. A large multicolored area rug covered the hardwood floor.

Roxanne unpacked the clothes she had purchased that afternoon with her mother: a tight-fitting distressed denim jacket with roll-up sleeves; a black zip-up hoodie; three tops; a couple of pairs of skinny jeans; a brown heavy-knit turtleneck sweater; a baby blue cardigan with embedded rhinestones; and a couple of pairs of shoes, including a pair of silver Bella Metallic sneakers by Ralph Lauren.

As she unpacked and hung up her clothes, Roxanne tried to make sense of the feelings that roiled inside her. When the moment of truth had come and Uncle Alexander had asked for her thoughts about Andor, she had suddenly reared up, like a horse that was being forced to jump into a chasm. Her solar plexus had tightened, her body had pulled back, and her spirit had said no. Why had she done that?

Even though alone in her room, she suddenly became self-conscious. Was someone listening in on her thoughts? She raised her shield, walling herself off and protecting from intrusion.

Why had she resisted sharing her feelings with her family? Andor Lysenko was a boy she had spent a total of thirty-three minutes with. Why should she choose him over the people she loved the most? Or maybe she wasn't choosing Andor. She was choosing herself.

I'm not a child, as much as you'd like to treat me like one, she thought in an imaginary conversation with the three adults. *I'm entitled to make my own judgments of people, including my feelings about this boy. I also have the right to decide if I'm ready to share my thoughts, and even how much I want to say.*

In that moment, Roxanne realized she had crossed some divide in her life. She had chosen herself over her parents and Uncle Alexander. In doing so, she had gained a sense of power and independence. Somehow, Andor had helped her do this.

Again, she became protective of her thoughts, retreating even further into her inner world.

What was it about Andor that had compelled her to make such a stand? The answer came to her immediately: there was more to Andor than what her family saw. He wasn't the one-dimensional figure they were making him out to be. On the surface, he seemed purposeful and strong. He wanted to appear brave, witty, and even suave, as if he were in complete control of any situation. But he was acting. Of this, Roxanne was certain. Had he continued talking, she realized, his brave facade would show cracks of uncertainty, perhaps even fear. That was what she had sensed beneath all that show of confidence—fear. It had been apparent as they walked down the stairs from Dean Murphy's office. It had been even more evident when they stood outside the Laurel building and he had struggled to find something to say to her. He'd been reaching out—she'd felt it!—but he didn't know how. What had he really been asking her? She wondered. Was it just a date? Or was it something more? Was he perhaps looking for a confidante in a dangerous and scary world?

He might be a spy, as her father had said. But he was more. He was a terrified boy looking for safety, friendship, and someone with whom he could share his inner world. He didn't fully trust the adults in his world, either, but he didn't know where to turn for support or help. There was no one he could trust.

Roxanne suddenly felt a special bond with Andor. They were alike in so many ways, including the need to share their inner worlds with someone who could truly understand what the other was going through. Her heart opened and she felt an irresistible pull toward this awkward boy. She wanted him to call and to be with him that night. Surely, he must feel that, wherever he was. Did she dare open up and send out that thought? She had no doubt that he would receive it immediately.

Suddenly her cell phone rang and she jumped. The excitement and hope that Andor was calling obscured her ability to know who was actually on the line. In fact, it was Paul Grinsky, and when she realized that, her heart sank. She took a breath and answered her phone.

"Hi, Paul, this is a surprise," she said, trying to sound upbeat. It wasn't his fault he wasn't Andor. "Don't you have something better to do on a Saturday night than call me? *Isn't there someone else you'd rather be calling, Paul?*"

"Well, yeah, I guess so, Roxanne," he said. "That's why I'm calling you, because you're the only girl I can confide in. What if Sarah doesn't want me to call? I don't want to get rejected. And the truth is, I get tongue-tied when I speak to her. I make a mess of the words. What should I do?"

Roxanne felt on the spot. She knew Sarah wanted Paul to call her, but she didn't want to betray her friend's confidence.

"Paul, you're one of the smartest guys in our class, and everybody likes you. Sarah's not going to reject you. She's not that kind of girl."

"Yeah, I know she's nice and all. I guess I'm worried that she'd be nice to me, but she doesn't want me to ask her out."

Roxanne considered sending him a series of impulses that would increase his dopamine levels and give him an instant jolt of energy and courage. She decided against it. *Restraint, remember?* She told herself. He would have to do this on his own—or at least with only minimal help from her.

"Tell you what, Paul. Would you like me to ask her if it would be okay if you called?"

"Would you do that, Roxanne? You are such a good friend, really."

"No problem. Besides, I owe you for getting me through all those tests." Roxanne resisted the urge to roll her eyes.

"Oh, that was no problem, Roxanne. You know, you're a lot smarter than you think."

You don't know the half of it, Paul.

"Okay, let's get off the phone so that I can call Sarah and then call you back. Give me five minutes."

"Okay, great, I'll wait for your call in five minutes," Paul said.

Roxanne telephoned Sarah, but the call went immediately to voice mail.

"Rats," Roxanne said out loud. "Where could she be?"

She scanned the city looking for Sarah's thought patterns and soon found her at the cinema downtown.

"Oh, Sarah, you don't want to be in the movies right now. You want to be talking to Paul Grinsky. This is your night to hook up with him, girl."

She had options. She could place a thought in Sarah's mind that would compel her to call Roxanne, but that was far too invasive. Sarah was her friend; Roxanne felt protective toward her. But there were even deeper reasons for Roxanne's restraint. She needed real friends like Sarah. If she invaded her friends' thoughts, they would become an extension of her, which would make her feel even more alone and lonely in the world. Roxanne needed her friends to be independent of her. That was the only way she could trust their friendship and love. No, invading Sarah's mind was out of the question. But there was another option.

She sent an electromagnetic pulse to Sarah's phone, overriding the off switch, then dialed Sarah again. Silently, she apologized to all the other people at the movie who would suddenly be treated to Sarah's loud hip hop ring tone.

The phone rang a few times and then the call was ignored. Roxanne knew Sarah wouldn't be able to resist calling her back, though. She just had to be patient.

About two minutes passed before her phone rang.

"Roxanne?" Sarah said. "You called?"

"Oh, I'm so glad you called me back, Sarah. Listen, Paul Grinsky called me tonight. He wants to call you and ask you out, but he's afraid you're going to reject him. I told him I would ask you if it would be okay if he called you. I'm supposed to call him back right away. So is it okay if he calls you now?"

"Roxanne, are you kidding me? Absolutely. Yes! No! Wait! Is that what I'm supposed to do, Roxanne? Aren't there some kind of rules about this? I don't know the rules. I never read that book! Should you tell him I'm busy tonight, make him wonder and want me more? Tell me what I'm supposed to do, Roxanne. I don't want to blow it."

"Sarah, you nut," Roxanne replied. "The only rule is to follow your heart.

You've wanted this guy to call you since the semester began. This is your chance. He's dying to ask you out. You can't blow it unless you say no."

"Yeah, I know, but I get all nervous when I talk to him."

"Don't talk too much. Let him do the talking. He gets nervous too, but at least he'll be the one embarrassing himself."

"You're right, Roxanne. You're always right. Okay, call him back and tell him that I'm at the movies but I'm buying more popcorn and I can talk to him for a few minutes now."

"Okay, I'll call him now."

As soon as Paul answered his phone, Roxanne told him Sarah was at the movies but she happened to catch her as she was buying popcorn. "You can call her now and she can talk for a few minutes."

"Maybe I should wait, Roxanne. She's at the movies. She probably doesn't want to talk to me now."

"Paul, she's waiting for you to call. This is your chance. Don't be a wuss. And don't stand her up."

"You're right, I'm being a wuss. I think I could go to war sooner than call the girl I like."

"Paul, there's a little window here. Make the call."

"Okay, Roxanne. I'll call her."

Roxanne rang off. She sat down at her desk and checked her e-mail and Facebook. She was writing an e-mail to Lyla when her phone rang again.

"Roxanne, we're going out next Saturday night!" Sarah screamed into the phone. "Isn't that great!? Roxanne, I owe it all to you. You are so wonderful. Isn't it great?"

"I'm so happy for you, Sarah. Yes, it's so great," Roxanne said.

"Okay, gotta go. I left Lyla alone in the movies. She's probably wondering if I skipped out on her."

"Okay, let's talk tomorrow," Roxanne said.

"See ya," Sarah said.

Roxanne went back to her e-mail, but her phone rang again.

"She said yes!" Paul said. "Can you believe it? We're going out next Saturday. Can you believe it? But, Roxanne, I need you to tell me where I should take her. I'm not good with these kinds of things. You know that."

"Paul, you'll be fine. Take her to the movies. and then to Antonio's for pizza. She likes that place."

"Okay, Roxanne. That's great. Yes, that's what I'm going to do. I can't wait. But listen, we'll talk during school on Monday, okay? Thanks, Roxanne. You're the greatest."

Roxanne put her phone down and stared at her computer, completely empty of any enthusiasm for the e-mail she had been writing. She couldn't type another word. *Forget it*, she told herself. *I can't be bothered right now.*

Throwing herself down on her bed, she thought of a song from the musical *Avenue Q*, which expressed how she felt perfectly. "It sucks to be me," she said out loud. "It sucks to be me."

Her phone rang again. Her emotions blocked her prescience. Besides, the desk seemed like it sat on the other side of the world.

"No, I'm done playing matchmaker for tonight, you guys," she said to the phone. "You can take it from here."

The phone continued to ring until her voice mail picked up. A minute later it beeped, indicating someone had left a message. Roxanne sighed. Suddenly it hit her. That last call was not from Paul or Sarah. She jumped off the bed and ran to her desk, already knowing who had called.

Before she could open the phone, it rang again. She answered without looking at the caller ID. She recognized his voice instantly.

"Roxanne, it's me, Andor."

"Andor? Why are you calling?" she asked, trying to sound both calm and surprised.

"Well, I thought it would be more polite and less intrusive if I called you, rather than break into your thoughts," he said.

"That's considerate of you," she said.

"I'm calling because I'd like to talk to you tomorrow, if that's possible. Do you have some time, maybe at lunch or something?"

"Yes, sure. We can have lunch together. Do you bring lunch or do you buy at the cafeteria?"

"I can bring lunch and maybe we could go somewhere that's less noisy. Is that okay with you?"

"Yes, we can do that. Let's meet at the snack bar in the student center."

"That sounds great. See you then."

"See you then, Andor," Roxanne said.

She closed her phone and threw herself on her bed again, but this time she was smiling.

Her phone rang once more. Her first thought was that Andor was calling to cancel, but then she focused and realized it was George Jackson, the high school basketball star, on the line.

"George? Hi, how are you?" she said.

"Hi, Roxanne. Hey, listen, the reason I'm calling is to tell you that we've got our first basketball game in a week and I was wondering if you would come to the game and then go out with me afterwards. We could, you know, go to Antonio's or something. Would that be okay?"

"Sure, George," Roxanne said, suddenly thrown into conflict. She had forgotten all about her crush on George. "I'd like that. When exactly is the game?"

"The game starts at five on Saturday."

"Okay. I'll see you at the game and we can go out afterwards."

"That's great, Roxanne. Thanks. See you then."

She closed her phone, took a deep breath, and let out a long exhalation. Then she lay down on her bed and stared into space. Suddenly, she smiled.

"It's good to be hot," she said out loud.

Chapter 7
Roger's Team

Westminster Abbey had stood proud against a thousand years of mostly gloomy weather, but the stretch of rain storms that had battered the United Kingdom and much of the rest of the world recently seemed to diminish even the great church's glory. The building was colder, the air heavier, its light dimmer, its stone walls harder to the touch. Now, indeed, it was more crypt than cathedral.

Even Roger and his team seemed subdued as they entered their high-ceilinged conference room in their special wing of the abbey and took their places around a large oak table. Like King Arthur, Roger had had a special round table constructed for the conference room. No doubt, it wasn't as grand as the king's must have been. It only sat ten people at most; Roger's team consisted of seven, counting Roger. Nor was it empty, as Arthur's must have been. Usually coffee mugs and teacups and whatever food that might be served during their longer meetings were scattered across the table.

Roger and his kind knew the details of King Arthur's life not from legend and myth, but from historical records. Arthur had been guided by Geniuses, including Merlin and Roger's own ancestor, Reginald Reynolds.

Like all of their offices, the conference room was protected by a sophisticated array of electromagnetic firewalls that prevented all forms of eavesdropping.

Roger and the others took their seats, prepared for the latest round of battles against their rivals of the East. Of the five members of Roger's team, four had been with him for most of the twentieth century. Stephen Elliot was relatively new to the group.

Roger had known Stephen since birth. Stephen's parents, both Geniuses, were professors at Oxford University. Early on, Stephen developed a passion for military history and strategy. He studied the great conquerors and generals, including Alexander the Great, Napoleon, Wellington, Grant, Lee, Patton, Montgomery, and Rommel. By the time he was fourteen, he could explain in detail the reasons for the success or failure of every significant battle since the time of Alexander.

He was also the most advanced computer geek in all of the United Kingdom. At fifteen years of age, he was building computers that moved beyond the single processor design, utilizing instead multiple parallel processors. He also designed software that, in combination with his own brilliant insight and analysis, could develop strategies that would have changed the outcome of every major war.

Stephen's parents were exceedingly old when he came along and died when he was seventeen. Roger took over as his mentor, making sure he got the appropriate education that would allow him to make full use of his abilities. Thirty years earlier, when he was twenty-two, Stephen came to work for Roger and had been with him ever since.

Denise Parker, among the most senior of Roger's team, had been with Roger since just before the First World War. He found her in Pittsburgh when she was twelve. Her parents, both Ordinaries, worked in the Pennsylvania steel industry. When a fire at the mill killed both her parents, Denise was sent to an orphanage. Within a few weeks she had run away and lived a hardscrabble life on the streets of Pittsburgh. One day, hungry and cold, she turned up at a soup kitchen run by the Salvation Army. One of the volunteers there was Jason Phillips, who was teaching at the University of Pittsburgh. When Denise arrived, Jason recognized the source of the ping immediately. Soon, Denise was living with a married couple who were Geniuses. Phillips also told Roger about

Denise, and he helped her get an education. When she graduated, she came to work for him.

Denise was in charge of operations for the northern hemisphere. She monitored all communications north of the equator, especially between Geniuses. She also helped to plan all Genius operations in the United States, Europe, Asia, and North Africa.

Willie Mayfield was a military and weapons expert and an adept covert operative. He headed security for the London team. And since Roger had ordered it a day ago, Willie was now responsible for monitoring every thought, emotion, action, and ambition of Victor Grozny, the president of Slavistan.

Willie, who was a British national but a black South African by birth, came to Roger just before World War II when he was fifteen years old and living by his wits on the streets of London. His primary source of income was poker, blackjack, and three-card monte. Since he could count cards and read the minds of the people he played, he knew the cards in every opponent's hand. He made a good living playing cards on his little wooden box, which he set up in Hyde Park every day. He learned early that he had to hide his gifts, however. When he was young, a couple of unhappy players beat him senseless, and twice he got his fingers broken. Those hard lessons led him to local gyms where he learned to box and even mastered a couple of martial arts. Willie loved his freedom and thrived on dangerous challenges, which made life on the streets a bit of heaven for him.

One sunny afternoon, while strolling through Hyde Park just before the war, Roger heard the ping and spotted Willie using a three-card monte game to take three university lads to the cleaners. All three were privileged Londoners, far above the likes of Willie, as far as they were concerned, They wore expensive suits and good shoes, while Willie was dressed in battered boots, black trousers with holes at the knees, and a grungy brown overcoat and cap that were straight out of *Oliver Twist*. That was part of Willie's con, Roger realized instantly. He wanted to look every bit the street urchin, the loser.

The four were crouched down around Willie's box, which sat on the grass. Willie worked his magic, rotating the three cards in circles and then alternately placing one card on top of another. He set them in a line again, swept them in circles once more, and finally set all three cards into position so that his pigeon could choose a card, which of course was the wrong card yet again.

"Bloody hell!" one of the students yelled after losing. "That's one more quid gone."

"So sorry, mate," Willie said, his voice so full of sympathy, you'd think someone had died. He swept the coins off his small box and gave the three larger young men an embarrassed smile. "Try your luck again, governor?" Willie said. "I'm on some kind of wanky winning streak, but my luck's never been this good for long. Wha'ya say?" He placed the three cards facedown on the box and looked at them with pure innocence. "Another go, sir?"

The other three had already lost £5 to Willie and were about to explode with frustration.

"Bollocks," one said. "I think you're sodding us, you bloody black blighter. How about we stand you on your head and shake your arse until we get our money back?"

All four stood up, the three Cambridge men preparing to jump on Willie.

"No need for that, guv. How's about double or nothin'?" Willie said with an unctuous smile. "I'm sure you can get your money back without violence. Wha' ya say? We'll each put down two quid and do the dance one more time?"

Roger, leaning against a tree nearby, watched the events unfold with an amused smile. The kid had guts, but he was too smart for his own good, Roger thought. If he wasn't careful, he'd get himself killed before he realized who he was.

"How's about we break your jaw instead, eh, *guv*?" another boy said, leaning close and sneering.

"He's got our five quid, plus another five that we should have won," the third one said. "What say we get our money back, lads."

The three of them were about to pounce when Roger intervened. In the blink of an eye, the three young men were lying on the ground, fast asleep. Roger stepped over them and approached the awestruck Willie.

"William Mayfield," Roger said. "Why don't we talk? Quite a game you've got here, but the rewards seem pretty small for a man of your talents."

"Did you do that to them?" Willie asked, his eyes wide with fear that he would be next.

"Yes," Roger said. "I can show you how to use your abilities for games that have a lot more at stake than a few quid."

"Are they ...?"

"No," Roger said. "They're not dead. They're just having a little nap. They'll wake up when you and I leave."

"Can you teach me how to do that?" Willie asked.

"That and a lot more," Roger said.

The three cards still lay face down on Willie's box. Roger looked directly into Willie's eyes. Without moving, using only his telekinetic powers, he flipped over the money card. The ace of spades stared up at both of them.

Willie looked down at the card and then back at Roger. The two locked eyes, and Roger spoke telepathically to the boy. "It's now or never, William."

Willie picked up his cards and his box, gave Roger a smile, and said, "Lead the way, governor."

The next thing Willie knew, he was attending secret classes at the University of Oxford and developing abilities he never knew he had.

Felix Novak was in charge of procurement, financing, and medical support. Like Willie, he was a soldier at heart. He and Willie ran all covert operations. Occasionally, Roger accompanied them, when the circumstances warranted.

Felix was raised by a Genius single mother who never fully understood her own gifts, let alone her son's. She sent her son to public school, where he tested off the charts. He won numerous scholarships to private schools and was enrolled at the University of California at Berkeley at the age of twelve. By the time he was fifteen, he had graduated with degrees in biology, chemistry, physics, and mathematics. By seventeen, he had finished his medical training at Stanford. His mother was a lioness when it came to protecting him from the public glare. Media organizations wanted to do reports on his brilliance, but she refused them all. She forbade Felix from speaking to reporters when he was at school and told his teachers that her son needed and deserved his privacy. Indeed, Felix was a loner by nature and found social situations nearly impossible to bear. He had no friends in college and initially didn't show any interest in girls. He abhorred the limelight, preferring his solitary world of books and academic pursuits.

Once out of school, Felix realized he had no interest in practicing medicine. It had been merely an intellectual exercise, he told his mother, like so many other academic subjects. He longed for new challenges and needed to get away. He went to Washington, DC, and got a job at a think tank for foreign policy. There he came to the attention of Lionel Clearwater, head of security for the Western Council of Geniuses. Clearwater felt the ping in a coffee shop on Connecticut Avenue. He had Felix followed for three weeks before he approached him and offered him a new life. Felix, already bored with the think tank, took Clearwater up on his offer to come to COG headquarters and complete his training. Under Clearwater's tutelage, Felix mastered advanced mathematics, computer technology, self-defense, military strategy, and covert operations. He took to the training like a squirrel to a tree. The secret world was the life he was born for; it was an extension of his inner nature. He joined Roger in 1933, when Hitler was just coming to power and the team was gearing up for their work with the French resistance and British war effort. He had been with Roger ever since.

Finally, there was Roger's closest and longest serving colleague, Simone Laurent. Simone was the coordinator of all incoming information, especially what came from London Center's field operations. She analyzed all the data, put the puzzle pieces together, suggested likely scenarios, and constructed a big picture of what was taking place in any single part of the world. She also worked with Denise at planning operations.

Simone was as old as Roger, now more than a century-and-a-half, and looked perhaps forty. She was every bit the French beauty—long dark hair, large dark eyes, high cheekbones, pouting lips, and a long curvaceous body. Glamorous and sensual, Simone radiated sexual energy, but like so many French beauties, she also had that allure of being untouchable. She attracted men by the hundreds, but was too ethereal to be fully reached. That quality determined her fate. Ever chased by men, she had never been caught and thus never found lasting love.

Her ethereal nature brought with it a remarkable set of talents, however. She was the most brilliant analyst and code breaker on Roger's team. She could see connections between bits of information that no computer could match. She was a gifted intuitive, a female Sherlock Holmes, who could walk into a home and tell the life story of the man or woman who lived there without ever meeting the person. For Simone, everything a person touched left an etheric trace of that person's mind and heart. Everything a person said revealed a connection to the person's past or some inner state—a conflict or a particularly joyful memory— that told the story of that person's larger life. She lived between worlds, between heaven and earth, never fully grounded yet intuitively aware of the unity of all that was around her.

No doubt adding to this aspect of Simone's character was another of her mental abilities. Long before she met Roger, she lived for years in the Brazilian rainforest where she studied with a medicine man/shaman. From him she had learned how to harness natural forces to transport herself and others to any spot on the planet. Before long, Simone's skills far exceeded those of her mentor, including her ability to create an exact double of herself, and project it to any location she desired. In this way she could actually be in two places at the same time.

Once for a few weeks she had tried to train Roger in certain of these skills. The training was too brief for him to master all of what she tried to teach him, but he did manage with difficulty to project himself a relatively short distance. He had never tried to do it again.

Simone loved Roger. In fact, they had been lovers for more than a decade. But in the end, they were too much alike. Both were unreachable to virtually everyone, including each other. Not surprisingly, their love was never enough to bring them fully together.

Simone was the first to recognize this fact. One day in early July 1914, just before war broke out in Europe, she and Roger were sitting together at an outdoor café on the Champs-Élysées in Paris. The sun shone brilliantly as people strolled along the grand boulevard.

The two sat in silence until Simone said, "You know, we never fight."

"Yes," Roger said, reading her thoughts and suddenly conscious of where she was going. "I suppose that does reveal a lot."

"We're two of a kind, you and me. We have the same priority—safety in a relationship. We don't go near the vulnerable places in our souls. We protect each other's wounds. We don't push each other to face our demons.

"I love you, Roger," she continued, "but if we stay together, our love will die from too much safety and boredom. Eventually, we'll lose our hunger for meaning. We could grow old and come to hate each other for being cowards, for never going into the places in our inner worlds that frighten us. Neither one of us wants that."

Roger let out a long exhalation and then reached across the table and held her hand.

"I don't want to lose you," he said. "We're not only lovers, but we're friends and colleagues."

"We will always be friends and colleagues. But we both need more from a lover."

"You've always been braver than I," he said.

"When it comes to the dangers in the world, you are the bravest man I have ever met. But we need to find partners who have a different kind of courage."

From that day on, their love became platonic.

Years after the two split, Roger met Rebecca and found the only woman to whom he could fully give his heart. Simone embraced Rebecca completely—that was the mark of how much she loved Roger—and had supported the two of them ever since.

She was still his right arm in London, and his most faithful and respected colleague.

As they all took their places at the round table, Roger saw the looks they sent him, mixtures of concern and anticipation. They knew this mission was different from any other that they had taken on. All that Roger held dearest was on the line.

Roger, for his part, was more reserved than usual. Whenever he assembled the team to deal with a threat from the Eastern Council, he felt the thrill of battle, especially when he was about to face off against Karl and Klaus Kleper. He became animated, more engaged and engaging. His concern for each member of his team burned brighter in this room. They all felt closer, more protective of each other, more like family. In this room, from which all their missions were launched, they were not seven people. They were a team.

Roger felt differently this time, and he knew it showed. His body was tense, his expression fixed. His enormous intellectual powers were tightly focused. He wasn't surprised that his condition seemed to make everyone else more tense and focused as well.

"Denise, why don't we start with you?" he began. "What have you got for us?"

"There is no doubt that Andor Lysenko is an operative of the Klepers," Denise began. "There is a powerful telepathic link between the Klepers and Lysenko and a fairly constant flow of communications along the link. They won't leave the kid alone. Obviously, they want us to know that Andor is their man, which means they want you to know.

"The thought patterns are highly protected by a stealth shield that surrounds all communications to and from the kid. The Klepers have also encoded their messages to the boy's DNA, which is the key that unlocks the coded communication they're sending to him. You will recall, Roger, this is the same strategy they used during both world wars. It was especially effective in their links to Adolph Hitler and Joseph Stalin. Of course with both of those men, the constant barrage on their DNA from the Klepers' thought patterns caused severe mental illness in both men, and their eventual destruction. Before they died, both had lost their individuality and any independence from the Klepers. They became puppets of the Eastern Council. We, of course, broke the code long before both men lost the capacity for self-directed thought and we were able to intercept the messages from the Klepers.

"The Eastern Council has since learned from that experience," Denise continued. "They are now utilizing the immense amount of electromagnetic radiation in the earth's atmosphere—especially human generated radiation from cell phones, microwaves, satellites, radio, and television—as background noise, concentrating it as a kind of shield around their communication with the boy.

"He's young and strong, but at this rate, communication with the Klepers and their assault upon his nervous system will cause him to lose all independence from them within months. Eventually, he will lose his mind and possibly become violent. He'll suicide, of course, but he could be a danger to those around him before he goes, especially if he is ordered to kill before he kills himself."

"What kind of progress are we making in breaking the white-noise shield and his DNA code?" Roger asked.

"We're working on it," Denise said. "Simone and I are combining our mental powers in order to create a set of wave patterns that are the exact opposite of the white-noise waves. In effect, we're trying to create a set of standing waves that are the mirror images of the white-noise patterns. If we can align our wave patterns with theirs at precisely the opposite frequency, our waves should cancel out the Klepers' shield around the boy. That would expose the Klepers' communication. If we also have the DNA code, we can intercept. We think it's going to work, but we both need time to study their shielding pattern and understand its frequency. Of course, we need a sampling of the boy's DNA too."

"If you have the DNA breakdown by, say, tomorrow afternoon," Roger said, "how long before you can start tapping into the communication?"

"A few days, Chief."

"We have to break the shield, and the code, and save the boy," Roger said. "Understood?"

"Yes," Denise said.

He knew they all understood what he feared the most—that if Andor wasn't rescued from the Klepers, he might be ordered to kill Roxanne. He also knew the other six were studying him for signs of stress, but he shielded them from his inner world and remained very much in charge of himself and the moment.

"Simone, what have you come up with?" he asked.

"We are currently trying to put together the boy's mission," she began. "Laurel Glen, as you know, is a target-rich environment for an operative such as our young Mr. Lysenko. The place is chockfull of students whose parents are rich industrialists, financiers, bankers, and high-tech innovators. As you know, I've been working with Stephen on this and we have narrowed it down to one possible target and two likely ones. We are also laying out the goals, scenarios, and steps involved in any plan that might be associated with each of these students. Let me deal with the one possible first."

Simone continued. "Rudolf Moore, is the chairman of the board at Universal Airlines. His son Henry is in Lysenko's year at Laurel Glen. Control the kid and you've got a whole fleet of aircraft at your disposal. We've already seen what that can mean with 9/11. Whether or not young Moore is a target, I think we need to be prepared for possible terror scenarios that involve aircraft. We're working on that end of things."

"Perhaps Rebecca can help you with North America," Roger suggested.

"That would be lovely," Simone said.

"Let's pay particular attention to Washington, DC," he went on. "I'm concerned about the big airports in the Washington, Virginia, and Maryland areas, as well as the smaller ones, where a plane can be hijacked and make a short flight to its target. Please look at military bases that are also airports."

"Will do, Roger," Simone said, and then continued with her analysis.

So, Henry Moore is the most likely alternate to what we believe are the primary targets.

"The first is Stewart Thompson, son of Stewart senior, who is a US senator. Stewart senior is chairman of the Senate Foreign Relations

Committee, which provides Congressional oversight over all US foreign policy. He's supremely ambitious and calculating and has no guiding principles except to promote his personal ambitions. He cheats at everything and on everyone, including his wife. All of which makes him extremely vulnerable to outside control. The senator has made it known to numerous intimates that he wants to be president of the United States. He has already made promises to numerous powerful figures in the US, Europe, and the Arab world that he would trade favors for their backing. He's raising money now for his campaign.

"Young Stewart is a senior at Laurel Glen. He's highly sensitive and shy, and has enormous doubts about himself. He's also very impressionable. For someone like Lysenko, he's easy pickings. Through young Stewart, Lysenko can get to the senator. Once he's inside the senator's world, he could run the candidate and possibly the eventual president."

"Isn't Thompson also a member of the Senate Banking Committee?" Roger asked.

"Yes, I was getting to that. In fact, he's now looking for a domestic issue that he can climb aboard in order to promote himself as the savior of the US economy. We're already way ahead of him. We've played out fifty potential scenarios and have narrowed them down to five. Once he chooses a particular issue, we'll know his moves before he does. Meanwhile, we're listening in."

Simone paused before mentioning the other likely target.

"The other target, of course, is Roxanne. Lysenko may be being guided by the Klepers to bring her under his control in order to bring you—and by extension all of us—under their control. The Klepers know that Alexander Astrakhan and all of us are the greatest threat to their ambitions. You and Alexander Astrakhan are their primary adversaries. Find a way to neutralize you, Alexander, and us—or even delay us—and the game is all theirs."

"What are your recommendations for stopping Andor?" Roger asked.

"I don't think we can afford to stop him now," Simone said. "It's possible that the boy's play is an elaborate theater to distract us from a more dangerous plot that is unfolding in the background. We can easily intercept Thompson and either override the boy's influence or neutralize the senator entirely. If controlling a future President Thompson is their goal, then how do the Klepers plan on stopping us from derailing them? The answer is they can't. Lysenko's role with Thompson is too obvious and too easily disrupted. Something else is going on here, and Lysenko's assignment may be to lead us away from the Klepers' true ambitions. All of which means that we need time in order to let Lysenko play his hand and allow us to uncover the Klepers' real purpose.

"Having said that, I see a very real danger in giving the boy more time. The longer we allow Lysenko to move freely, the more time he has to bring Roxanne under his influence. The real danger to her is if she falls for Lysenko and they develop a romantic relationship. If she drops her shield with him, he could hurt her badly. The Klepers would hope that that would neutralize you and weaken all of us. I don't need to point out that the mere threat to Roxanne is already distracting all of us."

Simone paused, and her voice dropped from her cool, professional tone into a more intimate and caring range.

"Time is not our friend on this, Roger. We have to give Lysenko enough time to reveal the Klepers' real intentions, but not enough time to bring Roxanne under his control. We've got to expose the plot before he can be a real threat to her."

"Any idea what that plot might be?" Roger asked Simone.

"No, not yet. But Denise and I are monitoring the boy carefully, and if we can break the code and intercept their messages, we will likely see the bigger picture."

Roger thanked Simone and turned to Stephen, asked him what information he had.

"Well, Chief, we have a better understanding of this satellite the Klepers launched in Slavistan and what its likely purpose is. Code named Archangel, the satellite was launched on May 19, 2010, from the city of Archangel, Slavistan. It's equipped with multifunctional capabilities, including the power to launch a high-intensity pulse beam. As you know, that could take out an electromagnetic grid and wipe out computer communications for hours or even days. The satellite has the capability to reload, so a series of pulses could hit several targets—obviously, New York, Washington, Los Angeles, London, and Geneva. This would cripple the world for weeks, perhaps months.

"That's its potential. However, we think another capability may be hidden in the satellite. Willie and I have been studying the thing carefully and have noted that it is already sending out a low-intensity radio beam that is having a widespread effect on the earth's electromagnetic field. It's possible this radio beam is the cause of the bizarre weather patterns the world has been experiencing recently.

"We've also studied the beam. I should really say played with it. We found some disturbing potential patterns which, if they're amplified in a certain way, could have other major impacts on the earth's electromagnetic field, with potentially serious consequences. One obvious concern would be any interference with the delicate system that results in the warning ping we all experience in the presence of other Geniuses. We're only speculating at this point, but it's a possibility we can't ignore."

Roger had already recognized the same danger. "If we can confirm this with further analysis, then the satellite's real purpose …?"

"Is that all of us have been marked for assassination," Stephen said without emotion. "Very likely, Alexander Astrakhan and our other brothers and sisters at the Washington headquarters are also targets."

"Thank you, Stephen," Roger said, also without emotion. "Whatever the purpose of this thing is, we're going to have to take it out, or better yet, gain control over it. Stephen and William, we need all the information you can gather on the Klepers' new toy, and we need a plan to turn the tables on them."

Roger turned to Felix. "Felix, we're going to need significant funding to create a device that will bring this Archangel to our side. That means Volk, of course. Let's be cautious. We're not going to tell him anything about what we're doing or what we're up against. We can get around Volk, but we need the numbers and a cover story. When the time comes, I'll be the one to deal with him."

"Will do, Chief," Felix replied.

Helmut Volk was the finance minister for the Council of Western Geniuses. He controlled the council's purse strings, which meant that every operation that needed funding beyond standard budget allocations had to go through his office. Roger had a significant budget of his own, but he knew he would need additional funding to take on the Klepers. Since Volk reported to Alexander Astrakhan, Roger could always go over Volk's head and directly to Alexander, but he was reluctant to play that card and bring another problem to Alexander's door.

Going to Volk with funding requests was never an easy task, no matter how important the job might be. Egotistical, petty, and power hungry, Volk was the consummate bureaucratic functionary. He had no creativity, and his only power derived from being able to stop others from doing their jobs. As far as Roger was concerned, Volk was a walking reminder of the superiority of character over intelligence. Volk had plenty of the latter and very little of the former. He saw every human interaction as a struggle for power. Whenever someone went to him with a funding request, he always first informed his colleague that he had the power to say no. And he loved saying no. Still, Roger outranked him and, if he had to, could simply order Volk to fund his project. But Roger never liked to take that approach. And this was an especially delicate moment. Better to be careful and circumspect.

"As of right now," he said, returning his attention to the meeting, "nothing of what we've discussed leaves our offices, and nothing is shared with Washington headquarters."

They all looked at one another in surprise.

"You realize," Denise said, "that if anyone in Washington has been targeted, we're keeping them in the dark and unprepared for an attack."

"And it's absolutely the right thing to do, Denise," Simone said. "Someone at the Western Council of Geniuses may be running Lysenko in the US, which means we could have a mole. We have to know more before we share any of this."

"What about Alexander?" Denise asked. "Surely our information must be shared with him."

"I've already decided to share that information with Alexander myself," Roger said. "And I'll explain to him the sensitive nature of all of this and that it shouldn't be widely disseminated throughout headquarters. At least not yet. I want the Klepers to think we're still very much in the dark about their plans, and Archangel."

He turned to Willie and asked what information he had on Victor Grozny.

"You mean besides a case of vicarious STD?" Willie said. Everyone laughed, and Willie went on.

"Victor Grozny, the so-called President of Slavistan, is under heavy telepathic protection by the Klepers and the Eastern Council. They block all intrusions into the parts of his mind that are responsible for governing the country, including any plans he may have for the future. It's possible the Klepers so fully occupy Grozny's cerebrum that breaking into Grozny's rational faculties really means breaking into the minds of the Klepers."

Willie let out a little laugh. "The rest of his life is an open book—and it ain't *Wuthering Heights*. Watching Victor Grozny is like spending way too many hours in a porn shop that's hooked up to a distillery. Blimey, the man spends his day consuming women and endless bottles of vodka." Willie shook his head. "His appetites are immense.

"Since we can't expect to get too much from Grozny, we shifted our attention to Lysenko's parents. Or rather, the two KGB agents the boy is living with in Silver Spring, Maryland. Bottom-of-the-barrel thugs, these two. Basically, they're his jailers. They have no idea who the kid is and what he's capable of. They've been told to keep him on a short leash. As if they could. So where are his real parents? We're hunting for them now. But the facts point to some kind of blackmail of the kid—either you play ball according to our rules or your parents die."

"We need to find his parents soon, Willie," Roger said. "Meanwhile, let's stay on Grozny. He may still give us something."

Willie nodded. "We're on it, Chief. They can't hide the parents much longer. And I'll keep an eye on Grozny, though I may need anti-nausea medicine pretty soon."

Roger grinned. "Thanks, Willie." He turned to Simone. "Can you get us a DNA sample from Andor?"

"Yes," she said. "It would be best if I pay him a visit while he's sleeping. Otherwise, he could be tipped off and alert the Klepers. I can go tonight."

"Run the sample through our computer and provide Denise with the boy's genome by tomorrow morning."

Roger looked around the table at his team. "There's a lot that has to be done. As Simone said, time is not on our side. Godspeed!"

Everyone went off in different directions, and Roger walked quickly to his office. As he sat down in his chair, he projected his thoughts out to Freddy and Ellis. Soon he felt their presence.

"Hi, guys," Roger said. "There's news and it isn't exactly good."

"Wouldn't have it any other way," Ellis said.

"Yeah," Freddy said. "Otherwise, where's the fun?"

Chapter 8
Roxanne's Morning

For all of his brilliance and power, Jason Phillips could not control the headaches. Neither could the powerful remedies his Genius doctors prescribed. In fact, none of his doctors could determine the cause of the headaches. This was especially perplexing, since Genius medicine could diagnose and cure virtually every known illness. At times, the pain was so intense, Phillips was completely incapacitated. The headaches started in his forehead, spread to the backs of his eyes, ran along the sides of his head, and then down the back of his neck. The pain was blinding and sent his upper body into a vice-like tension. His only option was to go to bed. After a fitful night's sleep, the headache would disappear, often for days. Not a trace of pain anywhere in his body. There was one unfortunate side effect in the aftermath of the headaches: he experienced a kind of brain fog, some degree of forgetfulness and disorientation, for several hours or even a day or two. He had noticed a pattern, which he was trying to understand. Certain thoughts seemed to bring the headaches on.

That morning, three weeks into September, Phillips awoke early, feeling well. He had lots of energy and felt a rush of enthusiasm for what he expected to be a headache-free, productive day at Laurel Glen.

Roxanne was up early that morning as well. By 6:30 she had already - for over an hour – been working on her thought-activated, Genius-invented, multi-screened computer. It was built into the clear contact lens which she wore in her left eye. As she ate her oatmeal, she read eight newspapers from around the world, all projected onto her computer screens. The papers were: the *New York Times*, *Washington Post*, *The London Times*, *Le Monde*, *Pravda*, *China Daily*, Aljazeera.com, and Haaretz.com, the Israeli online newspaper. At 7:40, she walked out her front door, her backpack slung over her shoulder. The day was gray, the sky heavy with the portent of rain. In her right hand, she carried several slices of whole wheat bread. She walked to the tall oak tree in the front of her house, looked up into the tree, and called out telepathically, in the language of squirrels, "Good morning, Jack, I have breakfast if you're interested."

Jack scampered down the tree and landed on a branch just above Roxanne's head.

"Good morning, Roxanne. How are you today?" chirped the squirrel.

"Very well, Jack. How's your family?"

"Very busy, Roxanne, very busy," Jack said in his usual rapid fire cadence.

"Anything I should know about today?"

"The weather Roxanne, the weather! It's not good. All the animals are disturbed. We're upset. If the rain keeps up, the acorns are going to rot. We're all worried about our food, Roxanne, very worried."

"I'll talk to my father about it, Jack. We'll see what we can do."

"Thank you, Roxanne."

"Anything else I should know?"

"The fishers are fighting again, but not about anything important. Just sex."

Roxanne laughed. "Sex is pretty important, Jack. At least it is to us humans."

"It's important to us squirrels too, Roxanne, but we don't fight about it."

"We're more complicated than you guys, Jack."

"That's your problem, Roxanne, that's your problem. You humans complicate everything, even the weather."

"Yes, we do make things complicated, Jack. I'll just leave the bread here, but I'm going to break up a few pieces for the sparrows and spread them around, okay? So don't take it all, understood?"

"Can't promise anything, Roxanne. You know that, can't promise anything."

"Jack, be good, or I'll tell the sparrows to sing past seven tonight and keep you awake. Okay?" She broke up a few pieces of bread and threw them on the front lawn. "I'm off, Jack. Happy acorn hunting."

"Thank you, Roxanne. Enjoy your complicated day."

As Roxanne walked to her car, a crow named Charles landed on a neighbor's lawn.

"Caw, caw," Charles shouted.

"Hi, Charles, how are things today?" Roxanne asked telepathically, switching to the language of the crow.

"The lines are all bad at Main and Maple Streets, Roxanne. Be careful today. There will be a traffic accident there unless the lines get harmonized."

Roxanne loved crows and ravens, knowing full well their amazing intelligence and mysterious ability to see dimensions of the electromagnetic spectrum that humans, even Geniuses, could not see. She regularly counted on Charles and other crows to inform her of the harmonies and disharmonies that might lie in her path. Charles had said the corner of Main and Maple was in an acute state of disharmony, and she took the warning seriously.

"Maybe I can do something there, Charles. It's on my way to school."

"Yes, it is, Roxanne. We will wait for you."

"Good. I'll be there in twelve minutes."

With that, Roxanne got into her car and headed for school. Her route went through the center of town, along Main Street, but just before she got to Main and Maple, she decided to get a small cappuccino at the local coffee shop. She sent a thought to the manager, John Barber, to prepare a cappuccino-to-go for Roxanne. John never questioned his suddenly realizations that Roxanne would be along any minute. The coffee was sitting on the counter when she entered the shop.

The place was crowded with people sitting on the sofas and around the many small tables spread throughout the café. Eight customers stood in a line waiting to give their orders to the woman behind the counter. Next to her was John, the manager.

"Hi, Roxanne," he said when she walked in. "Your cappuccino is on the counter." He smiled, proud of his prescience.

"John, you are amazing," Roxanne said, handing him the exact change for the coffee. "How did you know that that's exactly what I wanted today?"

"You know me, Roxanne." He tapped the side of his head. "Psychic John…at least when it comes to my customers. Don't ask me about the stock market or the Redskins. I'm hopeless when it comes to using my powers to make money."

Roxanne laughed. She enjoyed watching sports from time to time, but her real passion was creating computer algorithms that analyzed players' performances based on their biorhythms, their abilities against specific opponents, field conditions, and other relevant factors. Her program analyzed all the data and accurately predicted the games' outcomes, as well as the point spread. By mid-November she knew which two football teams would go to the Super Bowl and which team would likely win.

"How about I give you a tip for this week?" she said. "I'm feeling lucky."

"Okay." John leaned on the counter toward her. "What ya got?"

"Take the Redskins and ten against the Eagles this weekend. They'll win and they'll cover the spread."

"That's not a good bet, Roxanne," John said incredulously. "The Redskins stink. So do the Eagles, of course, but all the experts say the Eagles are better than the Redskins, and they'll win this weekend."

"John, have you ever heard of the word *upset?*" Roxanne said, smiling mischievously. "Put ten dollars on them as a lark, okay?"

"Okay, but only because you said so."

She winked at him and left the coffee shop.

Back in her car, Roxanne continued on to school, heading for Main and Maple, her senses on high alert. She didn't get far before she realized she had gone too far with John—placing her coffee order in his head and giving him betting advice. None of that felt right, she realized. She had to stop interfering with Ordinaries.

She turned her focus to Main and Maple and in two minutes she was there. She parked her car and got out, walking to the corner. Main ran north and south; Maple ran east and west. Roxanne closed her eyes, directing her awareness to the center of her being and allowing herself to feel the atmosphere of the corner. The rumble of passing cars and trucks reverberated within her. The wind rushed against her skin and brushed her hair. The play of light, the streams of energy, and the prevailing feelings that dominated the corner revealed themselves to her.

Opening her eyes, she watched the people walking along the streets and the cars heading in both directions. Her mind processed the speeds at which the people walked, as well as the speeds of the cars. Instantly running a series of complex mathematical formulas in her brain, she realized the little boy walking with his mother was about to die.

The boy was perhaps five years old. His right hand grasped his mother's hand while his left held a rubber ball. Roxanne read the child's mind and realized he was about to throw his ball toward Maple Street. Another series of mathematical calculations determined the trajectory of the ball and its subsequent bounces. The pavement was irregular and the ball would bounce wildly into the street. Even an Ordinary could guess what would happen next--the boy would free himself from his mother's grasp and run out into the street after the ball.

Roxanne looked up Maple Street. A Honda traveling at a speed of 25.7 miles per hour was heading toward her, driven by a teenage girl, who was laughing and turning toward her friend in the passenger seat. Between the speed of the car and the girl looking away, she would not have enough time to see the boy step into the street and stop her car.

In horror, Roxanne hurried across Maple Street, walking rapidly toward the mother and child. The mother was late for an appointment, Roxanne realized, and wanted to hurry along. Roxanne sent a series of thoughts to the child, ordering him to look at Roxanne and hold his ball aloft. She stopped in front of both mother and child, blocking them as she responded to the boy's offer of his ball.

"Hello," she said, smiling at the boy. "That is a really nice ball you have." She looked at the mother. "He is so cute."

The mother smiled back, but more in an effort to move the encounter along and get to her appointment.

"Can I see your ball?" Roxanne asked.

She was aware of the mother's impatience and growing annoyance. The little boy hesitated but then handed her the ball. Roxanne pretended to admire the ball as the Honda approached the corner of Maple and Main. The girl, paying attention now, stopped at the stop sign, and then turned right onto Main Street.

Roxanne said to the boy, "Someday you're going to be a wonderful baseball player." She handed the ball to the mother. "He's beautiful," she said, and stepped aside, allowing the two to pass.

Roxanne exhaled and watched mother and son cross Maple and proceed on their way, unaware of the tragedy that had just been averted. The mother still held the ball.

Roxanne returned to the corner of Maple and Main and could now perceive some of what Charles had spoken about. The corner was bathed in a strange light. It was as if the light contained a shadow, or rather, dark lines that swirled and eddied and crashed into one another. The lines were discrete forms of disembodied consciousness. Chaotic thoughts dominated, along with whatever anger and fear people had experienced as they came to a stop at the corner, and then left behind as they drove away. The emotions and confusion had collected in whirlpools and crashing waves, taking on a life of their own and affecting the drivers who approached the corner. An accident was inevitable.

Roxanne knew what to do. She surrounded herself with her shield, making herself inconspicuous to those around her. She was visible, but those who passed her were distracted by other stimuli so that they didn't notice her. Then she began to hum a tune, ever so softly. Soon her humming turned into a song, a song written by a Genius about love and beauty and truth—a song that affected every person and everything on that corner. People who passed by found themselves mysteriously uplifted. Thoughts of nature—lush green forests, frolicking rivers, glistening lakes, sandy beaches—arose in their minds. Images of holidays with family and friends filled their hearts. It was rush hour and lots of people passed the corner. And every one of them unconsciously experienced love, joy, and tranquility, and then released those thoughts into the atmosphere.

Those powerful energies, generated by so many hearts and minds, filled the intersection. They interacted with the dark light and the lines of conflict and confusion, harmonizing them and restoring peace to the corner of Main and Maple.

Roxanne saw the dark lines turn into waves of golden light that embraced all who passed through the intersection. As the people released the positive waves into the environment, the waves returned and fed the people. It was a cycle of good will and love.

Roxanne came out of her reverie as she ended her song. She looked around and saw that every person who passed by was contributing to the beauty and peace of the intersection. Together, they had restored its harmony.

Under her breath, she said to the passing crowd, "Thank you, everyone."

A flock of crows cawed in celebration. Roxanne smiled and waved to Charles and his friends. She got into her car, took a sip of her coffee, and drove to school, the excitement of seeing Andor at lunch rising within her.

Chapter 9
A Day at School

"There they are, bro," Ellis said to Freddy. He indicated Andor and Roxanne as they entered the snack bar at the student center, their lunches and drinks in hand. They took a table by the window, which gave a view of the rain falling on the western part of the campus.

"Got 'em," Freddy replied.

Ellis lay in a small wood to the west of the student center, a blanket of powerful thoughts camouflaging him from any passerby. He had a direct view of Andor and Roxanne through the windows of the snack bar.

Freddy was to the northwest and also had a clear view of Andor and Roxanne. He, too, lay in a wooded area, hidden from view in the same way. They were both a little more than a hundred yards from the student center, just out of ping range. They were looking through Genius-designed goggles that not only acted as binoculars, but picked up each person's unique infrared heat signature.

After listening in on Andor's and Roxanne's telephone call the previous night, Ellis and Fred placed tiny listening devices throughout both the student center and the cafeteria, just in case the two changed their plans and met in the cafeteria instead. The brothers could now hear every word that Roxanne and Andor spoke. They were also breaking into Roxanne's and Andor's telepathic communication, as were Denise and Simone from London.

"What's Max doing?" Ellis asked Freddy.

"He's doing the same things we're doing, only he doesn't know we're out here," Freddy replied.

From Freddy's hiding place, he also had a clear view of Max Louri, the security man whom Lionel Clearwater had assigned to watch Roxanne. Freddy, Ellis, and Max were old friends, though Max was not in the same league as the Davies brothers as far as security and covert work were concerned. Max was 125 years old and pretty much looked it. Well wrinkled and more than a little worn, Max had five failed marriages, fifteen children—eight of them Geniuses, the rest Ordinaries—and more short-term relationships than anyone could remember. For many years he'd had a problem with alcohol, but after multiple stints at Genius rehab he was finally put right, at least with the booze. Like a lot of old cops, he was a tough guy, at least on the outside, but he still did good, competent work and both brothers were fond of him.

Max was stationed to the southwest of the student center. Thanks to the turret shape of the windows, he also had a clear view of Andor and Roxanne. Like the Davies brothers, Max was out of ping range.

"I'd kind of like to sit down with old Max," Freddy said to Ellis. "Stroll down memory lane a bit."

"Yeah, me too," Ellis replied, "but we've got strict orders from the chief. No interaction with Clearwater's man, no matter who he is."

"Anyway, Max is a lot more serious since he gave up the sauce, though it would be kind of fun to lure him into a bar and get him drunk. Serve him right after what he did to us in Tangier."

"That was fifty years ago, bro," Ellis said. "You gotta let it go."

In 1961, French President Charles de Gaulle was in the process of handing Algeria its independence. A quartet of generals opposed de Gaulle and planned a coup d'état that would allow them to seize control of Algeria and assassinate de Gaulle in Paris.

The Klepers wanted to take full advantage of the coup attempt. They sent Vladimir Ubitzov, a Genius and one of their senior lieutenants, to recruit an assassination squad of highly qualified Ordinaries. Ubitzov, who had already planned and executed several assassinations, arranged for his team to meet in Tangier, where they would be briefed on the plot details and their assignments. The plan was for the French police and secret service to become preoccupied with the generals' putsch, which would provide cover for Ubitzov's hit team. The generals had no knowledge of Ubitzov's involvement.

Roger realized early on that Algerian liberation was the perfect cover for the Klepers to try to unseat de Gaulle, who was staunchly opposed to Slavistan and any attempt by that nation to influence French politics and its economy.

From London, Roger and his colleagues intercepted Eastern Council communications and discovered the plot. Roger asked the Davies brothers to put together a team that could thwart the attempt on de Gaulle's life. Among the members of that team was Max Louri.

Ubitzov and his hit squad were scheduled to leave for Paris on April 10, 1961, but the week before they left, Freddy and Ellis were taking out the hit team, one by one, on the streets of Tangier. Three remaining assassins made it to a small air strip outside the city, where they boarded a private flight for Paris. Max had already booby-trapped the plane and it exploded once it reached altitude. In Paris, the generals' putsch failed miserably and Ubitzov's backup team never reached the city. Ubitzov himself escaped back to Slavistan, humiliated.

That night, after the assassins' plane went down, Freddy, Ellis, and Max met in a bar in Tangier to relax. Max had arrived early and already was well into his cups. Pretty soon, he was looking for female company and managed to attract the attention of three beautiful women who happened to work in Moroccan state security. At one point Freddy got on the dance floor with one of the women while Ellis went to the bar with another woman for a round of drinks. That left Max alone with the third woman, who was named Sabine.

"What are you men doing in Tangier?" Sabine asked.

One of Max's problems was overconfidence, which was understandable, given that he could erase the memories of Ordinaries. He also loved to impress beautiful women with his tales of derring-do. All of which added up to a lifetime of indiscretions, made worse by the booze.

"Well, my dear, do you know Charles de Gaulle?" Max began, more than a little pedantic and inebriated.

"Not personally, no," Sabine said, deadpan.

"No, no, I'm sorry. What I meant to say was, do you know who he is?"

"I've heard of him," Sabine said, now realizing she was in the company of a complete idiot.

"You know, you really are a beautiful woman," Max continued.

"You were talking about de Gaulle," Sabine replied.

"Oh, yeah. De Gaulle. Right. Well, my friends here—Ellis and Freddy—we came to Tangier to bump off a team of assassins who wanted to kill de Gaulle. So we killed them first. That is, before they killed de Gaulle. That'll teach 'em."

He belched and then threw back another whiskey. Sabine rolled her eyes.

"Yup!" he went on. "We saved the great man's life, and the life of an entire nation. We're heroes. Only one little problem," Max lamented. "Nobody's ever going to know about it. We'll never be written up in any of your history books, at least none that you Ordinary people read. Oh well, here's to saving the world yet again."

Max raised his glass. Seeing it was empty, he signaled a waitress for three more doubles.

As a state security agent, Sabine was already aware that nine men with lengthy criminal backgrounds had turned up dead in the city. All of the men were relatively young—in their late thirties and early forties—and seemingly in good health. Certainly they seemed physically fit, but all nine had died of massive strokes. Even more mysterious, all of the men exhibited the same remarkable and inscrutable symptom: their nervous systems had been destroyed by electrocution, which apparently had brought on massive brain hemorrhages.

"And how exactly did you dispose of these assassins?" she asked Max, watching him like a fox watches a rabbit.

"We gave them the death touch," Max said. "We sent a high-energy pulse into their bodies, which fried their nervous systems and burst the vessels in their brains. I say we, but the truth is, it was Freddy and Ellis that did that. I took care of the remaining three by blowing up their airplane. Neat little trick, really. I'd explain the technology to you, but you probably wouldn't understand it."

"Probably not," Sabine said.

"Say, you know, you're beautiful. Did you know that? How about you come back to my place? What do you say about that?"

"How about you come to my place?" Sabine answered. She pulled out a pair of handcuffs and slapped them on Max's wrists. Swiftly and deftly, she stood up and pulled a revolver from a holster at her back and pointed the gun at Max.

Freddy and Ellis were just returning to the table and realized instantly what was going on. Sabine turned the gun on them, and they looked at each other and rolled their eyes.

"Put your hands out where I can see them and get down on the floor," Sabine yelled.

The other two women, obviously baffled but trusting their partner, pulled their guns out as well and ordered Freddy and Ellis to get down.

Nearby patrons became aware of the commotion, and several started screaming at the sight of the guns.

"Looks like old Max's been talking too much again," Freddy said to Ellis.

"He does have a tendency to do that," Ellis replied.

The next thing anyone in the bar could remember—including the three state-security women—was waking up from a deep and disorienting sleep. Freddy, Ellis, and Max were long gone.

On their flight back to the United States, Max remembered little of that night, but the newspapers in Morocco were full of reports about a mysterious gas leak in a popular nightspot that apparently was responsible for putting 120 people to sleep.

As he and his brother watched Andor and Roxanne, Freddy couldn't help but reminisce about old Max. "He was always good for a few laughs," Freddy said. "That is, when he wasn't getting himself and everyone else into trouble."

Inside the snack bar Roxanne and Andor had both begun to eat the sandwiches they'd brought from home. They had been speaking directly, without a telepathic subtext, but now they switched to mind-to-mind communication. They covered their real conversation with occasional small talk in order to make it appear to anyone watching that they were having a perfectly normal conversation.

"This must be such a huge adjustment for you, Andor," Roxanne communicated to him. "How do you like it here, you know, the school and living in the US?"

"I'm managing okay, but I miss Slavistan and my friends. I'll make new friends here, I'm sure. So far, I think it's going pretty well."

"Were your friends like us or were they Ordinaries?" Roxanne asked.

"Mostly they're Ordinaries. I've only met a few young people like us."

"So what did you do with your friends?"

"We played football—what you Americans call soccer, we also skied and ice skated and snowboarded. We hung out a lot. We did a lot of the same things kids do here."

"Did you have a girlfriend?" Roxanne asked shyly.

"Not a steady one," he said. "I went out, but, you know, it's different being us. I really have trouble relating to Ordinaries in any sort of intimate way. There's such a gulf. I'd have to keep so much to myself. It's like having this secret life that you can't share with anyone except the rare adult, but even then, you really can't share it with adults, either."

"I know what you mean," Roxanne said. "I feel that way too. If I didn't have my mother, I'd go crazy."

Andor's face fell and a shadow covered his countenance. Roxanne felt a sudden dread come over him. She immediately scanned Andor's inner world, but encountered his shield, which was strong and dense. She couldn't penetrate it.

"Are you all right?" she asked. "What's wrong?"

He was silent for a moment. When he spoke, he changed the subject. "It's obvious how smart you are and how powerful your mind is. But when I asked some of the kids about you, they all say you're a dumb blonde. Why do you take the persona to such an extreme?"

"Ever since I was little, my parents, who are both Geniuses, taught me to hide my abilities. They referred to the Old Ones, our ancient predecessors, as our role models. The Old Ones learned to conceal their great intelligence and mental abilities from the rest of the population, who would have envied and hated them if they'd known the truth."

"Is that the only reason?" Andor asked. "You could pretend to be just average, not dumb."

"You're right. Everything is much more complicated than the principles that our parents teach us and would like us to follow, isn't it?" she said with a small smile. "Okay … well … this is totally awkward, but most boys find me pretty." She cast Andor an assessing glance. "Many of them feel insecure around me. Pretending to be dumb, I mean, really dumb, makes guys feel more comfortable with me. They feel more confident about approaching me. If I rebuff them, they can always tell themselves that I'm just a dumb blonde who doesn't know anything. I don't know how it is in Slavistan, but here if the boys think a girl is too good looking and too smart, that girl can spend a lot of Friday and Saturday nights alone.

"Also, if you're pretty and smart, other girls become jealous and hate you. There are girls here who attack me every chance they get. It could be a lot worse if I seemed to be even average in intelligence. I'm isolated, like you. I don't want to make things even worse."

"I completely get it," Andor said, smiling broadly. "You're so smart to act dumb."

Both of them laughed. "It's a brilliant strategy to be dumb," Roxanne communicated.

Again, both laughed, and as they did, each spontaneously reached out to the other. Their hands touched for just an instant, and a powerful charge passed between them. They pretended not to notice, but the energy left a strong impression on them.

They were silent for a while as they ate their lunches.

Finally, Andor said, "You know, we've got a lot in common. Would it be okay if we went out some time, maybe for a movie or something?"

Roxanne's heart pounded. It was what she wanted too. "Okay," she said demurely.

"How about this coming Saturday?"

The night she had agreed to go out with George Jackson after the basketball game. "I'm sorry, Andor, but I'm busy Saturday night."

"What about the following Saturday then?"

"Okay," she said. "Sure, next Saturday would be fine."

"We've got to get back," Andor said. "Fourth period is about to begin."

As the two left the student center, Freddy said to Ellis, "They're a couple, bro."

"Yeah, I guess so, Fred. The chief is not going to like it."

In English class, Mrs. Van Doren introduced the famed epic poem *Beowulf*, and out of the blue called on Roxanne and asked if she might know what the poem was about.

"I think so," Roxanne said. "Is that the book about werewolves and vampires?"

A few kids giggled, none louder than Diane.

"No, no," Mrs. Van Doren said, smiling. "It's not about werewolves. Actually, it's an ancient heroic journey set in Scandinavia and written in the seventh century." She addressed the whole class. "That's your assignment. I'd like you all to read the first main part of *Beowulf* over the weekend. It's the section that deals with his struggle with the monster Grendel, and we'll discuss it on Monday."

The bell rang and people began filing out of the room.

Diane waited in the hallway for Roxanne.

"So, Lady Duh Duh, *Beowulf* is a story about werewolves? Are you kidding me? Was that some kind of brilliant on-the-spot guess you came up with?"

Susannah, a tall, thin blonde, snickered, while Linda, a short and slightly overweight brunette, laughed out loud.

Roxanne looked at all three and instantly read their thoughts. Susannah was still reeling in pain and anger after her father hit her mother twice the night before. He had been drunk and angry and, as he had done so many times before, took out his rage on his wife. Susannah had little interest in Roxanne personally, but she wanted an outlet for her anger and Roxanne was as good a target as any.

Linda felt bloated and uncomfortable from having eaten too much at lunch. She was planning to be late for class so that she could be alone in the bathroom and vomit up lunch. Linda had nothing against Roxanne, either. In fact, she admired her and would have been friends with her had she not fallen in first with Diane and Susannah. Only Diane had a true enmity for Roxanne.

Roxanne looked deeply at Diane and in an instant downloaded a conversation she'd had with Susannah during lunch. A series of images ran through Roxanne's mind, giving her a picture of what had taken place just ninety minutes before.

Diane and Susannah had finished eating and were sitting in a corner of the café drinking soda and talking about Roxanne.

"You know, Susannah," Diane said, "I really can't stand her. I really think I hate her."

"Me too," Susannah said remotely. She was staring out the window, thinking about her father and how much she hated him for hitting her mother.

"I can't stand how she gives all those dumb answers," Diane went on. "I mean she's so stupid, but people still want to hang out with her. I can't believe she's that popular. And all the boys think she's such hot shit. Why isn't she, like, laughed at every day?

"Do you think she's pretty?" she asked Susannah, but didn't wait for an answer. "I don't. I don't think she's pretty. I was looking at her in Dr. Phillips's class the other day, you know, when she wasn't looking, and get this—I don't even think *she* thinks she's pretty. I could see she was hiding in class, like she didn't want to be seen or called on. That made me really sick. Like she's this wallflower and all these people think she's such hot stuff.

"Last night, when I was thinking about how this dumb creep has the whole school fooled, I got some kind of lightning-bolt idea, like I just had a hit of Ecstasy or something. It's my job to, like, expose Lady Duh Duh for what she is. To let everyone know she's this stupid creep, this horrible person, and that the entire school should, like, reject the hell out of her because she's such a dumb, stupid creep."

Diane's mood suddenly brightened. "So get this, Susannah! I am the Lady Duh Duh police! This just came to me out of thin air. I am going to show the world who she really is. And I'm going to make her life miserable as I do it."

Laughter poured from her. Susannah, still far away, offered a thin smile.

"No guy's gonna want to be with her. She'll be, like, toxic waste. No one is going to want to get near her. Guys are going to know that they would have to be a total loser to want to date her or take her to the prom.

"As I was thinking about this, I realized that if I really succeeded—I mean if I totally humiliate her—she might decide to leave the school. Oh, my God, that would be total victory."

Now, some ninety minutes later Diane had an opportunity to humiliate her in front of a crowd of people, and she wasn't going to miss it.

"You know, Lady Duh Duh, if you play your cards right, you might just get an A in Mrs. Rogers's class, you little apple polisher."

"Or she might get a C for clown," Susannah said.

"Or a D for dumb creep," Diane went on.

Diane turned to Susannah and gave her a high five, and they both laughed as if they had just heard the funniest joke of their lives. Linda joined in the laughter, but only half-heartedly.

Roxanne tried to get away, but the crowd of students on their way to their next class blocked her. Suddenly, the crowd parted, and Roxanne saw three of the basketball team's stars—Roland Evers, Ronnie Schulman, and George Jackson—strolling toward her. All three looked at Roxanne, and the expression on George's face revealed his genuine affection for her.

Diane turned and saw the basketball players too, and she noticed how George was looking at Roxanne and realized that he was interested in her. "Hi George," Diane said, giving him a foxy look as she stepped between George and Roxanne. But her movement was awkward and she somehow tripped over her own feet. She started to fall, and as she did, her body inexplicably picked up speed. She hurtled headfirst into a set of lockers, hitting a locker door that was slightly ajar. The impact slammed the locker shut, causing an explosion of metal against metal that reverberated up and down the hallway.

Everyone turned in shock toward the sound. Dozens of people ran toward Diane and gathered around her, wondering aloud if she was hurt. Diane lay stunned for a moment and then opened her eyes. Rolling onto her back, she moaned and touched her forehead. A red mound was swelling already, but she seemed all right. Everyone let out sighs of relief, and then someone called out, "That's using your head, Diane."

As people laughed, other comedians let fly.

"Hey, Diane, next time use the doorway. The walls in this place are six inches thick."

"Hey Diane, how was your flight? Rough landing, huh?"

"Is that, like, some kind of mountainous zit coming out of your forehead, Diane?"

Susannah and Linda hid their laughter as they backed away from Diane as if she were radioactive.

Roxanne scanned Diane for internal injuries, knowing she had contributed to Diane's fall. She had only wanted Diane to stumble out of George's path and perhaps suffer the embarrassment of looking awkward. But when Diane's balance faltered, the small humiliation Roxanne had intended turned into a potentially dangerous fall. Feeling more than a little guilty, Roxanne was relieved that Diane was fine—at least physically. Her pride was another matter.

George and Roxanne knelt down next to Diane.

"Maybe you should see the nurse," Roxanne said, her concern for her antagonist sincere.

Despite being dazed, Diane shifted into attack mode. Rubbing her head, she focused all her rage at Roxanne. "You tripped me, you slut!"

"Nobody tripped you," George said. "Roxanne wasn't within ten feet of you. You stumbled over your own two feet."

Diane glared at Roxanne, her eyes full of the promise of vengeance. Her wickedness gave Roxanne new resolve. With all the purity of new snow, Roxanne said, "Maybe you should tie your sneakers, Diane." Diane looked down at her shoes and saw that the long laces were dangling.

Mrs. Van Doren hurried over and told everyone to break it up and get to class. She helped Diane get to her feet and escorted her to the nurse.

George turned to Roxanne. "We're still on for Saturday night, right?"

"Yes, absolutely," Roxanne said, smiling now and satisfied with how things turned out.

"Looking forward to it," George said, and hurried off to class.

Chapter 10
The Basketball Game, Roxanne's Date with George

The instant Roxanne got out of her car in the school parking lot, she heard cheers and shouting, clapping hands and stomping feet, and the high-pitched voices of the cheerleaders as they led the crowd in a pregame chant. The full effect of the pandemonium didn't hit her until she entered the gymnasium and felt the thrilling rush of sensory overload. In an instant she took in the noise, the faces, the clothing, the smell of sweat and rubber and floor wax, the squeaking of basketball shoes on the gleaming surface of the court, the brightly lit scoreboard, and in the center of it all, the players.

Dressed in red and gold warm-up suits, the Laurel Glen players were practicing layups like languid demigods. One by one, they glided to the hoop with the ball on their fingertips. Each young man effortlessly launched himself into the air and either shot the ball directly into the basket or bounced it off the glass backboard, and then returned to earth as if he hardly touched the floor. In the center was George Jackson, seemingly oblivious to the excitement and the pressure, apparently in the kind of trance that only an abundance of athletic talent and confidence can convey. His layups were pure ballet. When the Laurel Glen team broke their layup drill and began shooting from all over the court, George fired long-range jumpers that seemed like guided missiles programmed to fall into the net. To the parents and nonathletic students, he looked like a Formula One race car idling in its own perfection. Roxanne couldn't take her eyes off him. She hurried to the Laurel Glen side of the bleachers and watched George for another minute. *I'm going out with him tonight,* she thought. *He wants me!*

At the other end of the court were Laurel Glen's arch rivals, Bloomfield High, dressed in purple and yellow sweats. They, too, took layups and then broke into a free-wheeling warm-up, shooting jump shots, foul shots, and more layups. Her gaze still fixed on the players, Roxanne hurried along the line of bleacher seats and bumped into Sarah Doherty.

"Sarah, hi!" Roxanne shouted above the crowd noise. "Where are we sitting?"

"We're over here," Sarah said, pointing. "Lyla is holding our seats."

Lyla was standing up and waving her hands in the middle of a crowd. Roxanne and Sarah made their way up to her.

"How are you, Lyla?" Roxanne asked when she reached her friend.

"Nearly hoarse," Lyla said, laughing. "This is so exciting. I want to get down there and kick some butt too."

"Let's hope they don't need you tonight," Roxanne said.

"I'm ready if they do. All Coach Smith has to do is look up here and give me the sign. I'll play in my bare feet if I have to."

"Semper Fi, sister," Roxanne said. "Semper Fi."

Lyla and Sarah laughed. Lyla held up her hands and received high fives from Roxanne and Sarah. "You got that right, girl," Lyla said. "I'm all over that stuff."

The three girls remained standing, as did the rest of the crowd. Roxanne looked to her right and saw Jason Phillips standing in a row just above hers, some thirty feet away. She smiled and he gave a polite wave.

Down on the court, the players finished their warm-ups and went to their benches for last-minute instructions from their coaches. The cheerleaders took center stage. Diane led the cheerleading team—composed of eight girls and two strong boys—in chants, high kicking, and then the formation of a pyramid, with Diane at the top. When she reached the summit, Diane looked up into the stands and saw Roxanne. The cheerleader tossed her head back in triumph and stretched out both her hands, a pose that, Roxanne thought, was vaguely reminiscent of Richard Nixon. The crowd roared. The pyramid broke up on cue, and Diane fell into the waiting arms of the two male cheerleaders. She bounced around the court, shaking her pompoms wildly, and led the cheerleaders and the crowd in a rousing chorus of victory chants for Laurel Glen.

Roxanne was tempted to play Jim Carrey to Diane's Steve Carrel, but suppressed the thought. Instead, she turned to Sarah, who was rolling her eyes and laughing.

"Don't forget," Sarah said in Roxanne's ear. "George is going out with you tonight, and that's driving her nuts."

Roxanne smiled. "I wonder if Prozac plus a heavy dose of arsenic would help her?"

The cheerleaders ran to the sidelines as five players from each team took the court.

Bloomfield High, located in Bloomfield, Maryland, and also a Washington, DC, suburb, was a perennial force in the region's high school basketball conference. Bloomfield and Laurel Glen met twice a year, and Bloomfield had won the last ten games. The reason was simple: Bloomfield's players were bigger, stronger, and more talented than the Laurel Glen team. This was the first meeting of the 2010 season, and the Laurel Glen coach and his players believed they had a good shot at changing their fortunes, finally.

Laurel Glen's starters had matured, both individually and as a team. Ronnie Schulman was the point guard, Steven Davis played shooting guard. Roland Evers, who was six foot six and had long arms and a kangaroo's ability to jump, was at center. Isaiah Brown, a six-foot-four power forward, was fast, had a good medium-range jumper, and could rebound. And then there was George, who was also six four and could hit from any place on the court. He was deadly from twenty feet, tough on the boards, and he could score inside. His defense was pretty good too.

Bloomfield was taller than Laurel Glen, thanks to Wagner Rivers, a six foot eight inch senior who had already pledged to Georgetown on a full scholarship. Bloomfield had another star in Henry Banks, big-bodied guard with blinding speed and a consistent jump shot.

The two referees went to center court. One blew his whistle and both teams took the floor, collecting in a circle around their respective centers, who would jump to start the game. Not surprisingly, Bloomfield won the tap. The ball was flipped to Banks, who took off like a gunshot toward his own basket. He flung an alley-oops pass to Rivers, who emphatically jammed the ball home. The crowd was stunned. The game was underway.

Basketball is a game in which primitive instincts are elevated to high art. The dark passions that reside in the shadowy worlds within humans—the impulses for aggression, violence, and conquest—are tempered and ultimately transformed by the boundaries of the court and the laws of the game, the grace and power of athletic ballet, the focus on a single goal, and the awesome beauty of five humans acting as one.

When played well, the players move the ball around the key as if directed by intuition. The ball seems to take on a life of its own, moving with electrifying precision from the point guard at the top of the key, to the center at the low post, back to the point guard, who fires a no-look pass to the forward at the left-corner baseline, who, after barely touching the ball, threads a bounce pass back to the center, who in turn relays the ball to the point guard at the top of the key. Seeing the defense coming at him, the point guard fires the ball to the right low post and the in-motion forward, who catches the ball on the fly and lays it in for an easy layup, or jams it through the hoop for a slam dunk.

The crowd erupts with a giddy thrill after participating vicariously,

For more than three quarters of the game, the crowd was treated to that kind of beauty. Long jump shots from the baseline, the top of the key, and the left and right flanks. Players driving to the hoop with the determination of the kamikaze. Hard fouls under the basket followed by boos and whistles from the crowd. Shoes squeaking at every cut and run. Errant passes. Blocked shots. Lots of hustle. Referees whistling the ball dead for brief moments of relief. Foul shots made and missed.

Coaches strategizing on small chalk boards and gesticulating wildly on the sidelines. Screaming crowds, who do not dare to sit for fear they might miss a pivotal moment or fail to convey their collective energy to their heroes on the court. It was no small feat that in this pressure cooker of noise and confusion, the players performed with concentration and courage.

Roxanne, Sarah, and Lyla alternately struck the classic poses of fans everywhere—fists at their mouths, biting hard in hope and fear; arms down at their sides, screaming at their team, the opposition, the referees; determined pointing at the players, conveying blessings on their home team or sending vitriol at the opponents; and bursts of applause, especially when a ref got it right or one of the hometown heroes scored or rebounded or made a good pass.

Because the game was played well, it all came down to the last few minutes of play. That was when things got dicey for Roxanne. Throughout the game, she had been tempted to influence the players just enough to keep Laurel Glen ahead. Oh, how easy it would be to interfere just enough with Wagner River's nervous system so that he dropped the ball as he flew to the hoop, or to confuse Henry Banks so that he threw a bad pass that would be intercepted by a Laurel Glen player. Again and again, Roxanne resisted the temptation, instead biting her fist hard and then jumping up and down, screaming, "Come on, you guys. You can do it!"

Every fan in these stands is trying to do what I can do, she told herself. *Give our players an edge. But it's wrong for me to do that. Get a grip on yourself, Roxanne. It's the law of our kind: don't interfere with Ordinaries except under dire circumstances, matters of life and death! Don't interfere! They can do it on their own! Let them play.*

With just two minutes left, Bloomfield was up by three points. Banks brought up the ball for the visiting team. All he had to do was run out the clock. Laurel Glen's coach called for a full-court press, with a double team on the man with the ball. Steven Davis and George pinned Banks along the right sideline. Wagner Rivers came up to help Banks, but Laurel Glen's Roland Evers shadowed Rivers. As Banks tried to protect the ball on his hip, George slapped it hard and dislodged it. The ball rolled free on the court. Steven Davis dove to the floor and in a single motion scooped the ball toward George. He caught it and lofted a perfect pass over Rivers and into the waiting arms of Roland Evers, who took a step and a half and slammed the ball through the hoop. The crowd went crazy.

Laurel Glen was down by one point with thirty seconds left. Bloomfield called time out, and both teams went to their respective benches to talk to their coaches. The cheerleaders ran onto the center of the court, danced frantically, and then shook their pompoms in a gesture of blessing at their Laurel Glen heroes. Then they turned on Bloomfield, shook their pompoms again, and chanted doom on the enemy.

A horn sounded and brought both teams back to the floor. Bloomfield took the ball out from the left side line. Coach Smith had instructed his players to foul the man with the ball. But when Banks received the ball on the in-bounds pass, he hurried away from the Laurel Glen players in order to kill as much time as he could.

Do I do something? Roxanne wondered desperately. *No, it'll be all right if they lose. I'm not going to interfere! But they can't lose. They just can't.*

And then it happened. As Banks dribbled to his left, he bounced the ball off his foot. A mad scramble ensued, with players from both sides diving at the ball. Ronnie Schulman reached it first. He stayed on his feet, gathered the ball into his arms, and with brilliant presence of mind immediately called time out. Ten seconds left. Time for one more shot.

The crowd went into pandemonium as both teams trotted to their benches.

Did I do that? Roxanne asked herself, suddenly overcome with guilt, terror, and remorse. *Did I cause the ball to go off his foot? I don't think so. But maybe I did. Oh, God, I don't want to believe that I did that. I don't think I did that.*

Reflexively, she turned to her right and looked at Jason Phillips, who was looking back at her with an expression of concern. His shield was up and she could not read his thoughts. *Oh no, I must have done that,* Roxanne thought. She sat down on the bleacher while the rest of the crowd remained standing.

Sarah bent over. "Are you all right?"

"Yes, I'm fine. Just exhausted."

"Me too," Sarah said. "Isn't it great?"

Roxanne gave a small smile. "Yes, it's great." She stood up again and looked down on the court.

The scoreboard horn brought both teams back onto the floor. Roland Evers stood outside the left side line, took the ball from the referee, and threw the in-bounds pass to Ronnie Schulman. Eight seconds left. Schulman dribbled to his right. Roland Evers ran down court and set a pick for George Jackson, who was standing along the right baseline. George raced from the baseline toward the top of the key, brushing the Bloomfield defender who was guarding him. For an instant, George was free on the right side of the court. Schulman fired the ball to George, who caught it, turned toward the basket, and lifted into the air. His eyes focused on the hoop, both arms extended above his head, George released the ball in a perfect arc. Cameras flashed. The crowd hushed. Bloomfield players grimaced as they rushed at him, attempting to block the shot or foul him. They were too late. The shot was perfect and the ball found its target. The game-ending buzzer sounded as the ball swooshed through the netting of the hoop. The crowd erupted in hysterical cheers. A great rush of energy and relief filled the gym as the Laurel Glen players mobbed George and then hugged one another. The fans jumped up and down and engaged in their own lovefest. Sarah and Lyla and Roxanne all embraced and screamed and raised their arms in celebration. Roxanne put aside her guilt. She'd had nothing to do with George's shot. For the moment, she felt redeemed, if only partially so.

After the game had concluded, Roxanne waited about forty-five minutes outside the boy's locker room before George emerged, freshly showered and groomed, exhausted but happy.

"I'm so sorry that took so long," he said to her.

"It's no problem," she said. "Lyla and Sarah waited with me for a lot of the time. We couldn't stop celebrating the game." She took George's arm and they walked out of the building.

"You were amazing tonight," she said. She looked into his eyes and searched his thoughts to see what his inner world was like.

"Thanks," said George. "I guess I was lucky with that last shot."

"George, you are a fantastic basketball player. That wasn't luck, that was pure ability."

He smiled as they walked into the school parking lot. "If it's okay, we'll take my car," he said. "I'll can take you home tonight and then pick you up for school tomorrow morning. Or I can drive you back here tonight and you can drive yourself home."

"Either way is fine," Roxanne said. She liked him even more now. He was considerate and modest and handsome. A prince!

They got into George's Ford Explorer and drove toward Antonio's Italian restaurant.

"What did Coach Smith say to you guys when you all got into the locker room?" Roxanne asked.

"He told us how proud he was, how hard we've worked in practice and how it all paid off in the game. Also, that we never gave up."

Roxanne laughed. "In other words, coach-speak."

"Yeah, I guess so," George said with a smile. "But you know, he means it. He's a really great guy, and he's helping me a lot with college and all."

"How is he helping you?"

"Well, there are a few schools that are offering me scholarships. He's writing letters to college coaches, telling them how easy it is to coach me and how great I'd be on their team. He's also helping me decide where I might like to go to school."

They parked in front of Antonio's and walked into the restaurant. The moment they entered, the patrons started clapping. A few got out of their booths and walked over to shake George's hand and pat him on the back.

"Let's hear it for George Jackson!" someone called out. Suddenly, everyone was clapping and people were calling out, "Hooray, George!", "What a shot, George," and "Buzzer-beater George."

"Thank you all," George said, with a self-deprecating wave of his hand. He turned his head down ever so slightly, as if to avoid further adulation, and pointed to an empty booth.

A young waitress hurried over with menus in hand, smiling broadly, obviously happy to be waiting on the famous George Jackson. She introduced herself as Connie as she put their menus down and asked if they'd like anything to drink. They both ordered sodas.

"I'm sorry," George said to Roxanne as Connie hurried off. "Maybe this wasn't the best place to have dinner after a game."

"George, what are you talking about? They love you and you deserve it. You scored the game-winning shot. You're a hero in their eyes, and rightfully so."

He paused a minute. "Yeah, you're right, but it's a team game. If Steven doesn't save the ball from going out of bounds, then I don't pass to Ro, and if he messes up the dunk, then there's no chance at the end. And if Ronnie doesn't get me the ball, and Ro doesn't set that pick for me, then I don't get a clear look at the rim. So a lot of things have to come together, and a lot of people have to perform in order for me to be the hero."

Roxanne was amazed. She had seen a lot of professional athletes interviewed on television and so many of them spoke in the very same terms as George just had. Many of these gifted athletes apparently were humble people. They performed feats of magic before enormous crowds, but became shy and even introverted when interviewed afterward. What was it that made some really talented athletes this way? She wondered.

She read the menu as thoughts flooded her head. Of course, the coaches molded young athletes into team players, she told herself. But special athletes also had incredible body wisdom. Their gifts resided in the old brain, the cerebellum, with the special programming that gave them such amazing physical coordination. They were able to turn off their minds so that their physical gifts could perform under great stress. Talk to them later and they didn't have a clue how they had done what they did. But put them in the heat of battle and they could dance and spin and, for short distances, even fly.

Connie was back and placed the drinks in front of them. The tall, cold glasses sweated beads of condensation that formed small pools of water around the bottoms of the glasses. George asked Roxanne if she knew what she wanted, and she suggested a slice of cheese pizza with sun-dried tomatoes and broccoli."

George looked up at Connie. "How about we have a medium pizza, half with sun-dried tomatoes and broccoli, and the other half with pepperoni?"

Connie made notes on her pad. "Coming right up."

Roxanne sipped her drink. "Your parents must be really proud of you. Were they there tonight?"

"Well, my father died when I was ten, and my mother works an evening shift, so she doesn't come to too many games."

"I'm so sorry, George. I had no idea. That's terrible."

"It's not so bad." He drank some of his soda. "We're all doing fine."

"We?"

"Well, my sister and brother and me. I'm the oldest, my brother's the youngest."

"What are your plans for after high school?"

"Well, I'm going to college on a scholarship, unless I really mess up this season," He smiled.

"You're going to have a great season, believe me," Roxanne said. "Where do you think you'll go to school?"

"I'll probably choose University of Maryland, which is Division One. That's the highest level of college sports," he added, as if she wouldn't know that.

Roxanne read his thoughts, tilting her head to one side as if sifting through her inner files. "Hmmm, University of Maryland. Oh, yes, head coach Gary Williams, whom I like, has been there since 1989, coached them to eleven straight NCAA tournaments, made the final four in 2001, and won the National Championship in 2002. They beat Indiana 64-52. The game wasn't that close, actually. A lot of people still believe that Maryland's loss to NC State in the 1974 ACC championship tournament was the greatest college basketball game ever played. But they're wrong, George." She leaned over the table toward him. "The greatest college basketball game ever played was the 1992 NCAA Eastern Regional Finals, when Duke beat Kentucky on Christian Laettner's last-second jump shot from the top of the key. Laettner went ten-for-ten from the field, and ten-for-ten from the foul line, and hit the game winner at the buzzer. I'm sure you agree that that's the greatest performance by a college athlete ever. Anyway, I think Maryland would be perfect for you, George, but don't expect Gary Williams to be there much longer. I think he'll retire in another year. At least that's what he's been saying recently."

George sat back and shook his head in utter astonishment. His smile was full of wonder. "How do you know all that, Roxanne?"

She gave him a flirtatious smile. "Oh, I read the sports pages too, George."

"You are amazing."

"So, you think you can make it to the NBA?"

"I don't know, but to be honest, I don't think so. I could play in Europe for a few years after college, if I really wanted to play pro ball. But that's not my plan. Do you want to know what I really want to do?" he asked, his voice dropping to just above a whisper.

Roxanne drew closer to him. "I can't wait to hear," she said, smiling in anticipation. George was about to reveal his secret ambition—something even greater than the NBA! She was thrilled with the intimacy of the conversation.

"Well, I'm going to try to make a name for myself while I'm at Maryland," he began. "If I play well, the whole state will know who I am."

She nodded in agreement. "That's for sure, George."

"Once I graduate from college, I'm going to come back here, get some investors together, and start a new car dealership, right here in Laurel Glen. I'll do one of those combination dealerships, you know, Chevrolet and Nissan, or GM and Toyota. Everyone will want to buy a car from George Jackson. I'll even have basketballs as my logo. I read an article recently that those guys who own car dealerships make a lot of money. I'll set my mother up in a new house, let her retire. I'll hire my brother and sister, get married myself, and have some kids. I'll live a nice life right here in Laurel Glen."

Roxanne sat back in her booth, suddenly crestfallen. She didn't know what to say. Could anything be more boring than a car salesman? And then she saw George for who he really was—how wounded he was from the loss of his father; how he had stepped into the family's father role even before he was capable of fathering anyone, including himself; how much he loved his mother and dreamed of providing a good life for her, after all that she had sacrificed and suffered; and how much he wanted to provide for his brother and sister. Above all else, George was his family's hero. She smiled warmly, compassionately, at him.

"That sounds really nice," she said. She felt her heart open for this beautiful young man, but they were light years apart. He could no more understand her than he could the planet Venus. George epitomized all that was good in people, but his life and his dreams had been fixed by tragedy. His goals, though admirable, would never interest her, much less give her the least excitement. Their worlds would never meet.

Their pizza arrived. They ate and talked about college basketball, high school gossip, and George's thoughts about the next few games on the team's schedule. They laughed a lot, becoming friends. When the evening concluded, Roxanne asked George to drive her back to the school parking lot. She'd get her car and drive herself home.

George pulled up next to Roxanne's Honda. Before she got into her car, they embraced. He held her in his arms and kissed her gently on the lips. Roxanne responded with warmth and affection, but there were no sparks for either one of them.

When their lips parted, Roxanne smiled and said, "Thank you, George, for a great night."

"Thank you, Roxanne. You know, the other kids have you all wrong. You're so much more than what people think."

"Thank you, George."

Rebecca was waiting up for Roxanne when she got home. Two cups of chamomile tea sat steaming on the coffee table in the living room as Roxanne sat down next to her mother on the sofa.

"So, kind of a mixed night, huh," Rebecca said.

"Yeah. Did I cause that kid to lose the basketball at the end of the game?"

"I really don't know, honey. What do you think?"

"I thought about it all night long," Roxanne said. "I was trying so hard not to interfere, but I have to admit that I really got involved in the game. I don't believe I interfered. That's my honest answer, but I cannot be absolutely certain. All I do know is that George made the game-winning shot all by himself."

"Well, Uncle Alex is coming over for dinner tomorrow evening, and your dad is coming home later tomorrow night, so among the four of us, we should be able to figure it out."

"Oh, no, Mom, this isn't going to be the Inquisition, is it?"

"Absolutely not," Rebecca said. "No one wants that." She pulled Roxanne close to her and Roxanne dropped her head onto her mother's shoulder.

"George isn't boyfriend material, is he?" Rebecca asked.

"No, not even close. Mom, how did you deal with being married to an Ordinary before you met Dad? I really don't know how you managed living with someone who didn't understand you."

Rebecca stroked Roxanne's hair. "It was very hard," she said. "And I know all too well the loneliness you're feeling right now. It wasn't until I met your father that life began to make any sense to me. But then, you know that story, don't you?"

"Tell it to me again. It gives me hope."

"You're tired now," Rebecca replied. "Everything will look better in the morning."

"Okay." Roxanne got up from the sofa and realized how deeply tired she was. She hugged her mother and then went upstairs to bed.

Rebecca remained on the couch, looking into empty space as she recalled life with her first husband and how much she had changed since Roger Reynolds had come into her life.

Chapter 11
Rebecca's Story, Meeting Roger

W alter Combs and Rebecca Sullivan met in 1934, when Rebecca was nineteen years old, just months after her parents had been killed when a gas leak caused a fire that destroyed their entire apartment building. Rebecca had been born and raised in San Francisco. Both of her parents were Ordinaries. She got her gifts from a great-grandfather who, after fathering children, left his family to live in the wilds of northwest Canada. Both of Rebecca's parents recognized that their daughter possessed amazing talents, but neither suspected the breadth and depth of her abilities. Nor did they expect her to amount to anything more than a conventional woman—to marry young, have children, and live out her life as a housewife. That was what they wanted for her, so they urged her to keep secret her special abilities in math and science, and her uncanny knack for recalling vast stores of information.

"Be a good girl," her father would tell her. "Mind your place. People don't like it when a little girl acts smart."

As a child, Rebecca was shy to the point of hiding, but intellectually, she was beyond anyone's capacity to teach. She was reading Einstein's general theory of relativity when she was seven years of age, and by ten she was working on mathematical formulas that attempted to reconcile the macroscopic world of relativity—which described the behavior of stars and galaxies—with the quantum world of atoms and electrons. She read novels in the hope of finding characters, especially female characters, with whom she could relate and who perhaps could illuminate some of her inner world. She loved Jane Austen, Emily Brontë, and George Eliot—any writer or character who explored the themes of alienation and female independence.

Still, there were aspects of her life that no author, not even Sigmund Freud or Carl Jung, could shed light upon, especially the moments of *blending*, as she called them, when she inadvertently opened up her mind and experienced the thoughts and emotions of another person. It was as if she disappeared and moved inside the life of one of her classmates or a teacher or some other person, directly experiencing their minds and emotions. In the process, she—Rebecca—disappeared entirely. Only the other person existed. During a blending, she feared she was losing her mind.

Hence, she hid her real life from others and retreated into her books and long ruminations in her room or in nature. In the end, she was a foreigner, an outcast, even within her own family.

When her parents died, she was alone in the world. Walter was a twenty-eight-year-old naval officer and completely in love with her. A few months after the fire, he asked Rebecca to marry him and she agreed.

The navy posted them to San Diego first, and then Walter was sent to Hawaii. He and Rebecca made a home there, but their marriage did not develop well. Walter wanted her to be the ideal navy officer's wife—a social butterfly that would help him move up the chain of command. But tea parties, gossip, and evenings at the officers' club alternately bored and infuriated Rebecca. What was far worse was that Walter had no interest in his inner feelings and thoughts, so they had no real intimacy. His life was based entirely on appearances, which, Rebecca came to realize, was essentially a life of lies.

Late in November 1941, Rebecca decided to visit a friend in San Francisco. The trip would give her time to reflect and help her decide what she wanted for her life. Walter arranged for her to get a seat on a military flight back to her hometown.

On Sunday morning, December 7, 1941, she woke up with a deep sense of terror. She didn't know why, but later that morning, as she walked along Market Street in downtown San Francisco and saw a crowd gathering in front of an outdoor food market, she knew she was about to have her answer. A radio on top of a large basket of apples was announcing the news that the Japanese had bombed Pearl Harbor, Hawaii, at 7:55 a.m. Authorities estimated that thousands had been killed, though no one knew the extent of the carnage. The instant she heard the report, Rebecca knew Walter was dead.

In the chaos that ensued, it was difficult for her to get back to Hawaii, but within days of the bombing, Rebecca gathered with other military families and personnel at San Francisco airport for a flight to Hawaii. While she sat in the terminal waiting area, she heard a strange sound in her head, a musical note of sorts. She had never heard the sound before. It was a soft sensation, not unpleasant, as if someone had plucked a guitar string within her nervous system. She intuitively knew it was important, but didn't understand its significance. She looked around the terminal and saw a tall golden-haired man walking across the waiting area. He seemed to be looking for someone. For reasons she did not understand, Rebecca felt sure the ping had something to do with this man.

When her flight was called, she boarded and took her seat. The tall man took the seat directly behind her. When the plane had reached cruising altitude, Rebecca had her second bizarre experience of the morning—she heard a man's voice *speaking inside her head*. She wasn't hearing him with her ears but was experiencing his voice within her nervous system, as if he was speaking inside her. Just as bizarre, she knew it was the voice of the man sitting behind her. How any of this was happening, she did not know. All she knew was that she heard the words clearly and knew who was speaking to her.

"I'm the reason you heard the ping in the airport terminal," he said. "My name is Roger Reynolds. We should talk. You are not losing your mind and this is no hallucination. You have rare abilities that are shared by only a few hundred people on earth. I am like you. There are empty seats at the back of the plane. I'm going to get up and go sit in one of those seats. Please join me."

Rebecca turned around and watched the man get up and walk to the back of the plane, sitting in an otherwise empty row of seats. She got up and walked to the back of the plane too. The man was sitting in the window seat. "Please, join me," he said aloud.

When she sat down, he switched back to telepathic communication. "I'm going to communicate with you telepathically because what I'm about to say should not be overheard. I realize this form of communication may feel awkward at first, but soon it will be second nature to you."

As she looked into Roger's piercing blue eyes, he explained to her who she was.

"You are what we call a Genius," he began. "Not the kind of genius you're used to reading about, but someone who is even more rare, a person with advanced and special abilities that transcend what you have been trained to think of as normal human talents. You can read other people's minds, their thoughts and emotions. I can teach you how to alter the biochemistry of others, how to change their thoughts and feelings. With time, you can learn to transmit enormous bundles of energy, either as a way to heal or as a means of self-defense. You may be able to move objects with your mind, as well.

"You are not a freak, but part of a tiny minority of people who are at the extreme end of a normal bell-shaped intelligence curve. If you shuffle the human genetic deck enough times, eventually you'll come up with a genetic arrangement that confers very special abilities. Those of us who have already found each other are organized under a kind of governing body, which we call the Council of Western Geniuses. We are stationed in places around the world, but our headquarters is in Washington, DC.

"I know this conversation is shocking to you and it's hard to digest all that I've said, though I assure you that you will remember every word I've spoken. I have an office in Hawaii, but I spend most of my time in London. I can help you learn more about who you are, how to use your innate abilities, and how you can develop a life among people just like you."

He reached into his suit jacket pocket and pulled out his business card, which he handed to Rebecca.

"When you are ready, please contact me," he said. "Also, I want to offer my condolences. I am very sorry for your loss."

Rebecca took the card from Roger, thanked him, and walked back to her seat. At first, she thought she might pass out from shock, but a stream of energy flowed to her like a gentle breeze and gave her the strength to find her seat. As she sat, another wave of support washed through her, giving her an amazing sense of well-being. Instinctively, she turned around and saw Roger still at the back of the plane, looking pensively out the window. As she stared at him, she was aware that she had never felt more physically well and at peace in her life. She knew the supportive flow came from Roger Reynolds.

Once she was back in Hawaii, Rebecca made the funeral arrangements for Walter, contacted his family members, and participated in various memorial services. The war had begun and she got a job working for the Red Cross. Months later, when she had regained her emotional footing, she decided it was time to meet Roger Reynolds again.

She found his card—but then realized she didn't need it. She recalled his contact information instantly. She called his office and arranged to meet him at a nearby restaurant that had not been damaged by the bombing.

Roger was waiting at a table when she entered the restaurant. He got up and offered his hand. Rebecca gave him a firm handshake and sat down.

"Thank you for meeting me," she said. "I have hundreds of questions for you, but I guess you already know that." She gave him a slightly embarrassed smile, uncertain how much he might already know about her and her inner life.

"It's only natural," he said. "Everyone alive wants to know who they are and why they are here."

"Can you tell me who I am?" she asked. Before he could answer, she said, "I'm not sure I'm comfortable with someone else telling me who I am."

"No," he said, "I cannot tell you who you are, at least not in the way you mean. But I can tell you a lot about yourself, and I can offer you a place within a community of people just like you who are searching for the same answers you are."

"What do I have to do to become part of that community?" she asked.

"There are several options, but one of them is to come and work for me."

"What would I be doing?"

"There's a war to win, Rebecca."

"Whose side are you on?"

"My colleagues and I are on the side of human freedom," Roger said. "We don't normally participate in the affairs of ordinary humans, but we are inherently opposed to totalitarianism and the restriction of people's right to discover their own destiny. So, to answer your question directly, we are on the same side Walter was on."

Rebecca studied Roger for a moment and then felt compelled to look away. She had never felt so understood, so comfortable, so at home with anyone as she did with this man. It was as if she had known him her entire life. And yet, communicating with him was so awkward. Not just because of the telepathy, which was entirely new to her, but because of the intimacy. He was inside her; she was inside him. It was shocking and at the same time exhilarating. But what made the experience so satisfying, so fulfilling, was that she trusted him. As with mind-to-mind communication, trust was a new experience for her. It was foreign and yet at the same time, the closest thing she had felt to safety and love.

"When do I start?" she asked.

Roger smiled. He was aware of all that was going on inside Rebecca. In fact, he was having his own version of the same experience. He could not resist her. He shielded his thoughts, because he realized his proposal wasn't merely for a job. It was for life.

"How does right now feel to you?" he asked.

She smiled. "Right now feels fine."

And that was how it began, under the safe cover story that they were colleagues, which gave both of them time to become comfortable with the realization that they were soul mates.

Chapter 12

Rebecca and Roxanne Have Dinner with Alexander Astrakhan

T he table was set for three—Rebecca, Roxanne, and their guest of honor, Alexander Astrakhan. Outside, a heavy rain fell. Punctual as always, Alexander rang the doorbell at 6:30 sharp. Before entering the house, he folded his umbrella, shook some of the water from his raincoat, and then handed his coat to Rebecca. She directed him to the dining room and seated him at the head of the table, where Roger normally sat.

As she returned to the kitchen to put the final touches on the meal, Alexander telepathically asked her where Roger was.

"I understood he would be coming home tonight."

"He'll be late, Alexander," Rebecca said as she carried into the dining room a large serving plate of salmon steaks, dressed in a tamari-ginger sauce, with leeks, garlic, scallions, and grape tomatoes. "We expect him around eleven."

"Can I help you with anything?" Alexander asked, again communicating telepathically.

"No, I'm fine," Rebecca replied in kind. "I'll have everything on the table in a minute."

Alexander got up from his chair and walked around, looking for something to occupy his thoughts. He strolled into the small den situated off the dining room, studying some books and then walking over to the small hearth. Above it hung a large crest of the Reynolds coat of arms, with its distinctive double *R* at its center. One of the *R*s was reversed, so that the two *R*s opposed each other, as mirror images. It was made of stone and had been carved many hundreds of years before. Alexander had seen it many times and knew the salient facts about it, including the double *R* prophecy.

Roger's ancestry went back thousands of years. His ancestors had served as advisers to many great leaders, kings and queens. Some eighty generations back, Reginald Reynolds had been a close adviser to King Arthur. He had also been a friend of Arthur's closest counselor, the great Genius Merlin, who had been considered a wizard because of his powers of mind control, telekinesis, and prophecy. Merlin had been present as a mortally wounded Reginald lay dying, and consoled his friend with a prophecy: one of your progeny will attain great powers and will avenge your death by destroying the descendant of your attacker.

"Have faith and rest easy, my friend," Merlin had assured Reginald. "One of your heirs will exact justice for your family, and for the lives of many thousands of others."

After Arthur passed and Camelot fell, Merlin went into seclusion and wrote his memoirs, which contained a long series of prophecies. He gave the book to an apprentice with instructions on where to hide it. No one knew where the apprentice secreted the book, or if it existed, but apparently it turned up centuries later and formed the basis for many predictions that would prove true, including the mysterious quatrains of the sixteenth century seer, Nostradamus. Among the legends passed down through generations of Geniuses was Merlin's vision of a heroic descendant of Reginald Reynolds, a prediction that came to be known as the "Double *R* Prophecy". Legend had it that there was more to the prophecy, but it had been lost in time.

Alexander studied the coat of arms and then looked into the fireplace, which held some recently burned cinders and ash. He wasn't much for prophecy, although some Geniuses did indeed have that gift. Nor did he dwell much on the past. He was a practical man, who believed that one should learn from the past and then use all powers to shape the present and the future. He studied the ashes in the fireplace, thinking that this was where so many predictions and prophecies wound up.

He strolled back into the dining room as Roxanne burst into the room. She smiled warmly and kissed him on the cheek. She was dressed in a pink cardigan sweater over a white cotton blouse and, of course, jeans and sneakers.

"My dear, you look beautiful," he said verbally.

She assessed his charcoal gray suit, matched with a light-blue shirt and electric-blue ascot. "And you look … Hmmm, how shall I put it? Like the leader of the free world."

Alexander raised his eyebrows in surprise and then winked at her in playful recognition.

Roxanne went into the kitchen to help her mother. The two emerged carrying serving plates of roasted potatoes, broccoli, carrots, and winter squash. Rebecca asked Roxanne to pour water for everyone while she poured red wine for herself and Alexander.

"Give your wonderful husband my greetings when you see him," Alexander said when they were all seated.

"I think he may drop by your office before he heads back, either late tomorrow or the day after," Rebecca said.

"I look forward to seeing him," Alexander said. "Perhaps we can talk about something other than saving the world this time. Although with this latest Kleper escapade, I rather doubt our meeting will allow for light conversation."

Rebecca served Alexander a salmon steak and an array of the vegetables. After she had served herself, Roxanne did the same.

When everyone was ready to eat, Alexander proposed a toast, "To love and family. Even though I am not a relative by blood, I feel that all three of you are my adopted family."

"To love and family," Rebecca said, and Roxanne repeated the toast. All three began eating, and Alexander was effusive in his praise of the food.

After they had caught up on the news, Alexander turned to Roxanne with a conspiratorial smile. "Did your parents ever tell you about the time the three of us conspired to drive Hitler and Stalin apart? We are the reason the two megalomaniacs never formed a lasting alliance, which, as you know, would have secured World War II for the Axis powers."

Roxanne glanced at her mother. "No, they never bothered to tell me how you all changed the world. But I would love to hear it."

"Oh, they saved the world many times," Alexander said, "but this was a particularly wonderful experience for all three of us. Not only because we sowed the seeds of Germany's defeat, but we also thwarted the Klepers, which is always such satisfying fun.

"Anyway, let me tell you what happened. The Klepers had formulated a brilliant plan to take over the world by having Adolph Hitler join forces with Joseph Stalin. Together, the two would be unbeatable, at least that was the Klepers' belief, and I must say there was good evidence for it.

"I should probably explain before going further," Alexander interrupted himself to add, "that even though the Klepers were trying to control Hitler and Stalin to achieve their dream of world domination, to this day I believe that most of the senseless and evil murdering and other horrors those two fiends perpetrated was a product of their own insanity, and not directed by the Eastern Council. At least, that's what I'd like to believe."

"Now where was I?" "Oh yes." But getting Hitler and Stalin to do what they wanted wasn't easy for the Klepers. The trouble was those two tyrants hated each other. Hitler, the more ideological of the two, absolutely hated communism. And Stalin, the butcher that he was, hated everybody.

"So the Klepers had a problem. They had to overcome the natural antipathy between these two killers.

"As you know, Roxanne, no matter how powerful a Genius is, it's hard to control the mind of a madman, and these two were off-the-charts insane. So controlling them for the long-term was a long shot at best.

"But the Klepers managed to do it, at least for a while. They got the whole Eastern Council to work on it, focusing on the two of them day and night. And in 1939, as you know, Germany and the Soviet Union signed a nonaggression pact. Neither side would go to war against the other, and neither would support any country that went to war with either of them. Finally, both pledged to support each other in the event of war. The next thing you know, Germany invades Poland and the two nations divide up Poland for themselves.

"Of course, we of the Western Council knew what they were up to—it wasn't hard to figure it out—so your parents, some of my staff, and I sat down to formulate a plan."

Rebecca interrupted. "It would be more accurate to say Alexander formulated the plan. And it was brilliant. He saw immediately where the weak link was and gave us our assignments."

Alexander resumed. "Well, anyway, we knew that the next big step for Hitler was Britain, of course. Hitler pounded the British with his blitzkrieg bombing, and by 1940 the British were pretty much flat on their backs.

"The Klepers wanted to seal the deal by having Hitler invade England. Trouble was, Hitler didn't like the idea. Among other things, he feared launching an invasion across the English Channel, and much to the horror of the Klepers, he secretly leaned toward invading Russia. That, of course, would ruin the Klepers' plans for the alliance and world domination, so they decided to have the two leaders meet. Let them get to know each other, form some kind of unholy friendship, and then the Klepers would direct their attention to the West.

"Now every history book written by Ordinaries says that Hitler and Stalin never met, but we know the truth. The Klepers arranged to have the men meet secretly in Lodz, Poland, which was right on the line that had been established to divide Poland between Germany and Russia. Lodz was on the German side, barely, and there was a resort outside the city that was so close to Russian territory, it might as well have been Russian. So both men felt comfortable meeting there.

"Your parents were the sole members of our team in Lodz, but we faced some challenges too. We couldn't actually be on site. The Klepers were there, and if Geniuses from our side were part of either entourage, we would instantly set off the Klepers' warning pings. There would be a firefight and the meeting would be over.

"We also knew we couldn't kill Hitler or Stalin. The Klepers had surrounded both with impenetrable shields. As much as we might have liked to take out one or both of them, killing them was going to be extremely difficult, if not impossible.

"So the two entourages gathered in Lodz—diplomats, translators, medical doctors, and security forces from both sides. Karl and Klaus Kleper, along with other members of the Eastern Council, were always present. Your parents were well-equipped with visual and audio devices, so they could watch and hear everything that mattered. And everything was being beamed back to us in Washington, so I could watch it all too.

"After first meeting, Hitler and Stalin took a walk in a large garden, making jokes through their translators. They discussed coming to the other's aid should the need arise. Everything appeared to be going well for the Klepers. Finally, the two sides sat down for dinner, Hitler at one end, Stalin at the other.

"Now, as you may know, Stalin was intensely paranoid. He was not going to eat anything that might make him sick or possibly kill him. He had his own chefs in the kitchen and his food taster at the table. When the meal was placed before him, his food-tester tasted a little bit of everything.

"The food tester's name was Vladimir Vagoyovich. He was a nice man, with a wife and three children back in Ukraine. Vladimir was the weak link in the Klepers' plan."

Alexander smiled gleefully at Roxanne. "And that's when your parents changed the world." He looked at Rebecca, allowing her to take over the story.

"Your father was positioned on a hilltop about one hundred meters away. His binoculars, equipped with night vision and X-ray, allowed him to see everything clearly. Vagoyovich put some of the food in his mouth, savored it for a moment, and then keeled over and fell to the floor. He appeared to be dead, poisoned by the food. In fact, your father had slowed down all of his vital functions to just above stasis. He was in a state of suspended animation."

Alexander cut in. "We didn't want to kill him. He wasn't a soldier or any kind of combatant. He was an innocent."

"I was in the garden," Rebecca went on, "out of ping range, and could see the events too. When Vagoyovich dropped to the floor, everyone in the room went into shock. Two doctors, one German, the other Russian, ran over to Vagoyovich and checked his pulse and eyes. I intervened and placed the thought in their heads that poor Vladimir was dead. The doctors looked up and gravely announced the news. 'Our comrade food-taster is dead,' the Russian doctor said."

Alexander resumed telling the story. "The instant the doctors said that, Stalin went into apoplexy. He thought Hitler had tried to poison him. In a fit of rage, he picked up a dinner knife and flung it across the room at Hitler! And your mother, with brilliant presence of mind, guided the knife so that it was aimed directly at Hitler's heart. The Klepers' protective shield blocked the knife, of course. It bounced off the shield and stabbed one of the German generals in the shoulder. Hitler was stunned, and then pandemonium broke out. Hitler grabbed a machine gun from one of the German security guards. He wanted to shoot Stalin. Everyone was screaming in German and Russian. Stalin's bodyguards lined up in front of him, picked him up, and literally carried him out of the resort to a line of cars waiting outside the compound. In no time flat, he was back in Russian territory. Hitler was whisked away by his team as well.

"Everybody was gone. The place was silent, except for poor Vladimir, who was still on the floor, fast asleep. At 7:30 the next morning, Vladimir woke up, looked around the empty dining room, and said, 'Where is everybody?'"

Rebecca, Roxanne, and Alexander all laughed at poor Vladimir's confusion.

"So you see, Roxanne," Alexander said, still chuckling, "having a major impact on history can be a lot of fun—when you do it for the right reasons".

"And just to finish the story, after spending months considering his options, and still seething from the events at Lodz, Hitler told his generals to prepare to invade the Soviet Union. And that, my dear, was the beginning of the end for Hitler."

Roxanne applauded and beamed with pride in her parents.

After they had finished dinner, Rebecca made tea and set out a plate of marzipan cookies. "These are not as good as the ones you served us at your office," she said to Alexander, "but they are fresh from the bakery today. I hope you enjoy them."

"Rebecca, anything from your table is heaven sent," Alexander said.

As they drank their tea, Alexander became pensive. Finally, he said, "So, there was a big basketball game last night, Roxanne. Laurel Glen won. And you're concerned that you might have intervened. Tell me what happened."

Roxanne, who'd been dreading this moment, retreated into herself as she recounted the events and described how emotionally involved she became in the game.

"Completely understandable, my dear, completely understandable," Alexander said with a reassuring tone. "I don't believe for an instant that you consciously attempted to change the outcome of the game. Not for a second. But we have to be extremely vigilant with the powers that we possess. It's one thing to alter history when so many lives are at stake, and even the fate of the world, and quite another to do it when it suits our whimsy or our passions. Do you know why I say that?"

"Yes, of course, Uncle. If we fall victim to such temptations, we will not stop before we try to control everything. And Ordinaries have the right to live their own lives free from our interference."

"That's right," Alexander said. "Otherwise, in no time we'd be no different from Hitler or Stalin, or the Klepers, for that matter, with their ambitions to dominate the world. Remember, megalomania begins with small acts."

Roxanne reflected on her many small uses of power, such as placing her cappuccino order in the mind of the café manager or causing everyone in her class to forget the answer she gave on Manifest Destiny.

Alexander continued. "But there are other reasons. If Ordinaries ever discovered who we are and what we are capable of, our entire community—all of our kind—would be in danger. Long ago, the Old Ones established a code of secrecy and protection. We can do a lot of good for the world, but the world must never know of our existence."

"I understand," Roxanne said. Finding her strength, she added, "But that's just it. I really don't believe I interfered with the game. It didn't feel like I entered the mind of the Bloomfield player and caused him to lose the ball."

Alexander was momentarily silent. "Well, there is one way to find out," he finally said. "If you allow me, I could use your thoughts to recreate the events right here on this dining table."

"You could create some kind of visual of what took place?" she asked.

"Yes. With your permission, I could turn your thoughts into a small hologram that would show us exactly what took place at the time the player lost the ball."

"I've heard of this kind of thing being done," Rebecca said to Alexander. "But what does it entail and what kind of effect might it have on Roxanne?"

"As you know, thoughts are bundles of electromagnetic energy, very like photons that come from the sun. Each bundle carries precise information. Roxanne has within her mind and brain an exact record of events she has been involved with. All she has to do is recall those specific events and project those thoughts into the outer layers of her electromagnetic field. I will gather them up and boost their energy density enough for us to see whatever Roxanne was thinking and seeing in her mind's eye. The events will play out directly in front of us. There's no danger or threat to Roxanne. She will merely be thinking about the events in the same way she is doing right now as she recounts them to us. The only difference will be that she'll deliberately project her thoughts outward, so that I can transform them into an image we all can see."

Rebecca looked at Roxanne and told her telepathically that it was her choice.

"I want to do it, Mom," Roxanne said. "I want to know what happened."

"All right then," Alexander said to Roxanne. "Please begin by thinking, as precisely as you can, about the events right before the critical moment when you might have intervened."

Roxanne closed her eyes and with total recall brought to mind the closing minutes of the game. As she recalled the events, she projected her thoughts into the outer layers of her field. Suddenly, a three-dimensional image appeared over the dining table. The players, the basketball court, and the people in the bleachers were all there in vibrant, high-definition color, and from Roxanne's vantage point, high in the bleachers.

"Good, Roxanne," Alexander said, focusing on the hologram over the table. "Continue to concentrate. Run the events forward."

Alexander and Rebecca watched as Steven Davis and George Jackson trapped Banks on the sideline. They saw George slap the ball free and Steven Davis scoop it up and toss it to George, who lofted a pass to Roland Evers for the dunk.

Cheerleaders ran onto the court, danced, and then ran off. The coaches shouted instructions. The restless crowd cheered. Both teams were back on the court. The in-bounds pass went to Banks, who dribbled to his right, running away from the Laurel Glen defenders. Banks then turned and went back to his left. And then the ball bounced off Banks's left foot. Right before the ball hit his foot, both Rebecca and Alexander saw a fleeting stream of light fly at Henry Banks.

Alexander reversed the hologram for less than a second and then froze the image. Rebecca looked at it and instantly realized she was seeing the critical piece of information. She dropped her shoulders, exhaled, and sat back in her chair.

Roxanne opened her eyes and stared at the hologram, shocked by what she saw. A golden chain of light ran from her forehead to the back of Henry Banks's head. The chain was made up of tiny individual beads, much like a string of golden pearls. She could see the golden chain linking her forehead with the back of Banks's head just as the ball bounced off his foot. The hologram left no doubt: Roxanne had sent a series of thoughts to Henry Banks that caused him to lose the ball, which had changed the outcome of the game.

Alexander sat back in his chair. The hologram collapsed and was gone.

Everyone was momentarily silent, each deep in thought. Roxanne was the first to speak.

"I'm so sorry," she said, still looking at the table where the hologram had been. "I didn't realize I had interfered. It all happened so fast. I suppose my emotions got the better of me."

"It's understandable," Alexander said kindly. "You're young and these things happen to all of us. When I was young, I did all kinds of things that I later regretted. The important thing, Roxanne, is that you learn from this experience. We must be extremely careful, ever vigilant. When everyone around us is excited, we must be calm and in control of our emotions *and our thoughts.*"

Rebecca reached out and grabbed Roxanne's hand. "Okay, you made a mistake. Live and learn."

"Do you think my mistake will have any lasting ramifications?" Roxanne asked Alexander.

"Unfortunately, yes. The ramifications will be endless. It's a different time line now. How much different, we will never know. But it's different."

The weight of her mistake bowed Roxanne's shoulder.

"Don't be too hard on yourself," Alexander said. "Every action we take changes the present and creates a new future. This is true for you, your mother, me, everyone. So let's not make too much of this. The best we can hope for is to act for the right reasons. But as your mother says, we must learn from our mistakes."

Roxanne turned to her mother and smiled apologetically and then looked again at Alexander. "I will be more careful. I promise."

"Of course you will," he said. "Of course you will."

He exhaled and said, "Well, it's time for me to be going. Thank you, Rebecca, for a beautiful meal, and thank you both for a special night. Do say hello to Roger for me, Rebecca, and tell him I look forward to seeing him soon."

"I will, Alexander, and thank you for tonight. You are a great teacher. You guide us, and you are always comforting."

He turned to Roxanne. "Don't be surprised if the day comes when you are sitting in my chair."

Roxanne grinned. "I think you've got another few hundred years in you, Uncle."

After Alexander left, Roxanne and Rebecca put the food away and cleaned the kitchen. When they were finished, Roxanne said she wasn't feeling well. She had a headache and wanted to go to bed.

"Yes, of course," Rebecca said. "You've been through a lot tonight. You'll feel better in the morning."

While Roxanne went to bed, Rebecca drew a hot bath and soaked for nearly an hour, most of the time thinking of Roger and how much she wanted him—needed him—tonight. When He got home at 11:30, she was wide awake. Later, after the two had made love and lay in bed, Roger said, "I was listening in on the conversation among the three of you. I'm still not convinced Roxanne influenced that basketball game."

Rebecca propped herself up on her elbow and looked at her husband, astonished by what he had just said.

"Neither am I," she said, gratified that Roger felt as she did. "But I saw the line of thought going from Roxanne to the Bloomfield player. What else could have happened? The facts tell us Roxanne changed the outcome of that game."

"The facts *as we know them* point to that conclusion," Roger said. "But I feel there's more going on here than meets the eye."

Rebecca brightened. "You suspect someone. I love it when you get this way. Who do you think is the real culprit? The Klepers? Or maybe this kid, Andor Lysenko?"

Roger affected a British accent. "My dear Watson, we mustn't jump to any conclusions just yet." He pulled her into his arms and kissed her. One hand ran along the side of her body. "This calls for further investigation," he whispered.

"Oh, God," Rebecca said, drawn into desire once again. "I love it when you investigate."

Chapter 13
Roxanne's Date with Andor

"Mom, I am going to go out with him and that's all there is to it," Roxanne said to her mother.

Roxanne was in the kitchen, having just come home from school, making a sandwich of lettuce, tomato, mustard, and vegan mayonnaise on rye bread. She poured herself a glass of apple juice, but didn't want to eat until her emotions settled. If she ate while she was upset, she would have to mentally adjust her biochemistry to avoid indigestion. That would require effort she didn't have the patience for at the moment. Her mother stood behind her, arms folded.

Roxanne had told her as soon as she got home that Andor asked her to go to the movies and she'd said yes. Rebecca had not been enthusiastic.

Roxanne turned away from her sandwich and faced her mother. "I like him, Mom," she said telepathically. "He's the only boy I've ever met who understands what it's like to be one of us."

"I didn't say you couldn't go out with him," Rebecca said. "All I said was that I wanted you to be careful."

"Mom, when you say 'be careful,' you're really saying that he's a danger to me. He's not the menace that you and Dad make him out to be."

"And what if he is an agent for the Eastern Council?" Rebecca asked. "What then? If you fall for him and lower your defenses, he could hurt you. And that may be exactly what they want you to do."

"Mom, how many times have you spoken to him?"

"Yes, you're right, I haven't met him. But I trust your father and Uncle Alex. And we all love you. How do you expect us to react?"

"Mom, I'm not going to lower my defenses, I promise. You and Dad worry too much. I'm not a fool and I'm not a little girl anymore. I'll be eighteen in a week. I'm past the phase of my life when being good means doing everything Mommy and Daddy tell me to do. I've got to find out for myself."

Rebecca dropped her arms to her side, her shoulders dropping with them. Roxanne could feel her resignation and frustration. She left the kitchen and sat down on the sofa in the living room.

Roxanne stared at her sandwich and apple juice, but had no appetite for either. For a minute, she wondered what to do. Then she went into the living room and sat down next to her mother.

For a time they sat silently, shoulder to shoulder, both looking down at their hands in their laps. Finally Rebecca looked at her daughter and said, "If he harms one hair on your head, I will track him down and rip his lungs out."

Both of them laughed, the kind of laughter that is full of relief and reconciliation. Rebecca put her arms around Roxanne and Roxanne placed her head on her mother's shoulder.

"Mom, don't worry. I'm not the little fawn you imagine me to be."

"You're right. And you're right about having to find out for yourself. But that doesn't make it any easier for your parents." She kissed Roxanne's forehead. "How did I get such a smart daughter?" she asked as if from far away.

"I'm *your* daughter," Roxanne answered. "I can't imagine someone telling you what to do and you just going along with it because you were afraid to find out for yourself."

The two fell silent again, both preparing in their own ways to face the future and all of its uncertainty.

"What time is he coming by to pick you up on Saturday?" Rebecca asked.

"Six-thirty. We're going to the movies and then to Antonio's for pizza."

"Okay. But you're back by midnight, right?"

"No problem. But don't wait up."

"Oh yeah, right. Like it's just another night. Don't kid yourself. I'll be sitting right here, wide awake when you get back — which will be at least two minutes before twelve. Understood?"

Roxanne smiled. "Yes, ma'am."

"Weren't you making yourself a snack?"

"I guess I can eat it now. My appetite is back."

The next day was Friday, and Andor and Roxanne met in the student center to have lunch together, as they had every day that week. The day was overcast, but a few short-lived openings in the cloud cover reminded everyone of what they had been missing.

"Let's go to the pond and eat lunch there," Roxanne suggested.

"Okay," Andor said. "Lead the way."

A small pond that was home to carp and some ducks was located on the northeast corner of the campus. A few benches stood along the edges of the pond. No one else was there. Andor and Roxanne sat down, unpacked their lunches, and began to eat. When Roxanne asked Andor how his classes were going, he rolled his eyes.

"Boring! Boring and frustrating. The other day, Mr. Saunders posed this question to Harry Traubridge: 'A triangle that can be written in the form of n-squared plus 1, n-squared minus 1, and 2n, where n is greater than 1, is right angled. Show that the converse is false by presenting a counterexample.' It was so simple."

Roxanne agreed, and they mentally exchanged a series of equations that elegantly satisfied what Mr. Saunders' had requested.

"But Harry was lost," Andor said. "I could see him sweating and looking around at the other kids in the room. Ugh. I couldn't bear it. 'C'mon dude, think,' I kept saying to myself. He didn't have a clue, and I'm really frustrated because the problem is so easy. And Mr. Saunders is, like, looking at Harry, and the sweat starts pouring down Harry's face. And Mr. Saunders's eyes are going to pop out any second. I sit to Harry's right, which means I'm in Mr. Saunders's direct line of sight.

I can feel Harry's distress, so I start sweating too. It's like one of those terrible moments when everything is stuck and you don't know what to do. And the feelings inside of you, and everyone around you, are just building toward an explosion of pain and fear and frustration. At that moment, all I could do was start daydreaming about home and wishing I was outside kicking a soccer ball through a window."

Roxanne closed her shield as she realized Andor's dilemma had not been because of Harry's intellectual deficits, but rather because Andor's empathy for Harry put him in a moral bind. If he saved Harry by placing the answer in his head, he'd be violating the Eastern Council of Genius's ethic against helping Ordinaries. But if he didn't help Harry, he'd have to suffer with Harry. There was no getting away from the realization that his heart—which did not make distinctions on the basis of intellect—felt a unity with all people, including Ordinaries. Unfortunately, Andor's training and the authorities had won out—this time.

Roxanne drew in a deep breath exhaled and looked at the pond. "Why didn't you just put the answer in Harry's head?"

"I was taught never to do that. My teachers were adamant. Never help an Ordinary…unless it was, like, your mother or father or a family member, of course."

Roxanne didn't reply. Instead, she let Andor's answer hang in the air for a moment. She wanted him to discover on his own how limited and ignorant that teaching was.

He broke the silence by saying, "Do you do that? I mean, put the answers in their heads?"

Roxanne smiled mischievously. "Sometimes. Why not? Harry's a good guy, and you're right, he's not the brightest kid in the class. I figure if he gets the answer, he'll know how to do the math in the future. As far as I'm concerned, it's just a quick little tutorial."

Andor looked as though he had just failed a test. Roxanne broke the tension by asking what Slavistan was like.

"It's the most beautiful country on earth," he said. "Some of the cities are bleak, sure, but the countryside is rolling hills and beautiful farms. We've also got the Urals, our Rocky Mountains. The Urals are older, rounder than the Rockies and not as tall, but they're beautiful. Many people in my country are poor, but things have been changing for the better. At least that was happening before people started worrying about war. I just hope people can work things out."

"How long do you think you'll stay here?" Roxanne asked.

"I don't know. I want to stay through university. I'm studying the stock market now and plan to be rich by the time I graduate from college."

"Yes, a lot of our kind do that," Roxanne said. "Are you motivated by money?"

"Of course," he said. "Don't you want to be rich?"

"Rich isn't really what motivates me, to be honest. Fulfillment, peace, finding love. Those are my real goals in life."

"Yes, those are the most important goals, but everything is made easier if you're rich."

"You sound like an American," Roxanne said, laughing. "Well, it's also possible that wealth can take you further away from the really important things in life. Just ask Elvis, or Howard Hughes, or Michael Jackson, if you can find any of them."

"What do you want?" Andor asked.

"I want my own version of what my parents have, but please don't tell them I said that. I'd be mortified."

"What do they have that's worth having?" Andor asked.

"Love, for one thing. They really love each other. Family for another. They've got me!" She burst out laughing. Andor laughed too. But after their laughter waned, Roxanne said seriously, "And they have purpose. Both of them have purpose in their lives."

"What purpose?" Andor asked.

"They're both committed to making the world a better place. They have a perception of something larger than themselves, even larger than this life. It's not just a belief. It's something more than belief, something felt by both of them. They feel connected to something that gives their lives meaning. And they believe that the good that one does contributes to a greater good that's implicit in life."

"Your parents have vision," Andor said. "Where I come from, most people are just trying to get by. We don't have the luxury of thinking in larger terms. And our history is a long story of oppression. That has caused many to turn toward a more material life. Which, of course, is understandable. Many Slavistanis are atheists."

"What about you? Don't you believe in anything ... other than getting rich?" she added with a smile.

"I believe in power, for one thing. It's good to have it and it's bad not to have it. Money brings some power. Not a lot, but some. People with real power can control and abuse other people, especially innocent people who have no power."

"I suppose you're right," Roxanne said. "Sometimes I need to be reminded of how lucky I've been to grow up in this culture. There's so much I take for granted."

"Yes, you're beautiful and smart and you've got parents you respect and love. I'd say that you're one of the richest people on earth."

She smiled at him, but he turned away.

"I think our lunch hour is up," he said.

"Wait," Roxanne said. "Before you go, let me introduce you to a friend of mine. Dennis."

"Dennis?" Andor asked, looking around as if worried someone was spying on them.

"Yes," she said. "Dennis the drake."

Floating on the water right in front of them was a male mallard with a brilliant emerald green head.

"Dennis," Roxanne said telepathically in duck language, "this is my new friend, Andor Lysenko."

Dennis replied aloud in the language of ducks, since he did not have the power of telepathy. "Good day, friend Andor. Any friend of Roxanne is a friend of mine."

Andor answered telepathically in duck language. "Dennis, it's a pleasure to meet you. Unfortunately, I'm late for class, but I look forward to getting to know you better on another occasion."

"Likewise," Dennis replied, and then said to Roxanne, "Andor speaks duck language pretty well."

"Yes, he does," Rebecca said telepathically. "But be careful, Dennis. Any more praise and Andor's head won't fit through the classroom door."

Roxanne and Andor walked back to the Laurel Building, grinning about Roxanne's last remark. As they walked Andor looked down at the ground as Roxanne greeted people she knew with a smile.

"What class do you have now?" Andor asked.

"English with Mrs. Van Doren. How about you?"

"Social studies with Dr. Phillips."

As they stepped inside the building, each heading in a different direction, Andor said, "See you tomorrow night."

"Yes," Roxanne. "See you tomorrow."

The following night, Andor arrived at Roxanne's house at 6:30 sharp. Rebecca, eager to meet Andor and size him up, opened the door and welcomed him into her home. The two shook hands.

"Mrs. Reynolds," Andor said verbally. "It's a pleasure to meet you." He was immediately impressed by her presence and beauty, both of which intimidated him.

"It's nice to meet you as well, Andor," Rebecca said, also out loud. "Roxanne is in her room getting ready. She'll only be a minute. Why don't you come sit down?"

Andor walked into the living and sat on the white sofa facing the fireplace. Rebecca followed him in and sat down on a stuffed chair to the right of the sofa. Andor looked around the room, taking in the decor.

The room was comfortable, lived-in and yet elegant at the same time. The walls were painted light green and trimmed in white. A large Oriental rug with myriad designs and colors—most of them red, green, and dark blue, with flecks of white—stretched over the hardwood floor. Original works of art hung on the walls by artists Andor had never heard of. He guessed they were local artists. A floor-to-ceiling bookcase stood to the left of the fireplace. He could make out some of the classic titles.

Andor felt more than a little uncomfortable in Rebecca's presence. She was clearly relaxed and self-possessed, and her confidence made him all the more self-conscious.

"So, you like books by Ordinaries," he said, continuing to speak aloud. He was afraid of Rebecca being too privy to his thoughts.

"Yes." She glanced at the bookcase. "Everyone in our family loves art, and especially books."

"Do you think Ordinaries have anything to say to us, much less teach us?"

"Oh, yes, definitely. In so many important ways, our lives are no different from theirs. We have to face the same questions they face. What is the meaning of life? What is love and how does it shape our lives? What do we become if we are driven by fear? Art addresses all the important questions. And artists attune themselves to a wisdom greater than their own. As T. S. Elliot said, a poem rains down on the poet. It comes from a higher source. I think that's true of all art. And that goes for Ordinaries as well as our kind."

"I guess you're right," Andor said. "But a lot of people don't have the time or the circumstances to consider those questions."

"Whether you take the time to consider them or not, your life is still shaped by them. You become the love or the fear you have lived."

At that moment, Roxanne came into the room, and Andor was momentarily stunned by her beauty. Her clothes seemed ordinary enough—a pair of black jeans, stylish black boots with a low heel, a white top cut low enough to reveal the upper swells of her breasts, a necklace of colorful stones, and a black sports jacket with the sleeves rolled up along her forearms.

Her long golden blond hair cascaded in waves upon her shoulders. Her large, almond-shaped blue eyes, beautiful smile, and radiant skin combined to create a luminescence that made her beauty immediate and immensely desirable, and at the same time beyond anyone's reach.

Andor couldn't help but lose himself in the moment. "You look amazing," he said.

"Thank you," she said modestly.

"Well, you two have a great time and enjoy the movie," Rebecca said.

"We will, Mom," Roxanne said.

"Thank you for inviting me into your home," Andor said to Rebecca as he headed out the door.

Rebecca smiled briefly and then said, "Take care, Andor, and drive carefully." Her words bore an unmistakable hint of steel and a message that went beyond the job of maneuvering a car around town. Her message was not lost on Andor.

They went to see *The Social Network*, a new movie about the creation of Facebook. Afterward, they drove to Antonio's Pizzeria, where they ordered a large pizza, half cheese and half with hot peppers and sausage. That was for Andor.

"In my country," he said, "we are so used to using food and vodka to keep warm that even when I'm in a more temperate climate, I can't help but crave foods that turn my insides hot and remind me of home."

"And the vodka?" Roxanne asked, smiling.

"Well, we have a saying in Slavistan. Vodka spoils everything but the glasses. I wouldn't want to spoil a minute when I'm with you."

Both of them were so surprised by Andor's openness and candor, neither spoke for a minute.

"How did you like the movie?" Roxanne asked, switching to mind-to-mind communication.

"I liked it very much. I love American films. And what would the world be like without Facebook? Look at its endless applications, from pure entertainment to the glue of revolutions. Mark Zuckerberg is an Ordinary whom even we can admire. Which brings me to a question I've wanted to ask you. How do you do it? How do you get along with Ordinaries so well?"

Since it was clear to them this would be a sensitive conversation, and that it would look odd if they sat for a long time without speaking, they shifted into a dual conversation mode, speaking aloud about the movie they had just seen while telepathically discussing what was really on their minds.

"You make Ordinaries sound like they're some alien species, that they're so different from us," Roxanne said mentally.

"Well, aren't they?" he asked.

"In a lot of ways, no, they aren't different. But I tend to react to people on the basis of whether I like them or not, and not whether they're Ordinaries or like me. Take Sarah, for example. She's one of my best friends. She has such a beautiful heart, she's honest, sincere, and she's so loyal to me. I can't help but love her. She's always trying to do something kind for me, and she seeks my advice, which makes me feel respected. And we go through a lot together. The fact that I can read some of her interior life and see how sincere she really is makes her even more special to me. And it's the same with Lyla and my other close friends. Sometimes I think my friends are the most precious gifts I have in my life…outside of my parents, of course."

"Maybe it's different for guys. We're always competing with each other."

"Oh, don't fool yourself. Girls compete with each other too. Some girls are like sisters to each other, but some are competitors. You learn to stay away from the competitors, because they're bad news, and you learn to love and cherish and hold onto your sisters, because they'll go through fire with you."

"Yes, as long as they don't find out who you really are."

"What do you mean?" Roxanne asked.

"If any one of these people, or their parents, ever found out who we are and what we're capable of, they'd burn us at the stake in a heartbeat."

"Many of them are afraid of what they don't understand, but it's not true about all of them."

Andor shook his head. "Can you imagine what would happen to us if they discovered our nature, that we're living among them? Can you imagine if enough of them banded together and came after us? They'd destroy us all overnight."

"Impossible," Roxanne said. "We would know about it early on and we'd be able to head off the trouble before things got out of control."

"No way. There are too many of them and they're too violent. The minute they face something they don't understand, they want to kill it. Or they want to turn it into a weapon, or convert it into some kind of money-making scheme. Ordinaries are primitive. They see life only through a very narrow lens."

"Part of our responsibility is to help them where we can. At least that's what my parents think. I guess I agree with them. Where would we be if we lost the freedoms that all of us—Ordinaries and Geniuses alike—need to be happy? I think all of us are responsible for doing something to keep those liberties alive."

"You mean democracy, right?" he said skeptically.

"Democracy, freedom of speech, the right to pursue your heart's direction and talents. Those are the values that make life worth living."

"Democracy is one of the greatest dangers on earth today. First, Ordinaries can't govern themselves because they aren't mature and disciplined enough to limit their behavior, even when it's in their own best interests. Look at what they're doing to the planet. They're going to destroy the earth, which means they're going to destroy themselves and us. Has anyone even thought about what's going to happen when one billion Chinese want to eat steak every night? Talk about greenhouse gases. And say good-bye to the ozone layer. There are a million other similar decisions that won't be made in the world's best interests because Ordinaries have no ability to limit themselves or control their greed. Which means that they—and we—are all headed for the proverbial cliff."

"So what's your alternative?" Roxanne asked. "Totalitarianism? And how do you propose we create a totalitarian state? Imprison or kill as many as we can until they submit to our control? Think about it, Andor. There are worse things to be afraid of than Ordinaries."

Those words stopped him in his tracks. Suddenly he realized he had gone too far. He had revealed too much and in the process had trapped himself in a corner. He reinforced his shield and protected his thoughts, which were now running amok. *You're such a hothead,* he told himself. *You're going to blow it, and the ramifications are going to be catastrophic.*

The trouble was, Roxanne had the advantage of possessing the sort of practical wisdom that made it possible for her to live comfortably in the world. Unlike himself, who wasn't at home anywhere in the world. He exhaled and wished he could take back all that he had said.

"I'm sorry," he said. "I get carried away."

Their pizza and drinks arrived and for a time they ate in silence. Both of them realized they had gotten too close. They retreated to their food and private thoughts, both shielding the other from their inner worlds.

Finally, in an effort to break the tension, Andor said aloud, "Where is that vodka when you need it?"

Roxanne laughed with relief. "My drug of choice is chocolate. Want to get some after the pizza?"

"You bet. Is there a place nearby?"

"There's a wonderful coffee shop just down the street that sells the best chocolate chip cookies and brownies. You're going to love it."

"I'm feeling better already. But mind you, please don't be put off by my gluttony." She grinned. "You haven't seen me eat chocolate yet."

Andor pulled up in front of Roxanne's house just before midnight. He offered to walk her to the door, but she told him it wasn't necessary and that she'd see him at school on Monday.

He watched as she went inside and closed the door behind her. She didn't look back.

Andor dropped his head onto his steering wheel. Straightening, he blew out a deep breath and then started the car and drove home.

That night, he tossed and turned in his bed, unable to fall asleep. Thoughts of the evening and the things Roxanne and Rebecca had said whirled in his head.

"You become the love or the fear you have lived," Rebecca had said.

Where is my life going? Andor asked himself. *What am I becoming?* Then he told himself to take a good look at the other seniors at Laurel Glen. He'd know exactly where he was going and what he was becoming. Was that what he wanted?

I don't have a choice, he thought. *Do the job and get home. That's all I can think about for now.*

Despite his best efforts at denial, Roxanne's words rose from deep within him.

"Think about it, Andor. There are worse things to be afraid of than Ordinaries."

She's right, he said to himself. *But, man, that hurt.*

Chapter 14
Karl and Klaus Kleper, Archangel, Other Plans

igh in the Caucasus Mountains of Slavistan, in a region fought over for centuries by Europeans, Arabs, and Slavs, a remarkable castle stood among the pine trees and sheer rock face. The castle was one of those architectural marvels, built at the very edge of a precipice and overlooking a drop of a several hundred feet. An enormous complex, it had stone walls as high as thirty feet, eight turrets, walkways along its ramparts, a large courtyard, and gardens. The main building, a sprawling, rectangular mansion, had guest rooms, a large dining room, and a kitchen worthy of four stars from Michelin. There was a spa and gym, a large swimming pool, and a heliport. And in the corners of the complex, well protected by inner walls and beautiful shrubbery, were two houses, the residences of Karl and Klaus Kleper.

In a vast office complex well below ground, deep within the mountain, Karl and Klaus directed the business of the Eastern Council of Geniuses. The brightly lit, ultramodern war rooms contained the most advanced Genius-designed computer and communications system available in the Eastern world. The castle was also equipped with advanced weapons systems, including electromagnetic-pulse weapons and missiles. Those weapons were capable of blasting invisible waves of electromagnetic energy that could wipe out entire armies and fleets of aircraft that might be so unwise as to approach the Council lair.

Seated at a highly polished conference table within the bunker were the key members of the Eastern Council. Karl and Klaus were twins in the same way Arnold Schwarzenegger and Danny DeVito were twins in the movie by the same name. Although born of the same mother and within minutes of each other, Karl and Klaus could not have been more different, especially in their appearances. Karl was six two, and possessed a powerful, menacing girth, a reflection of his insatiable appetite for every sensory pleasure. Like a black hole in a particularly dark region of the galaxy, he consumed everything in sight—food, drink, women, any object of value that might trigger his desire. He tossed the women and objects away, usually in a fit of rage and violence, when some brighter thing turned up. He had thick brown hair, a high forehead, heavy features, and a large nose that hung over his upper lip like a pelican's beak. His eyes were black and small and angled downward, as was his mouth, suggesting an unpleasant Asian ancestor. Together, his features revealed a personal history that was long and cruel.

Klaus, on the other hand, was short and slight, with sparse hair that revealed patches of scalp. His face was bony and frail. His eyes were small, active, and alert, in the same way the eyes of small animals dart this way and that in their constant lookout for predators. His mouth was small, as was his appetite for food and other sensory and sensual pleasures. His nose was the largest feature on his face, swollen at both the bridge and the bulb. On the whole, his body seemed in a state of perpetual wasting.

Not surprisingly, their clothing was consistent with their personalities. Karl enjoyed expensive suits, tailored to perfection by the most skilled hands on Savile Row. His shirts were made from Egyptian cotton and tailored in Spain. His shoes were Italian and made of the finest leather.

By contrast, Klaus's clothes, though always clean and pressed, appeared to be off the rack and never seemed to fully grasp the mysterious dimensions of his body. His shoulders didn't fill out his suit jacket, his shirts shifted left and right, his tie seemed permanently askew, and his pants were pulled up well above his navel. His shoes were simple black loafers.

Born in Leipzig, Germany, both brothers were abandoned by their parents at birth and placed in an orphanage located in a rough section of the old city. The year was 1825. The orphanage made its money by sending the children into the streets to beg for food and money. Whatever a child garnered during the day was considered his daily payment to remain in the orphanage. If a child returned without food or money, he was beaten and locked up in a tiny closet, where he usually passed out from heat exhaustion. Once a child reached the age of twelve or thirteen and was no longer an effective beggar, he was sold into slavery. That, in fact, was the orphanage's principal source of income.

On those streets of Leipzig, Karl and Klaus began to realize their power. Leipzig arose along two major trade routes that linked Asia with Europe. Lots of money passed through the city, and thus beggars and thieves alike collected along the city's main thoroughfares, especially in front of the University of Leipzig and along the Augustusplatz, where the city's merchants collected and did business every day. One day, in the heart of the Leipzig Trade Fair, where merchants from all over the world gathered to sell their wares, Karl approached a rich businessman and begged for a few marks, the German currency. The businessman looked down at Karl and said, "Get away from me, you dirty little pig." Rage was already a primary characteristic of the boy. At the orphanage, both he and Klaus had been beaten regularly and forced to spend days at a time in the tiny closet. The businessman's rebuff sparked Karl's already boiling hatred, and its power welled up inside him like a volcano. In that moment, some inner knowledge of who he was and what powers lay within him took possession of him. As he watched the rich man walk down the street, Karl focused his attention on the man's back and sent a beam of hatred directly into the man's heart. The man collapsed on the street and was dead of heart attack. Karl and Klaus both stood dumbfounded as the man lay motionless on the ground. They realized Karl had killed the man. They ran for cover and hid behind a building, watching as a crowd gathered around the man. People shook their heads, acknowledging that he was dead.

"What happened?" Klaus asked Karl.

"I killed that fat pig with an invisible dagger," Karl answered.

The boys were ten years old, and in that moment Karl had an epiphany—he was the most powerful boy on earth. And he knew immediately what he had to do next. That night, after Karl and Klaus returned to the large dormitory room at the orphanage, Karl waited for the nightly ritual in which he would be forced to give up the money he had collected earlier that day. Each night, Armundi, a forty-year-old Arab immigrant with hands of stone and a leathery, pock-marked face, arrived at the boys' beds and collected their earnings. If a child even hesitated to give over the coins, Armundi would beat him or her. Karl was lying on his bed when Armundi stood over him and demanded the money.

"No," Karl said. "Get away from me."

It was the first time any child had ever refused Armundi, and the older man was shocked. "What did you say?"

"Get away from me or you will die," Karl said to him.

Armundi raised his hand to strike Karl, but when he did, Karl focused all his thoughts on Armundi's chest and screamed. Armundi's arm was still high above his head when his eyes rolled back and he collapsed on the floor. Karl knew instantly that he was dead.

Klaus ran over to Karl and looked down at the fallen man. "You did it again, Karl," he said.

Karl got up from his bed and put on his shirt and shoes, telling Klaus to do the same. When the two were ready, Karl headed for the office where Brunhilde, the orphanage's director, worked. After taking whatever food the children brought home to the kitchen, Armundi would bring the money to Brunhilde. She would count it and place it in a locked metal box that she stored in a big drawer of her desk.

The office door was open when Karl and Klaus arrived. Sitting behind her desk, Brunhilde was counting her money.

"Give us the money or I will kill you," Karl told Brunhilde.

Brunhilde was forty-three years old but she could have passed for sixty-three. Her thick black and gray hair fanned out from her head. She was overweight, with greasy and mottled skin and not a trace of kindness in her eyes. After two decades of using children and selling them into various forms of slavery, she was as ugly as she was depraved.

She reached into a drawer and pulled out a gun. "Get back in your beds or Armundi will beat you bloody and put you both in the closet for the next two months."

Karl's hatred for this woman rose from his feet up to his dark heart, grew in intensity, traveled to his brain, and like a cobra sprang at Brunhilde. Karl and Klaus could actually see the illuminated line of energy hit Brunhilde in the face, throat, and chest. The power of the blast threw her back against the wall, causing the gun to fire into the ceiling. The shots woke the entire orphanage, and children began screaming.

Karl grabbed the cash Brunhilde had been counting and then searched the desk drawers until he found the metal box. Shoving the cash in his pocket, he tucked the metal box under his arm and told Klaus to follow him. Rather than run out the front door and into the street, which was what the frightened children were doing, Karl led Klaus through the kitchen and out the back door, where they disappeared in the alleyways of Leipzig.

Both brothers quickly learned what their minds were capable of. It was a bloody education, especially for Karl. He relished killing people in all sorts of creative ways. At first, he killed in the same way he had destroyed Armundi, Brunhilde, and the rich man on the street. In time, he realized he could get people to kill themselves by controlling their minds. He commanded people to walk into oncoming trains, or jump off buildings and bridges, or stab themselves with their own daggers, or eat poison. Killing people gave him a distinct satisfaction and pleasure, but controlling people's minds gave him money. Bank tellers handed over huge sums of cash, as did wealthy people on the street. Soon, Karl and Klaus were living in luxury. They also gathered a large army of orphans and street urchins. By the time they were fifteen, they were both powerful and rich.

Karl was always the one in charge. He saw himself as greater than Napoleon and all the czars. Klaus, the more sensitive of the two, wasn't as interested in controlling or killing people. He was fascinated by money, currency exchange, markets, and land speculation. The two moved their minions and power base to Turkey and established themselves as kings among the feudal tribes. In 1853, when war came yet again to the Ottoman Empire, the brothers disbanded their army and transferred their wealth to Spain, where they quickly established themselves as successful businessmen.

In Madrid they attracted other Geniuses with similar abilities, though none had the power that Karl did. The Klepers organized their Genius comrades into a council with the intention of establishing even greater power and wealth. At the top of the council was Karl, with Klaus as his second in command. Karl decided at that point to step back from the world and remain unknown. He would rule from the shadows, he told Klaus. That would give him freedom as well as protection from anyone who might attempt an assassination. With his identity secret from all but a handful of Geniuses on the council, Karl decided it was time to have governments start doing his bidding. His ambition was blinding: he meant to rule the world.

He started close to home, with the Spanish government, which had already established something of an empire in the Americas and the Pacific. Spain owned Cuba, Puerto Rico, Guam, and the Philippines. Karl formulated a plan to expand the Spanish empire and rule indirectly through the leaders he would control. So near the end of the nineteenth century, he decided to draw the United States into a war with Spain, hobble the US leadership by gaining control of their minds, and tip the balance of power in favor of Spain. He could then annex either part or all of the United States for Spain—which is to say, for himself.

After years of killing and controlling Ordinaries, Karl had become a megalomaniac. But he was inexperienced on the global stage, and he would later see that his plan was littered with stumbling blocks. The most important one was the Western Council of Geniuses, specifically Alexander Astrakhan and Roger Reynolds.

Karl had learned from his associations with Geniuses in Spain that two great councils of Geniuses—one in the East, located in Slavistan, and another in the West, located primarily in Washington—combined to form the great axis of power among their kind. But neither of these councils intimidated Karl in the least. He was always the most powerful man in the room, even when the room was filled with Geniuses. Why should it be any different when dealing with the Geniuses of the West? He could overpower and outwit them, just as he was doing in Spain.

Alexander Astrakhan, executive director of the Council of Western Geniuses, had just promoted Roger Reynolds to the position of operations director of the western hemisphere. Among the trends Roger was watching were events in Cuba, which was attempting to gain its independence from Spain. Spanish generals had responded to the insurrection by creating enormous concentration camps, where they incarcerated anyone who might be suspected of defying Spanish rule. In fact, by the late 1890s, much of Cuba's population was being relocated to the camps.

The United States was in an uproar over Spanish control of Cuba and its treatment of the Cuban people. Threats of war were a daily occurrence throughout 1896. The truth was, Spain did not want war with the United States and much of the Spanish leadership sympathized with the Cuban people. Karl couldn't control the minds of the entire country, nor all of its leaders. Free to follow its own inclinations, Spain gave Cuba its independence when Spanish leaders signed a peace treaty with the United States in January 1897. All seemed settled, without a single shot being fired.

That was not what Karl had in mind. He needed an event that would put the two countries at war, and fate gave him his opportunity when, in October 1897, it was announced that the *USS Maine* would dock in Havana and take US citizens out of Cuba.

Karl and Klaus traveled to Cuba, arriving in Havana just in time to watch the *Maine* come to port. Late the next night, from a safe distance on the harbor, Karl scanned the *Maine*. He perceived an enormous quantity of munitions stored in its hull and triggered it with a concentrated burst of energy directed at a single keg of dynamite. In no time, the *Maine* was a rubble of twisted metal, shot full of holes, shrapnel spraying all over the harbor. The ship went down and all 266 hands on board were killed.

Karl knew the people of the United States would blame Spain and the Spanish would blame the United States. And Karl would have his war.

The only problem was that Astrakhan, Reynolds, and the Council of Western Geniuses were watching.

The day after the *Maine* exploded, Roger went to Havana to investigate what had happened. Once he arrived, he inspected the site of the sinking, as well as the debris pattern that had resulted from the blast. He mentally ran an array of complex mathematical formulas to determine what the debris pattern of the blast would look like if the ship had been destroyed by a mine, by another vessel, or if the blast had occurred within the ship itself.

If a mine had been placed in the water, the debris pattern would have focused primarily in a single direction, opposite the location of the mine. One side of the ship—the part closest to the mine—would have suffered far more damage than the other. The same effects would have occurred if the ship had been fired upon by another vessel. Also, a torpedo or cannon shot would have caused damage in a discrete location on the ship.

The physical evidence did not match either of these scenarios. The debris pattern from the actual explosion was uniform in all directions, indicating the explosion occurred within the hull of the ship.

The ship's captain had placed guards on the ship and in the harbor itself, protecting the *Maine* from being boarded or attacked during the night. It was highly unlikely that a team of swimmers could have placed a series of mines around the ship without being noticed by the guards on board. The log indicated there had been no visitors to the ship and that nothing out of the ordinary had occurred during the night.

Could the ordinance have gone off by itself? Roger wondered.

The ship's manifest indicated that the munitions had been inspected after the ship arrived and that all explosive materials had been stored properly and safely. Moreover, the ship's munitions specialist was a master sergeant, a career soldier, and an extremely experienced and careful man. He was unlikely to make any kind of mistake that would have set off the explosion.

Roger deduced that the *Maine* had, indeed, been destroyed from inside the hull. He also concluded that the explosion was the result of the *Maine's* munitions. Something, or someone, had triggered that explosion. Who? And more importantly, how?

He perused the minds of the local police chief and his beat cops and discovered that a Cuban government official had been killed in a very strange way. Apparently, his nervous system had been destroyed by lightning or some other electrical source. Two other people had been killed that night in a similar fashion; one, a prostitute and the other a man who worked as a desk clerk at the Hotel Havana, the finest hotel in the city.

The pieces were falling into place. A single electromagnetic pulse from a Genius could have easily set off the explosion. That same kind of electromagnetic blast could have killed all three people the previous night. The facts spoke for themselves. Now Roger had to find the Genius behind the explosion and the killings. The obvious place to look was the hotel, where he decided to eat dinner.

The restaurant was brightly lit by hanging chandeliers and ensconced candles on the walls. Large works of art, most of them landscapes or pictures of famous Spanish leaders, hung on the walls. Perhaps fifty tables were spread throughout the large room, half of which were occupied.

The moment he stepped inside the restaurant, Roger felt the pings. Karl and Klaus, both seated at a table covered in white linen, experienced the same warning. The brothers looked up from their meals and saw Roger Reynolds standing at the entrance to the restaurant. Roger walked over to them, introduced himself, and asked if he could join them for dinner.

Karl, supremely confident, smiled mirthlessly and said, "Why not?"

Roger took a chair opposite Karl and Klaus. A waiter in a white jacket ran over and gave him a menu.

"Havana is a lovely city, is it not?" Roger said to Karl.

"It's hot," Karl said, concentrating again on his food. "And dusty."

"Rather like Madrid, wouldn't you say?" Roger looked from his menu, directly into Karl's eyes.

Karl sat back in his chair and took a long look at Roger. Instantly, he reinforced his shield as a chill ran through is body, something he had not felt in a long time. *This one is a lot more powerful than the Geniuses I am used to dealing with,* he said to himself.

Roger switched to telepathic communication. "Here on business?" he asked.

Karl took a sip of his coffee before answering. "My name is Karl Kleper and this is my brother Klaus. Who are you?"

"Roger Reynolds. I arrived about an hour ago. I was curious about what happened to the *Maine*. The Americans, of course, are blaming the Spanish and the Spanish are blaming the Americans. No doubt they'll go to war in a few months. It's too bad, really. Both sides just signed a peace treaty that would have avoided all that bloodshed."

Karl and Klaus remained silent. Karl looked deeply into Roger, taking his measure. Roger looked directly back at Karl. Neither man flinched, nor spoke for a long moment.

At last Karl returned his attention to his meal. "Since when do men like us worry about the blood of Ordinaries?"

The waiter approached and asked Roger what he'd like to eat.

"Nothing." He handed the menu back to the waiter but kept his gaze fixed on Karl. "I've got to get back to the States. Besides, I just lost my appetite."

He stood but then turned back to the brothers.

"You know, Klaus, if I were you I'd change my jacket. Even Ordinaries can spot a man who's been close to a fire."

Karl looked closely at Klaus's jacket and realized it was peppered with tiny singes and small traces of soot. They were imperceptible, except to the most observant eye.

"Well, I have no more business here," Roger added. "I've got the answers I came for." He nodded to both men. "No doubt, our paths will cross again."

"I look forward to it," Karl said.

Roger returned to his ship and Washington, knowing full well what he had to do.

The Western Council's only interest in relations between Spain and America was to help both parties avoid war. Unfortunately, after the destruction of the *Maine*, too many in the United States wanted war, which was set in motion in April of that year. From a military standpoint, the United States was far superior to its European adversary, and any war between the two nations wouldn't last long—especially if both countries were allowed to see things clearly. Rather than intervene in the war itself, Western Council leaders realized they had to keep Karl and Klaus Kleper from blinding the US and Spanish leadership. Alexander dispatched three teams of Geniuses—one to the US Capitol, a second to the White House, and a third to Madrid. Using advanced technology and the power of their own minds, the teams set up protective perimeters around the government buildings within both countries, thus protecting the leadership from Karl and Klaus's mind control.

The Klepers were new to the international game and did not yet have the support of other powerful Eastern Geniuses to counter the Western Council's technology and protective barriers. The consequence was that the war lasted a total of ten weeks before a peace treaty was signed in Paris. The Spanish-American war had ended.

After the treaty was signed, the Klepers went to Slavistan and soon gained control of the Eastern Council of Geniuses, a platform that gave them much more power, technological support, and opportunities for revenge.

The Western and Eastern Councils of Geniuses clashed on every battlefield that arose during the twentieth century, from World Wars I and II, to the Korean conflict and Vietnam. They battled in the dark streets of Europe and the Soviet Union during the Cold War, as well as in the ancient alleyways and modern highways of the Middle East. The twentieth century proved largely a stalemate, which as far as Roger and Alexander were concerned, was a victory of sorts. The Klepers were the aggressors, but the Western Council of Geniuses kept them in check. However, there was plenty of evidence to suggest the Klepers now believed they had the upper hand and were ready to go all in to win this latest series of battles for control of the world.

Deep in the bunker of their castle in Slavistan, Karl and Klaus were plotting their next steps to move themselves and their council closer to their goal.

Karl surveyed the five members of the council arrayed on either side of the table and asked Dominika Dementieva, the head of information and propaganda, to give her report.

"We have provided a set of documents and maps, all of them forgeries of the highest quality, to Victor Grozny, who is using the documents to show that large sections of Bulgaristan, Czeckostan, and Cossackia were once provinces of Slavistan. These documents, some of which are supposedly five hundred years old, call into question the sovereignty of these states and support Slavistan's right to annex them to the mother country. Grozny has petitioned the UN and is threatening war if these states are not restored as part of the homeland.

"Meantime, we are controlling the minds of journalists and radio and television commentators all over Eurasia, making the argument that the European Union is, a precursor to the creation of a United States of Europe. The unification of the currency and the fact that passports no longer are needed at border crossings are proof that Europe intends to become a unified entity, which will threaten all of Eurasia with economic and military domination unless a Eurasian entity of sufficient size and strength is created to counter the European hegemony. Our journalists, commentators, and key members of various legislative bodies are proposing the creation of a United Eurasia, a concept that is gaining popularity all across the two continents. You will recall that many people throughout Eurasia still yearn for the return of the Soviet system. A United Eurasia offers renewed hope that a new Soviet system soon will be established.

"These sentiments also support Victor Grozny's efforts to restore the unification of Bulgaristan, Czeckostan, and Cossackia with Slavistan. We are already drawing up a new constitution, which we will deliver to Grozny very soon.

"In the meantime, we are also building public support among the citizenry of Bulgaristan, Czeckostan, and Cossackia for reunification with Slavistan. We're providing live interviews with citizens in the satellite nations that demonstrate a longing among the people to be reunited with Slavistan and to be freed from the yoke of their corrupt and incompetent bureaucracies. These interviews are being presented to television and radio stations, newspaper and magazine reporters, which is turning public opinion in favor of reunification."

"Excellent," Karl said. "Please congratulate your team, Dominika. Of course, keep the whip at their backs until all is complete. Now, as for you, Alexei, what progress do you have to report?"

Alexei Zlovinsky, head of insurgencies and terrorism, was a legend among members of the Eastern Council. He was tall, thin, bookish, and balding. Behind his round eyeglasses and merciless eyes, he looked more like an effete wine connoisseur than a mastermind killer. Nonetheless, it was Zlovinsky who provided Osama bin Laden with intelligence, plans, and logistical support for his many acts of terrorism, including the one on New York's World Trade Center on September 11, 2001. The members of the Eastern Council regarded Zlovinsky as a Genius's Genius, a man of such advanced skill on the chessboard of life that no Western Genius could match him.

"Thank you, Comrade Kleper," Alexie began. "So far, we have engineered a series of assaults on both sides of the Slavistan's borders. Our teams have raided farms, burned buildings, committed an array of so-called atrocities in all three satellite states. We have also sent counterterrorism teams into Slavistan and committed similar acts of violence in the border villages and cities. People in all these countries are enraged and armies are arrayed on all borders. As we all know, the armies of Bulgaristan, Cossackia, and Czeckostan are small, too small to control their borders effectively. Death tolls are mounting and the horror stories are now on the front pages of every newspaper, every day, in all four countries. Recently, as most of you know, militias composed of farmers and factory workers have arisen and have made incursions into Slavistan, committing various acts of revenge. In short, the fuse has been lit.

"The United Nations will have to act soon if there is any chance of stopping the bloodshed. Grozny is a powerful and effective voice for ending hostilities. He is arguing that the only real solution is reunification of the four states under Slavistani rule. We have managed to drown out all the competing voices that argue for upholding the sovereignty of the other three countries. Assassination teams have been effective in silencing the voices of the opposition.

"We have placed our people in the leadership of the militias in the three countries. Those militias will begin a joint attack against Slavistan on November 1, at which point Grozny will launch a devastating counterattack that will bring all three satellites back under the control of Slavistan.

"With Dominika's teams already active, we will be able to create a larger parliamentary body that will offer representation to these border nations within the Slavistani government. Once the new provinces have been annexed, the Slavistan Parliament will announce the need for the creation of a United Eurasia. By the spring of next year, we should have an overpowering movement for the creation of a great new empire with our man, Victor Grozny, as its head."

Alexei Zlovinsky gave a slight bow of the head, which drew applause from all the others.

Klaus, who admired anyone who possessed true talent, looked positively moved. "As always, Comrade, it is an honor to be working with you," he said.

Karl nodded and then turned to Sergey Ivanov, the council's technological and computer genius. Ivanov was fifty years old and looked like a twenty-year-old boy. With unkempt blond hair, pale skin, blue eyes, and a frail build, Ivanov rarely went outdoors, even to take a walk. He spent most of his days in his basement computer center, working out new programs and algorithms designed to bring about various methods for death and destruction.

"Please brief the council on Archangel, Sergey," Karl said.

Ivanov pushed his unruly hair from his forehead and looked down at his papers. Shy and withdrawn, Ivanov hated speaking or communicating telepathically to any group, even one as small as six people. The reason was that he hated people, Geniuses and Ordinaries alike. They were far too much trouble and they bored him. On the other hand, technology and all technical challenges thrilled him. They were what he lived for.

"We launched a satellite, code name Archangel, on May 19, 2010, with the intention of silencing the warning signal emitted by our kind when in the presence of a Western Genius." Ivanov seemed to be speaking more to himself than to anyone in the room. "Ummm." His brow furrowed. He pulled a lock of hair from his forehead as he shifted more papers, finally pulling one from a seemingly chaotic stack. He continued, more than a little distracted.

"The satellite circled the earth for five months"—more paper shifting—"ah, yes, before we switched it on, at which time it began broadcasting microwaves that altered the earth's electromagnetic field, as well as the electromagnetic field that radiates from every living creature, including humans.

"We are altering the electromagnetic field of the earth," he reiterated, as if he were speaking to a bunch of idiots. "That's pretty cool. But one of the unintended consequences of altering the earth's magnetic field is the bizarre weather that we have recently been experiencing around the world... you know, storms, unusual temperatures, tornados, and hurricanes. That's us. We created those changes. Like I said, pretty cool.

"Anyway, the microwave beam is extremely precise," he continued, "capable of targeting specific geographical locations and altering specific frequencies within the earth's entire electromagnetic spectrum. By changing specific frequencies, we're able to affect the hearing of every living thing on earth."

Sergey looked up from his notes and around the table, wondering if anyone understood what he was saying. Why weren't they applauding? He decided they were just slow, though in fact, everyone in the room was shifting in their seats, at once impatient with Sergey's report and excited about where it was going.

Sergey shifted more papers, found the page he wanted, and continued. "There are large differences between the hearing of Ordinaries and the hearing capabilities of our kind. Even more important for our purposes, there are smaller but still significant differences between the hearing of Eastern and Western Geniuses. And the most important of these differences is the different wavelengths that Eastern versus Western Geniuses perceive as the warning signal in the presence of the other.

"We Eastern Geniuses perceive the warning signal of a Western Genius at twenty-three kilohertz. Western Geniuses perceive their warning signal at twenty-four kilohertz. Both are well beyond the range of Ordinary hearing, which means that our actions will go unnoticed by Ordinaries.

"Once I give the command, Archangel will alter the charged particles and waves within a specific geographical radius and thus neutralize the twenty-four kilohertz audio frequency. That means no Western Genius will hear the warning ping when an Eastern Genius approaches. We will be invisible to every Western Genius on the planet. They will not know us from—how do the Americans put it?—any Mikhail, Boris, or Yevgeny on the street. Archangel has the power to make every one of us silent predators. For the first time in human history, we have taken the warning signal away from Western Geniuses. When they realize we have that capability, they will be shitting in their pants, let me assure you of that."

"Now, here's where things get really interesting." He sorted through his papers again and then cleared his throat theatrically. "I have programmed the satellite so that I can turn off the warning signal within a certain area. For example, five square miles, the area around the US Capitol building or the White House. That means that any Western Genius within those five square miles would be deaf to the warning signal when approached by an Eastern Genius. However, any Genius outside those five square miles would have normal hearing and would therefore experience the warning tone as if nothing had changed. No one would know we had turned off the warning tone for Geniuses within a specific geographical area.

"On the other hand, I could command the satellite to wipe out the twenty-four kilohertz hearing range all over the earth, and thus take away the first line of defense for every Western Genius on earth. They would all be helpless before us. I'd say that is pretty cool."

With that, Sergey sat back in his chair and waited for his words to sink in.

Everyone in the room let out a collective sigh, grateful for both the information and the fact this trying boy was finally finished with his talk.

"Thank you, Sergey," Karl said. "Your work is a high-tension performance, but deeply satisfying. Yes, deeply satisfying."

Sergey didn't know what to make of Karl's remarks. It didn't matter. Karl bored him anyway.

"So, that leaves you, Vladimir Ubitzov," Karl said. "What do you have for us?"

Vladimir Ubitzov, the man in charge of assassinations, placed his large hands on the table and looked at each council member. His pale blue eyes sent an icy chill through the spines of those present. Ubitzov was machine-like in his bearing. He was six feet tall, with the body of a weight lifter and the movements of a cat. After so many years of killing, he had become devoid of anything resembling human feelings. Cold, robotic, and supremely efficient at his craft, he could terrify Geniuses and Ordinaries alike with his mere appearance. The only person he did not intimidate was Karl Kleper, who saw himself as more powerful, more lethal, and every bit as ruthless—if not necessarily as skilled—as Ubitzov.

"Tomorrow, Sergey will give Archangel the command to silence the twenty-four kilohertz frequency at exactly twelve hundred hours, Greenwich Mean Time, or 7 a.m. Washington, DC, time. My team has arranged for a group of Ordinaries to invade the campus of Laurel Glen High School at twelve hundred hours, EDT, tomorrow. Laurel Glen is the school attended by Roxanne Reynolds, daughter of our adversary, as well as the location of our asset, Andor Lysenko. The invading students will kill as many Ordinaries as possible. Ultimately, they will be stopped by Andor and Roxanne, which will give Andor the opportunity to come to public attention...especially the attention of US Senator Stewart Thompson.

"In the confusion created by the attacking students, and in the absence of any warning signal, Roxanne Reynolds's bodyguard will be assassinated. This will send a message to Roger Reynolds and his entire London team. Reynolds will know that we can kill his daughter at any moment we choose. That will affect his judgment and the judgment of those around him."

Ubitzov stopped talking and let his cold stare fall on the council members. "Not only will we accomplish a great step in our larger plan, but the exercise will serve as preparation for the series of attacks against the Western Geniuses later on."

Karl waited a moment before he commented on Ubitzov's presentation. He wanted his words to have maximum impact on Ubitzov.

"Vladimir," he began, "our collaborator in the West informed me only yesterday that the Reynolds bodyguard is none other than Max Louri. I thought you would like to know that." Karl was well aware that the memory of Tangier still burned in Ubitzov. He wanted the assassin to be hungry for revenge.

Ubitzov looked at Kleper and then looked away.

Karl smiled, enjoying the game of rubbing Ubitzov's face in an old, shameful memory, and then he went on. "Vladimir, how are your plans going for the assassination of the Reynolds team in London?"

"All is proceeding on schedule."

"Good. Remember, you are to take out every member of the team except Reynolds himself. The collaborator has something special waiting for him and his family."

"Understood," said Ubitzov. "You will remember, Comrade, that I will be personally involved in the killing of every one of his staff."

Karl smiled again. "I wouldn't have it any other way."

Chapter 15
Assault on Laurel Glen High School

He awoke precisely at 5 a.m. in a small out-of-the-way hotel in the Adams Morgan section of Washington, DC, just a thirty-minute drive from the campus of Laurel Glen. He went into the bathroom and twenty minutes later was dressing in dark blue slacks, black loafers, a white shirt, a dark blue tie, and a shoulder holster for his Glock 17. The holster also carried a magazine of rounds and a silencer. He then wrapped a Velcro holster around his right ankle, into which he inserted a Beretta 21A Bobcat, a smaller, lighter weapon, easily concealed beneath his trousers.

The weapons were those of Ordinaries, but he had a lot of experience with both guns and trusted them implicitly. Besides, he would discard them at the scene and the police would link the weapons with the young assailants.

He wiped down the entire room, making sure he didn't leave a single fingerprint. He put his few pieces of clothing into a small duffle, threw on a dark sports jacket, and strode out of the room.

His real name was Drazan Andelko, originally from Croatia, but that was long ago. He had no real home, nor any allegiance. He was of average height with a frame of pure muscle, bone, and sinew. His dark, deep-set eyes looked out from the shadows cast by a heavy brow. He had dark hair cut short, a wide nose, and a long, thin mouth that was usually tightly closed. Like most in his profession, he was silent and reclusive, more at home in the dark and fog than in the light of day. He was neither alive nor dead, he would tell himself. He was in the netherworld between the two. And because he lived in that mythic realm, he saw himself as a kind of priest, ferrying the living across the River Styx. His last name meant *messenger* in Croatian, and he saw himself as exactly that, though his was not a message of hope.

He had been in the Washington area for the past month in order to recruit a team of young, disaffected Ordinaries. That job was easy. All he had to do was spend some time in one of the poorer sections of the city, pick out four tough, angry high school boys, entice them with drugs—mostly marijuana and methamphetamine—and take control of their minds. He then gave them their instructions, armed them to the teeth, and loaded them up with enough meth to bring them to the border of insanity. His team of young thugs was eager to take out their hatred on the privileged youths at Laurel Glen.

As he walked down the street and got into the white Ford Taurus he'd stolen five weeks before in Lexington, Kentucky, he felt confident that all was in order. The sky was still dark and the pavement glistened from an overnight rain. No one was on the street and the few cars that passed were driven by bleary-eyed men and women who were either coming home from work or heading to their early-morning shifts. He got into the Taurus and headed north toward Maryland.

Ellis and Freddy Davies were also awake at 5 a.m. They had rented a house in Golden Gables, just a ten-minute walk from the campus. Ellis, usually the first one up, dressed in running clothes and shoes and checked the monitors in his office that revealed what was taking place on the Laurel Glen campus. Weeks before, he and Freddy had placed cameras and listening devices in key areas throughout the campus. All was quiet, for the moment. He knew it was the calm before the storm.

Meanwhile, Freddy made breakfast. Thirty minutes later, both were running through the streets of Golden Gables on their way to the athletic fields behind the Laurel Glen campus. The sky was still dark, the temperature in the low forties. Fog and mist hung in the air. Both were on edge but ready for what lay ahead.

At 6 a.m., Andor was already awake, receiving a final briefing for the day's events from Karl Kleper. Karl had telepathically gone over the operation in detail with Andor, but Karl was a careful man and a stickler for detail. He wanted to make sure everything went according to plan.

"Do you understand what you have to do?" he asked Andor one last time.

"Yes, Comrade," Andor said. "I understand."

"Good. No slip-ups. When you are in the cafeteria and young Thompson is present, you strike relentlessly. Understood?"

"Yes, Comrade. Understood."

At 7 a.m., Roxanne awoke, stretched, and looked out her window to check the weather. The view was not promising. The fog lingered, and it was a gray and misty day.

Once she was up and dressed, she made her usual breakfast of oatmeal with walnuts and fruit, herbal tea, and ate as she read her daily newspapers.

At the Laurel Glen campus, Freddy and Ellis decided to do a reconnaissance around the campus, careful to keep a wide perimeter in order to remain undetected by any of their own kind. Soon they were back at their house, and they showered and dressed in cotton trousers and sport coats, rather than their standard camouflage gear. Both had to be free to move when necessary, but could pass for parents or teachers, if need be. From their portable devices, they accessed their video and audio equipment installed around the campus. All was still quiet. They checked in with London and then completed their preparations for the day ahead.

The Davies brothers were already home when Drazan Andelko arrived at the campus. In about five hours, the Western Geniuses would be deaf to the warning ping. Most people, even Roxanne Reynolds and her bodyguard, Max Louri, would mistake him for a visiting parent or perhaps a substitute teacher, if they noticed him at all. Louri was his target and he was counting on the element of surprise to give him all the advantage he needed.

Max arrived shortly after 7 a.m. in his specially designed Ford van and parked in the lot directly behind the Betsy. The van, emblazoned with the green and blue labeling of the Quest Food Service Corp., which provided the lunchroom fare, was in fact a mobile high-tech center. Like Freddy and Ellis, Max had set up video and listening devices in every one of Roxanne's classrooms, along with the bathrooms, hallways, lunchroom, student center, athletic fields, and the little pond that Roxanne and Andor had been frequenting of late. He was also able to access the school's computers and communication devices, which gave him another way of keeping track of what was happening on campus.

The weather remained grim. The fog and mist turned to showers and a strong wind kicked up. Despite the rain and gloom, the players took their places on the stage and awaited their moment and their collision with fate. The students began filing in at eight. Diane coached Susannah and Linda on her latest plan to embarrass Roxanne. Roxanne, perhaps taking her cue from the weather, planned to lie low that day. She had been spending so much time at lunch with Andor, she decided to catch up with Sarah and Lyla at lunch in the cafeteria. Drazan Andelko, well out of ping range, found Max's van and watched it carefully.

On the second floor of the student center, Mr. Henry, the biology teacher, made plans for his senior class to have lunch in the lab in order to prepare for their field trip to the pond, where they would collect microbial samples. In the Laurel, the teacher's lounge was vacant. The student center snack bar was quiet except for the few staff members. Max, ever alert to Roxanne's movements, was ready to play his part. Freddy and Ellis were nowhere in sight.

At 11:30, the rain abruptly stopped. During the next twenty minutes, the clouds thinned and patches of blue sky appeared. At noon, the bell sounded in the Laurel, signaling the end of third period and the lunch hour. Students walked en masse to the cafeteria in the student center. Roxanne, Sarah, and Lyla met outside Dr. Phillips's classroom and were walking to the cafeteria when Andor intercepted them.

"Hi, Roxanne," Andor said. He carried his lunch in one hand and a gym bag in the other.

"Hi, Andor," Roxanne said, surprised by his sudden appearance. "What's up?"

"Could we have lunch together today? There are a few things I wanted to say to you, in private, if it's okay." He cast an apologetic look at Lyla and Sarah.

Both girls looked at each other and smiled. More grist for their gossip mill.

"It's okay, Roxanne," Lyla said. "Go. We'll see you later."

"Are you sure?" Roxanne asked.

"Yeah, of course," Sarah said. "Go."

"Okay, Andor," Roxanne said. "Did you want to have lunch in the cafeteria or at the snack bar?"

"The weather is nicer, so why don't we go to the little pond?"

"It'll be wet," Roxanne said.

"No, no. I've got a towel right here in my gym bag. I'll wipe down the bench. It'll be fine."

As the two walked toward the main doors, Andor saw Diane, Susannah, and Linda standing near it, lying in wait for Roxanne. Shielding his thoughts from Roxanne, Andor sent a surge of energy directly into the intestines of all three girls. *Not today, you witches.* The three girls immediately looked at each other with panic in their eyes. As one, they turned to the nearest girl's room, hoping they'd make it in time.

Roxanne frowned as she watched the girls and then turned to Andor. He shrugged and smiled benignly, the picture of innocence.

"I have no idea what that was about,'" he said telepathically. Judging by her mischievous smile, she was well aware he had created the emergency in her three antagonists.

He escorted her to the pond, hurrying her along. After he'd wiped off the bench, he smiled at her, hoping his tension wasn't apparent. "It's dry now. It really is. Have a seat; you'll see."

Both sat down. Roxanne pulled out her sandwich.

"Aren't you eating, Andor?" she asked him.

"Oh, no, I'm not hungry."

"Andor, what's wrong?"

"Wrong? Nothing. Nothing's wrong."

"You're obviously upset. What's the matter?"

"Well, you know, I just wanted to talk to you about the other night at Antonio's and, you know, the way I acted. All that stuff about Ordinaries and democracy and the state of the world. What I'm trying to say is …" He paused and exhaled, trying to get a grip on his emotions. He looked at his watch, intensely aware of the time and desperate to say what he wanted to say before all hell broke loose.

"What I'm trying to say is … I'm sorry. I acted like such a jerk." He looked at Roxanne, his expression open, his eyes searching her face.

"You know, there's so much I want to say to you," he said, each second ticking in his mind. Again he looked at his watch. "I wish we weren't sitting here," he added, as much to himself as to her. "I wish we were someplace else, someplace far away from here so that I could tell you what I really feel. I thought about you all weekend long, what you said, what your mother said." Again, he paused, trying to clarify his thoughts within a storm of emotions.

"I'm sorry, I know I'm not making any sense," he said. "What I'm trying to say is, you're right. You're right about everything."

She placed her hand on his. "It's okay, Andor. Relax. Say what you want to say. We've got time. The lunch hour just started."

"Oh, man." He wiped perspiration from his brow with his sleeve. "You know, sometimes people are not what they seem. I mean, you've got every reason to think that I'm an idiot, that I'm narrow minded and arrogant, but I'm more than that. I want you to know that, okay? There's more to me than what you might think—what your parents might think, okay? Can you accept that, Roxanne? Can you?"

Before she had a chance to answer, Dennis, the mallard duck, stood up in the water and waved his wings wildly in a frantic dance. He quacked and squawked loudly.

"Danger!" he cried out. "Danger! Danger coming!"

In the same instant, Roxanne's inner alarm went off and she rapidly processed the information that flooded into her nervous system. Four teenage boys from the Northeast section of Washington were climbing the rise from the athletic field to the Laurel Building. She scanned their minds and bodies and realized all four were armed and driven by a violent rage that was fueled by large quantities of drugs.

Second, she felt a strange vacuum in her nervous system. Something wasn't right. And then it hit her. She could not hear the ping of Andor's presence. Somehow, the ping was silent.

She turned to him. "There are four of them. We've got to go!"

"Yes," Andor said.

"They're all carrying guns and hand grenades," Roxanne yelled in horror. "And they're crazy on methamphetamine. One of them is headed to the teachers' lounge in the Laurel." Instantly, she realized about a dozen teachers were eating lunch there.

"One is going to the cafeteria," she said to Andor. "That's where everyone is! The other two are splitting up. One's going for the second floor of the student center and the other is headed for the snack bar."

"You go to the Laurel," Andor said. "I'll go to the cafeteria. Meet me in the snack bar after you've taken care of the guy in the lounge."

As Andor and Roxanne ran off, Drazan Andelko waited for Max Louri between the student center and the Laurel building. He had expected Max to get to the Laurel before Roxanne in order to protect her from the assailant. The warning ping had been turned off on schedule and he knew he would catch Max by surprise. The only problem was, Max did not appear. Where was he?

At that moment, Andelko realized he was experiencing six warning pings, two more than he had expected and planned for. Roxanne and Andor were expected. So, too, were Jason Phillips and Max Louri. Who were the other two? And what were they doing on the campus?

Andelko ran to the Laurel building, well ahead of Roxanne, thinking Max would already be in the teacher's lounge before Roxanne got there. He threw open the main door and ran up the stairs, pulling the Glock out of its holster and fixed the silencer on it. He reached the second floor, arriving at a set of double doors that opened to the hallway. He threw open one of the doors and cautiously looked down the corridor. At the far end, he saw Max Louri pop out of a classroom. Max saw Andelko and ran toward the stairs at the opposite end of the hallway. Holding the Glock with both hands, Andelko fired twice at Max. Max's shield was up and both bullets missed him by inches. Max flew down the staircase, with Andelko in fast pursuit.

Max ran out of the Laurel and turned east toward the gymnasium. Andelko was down the stairs and out the door in time to see Max duck into the gym. Andelko ran into the gym, and as he did, he felt another ping. Who was it? Was it Lysenko? No, Lysenko had strict instructions to go to the cafeteria, where he was to take out an attacker. Was it the girl? No, she would never leave the teachers unguarded. Then who was the other ping? He exited the gym, aware the Max had run into the nearby dormitory. Cautiously, he approached the dormitory, holding his gun aloft while reinforcing his shield. He entered the dorm and crouched low in the foyer, where he was confronted by two staircases, one leading down, the other leading up. He began to ascend the stairs and heard a sound come from the third floor. Looking up he felt two pings coming from above. Max and the unknown were both on the third floor.

In the Laurel building, Roxanne raced up the stairs to the second floor where the teachers' lounge was located. As she reached the top of the stairs, she felt a ping. She opened one of the doors and a man appeared. He had to be the source of that ping and a Genius. As tall as her father and with a lean, athletic build, he was dressed like a teacher—sports jacket over a cotton shirt and chinos. He had dark hair and was roguishly good looking.

"I'm right with you, Roxanne," he said verbally. "Let's go."

"Who are you?" she asked as she ran toward the lounge.

"A friend."

At the door to the teachers' lounge, Roxanne paused to reinforce her shield. Glancing at her new friend, she told him she'd go in first.

"Okay," he said, but as soon as she turned the doorknob, he grabbed her arms and pulled her away. He opened the door himself and stepped into the doorway, blocking Roxanne's line of sight. Still, she heard the shot. The bullet missed her friend by a foot and hit a ceramic tile in the wall, shattering it. The friend crouched down, extended both of his hands, and hit the gunman with a blast of electromagnetic energy, throwing him across the room. He hit the wall hard and collapsed on the floor.

The friend pulled two plastic restraints from his jacket pocket and handed them to Roxanne. "Disarm him, tie his arms behind his back, and lock up his feet. Then wait for the police. I'm headed for the snack bar. Stay here. Understood?"

"Who are you?" she said, now more than a little annoyed.

"My name's Freddy. I'm a friend. I've gotta go." With that, he was out of the room.

About a dozen teachers huddled in the back of the room, as much in shock by what they had just seen as by the gunman holding them hostage. Roxanne looked at them and said, "I guess the drugs must have knocked him out. Can someone help me tie him up and disarm him?"

Several teachers rushed toward the gunman. One man took the revolver from the assailant's hand. Another man went through his pockets and relieved him of two more guns and two hand grenades. Several women were already on their cell phones calling the police.

Once the gunman was hogtied, Roxanne asked the men to stay with him until the police arrived. Then she ran from the teachers' lounge, heading for the student center.

Roxanne knew she wasn't nearly as powerful as her parents, or even this Freddy guy. She also knew that anyone high on methamphetamine would be extremely difficult to bring under control, especially for a young Genius who had no training in the fine art of incapacitating a hallucinating madman. She would have to be careful. But who was this Freddy anyway, and where did he come from?

She entered the student center and reached out with her intuition in order to feel where the gunman might be located. On the second floor of the center were science labs and a few small offices. The assailant was up there. As soon as she reached the second floor she heard whimpering from one of the labs, and then someone said, "Take what you want and leave."

She reached the doorway to the lab. Once again, she paused to reinforce her shield and then slowly and cautiously opened the door.

What she saw momentarily shocked her. A young man was holding a revolver and waving it at a group of fifteen students and the biology teacher, Mr. Henry, all of whom were lined up along the windows of the room. The gunman stood at the front of the room, his back to Roxanne.

"What a fucking waste of time school is," he was screaming. "What a waste of time all of your fucking lives are. Today I'm putting an end to all of that fucking waste of time and your fucking wasted lives. I'm going to enjoy shooting every one of you losers through the fucking head."

At first, the gunman didn't notice Roxanne enter the room, but he suddenly whirled on her as the door clicked closed. Roxanne made her posture small and contrite and adopted her dumb blonde routine in an attempt to demonstrate how harmless she was.

"Oh, I think I'm in the wrong room," she said. "Is this Mr. McDonald's art class?"

The gunman seemed stunned to see her. Before he could collect himself and start talking, Roxanne stepped into his mind.

Why are you throwing your life away, Richie Fredericks? She asked. *You have so much to live for, don't you realize that?*

As she spoke, Roxanne also sent a series of commands to Fredericks's nervous system, increasing production of serotonin and melatonin while decreasing dopamine and norepinephrine. She could see that Fredericks felt the effects immediately. He swayed on his feet, his eyes slowly closing.

"Who are you?" he asked her, obviously disoriented. "How do you know my name?"

"My name is Roxanne," she said. But telepathically, she sent a different message. *I used to watch you walk along Clifton Street on your way to Cardozo High School, Richie. That's where you go to school, right? You live on Seventh Street, isn't that right?*

"Yeah," Fredericks says. "But—but what do you mean, you used to watch me?"

Oh, I kind of had a crush on you, but I was too shy to approach you.

The young man's brain was wide open now, Roxanne realized, and completely vulnerable to her powers. She drastically elevated brain levels of melatonin, inducing an irresistible desire to sleep. At the same time, she reduced blood flow to two precise locations in his cerebrum. One site controlled motor function, so she disabled his ability to pull the trigger. The other in his frontal lobe lost any conscious connection he had to his plan to murder students and teachers.

Richie Fredericks suddenly collapsed on the floor, out cold and snoring like an old man.

Immediately, Roxanne ran over to him and took the gun out of his hand. Mr. Henry joined her and together they went through the gunman's pockets. They found two more guns and two hand grenades.

"You were amazing, young lady," Mr. Henry said. "That was one of the bravest things I have ever seen in my life."

"No, no," Roxanne said. "It must have been the drugs that overwhelmed him. I think he just passed out."

"Maybe. But I shudder to think what would have happened if you hadn't come along when you did."

"I think we should tie him up, don't you?" Roxanne said, staying in character.

Mr. Henry let out a small laugh, full of relief. "Yes, I think that would be a good idea."

On the third floor of the dormitory, Drazan Andelko kept his back against the wall as he crept down the hallway, both hands holding the Glock. The pings were louder and closer now, which meant that both Max Louri and the second Genius were in one of the bedrooms down the hall, on the right.

He reached out with his mind, trying to ascertain which room but could not perceive their exact whereabouts. Hearing a sound from the farthest room on the right, he quickened his approach. He reached the door and opened it just in time to see Max disappear into an adjoining room. Andelko fired two shots at the door, but Max was already out of sight.

Andelko cautiously entered the room Max had run into and saw an open window that let onto a fire escape. Racing to the window, Andelko saw Max running down the metal stairs. He fired twice, but both bullets ricocheted off the metal latticework as Max continued downward. Andelko got onto the fire escape and leaned over the edge as far as he could in an attempt to get a clear shot at Max.

As Andelko leaned over, Ellis dropped down on him from the roof. He landed directly on his back, and the force pushed both men off the fire escape, sending them into a free fall toward the pavement below. As they fell, Ellis wrapped his legs around Andelko's torso. With his left hand, he grabbed Andelko by the hair and pulled his head back. With his right, he grabbed the assassin's gun hand. Ellis rode Andelko like a man on a giant bird as they plummeted three stories to the ground.

At this particular moment, the crucial difference between Ellis and Andelko was that Ellis was tied to a bungee cord and Andelko wasn't.

Andelko hit the concrete walkway face first with a hideous thud, the side of his face, chest, and legs taking the direct impact of the fall. Just before he found the ground, the bungee cord yanked Ellis upward toward the roof. Like a giant rubber band, the cord raised Ellis and then gently lowered him again. While still eight feet in the air, Ellis released the grappling hook that kept him tied to the bungee cord. He landed, feet first, on the assassin's back. He felt the man's ribs and spine break. Quickly, he grabbed the assassin's neck and sent an electrical charge through his nervous system, electrocuting him.

Ellis stood over the body and caught his breath while Max assessed Andelko's condition. "Fractured skull, six broken ribs, a broken back, broken pelvis, two broken kneecaps, and a nervous system that's been burned to a crisp. I'd say he's dead. What about you, Ellis? You think we need to cut off his head or something?"

"That won't be necessary," Ellis said, still catching his breath but eager to get to his next stop. He looked down at the assassin. "Drazan Andelko. A very tough customer."

Max nodded in recognition, well aware that had it not been for Ellis, this would have been his last day on earth.

Freddy, meanwhile, had just finished taking care of the gunman in the student center without any loss of life. Ellis reached out to his brother for Roxanne's status.

"Roxanne's safe," Freddy said. "I left her in the teacher's lounge. The bad guy is out. Roxanne is babysitting the body."

"I'm scanning for her, bro, but I don't get her in the lounge. Could she be upstairs in the student center?"

Freddy searched with his mind for Roxanne. "You're right, she's there. I'm on my way."

Ellis turned to Max. "I need you to hide the body somewhere quickly and then come back for it once we're through here. When you've got the body hidden, meet me in the cafeteria and we'll take out the last bad guy, if Andor hasn't finished him off already."

"Got it. I'll be there in less than five minutes."

With that, Ellis ran to the cafeteria. On the way, he communicated with Freddy. "It feels like Roxanne's got things under control in the science lab, Fred."

"Feels that way to me too. I'm down the hall, nearly there."

When Freddy burst into the lab, Roxanne and Mr. Henry were trussing up Richie Fredericks. Breathing hard, Freddy knelt down next to Roxanne and Mr. Henry. He raised his eyebrows and gave her a tired smile. "Didn't I ask you to stay in the teachers' lounge, young lady?"

"Did you say that?" A sly smile crossed her lips. "I don't know," she said, shaking her head. "All that excitement, so much to think about, who knows what anyone said."

Freddy laughed, a little exasperated but feeling more than a little admiration for Roxanne. "Your parents would be proud of you," he said.

Suddenly Roxanne turned serious. "Andor's in the cafeteria with the last gunman. We should go."

"It's all right. Andor's fine and my brother is on his way."

"Well, let's go and see if your brother needs any help," she said, again with the sly smile.

"I'm going to tell him you said that," Freddy said.

When Andor arrived at the cafeteria, he was already attuned to the young man who was holding a few hundred students at gunpoint.

Karl Kleper had given Andor strict instructions about what must be accomplished in the cafeteria. But as he focused on the gunman and tried to bring the young man's brain chemistry into a calmer state, he found himself hoping that Roxanne wouldn't see what he was about to do.

He burst into the cafeteria as the gunman raised his weapon, about to start firing into the mass of terrified students. "No!" Andor screamed at the top of his lungs.

The gunman turned toward Andor and fired twice, both shots missing. Andor kept his composure and jolted the young man with a blast of energy, throwing him back on some chairs and a table.

At that moment, Andor telepathically spoke to the gunman. *Robert Amis, don't do it! You're better than this. You don't want to hurt anybody. And you don't want to spend the rest of your life in jail.*

Amis got up from the table, recovered his balance, and aimed his weapon at Andor again.

Andor sent a bolt of electromagnectic energy to Amis's bronchial passages and throat, which threw Amis into a convulsive state as he struggled to breathe. His hands clutched at his chest and throat.

"What are you doing to me?" Amis managed to say.

Andor responded telepathically again. *You don't want to hurt anyone, Amis. You're a good person and you don't want to kill anybody, or be killed yourself. But I will kill you if you force me to."*

With Amis struggling for breath, Andor manipulated his brain chemistry, inducing a profound state of confusion and exhaustion. *I know you're tired. All you want to do is rest. Why don't you just allow yourself to rest?*

Amis stopped struggling with his breath as he struggled instead to stand up straight. He looked confused and exhausted. As Andor approached him, he spotted Stewart Thompson, Jr., cowering behind a group of students against the cafeteria windows.

This is it, Andor said to himself. *Think of your parents. Do this for them.*

Andor grabbed the gun from Amis's hand and threw a right cross that landed directly on the gunman's jaw. He had planned to hit him only once, but the impact of his fist on the young man's face triggered a dark and volcanic rage inside Andor. All the fear, anger, and frustration he had felt the past many weeks; all the months of training and preparation under Karl Kleper's humiliating tutelage; all the hatred he felt for that man—all of that and more rushed up inside of him and threw him into hysteria. Andor pummeled the boy mercilessly until the assailant fell on the floor, unconscious, a bloody pulp.

A group of teachers ran to Andor's side and pulled him from the boy's limp body. "It's okay, it's okay, son," one of the teachers said. "It's over. We've got him. Relax. It's all over. You're a hero. You're a hero, son."

While a couple of teachers disarmed the unconscious youth, others telephoned the police, who by now were getting dozens of calls at once. People surrounded Andor as he struggled to regain his breath and composure. The cafeteria was filled with wild emotions, all of which were channeled into an explosion of relief and celebration that had people embracing one another and retelling the events over and over again. They all wanted to touch Andor, to slap him on the back, to shake his hand, and to tell him how great he was.

Stewart Thompson fought his way through the crowd, finally getting to Andor. He shook Andor's hand and said, "You saved our lives. Wait till I tell my father about this. He'll pin a medal on you!"

Involuntarily, Andor turned around and saw Roxanne standing at the entrance to the cafeteria. Shock and disappointment covered her face. Shaking her head, tears running down her cheeks, she telepathically sent him a single word—*Why?* Then she turned and left.

Freddy, Ellis, and Max, all driving separate vehicles, followed Roxanne as she drove home. In the back of Max's van lay the body of Drazan Andelko, which Max would dispose of in ways no one would discover.

In London, Roger had been following the events closely via the Davies brothers' monitoring devices and by tapping into all the participants' thoughts. Now, Ellis briefed him on the events, starting with Roxanne's safety. He stuck to the facts. He didn't have to tell Roger that the Klepers were sending him a message.

That done, Ellis, Freddy, and Max began to decompress.

Freddy was the first to assess the situation. "So, four objectives, as far as I can make out: kill Max, bring Stewart Thompson under Andor's influence, threaten the chief's family, and let us all know that our warning signal from Eastern Geniuses is gone."

"I'd say a partial success," Ellis replied.

"Yeah, except for Max," Freddy replied. "You're still breathing over there, right, Max?"

"Last time I checked. But I wouldn't be if it weren't for you two. Otherwise, the mission would have been a clean sweep."

"We get one out of four. A batting average of .250 is not stellar, gentlemen," Freddy said. "We must be slipping."

"Not by me, you're not," Max said. "Imagine my surprise when Ellis's voice came in loud and clear last night telling me that I'm Drazan Andelko's target, and that he very likely will be coming for me today."

"Sort of woke you up, eh, Max?" said Freddy.

"How did you guys know?"

"You were lucky, Max," Ellis said. "He was watching you, but so were we."

"Yeah, for the entertainment value," Freddy said.

"Once we caught him watching you," Ellis said, "we had to find out who was the primary target, Roxanne or you. Even if he was going after Roxanne, he'd have to go through you. We figured it out pretty quickly that you were his primary."

"How?"

"He wasn't very interested in Roxanne. Which makes perfect sense. As long as she's alive, the chief will be worried about her. They're hoping her vulnerability will cause him to take his eye off the ball, distract him from what they're doing elsewhere. By killing you, he'd send a message to the chief that the Klepers could kill Roxanne anytime they wanted. Besides, I'm betting it was Ubitzov who arranged the hit."

"You mean he hasn't forgotten Tangier?" Max said, grinning.

"That's right, Max," said Freddy with a little chuckle. "And neither have we."

"Anyway, gentlemen, score this round for the Klepers," Ellis said.

"Somehow, I don't think the Klepers are going to see things that way," Max said.

"Maybe. But I'm betting that this was a trial run. The next time they come at us, they'll be coming for all of us."

Chapter 16
The Assault's Aftermath

I n the aftermath of the assault, the peaceful campus life at Laurel Glen High School was turned into a three-ring circus. First came an army of psychologists and trauma experts, brought to the campus to help treat the students, teachers, and staff for post-traumatic stress disorder. Classrooms and offices, which were already in high demand, had to be turned over to therapists so they could see students and school personnel before, during, and after school hours. Each student, teacher, and staff member was required to attend lectures on coping in the aftermath of trauma. Meantime, there seemed no end to the "healers" and "experts" who wanted to get onto the campus in order to siphon off some of the emergency allocation funds being doled out for treatment. School administrators attempted to control the number of therapists on campus by insisting they would determine who was or wasn't allowed to treat students and teachers. Some distraught and angry parents insisted that their children be treated only by their own family therapists, which meant students were routinely leaving school in order to see outside psychologists. Attendance dropped precipitously, and senior administrators worried that the first semester of the school year might be lost entirely.

Then came the ambulance chasers—the hordes of lawyers eager to persuade parents to sue school administrators on the grounds that they failed to fulfill their responsibility to protect students. Given that these were the children of wealthy and important people, parents and their attorneys asked, why wasn't there a private security force present on the campus? Why wasn't such an incident, even a kidnapping, anticipated and prepared for? Hadn't the administration learned anything from Columbine and other schools that had been victimized by armed assaults? Why weren't the doors to the biology laboratory locked? Those were only a few of the difficult questions attorneys were asking.

Finally, there was the mob of television, radio, newspaper, magazine, and online reporters who surrounded the campus and camped out in the town. All the major networks were present—CNN, Fox News, ABC, NBC, CBS, and MSNBC. They arrived in their enormous vans, crowned by their satellite dishes and sprouting tentacles of thick black power and broadband cables. Along with their print and electronic media brethren, reporters from the *New York Times, Washington Post, Time* Magazine, *Newsweek, Rolling Stone, Huffington Post,* and the *Drudge Report* arrived, searching for fresh angles to report on. All of the reporters wanted interviews with students and teachers, anyone who had been an eyewitness to the attack. Of course, the most sought-after interview was with Andor Lysenko, who was being crowned the hero of Laurel Glen, the young man who had saved the lives of hundreds of students, teachers, and staff.

Andor burst into the national consciousness like Chinese fireworks. He wasn't an inarticulate doe-eyed boy who shyly struggled for the words to describe his heroism. No, he was handsome, poised, articulate, and even witty in a self-deprecating way. That he was Slavistani, with a slight accent, made him all the more exotic and charming. In short, he was made for the American media.

The Associated Press managed to snare the initial interview with Andor and its story captured some of the themes that would be retold and embellished by other reporters again and again. Its first headline and article shaped the story from the very start.

Teenage Hero Saves Hundreds in Attack on School

Golden Gables, MD (AP) September 25—Four male teenagers, all armed with automatic pistols and hand grenades, were thwarted in their attempts to kill students and teachers at Laurel Glen High School today by a combination of heroism and luck that saved the lives of hundreds of students, staff, and faculty members.

The four assailants, who range in age from 16 to 18, marched onto the campus at around 12:30 p.m., according to Golden Gables police. Each carried two 9 millimeter revolvers, more than 100 rounds of ammunition, and two hand grenades. According to police who interrogated at least one of the attackers on the scene, the four intended to shoot as many teachers and students as they could, and then blow up the administration offices. All four assailants have been arrested and are now in police custody.

The attack was intended to coincide with the lunch hour, when most of the students and teachers could be found in the cafeteria, the student center, and the teachers' lounge.

According to eyewitnesses in the cafeteria, one of the attackers, Robert Amis, 18, was about to start shooting into the crowd of students when Andor Lysenko, a senior at Laurel Glen, burst into the cafeteria and shouted at Amis to put down his gun.

Amis, who police said was under the influence of methamphetamine, turned on Lysenko and fired a single shot. The bullet missed Lysenko who then ran toward the gunman and struck him in the face before he could get off another shot, according to numerous witnesses. Lysenko struck Amis several more times, until he dropped his weapon, according to students and teachers on the scene.

"It was one of the bravest acts I have ever seen," said Ronald Whitman, a science teacher at Laurel Glen and veteran. "I've been in combat and I can tell you, only the bravest of the brave run into the line of fire in order to save the lives of others. If he were a soldier, he would get the Congressional Medal of Honor."

"I was scared out of my mind," said Stewart Thompson, Jr., a junior at Laurel Glen and the son of US Senator Stewart Thompson of Bethesda, Maryland. The younger Thompson was held at gunpoint in the cafeteria, along with hundreds of other students, and was present when Lysenko entered the cafeteria and confronted the gunman.

"The guy with the gun was just about to start shooting us when Andor came through those doors and yelled at the guy," Thompson said, still overcome with relief. "As soon as he heard Andor, the guy starts shooting at him. Andor put up his hands, like he was trying to protect himself, and then he ran right at the guy. Crazy, right? The guy goes down and Andor starts hitting him. When the guy dropped the gun, all these teachers rushed at them. The guy was unconscious."

Police reported Amis had another 9 millimeter revolver, five magazines of ammunition, and two hand grenades.

Two other assailants, one of them in the teachers' lounge and the other in a biology class laboratory, apparently passed out from the drugs in their systems. Eyewitnesses told reporters that in each case, the gunman started acting oddly and then collapsed. The gunman in the teacher's lounge appeared to undergo some kind of seizure, similar to an epileptic attack, police told reporters.

The fourth assailant, who held about forty students and staff hostage in the student center snack bar, was apparently overpowered by an unidentified man who walked into the snack bar just before the gunman started shooting. No one knows who the man was. Eyewitnesses reported that the man subdued the attacker, leaving him unconscious. He then removed weapons from the man's clothing and left the snack bar. Staff members say the man has not been seen since.

Winthrop B. Rutherford, Laurel Glen headmaster, announced today that October 10 would be designated Andor Lysenko Day. Lysenko's heroism will be commemorated in an assembly, and the school has already confirmed that Senator Stewart Thompson, the senior senator from Maryland, will be speaking.

Lysenko is a native of Slavistan and arrived in the United States in early September to begin his senior year at Laurel Glen. He maintains that he had no choice but to rush the gunman.

"I figured that if I turned and ran away, he would shoot me in the back," Lysenko said. "I'd be dead anyway. The only choice was to see if I could get to him before he got off another shot."

When asked if he were afraid, Lysenko replied, "It all happened too fast for me to be afraid. I'm more afraid now when I look back on it, but at the time something just took over me and I acted on instinct. I never ran so fast in my life."

Police spokesman Sergeant Elliot Vanderweghe stated that all four attackers are being held without bail, pending arraignment, which is scheduled to take place on September 26.

"Really, it's a miracle," said Vanderweghe. "Two of the assailants apparently overdosed on the drugs and passed out before they could hurt anyone. That alone potentially saved dozens of lives. Meanwhile, Mr. Lysenko's heroism prevented Amis from taking the lives of many others. It would have been a tragedy if Amis started shooting into the crowd in the cafeteria.

"We are also asking the man who disarmed the gunman in the student center to please come forward and identify himself. A grateful community would like to honor him for his courage."

No sooner had the AP story appeared than Andor was the darling of the American media, appearing first on all the major news programs. CNN reporter Wolf Blitzer asked Andor what he had been thinking right before he entered the cafeteria.

"I remember thinking that I was really hungry and hoping the cafeteria was serving sloppy joes that day," Andor said, smiling.

Blitzer smiled in return. "It's not often that a young man enters a cafeteria thinking about sloppy joes and ends up saving the lives of hundreds of people. Did you get your sloppy joe after the police arrived?"

"No, by that time I wasn't hungry anymore. I just wanted to lie down and sleep for a week."

After seeing the CNN report, a meat-packing company in Columbus, Ohio, sent Andor a certificate for a year's supply of sloppy joe mix.

Andor told Bill O'Reilly of Fox News that as soon as the gunman took a shot at him, he felt his legs go limp. "But in that instant I saw my teachers and classmates sort of cowering over by the cafeteria windows and something inside of me just exploded with power. Suddenly I had all this energy. Before I knew it, I was on the other side of the room, punching the guy. Something just took over me. It was like I was possessed."

O'Reilly looked at the camera and said with a wry smile, "My fourth grade teacher, Sister Mary Catherine, would have said that Andor Lysenko was possessed by St. Michael, the Archangel."

Andor even received a telephone call from the President of the United States, who praised Andor for his enormous courage and, on behalf of a grateful nation, thanked the young man for his bravery.

And so it was. America, hungry for heroes, derring-do, and happy endings, could not get enough of him. Invitations came from every quarter of the television, radio, and print media. Jay Leno, David Letterman, Conan O'Brian, and other television celebrities wanted interviews with Andor, and he obliged them all. He told Jay Leno that Leno was a big celebrity in Slavistan and that he should do a show sometime in Andor's home country.

Leno turned to the audience and said, "Well, there you have it, folks. If I ever leave the *Tonight Show* again, tune in to me in Slavistan. What channel would I be on in Slavistan, Andor?"

"You'd be on state television, Jay," Andor said smiling.

"State television? That sounds scary. Almost as scary as working for NBC."

From all outward appearances, Andor seemed to be enjoying himself. In fact, he was doing all that he had been trained to do. But with every interview he did, with every self-congratulating detail that he gave, he fell a little deeper into self-loathing. A voice inside him wanted to tell every reporter and interviewer who he really was—and more important, that the whole event had been staged so that he could be seen as a hero and attract the attention of single senator. A senator, who, because of his inflated ego and rampant ambition, would try to use Andor's celebrity for his own gain. Ironically, the senator would be used in a much bigger game than anything he could imagine.

You're all suckers, Andor wanted to tell the world. *I'm no hero. I'm a fraud.* He could have put that kid to sleep without anyone even knowing he was in the room. That was what Roxanne had done. She was the real heroine. She hadn't known the whole thing was prearranged and she could have been hurt, yet she acted with courage, with no thought of herself.

Her presence and all that she embodied haunted him. Every time he was interviewed or appeared on television, Andor hoped she would not read what he said or wouldn't see him speaking such lies. Her presence within him became stronger by the day.

At the very apex of his success, he was utterly sick in his soul.

He spent four days in New York City, having been brought to the city to make the rounds of the late-night talk shows. During the day, he walked around the city, his hands thrust into his pockets, his collar turned up against the wind and unseasonable chill. He gazed into store windows and stared down the long corridors of the city streets, and saw nothing but the emptiness of his own longing. He wanted to be with Roxanne, to confess the entire scam, to purge his soul of all that burdened him. What good was all of his intelligence and powerful mind now?

The two figures that loomed largest in his mind, Karl Kleper on one side and Roxanne on the other, had taken on a kind of spiritual symbolism. They represented two different paths, two very different destinies.

Karl had wanted those thugs to kill as many of the Laurel Glen students and teachers as they could. If not for Roxanne and some remarkable timing, he would have had his wish fulfilled.

Roxanne wanted love and purpose and an opportunity to make a difference in people's lives. "Why didn't you just put the answer in Harry's head?" she had asked him at the pond. Simple, straight, and right to the point—help them.

He could not escape his memories of their conversations. All too often, his own words returned to him like circling vultures. He wanted power and wealth, he'd told her. Now he was well on his way to having both, but her retort still stung him with the power of its truth. "Well," she had said, "it won't take you long to figure out that sometimes wealth takes you further away from the really important things in life."

His mind became an inescapable mirror, reflecting back at him who he had become. "Do you think Ordinaries have anything to say to us, much less teach us?" he had asked her. What arrogance, he realized now. How could he have been so blind and arrogant?

He remembered how, right before the raid began, when he and Roxanne were sitting at the pond, she had placed her hand on his and tried to reassure him that everything would be all right.

"It's okay, Andor," she had said. "Say what you want to say. We've got time."

Her innocence and purity had opened his heart. And the memory of her hand on his brought him to tears. What he wouldn't give to experience her touch right now.

Late in the evenings, he tried to contact her telepathically. Her shield was always up and reinforced. Every time he approached her with his feelings and found the door to her world closed, his heart broke a little more and his inner life collapsed in misery.

The worst memory was the expression on her face the last time he saw her. She had been standing at the cafeteria doors, tears of disappointment and heartbreak streaming down her face. In that instant he'd known beyond any doubt that he had made the wrong choice. Yet it had been his only choice. As long as Karl Kleper had his parents' lives in his power, he had to stay the course and be Karl's agent.

The four days he was in New York were the longest and loneliest of his life.

Of course, Karl knew what Andor was thinking and feeling. He could read the boy's inner world any time he wanted to. But for Karl, Andor's thoughts and feelings were meaningless. He could not have cared less that Andor hated him and wanted him dead. He was used to being hated. In fact, he wouldn't have it any other way. Being hated meant being feared, which was what he really wanted above all else. Fear made people do what you wanted them to do, and right now Andor feared Karl Kleper more than he hated him.

The truth was, Karl hated anyone who was powerless. Indeed, the three states that dominated Karl's psyche were: hatred of the powerless, satisfaction at getting what he wanted, and respect for the three people who had sufficient power to oppose him—Alexander Astrakhan, Roger Reynolds, and the Collaborator, whose identity was still a mystery to him. In fact, he wasn't sure if the Collaborator had any real power of his own. But he was a means to an end, just as Andor was. Both would be expendable when they had fulfilled their purposes.

So when Karl presided over a meeting of the Eastern Council in a conference room buried in the bowels of the Caucasus Mountains, he extolled the one success of the attack on Laurel Glen without any mention of Andor Lysenko. The boy was nothing more than an extension of Karl's hand. All the credit belonged to him alone, and he had absolutely no reservations about framing it as such. As for the rest of the mission, Karl was enraged. It had been a dismal failure in every other respect. His wrath was directed specifically at Vladimir Ubitzov, who had planned the assassination of Max Louri.

"Killing Louri was perhaps the easiest part of this mission, Comrade Ubitzov," Karl said out loud, which was characteristic of him. Whenever he was enraged, he communicated verbally. Rage was best expressed in a loud voice, and he was deeply enraged.

"Put me within a kilometer of him," he went on, "and I could kill him in my sleep. And yet not only did he get away, but he and everyone at the Western Council now know we have the technology to eliminate the warning signal. Had Louri been killed, only the girl would have experienced the loss of the alarm and she would have attributed it to some kind of atmospheric disturbance. It would have been overlooked. Not now. Now we have been found out."

Karl paused for effect. For a moment, he seemed to look within, as if deciding what to do with Ubitzov and the council's entire plan. The tension in the room soared to an unbearable level. Fear became palpable.

Karl resumed his monologue from an even deeper place within his being, as if he were thinking out loud.

"If we do not act quickly, we may lose our most important advantage in our effort to eliminate those who stand in our way."

Again the introspective pause, and then he turned to Ubitzov, still burning at the assassin's failure.

"After years of meticulous planning, after so many great minds working tirelessly to create this technology and put together a foolproof plan, we are undone by the fool we counted on. Our entire timetable must now be moved up because of your incompetence, Ubitzov. You have failed me and this entire council."

Those words landed on Ubitzov like a death sentence. He was lost in terror. He didn't know what to do at that moment except beg for his life.

"I had no way of knowing that the Davies brothers were on that campus, Comrade," Ubitzov said, his teeth nearly chattering with his fear. "You informed me that Louri was the only bodyguard for the girl. I sent one of my best men to take him out. Andelko expected to be opposed by Louri alone, who was no match for him. No one knew the Davies were on that campus—not even your Collaborator! We were misinformed by your source, Comrade. You must understand. Surely you realize that I should not be blamed for creating a plan on the basis of faulty information."

The council members were nearly as terrified as Ubitzov. Ubitzov was a frightening figure, a walking minister of death. A terrifying darkness seemed to pool around his deep-set eyes. He was not a man one dared to incite, ever. But today he was a powerless and frightened schoolboy, begging for his life. The humiliation was awesome and, at the same time, terrifying to witness. No member of the council wanted to look at Ubitzov for fear he might turn his wrath on them, but no one could take their eyes off him either. Ubitzov was the proverbial train wreck unfolding in slow motion before them. Mesmerizing and yet horrible to watch.

As his brother Karl prosecuted Ubitzov, Klaus sat silently in his chair, wondering if he should intervene and kill Ubitzov now, thus saving his brother the trouble of disposing of this fool and sparing the council from having to witness Ubitzov's humiliation.

"Ah, yes, the Davies brothers," Karl said. "You've had many run-ins with those two over the years, haven't you, Ubitzov? And as I recall, you have not had a single success against them. We all remember the Tangier affair, when we had that flabby-faced poseur de Gaulle in the palm of our hand. We were on the brink of another success then too, only to have it ripped from our grasp by those two pretty boys who wiped out your entire assassination team. You returned to the council empty-handed and complaining that you hadn't anticipated the Davies then either."

Karl stood and loomed over Ubitzov. Those seated at the table fairly gasped as Karl looked down on Ubitzov, almost daring him to strike.

"You should have anticipated that Reynolds would turn to those two. He's done it repeatedly for more than seventy years." Karl pounded the polished table with the flat of his hand, sending a shock wave through every person seated at the table.

The instant Karl's hand smacked the table, a massive barrage of electromagnetic energy emanated from Karl's enormous body and began electrocuting Ubitzov. Violent convulsions shook the assassin. His eyes, wide in horrified shock, nearly burst from their sockets. His mouth opened and his tongue shot out, as if it was trying to escape a burning building. Indeed, Ubitzov's hair started to singe and smoke, as did the leather of his chair. Ubitzov screamed, a cry like an animal being tortured.

Kleper was possessed. His eyes were insane, his smile demonic as he intentionally kept Ubitzov alive as he electrocuted him. He kept the electricity flowing, enjoying every second of the torture as Ubitzov screamed even louder.

The horror among the rest of the council members was unbearable. Dominika Dementieva, the head of propaganda, couldn't take it any longer. She covered her ears with both hands and looked down toward the table.

"Make it stop," she cried out. "Stop it, stop it, please!"

Finally, Klaus jumped up from his seat and placed both of his arms around his brother. In a shielded telepathic communication, he shouted at Karl, "If you want to kill him, kill him, but finish him!"

Karl released Ubitzov, who fell off his chair and landed hard on the floor. He was still alive, though barely.

Karl walked over to him and grabbed him by the front of his shirt. With the power of his mind, he lifted Ubitzov off the floor and threw him into the still-smoking chair.

He looked directly into Ubitzov's traumatized face. "That is my last warning, Comrade. Kill every member of Reynolds' team, kill the Davies brothers, or kill yourself. It will be easier than what I will do to you."

With that, Kleper released Ubitzov, who slumped into his chair and passed out.

Chapter 17
Roger's Answer to Archangel

Roger stood before his office window on the western side of Westminster Abbey and looked out on Parliament Square, Big Ben, and the Houses of Parliament, completely lost in thought. Rain crashed against the window and fell in long tears. He hadn't gone back to his flat the previous evening. Instead, he'd spent the night turning over every detail of the recent events, recalling every bit of relevant background information, and reasoning through his options, most of which he didn't like. Ellis and Freddy's report on the raid on Laurel Glen left him feeling isolated and vulnerable. Yes, Roxanne was safe—for the moment. He was proud of her bravery, but nonetheless afraid she might continue to take dangerous risks. He could talk to her about those concerns, but it probably wouldn't do any good. As with so many discussions he had had with his daughter of late, she'd see his concerns as an attempt to control her, or that he was disrespecting her maturity. Like her mother, she was headstrong and determined. Unlike her mother, she had little sympathy for his need to protect her. No doubt, she would berate him for placing Ellis and Freddy nearby without telling her.

Still, he would do what he had to do. The tragedy of his parents' death loomed ever larger for him, stalking him like a large black shadow. It was the curse of his past that justified his actions, he told himself. He would do all he had to do to protect Rebecca and Roxanne.

As for the Davies brothers, his trust in them was reaffirmed yet again. They would give their lives before they allowed anything happen to his daughter or his wife. But there were limits to what they could do; even to what Roger himself could do.

And then there was the new game-changing development. The Klepers had found a way to control the warning signal that Western Geniuses experienced in the presence of Eastern Geniuses.

Roger was certain the raid had been both a trial for Archangel and a way for the Klepers to demonstrate they could kill Roxanne, or any Western Genius, at any time they wanted. By controlling their innate, hereditary warning signal, the ping, the Klepers had made every Western Genius vulnerable to assassination. What was even more disturbing was that the Eastern Council could silence the warning signal within a specific geographical area, thus isolating a small number of Western Geniuses for attack.

Roger knew the Klepers had the capability to isolate a small area because reports had come in from all over the world that no other Geniuses outside the Laurel Glen campus had lost that warning tone when in proximity to Eastern Geniuses. The same was true for him and his team. None of them had experienced the silencing of the signal.

We must take that power from the Klepers—and right away, Roger told himself. The picture looked grim, but there had been some silver linings, some small bits of good luck.

For one, the Western Geniuses might not have known about the loss of the ping had the Davies brothers not been present, and had Max Louri been killed. In that case, Roxanne would have been the only Western Genius to report she hadn't heard a ping from any Eastern Genius, including Andor. In the heat of battle, would she have noticed its absence? If she did, would she have attributed it to some kind of atmospheric disturbance, a temporary alteration in the earth's electromagnetic field? Certainly that conclusion would have been reinforced if the Klepers restored the ping once the assault was over, which is exactly what they did. In the absence of corroborating experiences, Roxanne might have felt no need to mention the loss of the signal. Even if she had told Roger, he might have attributed the loss to some temporary anomaly in the atmosphere. But things had not gone as the Klepers had intended, which meant they were now exposed.

They know we know, Roger thought. That would change their game plan. Every step in their scenario would have to be moved up. No doubt, that would cause them problems. They would make mistakes. But, Roger acknowledged, it meant his team had less time to counter the Klepers' offensive.

Everything turned on a single factor, he realized. They either had to destroy Archangel or take control of it. Both objectives had to be pursued, but gaining control of Archangel was clearly the best option.

Naturally the Klepers would expect that from him. They would have to try to head him off, but how? What would they do to protect their satellite?

Roger put the second question aside for the moment and considered the satellite itself. Sitting in his big leather chair, he cleared and opened his mind. In an instant, a sequence of thoughts, a kind of logic train, was illuminated within his mind's eye. Begin at the beginning, the logic told him. Start with an understanding of the warning signal.

Whenever Roger confronted a challenge, he turned to the power of his brain to recall all relevant information he had encountered in the past. He could recall entire books, conversations, lectures, and the like word for word. And he could arrange the information into an integrated, holistic picture that would give him the basis for an effective strategy for solving the problem.

Reaching into his mind, he found a single volume that he had read many years before—*A Comparative Study of the Genius Versus Ordinary Nervous Systems*, written by Professor Albert Raushenbach. He brought Professor Raushenbach's book to his consciousness and recalled every word of it. In his mind's eye, he saw Dr. Raushenbach's words on the page.

"We can begin to understand the essential differences between the nervous systems of Geniuses and those of Ordinaries by understanding the different experiences of what *recall* means to the two types of human beings," Raushenbach had written. "An Ordinary *recalls* fragments of information gleaned from books that he or she read in the recent or distant past. For the ordinary person, time erodes recall. In a Genius, the passage of time has no influence on memory. A Genius can *recall* an entire book, as if he or she were taking it down from a shelf and reading it again."

In his mind, Roger breezed through the pages of Dr. Raushenbach's book, re-experiencing every word, pulling forth the relevant information that he needed.

> Any time vast supplies of energy and information are stored in a single container—in this case, in the nervous system of a Genius—there is necessarily a high degree of wave emissions or radiation. The emissions that emanate from the Genius nervous system collide with the highly charged particles in the earth's atmosphere. These collisions result in minute increases in energy that are audible at high frequency ranges. Just as a billiard ball gives off a familiar sound when struck by a cue ball, so does a Genius's wave emissions give off their own characteristic sound when they pass through the waves and particles that pack the earth's atmosphere and then collide with the wave emissions coming from the nervous system of another Genius.
>
> Geniuses refer to this sound as the warning signal, or ping.

Roger recalled that Dr. Raushenbach was always a bit pedantic.

> Our ability to hear the ping is made possible by our advanced hearing capabilities. We hear frequencies that Ordinaries do not hear. Ordinary hearing falls within the range from 20 cycles per second, or 20 hertz, to between 18,000 to 20,000 cycles per second, or 18 to 20

kilohertz. The hearing capabilities of Geniuses extend beyond these ranges. We can hear sounds up to 25 kilohertz, and for some, even higher.

Roger continued on reading, page after page of material passing before his mind's eye.

> Even among Geniuses, hearing capabilities vary. This is particularly true of Western versus Eastern Geniuses. Over many millennia, genetic variations have occurred in the West and East that have brought about small but significant differences in our respective hearing capabilities."

Roger knew that now he was almost there.

> Though these differences in hearing seem inconsequential, they nonetheless do affect a single factor: the frequencies at which Eastern and Western Geniuses hear the warning signal. In the presence of another Genius of their own kind, both Eastern and Western Geniuses hear the ping at the 23 kilohertz frequency. However, when Eastern and Western Geniuses are near each other, Eastern Geniuses hear the warning ping at 24 kilohertz and Western Geniuses hear it at 25 Kilohertz.

Roger sat back in his chair. So, that was how they did it. They found a way to affect the interaction between the Eastern Genius wave emissions and the atmospheric medium through which those emissions traveled in order to silence the 25 kilohertz frequency. Thanks to Archangel, the warning ping emitted by an Eastern Genius was gone, or at least inaudible to a Western Genius, which meant Western Geniuses were deaf to the presence of Eastern Geniuses.

Roger marveled at the technical know-how and ingenuity of the Eastern Council scientists. Now, how could he counteract their brilliance?

If his Western scientists could reprogram Archangel so that it reactivated the 25 kilohertz frequency and silenced 24 kilohertz, he could use Archangel to silence the warning ping Eastern Geniuses heard when a Western Genius was near. They could turn the tables on the Klepers and use the satellite for their own purposes. And they could spring the trap on the Klepers before they realized what was happening. But how?

Roger picked up a paper clip and began to rotate it in his fingers. Suddenly he looked down at the paper clip, and in that instant the *how* question was answered.

"We'll build a nanocomputer the size and shape of a paperclip," he said aloud as he looked closely at the paper clip. "We'll place it on a rocket that's already scheduled to launch and redirect the rocket to rendezvous with Archangel."

Now for the second question, he mused. What would the Klepers do, knowing that Roger now knew about Archangel?

They'll stick with their plan, he realized. It had been too long in the making for them just to scrap it overnight. But they would have to move their timetable up and try to anticipate Roger's next move.

And what was his next move? Of course, he would try to gain control of Archangel. And for that, he needed money to build a device that could do that. Getting the funds meant going to their banker, Helmut Volk. So the Klepers might try to take out Volk, just to slow Roger down. And if he was able to create the necessary device, they would attempt to destroy it. The Klepers just needed to slow him down enough to give them time to assassinate the Western Council leaders—eliminating the only real obstacle to their dream of world domination.

Roger's foresight gave him an immediate thrill. Not only did he know the Klepers' next two moves, he could use that knowledge to his advantage.

He was about to reach out telepathically to Stephen in order to get the young Genius to design the paper clip computer, when Simone broke into his thoughts.

"Roger, sorry to interrupt, but I have something important to tell you."

"Can it wait, Simone? I was about to meet with Stephen and I have to move quickly."

"No, Roger, it cannot wait."

"What's the problem?"

"We have a mole on our team and he's feeding information to the Klepers."

Roger's mind reeled as he considered who the traitor might be, what damage the spy might have already caused, and might cause in the future.

"Come to my office right now, Simone."

Chapter 18
The Collaborator

They met at Al Wigh, a desert oasis in the Southwest corner of Libya, about a thousand kilometers south of the Libyan capital of Tripoli. The place was a tiny dot in the vast south Sahara, near the border with Niger, but it had a military base and a good airfield where they could land their planes. The military base provided all the comforts the three needed, thanks to their generous host, Muammar Gadhafi, who had been under the influence of Karl and Klaus Kleper since Gadhafi took control of Libya in 1969.

The meeting was in the base commander's dining room, which doubled as a conference room when the need arose. The room was carpeted and decorated with tassels around the windows and along the ceiling. A large photograph of Gadhafi hung on one wall; otherwise the walls were bare. Only the northern wall provided a view through large windows and a sliding glass door that opened onto a large veranda and then the vast Sahara. The windows and door could be protected from the desert winds and sand by corrugated steel curtains that rolled down from the roof, but that day the curtains were up and the Sahara was calm. Even in tranquility, the Sahara was awe inspiring in its terrible barrenness and otherworldly power. The ceaseless wind flew along the desert's back, shifting her contours, and whispered seductively to the foolish soul who might be tempted to approach her.

The three had arrived late in the morning and eaten lunch separately in their respective quarters. After a short rest, they were now ready for their meeting. They had never met in person. The Klepers didn't even know the Collaborator's real name. But they didn't need such information, they decided. Once the Collaborator had established his bona fides to their satisfaction, the Klepers were content to formulate a plan with their new partner and let it unfold.

For the Collaborator, however, such trust was now lost. The recent debacle at Laurel Glen had raised concerns that had to be addressed. He had decided he would have to take the measure of the Klepers personally and *"re-inspire"* them, so to speak, by which he meant sticking his rather large boot firmly up their asses. He had no patience for incompetence and the Klepers had shown too much of that.

The base commander had replaced the conference table with a smaller dining table so the three could speak more intimately. Three cups and a plate of pastries were arrayed around a large ornate samovar that provided tea. Klaus Kleper sat to his left; Karl Kleper sat across from him.

The Collaborator made himself comfortable in the large leather chair. He poured tea for the three of them and, with a slight nod to the picture of Gadhafi, said telepathically to the Klepers, "Your boy is getting old and sloppy. He's got two years left, if he's lucky."

Karl nodded, as if the observation was obvious. "We have warned him many times. His appetites are too big for his bowels."

As Karl spoke, Klaus observed the Collaborator, who wore a wide-brimmed straw hat, a khaki shirt, dark trousers, and boots. Shifting light and kaleidoscopic energies surrounded his face and kept him from being seen clearly. Was he old, young, middle- aged? Yes, middle-aged, Klaus decided. His eyes were dark, deep set, and hidden. The nose was large and full, rather like de Gaulle, a man Klaus secretly admired. Of course he never dared admit as much to his brother. A dark, heavy beard covered the Collaborator's face and his mouth, wide and thin, was closed tight. Overall, his skin was dark, perhaps revealing some Middle Eastern ancestry. But his features seemed to shift and change moment to moment. Suddenly, his lips were fuller. The eyes were dark one moment, hazel the next. His skin lightened and then darkened. Even the nose seemed to change slightly as the Collaborator looked left or right. Klaus attempted to peer into the man's thoughts, but met a powerful shield that was impervious to anyone else's mind. Klaus marveled. *What power this man has that even I cannot discern his exact features.*

"I admire your camouflage," he said to the Collaborator. "Have our paths crossed before without our knowing?"

The Collaborator was silent for a beat and then said, "Once or twice."

Klaus knew his brother hated it whenever he expressed admiration for someone other than himself, so he wasn't surprised when Karl quickly changed the subject. "So, you called this meeting, Comrade. What is it that you'd like to discuss?"

Another pause, and then the Collaborator chose to speak verbally, an action that momentarily surprised both Klepers. "Do the two of you happen to recall the twentieth century?" he asked.

His tone was blatantly condescending. Klaus and Karl were used to deference.

The Collaborator went on. "Do names like Roosevelt, Churchill, Eisenhower, de Gaulle, Hitler, Stalin, Gandhi ..." His voice trailed off and he paused once more, as if he was already uninterested in speaking to the two of them. "How about Ben-Gurion, Mao, Lenin, Trotsky, Castro, Che Guevara, MLK? Do those names ring a bell with either of you?"

He speaks to us as if we're fools, Karl thought. He considered grabbing the Collaborator by the throat in order to shut him up and teach him a lesson or two.

The Collaborator continued. "You know, from 1900 to 1968, the average man on the street had a greater willingness to sacrifice for whatever ideal he might have believed in than all of the bloated fools who now occupy the great halls of power." The Collaborator paused to take a sip of tea.

"Of course, that presented us with a problem. There were too many men of will and substance. We couldn't control them all, so we were forced to bide our time.

"Over the past fifty years, everything's changed. Have you noticed? The world is suddenly devoid of greatness. It's being run by spineless thieves whose only motive is greed. They see life through their wallets, which are appropriately positioned on their asses. Which means, of course, that the table finally has been set for us. We have arrived at our moment."

The Collaborator took another sip of tea. His every gesture said that not only did he not fear the Klepers, he had no respect for them, either. Klaus marveled at the Collaborator's gravitas, his poise and control of the moment. Karl, his chest filling with hatred for the other man, could feel the power shifting away from him and to this impertinent actor. He couldn't wait to bring this man to his knees, to have him groveling for his life.

"With Ordinaries reduced to small-time crooks," the Collaborator said, "the only ones who stand in our way are those of the Western Council, specifically Alexander Astrakhan, Roger Reynolds, and those who abet them.

"We—the three of us—chose to seize the moment. We made a plan. I thought it was a good plan. But like all good plans, it hinged on one thing above all else: competent execution. Plans are only as good as those who carry them out."

At that moment, the Collaborator gave Karl a baleful, contemptuous look. Karl's fury rose to the surface, reddening his face. He leaned forward, prepared to strike. Klaus, who knew his brother's inner world as if it were his own, felt a chill run down his spine. The Collaborator had crossed a line. He was a dead man.

The Collaborator acted as if he were oblivious to all of this, as if he couldn't care less what the Klepers thought.

"And what we have discovered," he went on, "after that Keystone Cops affair at Laurel Glen, is that neither of you is very good at what you do."

Karl erupted. He jumped out of his chair and sent a lightning bolt at the Collaborator's throat. The Collaborator reacted as if Karl was moving in slow motion. He remained seated, held up his hand, and repelled the blast of electromagnetic energy as if it were a child's balloon. The fusillade bounced back at Karl and struck him in his chest. The blast tossed the obese man across the room, and he hit the wall behind him with a thud. Standing, the Collaborator sent a line of electromagnetic energy toward Karl that was an extension of the Collaborator's own hand. From twenty feet away, he grabbed Karl by the neck and dragged him back to the table, and then lifted the three-hundred pound man and dropped him like a sack of potatoes onto his chair. The battering momentarily knocked Karl unconscious.

Klaus, who had been shocked and mesmerized by what he had just witnessed, whirled on the Collaborator and fired an enormous blast of energy at him. The blast merely illuminated the Collaborator's shield. The Collaborator let out a hideous laugh that reverberated through the room, as if it had come from another dimension. Extending his left hand, he lifted Klaus into the air. Then he drove the skinny little man into his seat. Klaus's butt punched a hole through the bottom of the chair. He, too, was unconscious.

The Collaborator looked contemptuously at both men. He released a deep breath, as if he had expended more energy on the Klepers than they were worth. Turning his attention to the silver tray, he picked up a piece of baklava and walked over to the sliding door to study the Sahara and wait for the Klepers to wake up. *What a marvel*, he thought as he admired the great vastness that lay before him. *What power.* He took a bite of the baklava and savored its flavor. The crust was fresh and flaky. The baker had the sense to make it with olive oil rather than with butter. *Not bad*, he said to himself, *especially for being some distance from Athens.* He realized the commissary probably ordered their specialty items from Tunisia, which was significantly closer to this hell-hole.

Since the pastry made him thirsty, he walked back to the table and poured himself a fresh cup of tea from the samovar. The tea had lost some of its heat, but the taste was still delicious.

The Collaborator lifted the pot above Karl Kleper's head, and poured the tea over him. The top of the samovar, which contained the tea leaves, fell from the pot and comically hit Karl in the head. The hot tea, tea leaves, and silver top roused the fat man to consciousness. He screamed at the top of his lungs. The Collaborator then poured the rest of the tea over Klaus's head, awakening him in the same way.

"Nap time is over, children," he said. He wrapped both men in a chain of electromagnetic energy, paralyzing them. "I'm going to release you, but you're going to behave. Understand? No more shenanigans. Otherwise, I'll be forced to kill you both. Nod your heads if you understand me."

Both men nodded and the Collaborator released them. "Now, here's what you are going to do. Reynolds is going to attempt to take control of your little satellite, but he'll need funding for the technology he comes up with to do it. He'll also need to launch that technology (or the device containing it) into space so that it can dock onto your toy. Those are the two places where he is most vulnerable. The first thing he'll do is go to Helmut Volk for the money to create the computerized device that he will use to take over Archangel. The second will be to piggyback the device onto some kind of rocket that will be launched from Cape Canaveral. I want you to intercept him at Volk. Take Volk out. Failing that—and you will not fail—but if you do fail, you will destroy the device during its launch."

"He may have already gone to Volk," Karl said, his voice groggy.

"He hasn't," the Collaborator said.

"If we kill Volk, he will go to Astrakhan and Astrakhan will approve the funds."

"I will take care of Astrakhan. You stop him at Volk. But if Volk survives and Reynolds gets his funding, you will find out which rocket he will use to launch his device, and destroy the device and the rocket. Understood?"

"We have a spy on his team," Karl said. "We will know the details of the launch and we will take out the device."

The Collaborator was surprised. He had not been aware of the Klepers' spy within Roger's circle. He was impressed. "Very good, Karl," he said as if he were patting a child on the head. "Maybe you're not as incompetent as I feared. We will continue with our plan. Make sure you take out that device."

With that, the Collaborator turned and walked quickly out of the room.

Klaus looked at Karl. In Klaus's eyes, Karl was the greatest man alive. Klaus's heart nearly broke as he saw his brother beaten and humiliated. He looked away, desperate to protect his brother from further embarrassment.

"We will continue with our plan," Karl said. "And when we are ready, we will kill him." Then he added, as his upper lip curled into a sneer, "We will kill him slowly and painfully. I will have my revenge."

Klaus knew there was no other way.

Chapter 19
Geniuses also Need Money

On the twenty-ninth floor of a gray skyscraper in midtown Manhattan—one of those glass and granite monoliths that reek with anonymous power—ten men and two women, all in expensive suits, sat around an oblong conference table waiting for the man who would occupy the empty chair at the table's head. In front of each person was a leather-bound portfolio embossed with the participant's name, title, and firm.

Those seated around the table were either the principals or CEOs of a dozen of the world's largest banks, hedge funds, investment firms, and insurance companies. Every man and woman in the room had a personal wealth of more than $150 million, and they represented corporations with assets in the many billions.

Two of the walls of the oversized conference room were made entirely of glass. One of them provided a good view of the west side of Manhattan and, looking north, a small glimpse of Central Park. The other revealed the hallway where four powerfully built bodyguards had been stationed—two at the conference room door and one at each end of the hallway. More security men were in the lobby downstairs, two of them at the reception desk. All were there to protect the man for whom they all waited.

All the bankers and executives were familiar with one another, having done business together over many years. Some chatted amongst themselves, others read their portfolios. Occasionally, one or another of them cast a suspicious and slightly intimidated glance at the two bodyguards standing at the door.

Presently, they could see their host through the glass wall as he approached the doors to the conference room. One of the bodyguards held the door open for him and he breezed into the room, full of energy and purpose. Sitting at the head of the table, he placed his hands in a prayerful position and surveyed the room. It was a signal for everyone to be quiet and await his presentation.

His name was Lucius Webber. At least that was the name he had given in his correspondence when he arranged this meeting. No one had ever heard of him.

He had arranged the seating so that his back was to the west-facing windows. He'd known the light from the city would create an aura around his silhouette while obscuring his features. As best as the others could make out, he was middle-aged, perhaps in his late forties. He had dark hair and, like the other men in the room, he wore a dark tailored business suit. That was as much as people could agree on. Many weeks later, when those present in the room were asked by the police, the FBI, and the Securities and Exchange Commission to describe the man, confusion reigned. Some said that he was exceptionally tall, six foot six at least. Others claimed he was of average height, but broad shouldered and stocky. No one could recall a clear image of his face and there was even disagreement about coloring. Despite his European name, he appeared dark, perhaps Mediterranean, while others said northern European, even Scandinavian. The one feature two or three of them could agree on was that he wore a vintage Rolex on his left wrist.

Despite their inability to remember their host's appearance, everyone agreed that the people he represented were powerful, wealthy, and extremely effective players of the market. They seemed prescient in predicting the political, social, and natural events that would have a direct and significant impact on the stock market.

Webber stood up and began to speak.

"Thank you, ladies and gentlemen, for accepting our invitation today and for your willingness to facilitate the investment strategy I am about to present to you. As I stated in my earlier correspondence, I represent a consortium of wealthy and powerful individuals and families from around the world who have a long history of successful strategic investment.

"If you open your portfolios, you will see examples of what I mean. All of the many investments I am about to outline, as well as those described in your portfolios, have been verified by independent accounting firms.

"As described in those portfolios, we correctly anticipated the key events that have shaped global financial markets during the last century. I have detailed our strategies over the past twenty-five years, starting with our strategic moves leading up to the market crash of October 19, 1987. As you will see, we enjoyed significant returns on the crash of '87.

"We correctly anticipated and therefore reaped sizable rewards on the rise of the Chinese economy over the last decade; the rise and subsequent collapse of the dot-com bubble in March 2000; the September 11, 2001, attack on the World Trade Center; and the variability of the euro. Hurricane Katrina was, for us, an extremely profitable event, as were the collapse of debt securities backed by mortgages, the September 2008 stock market crash, and the subsequent rise in oil and gold commodities. You will also see that the BP Gulf oil spill of April 2010 was another event from which we enjoyed significant gains.

"In each of these cases, our strategies were both complex and precise. For example, in August of 2001 we shorted $10 billion on airline and insurance stocks, and bought puts on the S&P. We purchased a billion dollars' worth of euros and yen, and another billion of call options on gold and oil. Of course, on September 11, the Standard and Poor's index was closed and subsequently dropped sharply, as did the stocks for the airlines and insurance industry. Our profits on the latter stocks alone were greater than $500 billion.

"All of you have long practiced the art of profiting from other people's tragedies. Our group of investors feels strongly that we now stand at another turning point in history. The forces driving events are powerful and seemingly unpredictable. Let me assure you, the latter belief is an illusion. Blind forces do not make history. People in positions of great power create history. And our intelligence indicates that history is about to be written in capital letters during the next thirty days. We are not talking about the weather. We're talking about planned events.

"On page thirty-five of your portfolio, we have outlined a strategic investment plan designed to take full advantage of the coming opportunities. This morning, I will summarize our general protocol.

"We are instructing you to purchase thirty-day puts on, and to sell short, large quantities of securities issued by major international airline companies. In your portfolios are specific instructions to be carried out by your particular firms. We plan for you to sell short an aggregate of $30 billion of securities. Additionally, we want you to expend a total of $75 billion dollars acquiring thirty-day puts on the S&P."

"Finally, we wish to purchase thirty-day-call options for the shares of all of the major oil and oil service companies, including Exxon, Shell Oil, British Petroleum, Schlumberger, and Occidental. Total investment for these options is $50 billion. That brings our entire investment strategy to $180 billion.

"In order to impress upon you the magnitude of our confidence and commitment, I will tell you that we are employing similar strategies for the London, European, Shanghai, Nikkei, and Hong Kong stock exchanges as well."

As Webber spoke, those seated at the table underwent an array of disorienting sensory experiences. Though the room was well lit, Webber seemed to move in and out of shadow. His face became hidden at times. Most disturbing of all, Webber's voice stopped being an auditory experience and became an internal one, as if his voice emanated from within each participant's central nervous system. Though they were unaware of what was taking place, each participant was surrendering to Webber his and her ability to make independent decisions.

"You have all signed confidentiality agreements with our group," he continued. "No one outside essential personnel within your firms is permitted to know of our investment strategy. You are not permitted to make any trades along these lines for your own accounts or share them with clients. You will be handsomely compensated, and your commissions will more than make up for any losses that you or your firms incur. We are not Communists."

Webber looked into the faces of each person sitting at the table, and continued speaking in a matter-of-fact manner that was nonetheless chilling in its effect. "If any one of you fail to follow our instructions, even in the slightest detail, you will be subjected to extreme reprisals. Do not make the mistake of believing that the consequences of such violations will be restricted to the limits of the law. I hope that I am making myself absolutely clear on this point."

Webber's tone remained unchanged as he continued.

"If you look at page forty of your portfolios, you will find that an individual account has been established for the specific investment strategy that your firm has been assigned to carry out. You will draw on these accounts in order to complete the transactions. When the strategies have been fulfilled and have borne fruit, you will make the appropriate deposits into these same accounts. Needless to say, if any of these funds are mishandled or misappropriated, the consequences will be fatal. When you sign the agreement at the back of your portfolio, you will be taking personal responsibility for the handling of these funds.

"You may now ask any questions."

Those seated around the conference table looked at one another in both shock and dismay.

Robert Hanson, CEO of the Silverman and Bach investment bank, spoke first. "What you have laid out here is a strategy for controlling the market in the wake of a terrorist attack or a war in the Middle East, Mr. Webber. Obviously, you believe that within the next thirty days some history-making event will take place that will have a shattering effect on financial markets...on the entire world possibly. Do you mind telling us what kind of intelligence you base these predictions on? Your group has a remarkable record for predicting events before they happen. Shouldn't we know more about what you believe will happen and how you came by this information? We should know more before we make investment decisions for our firms and our favored clients—" Hanson caught himself, remembering Webber's warning. "That is, after we have carried out your instruction and these mysterious events have unfolded."

Even as Hanson was speaking, he was struggling to retain his clarity, to remember what he was trying to say. Strange sensations of fogginess kept overwhelming him.

"I am not at liberty to share that information, Mr. Hanson," Webber replied. "No doubt you will appreciate this simple fact: if you follow our instructions and continue to invest as if you had no knowledge of our protocol, you and your clients will appear innocent of any insider trading in the eyes of the SEC. Meantime, you will be compensated lavishly for any losses you may incur. Your financial statements will emerge from the coming events in a very healthy condition. I have already stated the dire consequences that would occur if you violate our requirement for strict confidentiality."

Leonard Bronfeld, the president of Carter Bellon investment bank, sat back in his chair and said, "You realize that if your predictions prove accurate, you will own a substantial percentage of all energy assets traded on the securities and commodities exchanges worldwide."

"That is correct, Mr. Bronfeld. And that is precisely our intention."

A chill went through the room.

"Mr. Webber," Carlson Benedict, the Chief Executive of Baxion Insurance Group, asked, "should your predictions prove true, how would you counsel those of us in the insurance industry?"

"I am sure you already have strategies in place that are designed to protect you against sudden, unexpected catastrophes. But if I were you, I would follow our instructions to the letter."

Webber turned his attention to the group at large. "Now, if you will turn to the back of your portfolios, you will find an agreement that binds you to the specific actions we have outlined for your firm. By signing it today, you are committing your firms to take the actions we have requested. Once you have signed the agreement, place it on the desk. At that point, you are free to leave."

All twelve executives turned to the back of their portfolios, read the agreement, and signed their contracts. Lucius Webber left the room before any of them had put down their pens.

On the other side of the Atlantic, Roger was briefing Stephen Elliot on his plan to convert the Kleper satellite to the side of the angels. He held up a paper clip and said, "This is what we need, Stephen."

"A paper clip?" Stephen asked, confused.

"We need a computer the size of this paper clip which we will send into space and dock onto the Klepers' new satellite. We'll piggyback our device on an existing rocket, one that's scheduled to launch within the next couple of days. Once the device is in space, it will need its own propulsion to travel from the launch rocket to other rockets, and then to the satellite. Once docked onto the satellite, it must have the capacity to bore into the craft, take over the satellite's control center, and then reprogram the satellite according to our instructions."

Roger then briefed Stephen on Archangel's ability to block the 25 kilohertz frequency and thus silence the warning ping Western Geniuses hear in the presence of Eastern Geniuses. The paper-clip-sized computer had to be capable of restoring the 25 kilohertz frequency and blocking the 24 kilohertz, thus silencing the ping Eastern Geniuses hear in the presence of Western Geniuses.

""It's got to accomplish all of this without the Klepers realizing we managed to pull off such a thing," Roger said. "And we've got to have all of this done quickly. I mean in a couple of days, tops. The lives of Western Geniuses all over the world are at stake, Stephen, including our own." He held out the paper clip. "Can you do it?"

Stephen took the paper clip from Roger and held it at both ends. "We're talking highly complex nanotechnology," he said. "We will also need an extremely small, extremely powerful battery in order to provide the energy needed to propel the paper clip and reprogram a large and complex computer. No doubt the Kleper's technicians have installed a firewall or two against any attempts to gain control of their device."

"Can you do it, Stephen?" Roger asked again.

Stephen paused to consider it and then said yes. "But it's going to be costly, well above our standard allocations. We'll have to go to Helmut Volk for the money."

"Design the thing tonight and let me know how much you need by tomorrow morning."

"You know what Volk is going to say."

Both men knew that Volk would initially reject the request in order to delay the program and gain control of it. He would do that to make Roger beg for the money, thus reminding Roger of Volk's power. In the end, Volk might provide half of what was needed. For Helmut Volk, the substance of the request meant nothing. The issue at the heart of every request for money was power—and he wanted everyone to know that he was the purveyor of that power.

"Yes, I know," Roger said. "Here's what I want you to do. Whatever the cost of the project is, multiply it by ten in your budgetary request."

Stephen was obviously taken aback. "That will be a big number, Chief. He's not going to like it."

"That will give us more than what we will need for the rest of this war with the Klepers," Roger said. "Come up with the plans, and let me worry about Volk."

After Stephen had gone, Roger looked out onto Parliament Square. He considered another aspect of his plan and reached out with his mind to Simone, asking her to come to his office

When she arrived, Simone joined Roger in the sitting area of his office.

"I have a very important assignment for you," he began. "I need you to visit Vladimir Ubitzov by night." By saying "by night," Roger meant that Simone should visit Ubitzov by astral projection.

"I need you to invade his thoughts and extract his plan for assassinating our team. Ubitzov will be under enormous pressure after his failure to kill Max Louri at Laurel Glen. Karl Kleper will be bearing down on him, and probably demanding that he share every single detail of his plan with other Council members. That alone will be humiliating to Ubitzov. But the entire Eastern Council is now under pressure to act quickly. They'll have to formulate a new plan of attack on us and launch that attack before they are completely comfortable. I hope. I have a plan for keeping them off balance.

"With Ubitzov under so much pressure, he'll be easier to read. He'll also be more vulnerable to you inserting ideas into his mind. Can you do this, Simone, with all the other things you're handling?"

"Yes, I can," Simone said. "I'll find him tonight and start monitoring his thoughts on a daily basis."

"Find out how many men will be coming and how he plans to get them here to London. You'll have to know his initial plan and then his back-up plan, which he will likely make after I change our plans. I will change our plans at the last minute in order to keep him off guard and hope that he makes mistakes.

"All of this means that once you've made contact with him, you'll have to stay connected with him right up until their assault on our team."

"Understood. Anything else?"

"I also need you to keep working on freeing Andor Lysenko from Karl Kleper's grasp. Can you do both assignments?"

"Absolutely, no problem." She smiled, having anticipated Roger's question. "I will create an astral double of myself who will work at strengthening Lysenko's shield while I focus my attention on Ubitzov."

"You still never cease to amaze me, Simone." Roger paused and then added, "Your assignment to extract the information from Ubitzov is of the highest priority, but it must also be kept from every other team member, Simone. No exceptions. Understood?"

"Yes, Roger, I do." She got up from her chair. "I will have that information for you in the next day or two."

Roger thanked her as Simone left his office.

It was still the small hours of the morning, the sky as black as night, but Alexander Astrakhan was at his computer working feverishly on a strategy to counteract the effects of global warming. The Council of Western Geniuses had long foreseen the problem and had plotted a series of steps that would be taken, surreptitiously, without Ordinaries knowing, to cool the earth's surface. Some of those steps involved changes in weather patterns that would get the attention of Ordinaries and force them to take responsible action. Other steps were intended to regulate the earth's temperature. Most of these events would appear to be natural disasters, such as tsunamis, earthquakes, and floods, but they would help to cool the earth's atmosphere and protect various species from extinction. Astrakhan and the Council were planning steps that would be taken over the next centuries that would rapidly release carbon dioxide and methane from the atmosphere, thus helping to cool the earth's surface. They would not implement their more overt strategies unless Ordinaries abdicated all responsibility for self-regulating their own behavior. Since that self-regulation seemed unlikely, the Council was prepared to take more drastic steps within the next forty years. Alexander wanted to create an approach that was effective but easily explained as naturally occurring events. In other words, he wanted to be sure Ordinaries never glimpsed the Council's fingerprints on events protecting the earth and the majority of its people.

As he worked, telepathic communications came in by the dozens. He instantly answered every communication while keeping his primary focus on the work at hand. Suddenly, his full attention was diverted from his project by a telepathic communication from Roger. Roger briefed Alexander on the discovery of the Klepers' satellite and its purpose. He then outlined his plan to create a powerful but tiny computer that would take control of the satellite. Time was of the essence, Roger told him, and he could not be slowed down by Volk's standard power plays. If Volk hesitated, he might have to turn to Alexander for the funds.

"Have no fear, Roger," Alexander assured him. "I will get you all the money you need. But try to work with Volk. We don't want to alienate him, for the simple reason that he's not going away and we'll be back at his door in six months with another request for his support."

"I understand, Alex. I'll handle it appropriately."

"As you always do, my dear friend."

With that, the two broke off communication.

Hours later, a gray morning rose over Golden Gables, Maryland. More unseasonably heavy rain was coming. Roxanne had risen early for school and had already had breakfast with her mother. Now alone in her room as she got ready, she once again thought about Andor and the assault on Laurel Glen.

As she had done so many times in the previous three days, she went over every detail of the conversation she'd had with Andor leading up to the raid. She replayed in her mind his every word, the fear in his manner and on his face, the loaded intonations in his voice, and finally—and most troubling to her heart—how he had treated her.

His behavior before the raid did not comport with the cool, calculating actions of an Eastern Council spy. He had been charged with emotion and visibly upset.

"There's so much I want to say to you," he had told her. She believed he had wanted to tell her what he was doing and why he was doing it.

"I wish we weren't sitting here," he had said. "I wish we were someplace else, someplace far away from here so that I could tell you what I really feel."

Before the raid, he had kept looking at his watch. She guessed he had known that in a matter of minutes, she would know for sure that he was a spy for the Eastern Council.

"There's more to me than what you might think," he had said—telling her in advance that he was not doing this because he wanted to.

And then, finally, "You're right about everything."

He wanted her to know he was no longer the same young man who had come to the United States on orders from the Eastern Council. He had changed.

Then why had he gone through with the raid?

And then it hit her. He was being coerced. Those who sent him were threatening him with something. But what? How could they force him to do what he didn't want to do—unless perhaps they were threatening him or people he loved. But his family was in the States with him. Maybe the Eastern Council has agents nearby by or even living with his family.

As she brushed her hair she considered that Andor had been trying to get in touch with her since the assault, but she wasn't ready to speak to him. Not yet. There was more she had to do before she was ready to confront him.

She thought about her next series of moves. When she saw clearly what she had to do, she relaxed a bit and put Andor out of her mind, turning instead to the next disturbing set of questions that pressed against her awareness, like pebbles stuck in her shoe.

Where had Jason Phillips been during the raid? Why hadn't he used his powers to protect the teachers and students? Was he part of the plot that Andor was mixed up in? If so, what role did he have to play in all of this? Was he the one running Andor or threatening him or his family?

She meant to find the answers to those questions.

And then there was that other mystery in all of this, the easiest one of all. Who were this Freddy and his brother? How had they suddenly appeared out of nowhere?

Roxanne smiled. She already knew the answer.

She gathered up her books, went downstairs, and kissed her mother on the cheek. "Tell Daddy I love him," she said, and headed off to school.

Chapter 20
Helmut Volk

reed. That was the word that came to Roger's mind when he considered Helmut Volk. Greed and lust for power. Certainly, Volk looked the part. He was a big man, and even in his expensive blue suit and colorful suspenders, he looked like he was composed of two spheres—his round, bald head sitting on top of his larger circular torso, from which his arms and legs emerged. Though overweight and rotund, his body gave the impression of being hard and strong. There was muscle below the lard. His hazel eyes, partially obscured by horn-rimmed glasses, were small, distant, and imperious. His mouth, thanks to an irregularly shaped upper lip, formed a perennial sneer. When he wanted to intimidate, he would often move his hard, protruding stomach close to a supplicant and then peer down on the person, as if from a mountain top, giving him a look that reduced him to the status of a bug. It was Volk's *you are nothing and I can make you disappear* look that had become something of a signature statement. It was whispered throughout the society of Western Geniuses that Helmut Volk had no heart, but that his blood coursed through his veins by virtue of a Genius-designed pump that had been installed decades before.

No one he ever dared to ask Volk, but if anyone did, he might have said he had no need of a heart. Indeed, he applied his genius to the business of making and managing money. He was among the richest men on earth. His gift for understanding finance and the world's markets was unparalleled. He had homes all over the globe, great modern castles in New York State, Florida, and in the English, French, Swiss, Polish, Hungarian, and Italian countrysides. Though his primary residences were in Manhattan and London, he did most of his business in the British capital, where he advised the Queen of England on her personal fortune. He also managed the wealth of the Belgian and Japanese royal families, for which he was paid enormous sums. He enjoyed the adoration and the accolades his wealthy clients showered on him; and he absolutely reveled in the power he had over them all, especially when the markets turned mercurial and his clients came running to him like frightened children, terrified their fortunes would suddenly shrink.

When his clients arrived at his London doorstep, they were in awe, because Volk's office complex was located in Parliament itself. By edict of the queen, Volk reigned under the great clock tower of Big Ben and behind the grand façade of Parliament. Of course, this proximity to British power seemed to give his guidance the imprimatur of the queen herself. Once he was ensconced in his Parliamentary wing, he was accepted by all who trafficked in those great halls.

As for his role within the Council of Western Geniuses, he held the post of chief financial officer. This meant that every project, secret endeavor, or major initiative that required funding above a department's standard budget had to go through him and receive his approval. This gave him enormous power, despite the puniness of his vision and character.

Volk had no wife or life partner, and no children whom he claimed. In short, he had no personal love—and no allegiance. One of the ways he remained in his position at the Western Council of Geniuses was that he channeled enormous sums of money into the council's bank accounts, which in turn funded important council projects. Not only was he the council's leading accountant, he was also one of its most important benefactors.

Roger and Volk had worked together for the last century. Volk was seventy-year years older than Roger, but he sometimes felt like Roger's junior. Indeed, deep inside his inner world, Volk felt inferior to Roger. Roger possessed what Volk saw as an impregnable dignity, which rested in part on his selfless dedication to the mission and the power of his facts.

That dedication removed him from the personal, which was Volk's entire world. Everything was personal for Volk. Life was a contest, a game of winners and losers. But that approach made him feel small whenever he did business with Roger. In fact, Roger was the only person on earth who could make Volk feel immoral, which was quite an accomplishment. In the presence of any other human being, Volk could not have cared less about the ethics or morality of his actions. Of course, he paid lip service to the values of the Western Council, but his words were empty—and obviously so in Roger's presence.

And now Roger was on his way to Volk's office with yet another allocation request, this one shrouded in more mystery than usual. Roger's explanation for the funding request had been: To halt the spread of Eastern Council hegemony and save the lives of Western Geniuses throughout the world.

Roger strode the grand hallways of Parliament and arrived at the large entrance to Volk's office. Two bodyguards, both Ordinaries, stood outside the office. They recognized Roger, and one of them opened the door to Volk's outer office. Upon entering the ornate chamber, Roger was immediately confronted with the cold countenance of Volk's secretary, Mrs. Flinch, a Genius who drew her bearing and conceit from her master.

"He will be with you momentarily, Mr. Reynolds," she said to Roger without directly looking at him. She busied herself at her computer.

Mrs. Flinch was making a point. Roger had originally scheduled the meeting for 11 a.m., but late the previous night he had requested that the meeting be rescheduled for two hours earlier.

He sat in a chair against the far wall, opposite the imperious Mrs. Flinch. He made no effort to charm her. His shield was up, as was hers, but he could read her every thought nonetheless. Despite her attempts at superiority, she was, like Volk, intimidated by Roger. He didn't kowtow, as did Volk's other supplicants, and his indifference to the trappings of power paradoxically gave him more power. Whenever she saw Roger, Mrs. Flinch felt not like the gatekeeper to a powerful man, but more like, well, a secretary. Roger, on the other hand, was the director of operations for the Western Council. Not only did he outrank her boss, he outranked virtually every other Western Genius.

When she thought about it, it made her feel exceedingly uncomfortable, even guilty, that her boss was keeping this great man waiting.

"Can I get you something, Mr. Reynolds?" she asked him. "A cup of coffee or tea, perhaps?" She regretted the haughty way she spoke to him. She couldn't help it, though; the pattern was too deeply engrained to escape.

"No, thank you, Mrs. Flinch. I'm fine."

"What weather we're experiencing this year. Terrible, wouldn't you say, Mr. Reynolds?" She was trying to get her tone right.

Roger smiled. "Yes, we're going to have to do something about that when we have the time."

Volk telepathically communicated to Mrs. Flinch that he was ready to meet Roger. Before she had a chance to relay Volk's communication, Roger was out of his chair and heading to the large door to Volk's inner office. *Oh, dear*, she told herself, *he can read my every thought. And Mr. Volk's too.* She turned back to her computer in order to distract herself from her embarrassment.

"Roger, so good of you to come by," Volk said, his smile small.

"Thank you, Helmut," Roger said, shaking Volk's hand. "And thanks for being flexible with the meeting time."

Of course, since Roger outranked him, Volk had been forced to accept the 9 a.m. meeting, but courtesy among senior officials among the Western Council of Geniuses required that they both pretend Volk had conveyed a small favor to Roger.

Volk extended his arm and directed Roger to a comfortable sitting area. They both sat in leather Queen Anne chairs that faced each other at a slight angle, a small coffee table between them. Directly in front of them were floor-to-ceiling windows and a pair of glass doors that opened onto a large terrace. Beyond the terrace flowed the River Thames.

"How are things over at the Abbey?" Volk said. He made it sound as if Roger worked in a cell at a convent.

"We're fine, Helmut, thank you," Roger replied, ignoring the subtext.

Mrs. Flinch entered carrying an ornate tea set that she set on the coffee table between the men. As she served the tea, she contritely glanced at Roger in the hope he might give her an approving look, but he was looking out the window, seemingly lost in thought. In fact, Roger was scanning the horizon, looking for the hover jet Willie was piloting. When he spotted the craft, he briefly communicated with Willie and then returned his attention to the room.

"So, this request of yours," Volk said after savoring his first sip of tea. "It's both large and mysterious. Tell me about it. I don't believe you have ever asked for this kind of funding on the basis of so little information."

Roger had no intention of telling Volk all that he knew. Nor would he say what specifically the allocation was for or what his plans were for responding to the Klepers. Still, he had to strike a delicate balance here. Roger knew there were pitfalls with being too oblique with Volk, and even bigger problems with being deceptive. He had to sustain the relationship into the future, but there were ethical reasons to be careful with this man. He and Volk had shared the same foxhole for a long time, and Roger was in no way ready to treat him like anything but a compatriot. Still, dealing with Volk was always a chess match, one made more complicated by the fact that when Volk's shield was up and reinforced, Roger could not read his thoughts. The man was full of secrets and hidden agendas.

So Roger had to be careful. He had already worked out what he would present to Volk, and he would not play his best cards up front.

"The first thing I have to say, Helmut," he began, "is that all of what I'm about to tell you must be held in the strictest of secrecy. No breaches. Not a whisper of this to anyone."

"Of course," Volk said in a tone that implied the request was beneath him.

"The Eastern Council has sent an agent to Washington, DC, in order to bring Senator Stewart Thompson under their influence. They plan to run Thompson for president of the United States. Meantime, they have started a war between Slavistan and its neighbors. Many hundreds have already been killed in all four nations. We believe they will eventually use Thompson to keep the United States and the United Nations from intervening, which would give them a free hand to keep the war going. The purpose of the war, we believe, is to annex the three border nations under Slavistan's rule."

Volk gave Roger a blank look as if to say, *So what?* Roger hadn't told him anything he didn't already know.

"How does this affect us?" he asked. "And what's all the money to be used for?" "We have to intercept their agent, expose Thompson without exposing ourselves, and somehow stop this war."

"How do you propose to do that?"

"At this point, we don't know. We have to expose Thompson when the time is right and get the UN to step in and arbitrate a ceasefire."

"Well, of course, but that does not require any real money. You don't have to come to me for those funds."

"Exactly," Roger said. "And the whole scheme from the Eastern Council seems thin as rice paper, which means something else is going on in the background, something we have only gotten glimpses of."

Volk glanced at his watch.

"Last week," Roger said, "an assassination attempt was made on Max Louri, an old friend of ours."

"I heard about it, little snippets of information. What happened?"

"Max was assigned as my daughter's bodyguard to protect her against a possible attack made by the Klepers' agent, an Eastern Genius teenager named Andor Lysenko who recently transferred into my daughter's high school. It turned out that Max was not attacked by Lysenko, but by a professional assassin, one of our kind. Fortunately, Max survived, as did my daughter."

"I am very glad to hear that," Volk said with blatant insincerity. In truth, he could not have cared less.

"But for two hours," Roger went on, "the warning signal that we typically experience in the presence of an Eastern Genius was silent. No Western Genius on the Laurel Glen campus experienced the warning ping during those two hours. However, we have reason to believe that the

Eastern Council's assassin did experience the warning ping. He was able to track Max, even when Max hid at a remote location."

"How was he able to experience the ping and our side could not?" Volk asked.

"Because the Eastern Council managed to silence the 24 kilohertz frequency, at which we hear the warning ping. They hear their warning ping at 23 kilohertz…so their warning signal was not affected." "How did they do it?"

"They obviously have created some form of technology that they can transport to a specific location, say in a large truck or van that then irradiates a specific geographical area and turns off the ping. Or the technology could have been created on such a small scale that it can be carried around in a person's pocket. We need to investigate the possibilities, counteract the effects, and find a way to destroy the technology."

Volk paused to consider what Roger had said, but then he shook his head. "I'm sorry, Roger, but none of this is getting my juices flowing. Why not just live without the warning signal?"

"By preventing us from hearing the warning ping, they could kill us all. And that's exactly what they mean to do."

Volk was suddenly still. Roger's statement hit closer to home than Volk had expected. Volk was a man of the financial world, of great offices and palaces. He enjoyed the soft life. He was not a man of action. His sword was the money he wielded, and he believed his enormous wealth protected him from the lower instincts of humanity.

Roger continued. "They're planning to restore some version of the old Soviet Union under Eastern Council control. In order to do that, they have to wipe out their main opposition, namely the Western Council. Eliminate the key figures of the Western Council and they will be free to bring the Western world under their control. In short, worldwide domination."

Volk retreated into his own thoughts. Of course, he knew more than he was letting on about the loss of the warning signal. He had informants all over the world and paid handsomely for information that kept him abreast of every important event within the East and West Genius communities. His vast financial reach had led him to do business with the Eastern Council from time to time—via intermediaries, of course. Money crossed all borders and neutralized ideologies. In any case, anyone doing business on the big stage couldn't help but stray into the other side's pond from time to time.

For a moment, he considered his own safety. He had made a lot of enemies over the decades, and he knew that many of them might like to kill him. Without the warning signal, he would indeed be vulnerable. Still, there were ways around the threat. He could beef up his security by hiring a small army of bodyguards, including some Geniuses who could be equipped with all the necessary detection and offensive technology. He might lose some privacy but he could also choose a few beautiful bodyguards, which might give the whole experience some added value.

"Roger, there are contingencies," he began. "And they would be, in my estimation, a great deal cheaper than the enormous funding request you have presented me with. Let me think about it for a few days, maybe a week or two. Perhaps we can dig up more funds in the meantime and give you some portion of the allocation."

Roger was silent. All of the planning for his meeting with Volk had been in preparation for this moment. He had relied on the mole in his office to convey to the Klepers the time of the meeting; he had relied on Simone and Denise to intercept most if not all of the messages the Klepers sent to the mole; he had relied on his team to place cameras throughout Parliament Square and Parliament itself. Even now he was relying on Willie to help him escape what was sure to be a life or death situation.

Before he played his strongest card, he had to give Volk one more chance. He decided to appeal to what little humanity the man had.

"Helmut, you do realize that if I am in any way slowed or hampered in my efforts to destroy the Klepers' technology, many Western Geniuses will die. We're talking about family members here, Helmut. Not just combatants, but spouses and children, innocent people. Do you understand that?"

He looked directly into Volk's eyes, but Volk looked away and reinforced his shield. Once again, Roger had maneuvered him into a moral corner and in the process had gained the upper hand. Roger wasn't begging, he was demanding that Volk give him the money. *How dare you, Reynolds!* Volk shouted inside his own mind. *No one demands money from me. I am the bank. Yes, you outrank me, but I am the one with the money and I control it.*

Volk was enraged, yet he was also conflicted. Roger had held up a mirror and revealed him as small and vain. He hated Reynolds for that.

With effort, he concealed his hatred, took another breath, and found familiar ground. This was still about power, he told himself. And he had the power. He was the one who decided who got the money and how much. Not Roger Reynolds.

"I'm sorry, Roger, but I don't see the need to hurry," he said. "Yes, there are some risks here, but we'll all muddle through. We'll just do what we have to do. Let's take some time and think this whole thing through, shall we?"

Suddenly, Willie broke in to Roger's thoughts. "They're here, Chief. An even dozen, heavily armed and in a hurry. They're in Parliament Square. You've got about four minutes."

"Thank you, Willie," Roger communicated. "I'll meet you on the terrace in three minutes."

"I'll be waiting."

Roger spoke aloud to Volk, his voice conveying urgency. "Helmut, I need to show you something now. May I open your wall computer screen?" Volk reluctantly agreed, as Roger directed a thought to a blank space on the wall to the left of the door. Instantly a large computer screen opened. Roger mentally directed the computer to show the images streaming from the cameras which Roger's team had strategically positioned.

Volk and Roger saw a dozen men, all dressed in commando gear and carrying duffle bags. They were hurrying toward Parliament.

"Who are they?" Volk asked, his tension clearly visible and growing.

"They're assassins and they're coming for you. I just discovered that the Klepers have a mole in my office who has informed them that you and I are to meet today at 11 a.m. They're here to kill you before that meeting. Your assassination is intended to keep you from approving my funding."

Volk quickly scanned the thoughts of the approaching commandos, and he knew Roger was telling the truth. Volk stared at Roger, his panic rising. "What are you going to do about it?"

"I am going to save you and Mrs. Flinch, but I can't guarantee I'll be there the next time they come for you—unless you sign my allocation."

"That's extortion, Roger. You can't do that, not under these circumstances."

"Unless I get those funds, every Western Genius's life is in jeopardy. My family, my team, you, Mrs. Flinch, all of us are about to be killed. The only way I can save them, and you, is by having the funding to combat the Klepers' technology. Now, are you going to be sensible?"

"All right, all right. I'll give you the money. Just get me out of here!"

"Go over to your computer, authorize the allocation, and transfer the funds. I'll get Mrs. Flinch."

Volk ran to his computer. His fingers had never moved so quickly. Finally, he hit the *execute* button. It was done. Meanwhile, Roger ordered Mrs. Flinch to come into Volk's office immediately. He pointed at the glass doors and with a single thought blew them open.

"Quickly, to the terrace, both of you," he told them telepathically.

Mrs. Flinch was paralyzed with shock. "Let's go, Marjorie!" Volk yelled as he took her by the arm. She came to her senses as the two ran onto the terrace.

Seemingly out of nowhere, a Genius craft—part jet, part hovercraft—descended on the terrace and floated just above its floor. Mrs. Flinch, Volk, and Roger hopped into the bird as the twelve commandos burst into Volk's office. With a mental command, Roger ordered his laptop to release an electronic pulse that blew all the commandos against the wall and at the same time destroyed all the hard drives within Volk's office. The gunmen were stunned and disoriented. Gradually, they rose from the floor and staggered out onto the terrace. A few managed to get off several shots at the departing jet, but the craft was out of reach.

"Wooweee!" Willie yelled as he turned the ship south along the Thames. "I love this job."

Chapter 21
Andor and Senator Stewart Thompson

O n the other side of the Atlantic, Andor Lysenko sat in the well-appointed office of Laurel Glen headmaster Winthrop B. Rutherford and listened to US Senator Thompson sing his praises. He wondered if he was going to make it through the meeting without getting sick to his stomach.

Andor sat on a yellow leather sofa next to Thompson's chief aide, Martin Chipulsky, To Andor's right sat Headmaster Rutherford and directly opposite him was the senator. Joining them was the senator's secretary, Molly Handwringer, a buxom brunette whose ample assets were nearly bursting from her white blouse.

"Andor, you are a symbol of today's youth," the senator was saying. He was a tall and big-boned man. His jowls hung like saddlebags and his wide mouth moved like a puppet's, seemingly independent from the rest of his face.

"Andor, in you I see the future of our world, a young man who was raised under an oppressive regime … Yes, I know your country is experimenting with democracy and a free-market system, but you're still a long way from the freedoms we enjoy in the United States of America. But Andor, you're an amalgam of so many great Slavistani, European, and American values. You're like the Mississippi River. Have you heard of the Mississippi River, Andor? Of course you have. The Mississippi is a great river that a lot of smaller rivers flow into. You're like that, Andor. Your background, a great background with lots of different ethnic groups, lots of different visions, lots of different experiences, all flowing into the great river that is you. And I want you to help me help America, Andor. I want you to help me help America see what's possible again."

Andor looked over at Martin Chipulsky and read his thoughts.

Oh God, here he goes again. Mississippi River. How many times have I told him he's got to stop using that asinine metaphor. This is why he needs me as his speechwriter because the guy's stuck in the eighth grade. Look at Handwringer. What a name. She's drooling over him like some kind of wide-eyed cow.

Andor glanced at Handwringer and saw Chipulsky was right. She was staring at Thompson as if he were John Kennedy to her Marilyn Monroe.

But when Andor read her thoughts, he realized her look was anything but sincere.

How much longer do I have to put up with this bull, before he introduces me to Tom Hanks and Mel Gibson like he promised me? I'm not getting any younger and having to be in bed with this guy, while he grunts and spits—it's like lying under a water buffalo. I'm an actress, for God's sake. How long do I have to keep pretending I'm his secretary? If he doesn't introduce me to Steven Spielberg in the next couple of months, I'm outta here.

Then Andor looked back at Thompson and read his thoughts.

I am going to ride this kid's fifteen minutes of fame all the way to the White House. This kid is perfect. He's good looking, naïve, innocent. I can use him as a poster child to remind Americans that we cannot engage in another war. Not after Iraq and Afghanistan, not after trillions of dollars poured down the drain and wasted. Don't forget to mention the deaths. Play up the lives lost, including those of our young people. I can use this kid as a symbol of young people everywhere and how war is not the answer, and all that crap. The American people are ripe for this kid and the antiwar message I can create around him.

All I need is a good domestic issue to go along with this, something to get this damn economy to pick up, something I can sell as a source of jobs, or better yet, a way I can blame the bad economic mess on my opponents. I'll have both the foreign and domestic fronts covered. I'll get the nomination and once I've got that, I'm all the way home.

Thompson turned to the headmaster. "Could you allow me to speak to Andor privately? Would that be okay with you, Headmaster Rutherford? And is that okay with you, Andor?"

Andor looked over at Rutherford, who was only too happy to oblige the senator. "Sure," Andor said with a shrug.

"Of course, Senator," Rutherford said. "Use my office and take all the time you need. I'll be just down the hall. Give a holler if you need me."

When Rutherford left the room, Thompson looked over at Andor and said, "Son, I've had you checked out. You're way ahead of your classmates in every one of your classes, they tell me. You're a smart boy, do you know that? Of course you do. What I'm getting at is that I'd like you to travel with me from time to time, just over the next six months or so. All the trips would be short, a couple of days, and everything would be paid for by my office. You wouldn't have to spend a dime. You'd be my protégé, sort of. You'd meet lots of famous people, lots of movie stars. Like Tom Hanks. Have you heard of him? Of course you have. Chuck Norris. I bet you've seen his TV show, *Walker, Texas Ranger*, right? Of course I'm right. Andor, you can have a very important role in helping people in this country, and in yours. We don't want America getting involved in Slavistan's internal affairs. That would be wrong, Andor. We don't have a right to meddle in your politics, do we? Of course not. You can help keep us from making that mistake."

Thompson lowered his voice. "By helping me, you can help save the lives of thousands of Americans and Slavistanis. Now that's important stuff, young man. I'm offering you a history-making role. Are you up for playing an historical role? What do you say, son?"

Andor had known for months that this moment was coming. His handlers had instructed him exactly what he had to say. Early in his training, he had looked forward to this moment with a certain thrill. Now he wasn't sure he could get the words out without throwing up his lunch on this overstuffed, overripe glutton.

"Yes, sir, I think I can help you in your mission," he said.

The well-rehearsed words echoed in his head, but it seemed as if he were having an out-of-body experience, as if someone else had uttered the words that left such a foul taste in his mouth.

Darkness fell upon his soul. The image of his parents came to his mind. They were calling out to him and urging him to come home. Then he saw Roxanne walking alone in a wood. He wanted to run to her, but then he was back in the headmaster's office and looking into the eyes of the devil, with whom he had just agreed to travel. He felt an overpowering urge to run...and to cry. But where could he go? And to whom could he run?

Andor felt as if he were experiencing a low-grade electrocution. His body and mind were wracked by emotional turmoil that flowed through him in waves of electrical currents. In the bearable moments, which were all too fleeting, he could lose himself in his computer, or on long walks, or in the complexities of mathematical proofs that had eluded Ordinary mathematicians for centuries. But as the turmoil rose and the electrical dial that seemed buried in his stomach was turned up, his mind became filled with imagery—Roxanne's hand on his knee, her radiant beauty the night the two went out to a movie, the pleasure of anticipation as he hurried to the cafeteria or the snack bar to have lunch with her. Inevitably, such memories pushed the turmoil to peaks of intensity and his mind to the edge of panic. He wanted to run, but there was no escape. Like a condemned man strapped to an electric chair, he was forced to accept his fate and the voltage that flowed through his veins and exploded in his heart.

Everything was made worse once Andor started traveling with the senator. He would stand on a stage with Thompson as he pleaded his case before hundreds and sometimes thousands of people. Andor knew many of them were bored to tears, but others were caught up in the grip of pandemonium as they waved signs that said, Thompson for President, and No More War!, and "Stay out of Slavistan!" There was even the occasional, "America First, the Rest of the World Can Go to Hell!"

The war in Slavistan was now on the front pages of newspapers throughout the nation. Experts on Slavistan and foreign affairs weighed in on CNN, Fox News, and the nightly television news broadcasts. The usual array of hawks called for UN sanctions against Slavistan and, if necessary, US support for the small border nations under attack. On the other side, a growing antiwar movement was springing up throughout the country. Senator Thompson was among its most popular voices.

Today, Thompson and his staff were in Phoenix, Arizona, suffering the heat of the southwestern sun while the senator tried to work everyone in the audience into a sweat over any sort of aggressive action by the United States. At least that was his ostensible reason for being there. His ultimate goal was to gain support for his inevitable run at the presidency.

They had arrived in Phoenix on a chartered jet around six the previous night. Even before the plane had taken off from Washington—before Thompson had even sat down—he asked the flight attendant to bring him a double whiskey. The drinking continued through the flight and by the time they arrived, Thompson was snoring loudly. When the plane descended into the Phoenix airport, the light was still bright enough to make out the Arizona desert. Andor had never seen a desert before, and for him arriving in Phoenix was like landing on the lunar surface. It was intensely foreign to him and utterly disorienting. The landscape was dark brown, mixed with shades of grays and hints of yellow and red from the low-hanging sun. He was already suffering from severe homesickness and a broken heart, and the sight of the parched and barren desert made his loneliness even more unbearable.

As he listened to Thompson, Andor realized he was caught between worlds. The little boy in him wanted to be held in his mother's arms and have his father tell him that everything would be all right. The man in him longed for Roxanne, to tell her how much he loved and needed her. He also knew he must find a way out of the web of lies that had trapped him. But how? He fought to stay focused on Thompson, knowing that every so often Karl Kleper tuned into him and his thoughts. *Stay focused on this overly ambitious fool*, he told himself. That way another part of his mind, which he kept hidden in the background of his consciousness, could plot a way out.

Thompson was working the crowd with his usual arsenal of empty clichés. Politician-speak, Andor called it. By Politician-speak Andor meant the language of lies, spoken with an actor's gift for false sincerity.

"We cannot afford another war," the sorry excuse for a public servant was saying. "Forty-four-hundred American men and women lost their lives in Iraq. So far, nearly two thousand Americans have been killed in Afghanistan. We're $14 trillion in debt, folks. The war in Iraq cost us $790 billion. Afghanistan has cost us $442 billion. Where's the money for another war going to come from? That's right—China! We cannot afford to borrow more money so that we can go to war again. At some point, we've got to say, 'Enough! 'Stop the bloodshed, turn off the money hose!'"

Loud applause rolled over the crowd. Little groups within the audience chanted, "No more war!" The senator's staff had planted people throughout the crowd to chant, "Thompson for president" at specific moments in his speech, and right on cue came the latest well-rehearsed belch of spontaneity from the crowd: "Thompson for President! Thompson for President! Thompson for President!" Thompson paused to let the slogan sink into the consciousness of the crowd.

"Now, as chairman of the senate foreign relations committee and a senior member of the senate banking committee, I assure you that I will not vote to send another American to a foreign war." His voice rose, as if he were possessed by a divinely inspired vision of a better world. "And I will not allocate another dollar that might involve us, directly or indirectly, in a foreign war. I will not allow our brave men and women to sacrifice their lives, to shed another drop of blood on foreign soil. We must bring our soldiers home and turn our talents and resources back to the work of rebuilding the United States of America!"

Wild and thunderous applause erupted. More chants of "Thompson for President!" were heard throughout the crowd. Thompson waited for the noise to rise to a crescendo, but it died down more quickly than he had hoped and then passed altogether. He resumed his speech.

"Today I brought with me a very special guest, a young man from a nation about to be torn apart by war. My guest is Andor Lysenko and he is a native of the great nation of Slavistan. Andor is going to tell you firsthand what US involvement in Slavistani affairs would mean to his country. Andor, why don't you come on up here and say a few words to this great American crowd" Thompson gave Andor a great, toothy smile, his fleshy cheeks flushed with too much booze and sun.

Andor strode to the podium. Thompson shook his hand as if the two had just met and then Thompson walked to the back of the dais and took a seat, leaving Andor alone at the podium. Andor adjusted the microphone downward and began his speech.

His talk had been written largely by Thompson's speechwriter, Martin Chipulsky. Andor had modified it, especially in places where Chipulsky was channeling his inner Thompson, infusing the speech with too many flourishes that were pompous, overbearing, and way too American.

"In Slavistan," he began, "for a very long time, we had no voice in our country's government. We lived under an oppressive dictatorship."

Someone in the crowd yelled, "No to dictatorship!" Andor ignored the fool.

"Now, we have a growing democracy. It's still a young democracy and some of the vestiges of the old Soviet system are still in place, but we have a free-market system that is starting to take hold and we have the vote. And we have a population of young people who want to turn our nation in a new direction. The young people of Slavistan are using the levers of power to gain greater control of our future. That future can be brighter than it was for our parents and their parents. The older generation knows this and so they are supporting young people to create a new Slavistan.

"If the United States uses its power to coerce the United Nations into imposing sanctions on Slavistan, many things in our country will change. Goods that you take for granted, like bread, butter, meats, and cheese, will be severely limited and the free market will dry up. The black market, which has always had a powerful grip on our economy, will become even stronger. Crime will increase and the government will use that rise in crime as an excuse to crack down on the fledgling democracy that we now possess. That crackdown will be especially hard on the young people of Slavistan, who represent the greatest threat to the old guard and their ambitions to return to the Soviet state.

"Sometimes we in Eastern Europe and those of us who live east of the Urals marvel at the power of the United States. We think about how much good can be done and what kind of new world we could inherit if the United States supports our democratic system.

"You Americans can do that by believing in the young people of Slavistan and our ability to work out our own problems. Be patient with us. Support us with your faith in democracy and your belief that people of good will can work out their differences. A new generation is rising in Slavistan, and with it will come many new policies that will bring a more peaceful and cooperative country. If America acts aggressively, that movement will be crushed. You can help us by giving us time and maintaining your faith in us. Thank you all."

Polite applause and sporadic cheering arose from the crowd. Someone yelled, "Yes to the young people of Slavistan!" Then there was more polite applause. Andor turned from the podium and resumed his seat. Thompson was eager to get back in front of the crowd.

"There you have it, folks," he said. "That young man would be among those we would be shooting at, dropping bombs on, and strafing from F-16s. You know, war looks a lot different to us when there's a human face on it. That young man is the face of Slavistan!"

Full-throated cheers went up in the crowd, along with more cries of "Yes to the young people of Slavistan!" and "No more war" and "Thompson for President!"

"Thank you all for coming today. Thank you. Thank you."

More applause and cheering followed, which Thompson acknowledged by waving his arms and smiling broadly. A local politician took over at the podium, thanking the senator and addressing the crowd as many headed for their cars. Thompson strode to the back of the dais and said to Chipulsky, "Let's get out of here. I need a drink."

Chapter 22
Shield and Sword, Operation Paper Clip

B ack at Westminster Abbey, palpable tension hung over those gathered at the round table. Everyone knew that Ubitzov's assassination team would be coming at them soon.

Roger had already handed out assignments days before and was now getting progress reports. Willie Mayfield and Felix Novak were working on a plan, code named Shield and Sword, to counter the hit team. Simone was trying to free Andor from Karl Kleper's telepathic grasp, a project they named Astral Dummy. Meanwhile, Stephen and Denise were working on Operation Paper Clip.

For all the tension in the room, Roger seemed completely relaxed, but the team knew that was characteristic of him. The more intense a situation got, the more he was in his element. It was when things were quiet that he became restless.

On the round table in front of each member of the team was a black leather pouch containing a small gadget, which the members inspected and then returned to the pouch. Roger began the meeting by asking for Willie and Felix's report.

"We're assuming," Willie began, "that the warning ping will be eliminated soon, which will give Ubitzov and his team the upper hand. The most vulnerable places and times of the day for any of us will be our trips back and forth between home and our offices.

"Here at the Abbey, we're safe. Our security systems will alert us to the presence of any intruder. We're also safe in our homes. Felix and I have seen to that. We've installed bulletproof windows and doors, sensors, cameras, and listening devices, as well as back-up electrical sources that can't be tampered with from outside the house. We've also installed technology that will take offensive action should anyone attempt to get into our homes."

"What kind of offensive technology?" Simone asked.

"Well, you know those electrical fly zappers that people hang in their backyards? If someone enters your house with a weapon or with a physiological signature that indicates violent intentions—sweat level, heightened hormones, that sort of thing—he's going to have a lot in common with the fly that gets caught in one of those electrical traps."

"Oh, I see," Simone said. "So I better be careful what I watch on my television." "The technology is highly specific. You're not going to trigger it inadvertently, even if you're really worked up over a big football match on your telly, darling. But just to be on the safe side, chamber music is safer than Rambo, okay? At least until all of the fuss with the Klepers is over."

Everyone smiled as Willie continued. "For our commutes, Felix and I have worked out a little seduction of sorts. We want to draw Ubitzov and his team into attacking us in places where they think they have the upper hand, but where we will have the advantage."

Willie telepathically triggered a switch in the table that displayed individual holographs before each member of the team.

"Those holographs depict your respective routes to and from the offices here at the Abbey. That route is shown in yellow. We're asking that you pair up in twos or threes and travel together along the blue route, which is lighting up now." A blue artery appeared within the holograph.

"Simone and Denise will come to work and go home together along the blue route that appears on their holographs. They can see each other off at their doorsteps. Stephen and Roger will also travel together. Chief, if you don't mind, you'll drop Stephen off at his place before proceeding home. Felix and I will travel together to and from our respective domiciles. If you have any shopping to do, do it together and along those blue routes. Felix and I have stocked significant supplies of food, water, and other essentials in our supply room and kitchen here.

"No one is to deviate from these blue travel routes for the duration of our battle with the Eastern Council.

"Of course, we're counting on Stephen and Denise's little gizmo to turn the Klepers' satellite in our favor. But if the gizmo doesn't work, we still have a viable plan to overtake the Eastern hit team.

"If you look again at your holographs," Willie continued, "you'll see small red dots appear along the blue routes. Felix and I have determined that these are the places where you are most vulnerable to attack. We've made contingency plans for each of these places, meaning they are now places where we want the Eastern team to attack us."

Willie then telepathically sent each of them a series of images that revealed his and Felix's plans to protect them. The tension rose to a new level of intensity.

"Of course, we must be vigilant," Willie said. "We're surmising that Ubitzov's goon squad will attack us at the red dots, but we could be wrong. Remember, we're most vulnerable in crowds, where their assassins can sneak up on us from behind without warning. Or conversely, in wide open spaces, where there's no cover from a sniper attack. You must keep your distance from groups of people. Walk around them, but you must also walk along routes where there is cover from sniper fire. The blue line routes will keep you free from crowds and give you plenty of places to duck into if you sense danger or someone takes a shot at you. Even when walking around groups, stay on the blue line. We all have to stay on our guard. Right?"

The holographs disappeared and as Roger thank Willie and asked Denise and Stephen how Operation Paper clip was going.

Denise fielded the question.

"The paper clip nanocomputer is completed and operational," Denise said. "We've also made a tiny rocket that will house the device and will essentially hopscotch on the backs of existing craft in order to find its way to Archangel."

"Not sure what you mean, Denise," Willie said.

"Well, we feared that if we fired a rocket at Klepers' satellite, the Eastern Council would instantly know what we were up to and take evasive measures. So using any launch that had not been scheduled months ago was out of the question. Instead, we came up with a kind of Rube Goldberg series of steps that will bring our package to the satellite without, I sincerely hope, alerting Eastern COG.

"First, we conceal the paper clip computer in a small rocket that will be hidden on a small weather balloon that's scheduled for liftoff tomorrow from the Kennedy Space Center in Florida. Taking into account all relevant factors—air currents, the weight of the balloon, the added weight of the rocket, the rotation of the earth, the balloon will be over Baltimore, Maryland, at 18:35 GMT at an altitude of 1318.5 meters, or 18 miles.

"An American XVS88 rocket carrying another secret US Star Wars satellite will be launched on Saturday from Edwards Air Force Base in California, at 13:00 GMT. At 18:35 GMT, it will be over New York City, exactly 230 kilometers from our weather balloon. The rocket containing our paper clip will fire at 18:05 GMT and traverse the 250 kilometers, rendezvousing with the rocket at 18:35.

"The composition of the rocket's surface material is highly magnetic and adhesive so that it will adhere to the surface of any rocket or satellite.

"The US missile will carry Paper Clip to an elevation of 881 kilometers above the earth. When it is over Reykjavik, Iceland, the rocket will fire again and intercept Slavistani Spy Satellite RU488, proceeding on its current orbit. At 23:07 GMT, the Slavistani spy satellite and our little package will be 44 kilometers above Klepers' bird. At that point, our little engine will fire again and make a soft landing on Archangel. The landing will be so soft, in fact, that it will not trip any sensors embedded in the satellite.

"Once Paper Clip is safely aboard the satellite, Stephen will order Paper Clip's nanocomputer to identify the location of Archangel's computer brain. Then a set of highly corrosive chemicals contained within Paper Clip will be released. Our device will bore through to

Archangel's main computer, where it will remain until Stephen orders it to reprogram Archangel to restore 25 Kilohertz and block the 24 kilohertz wave length.

"At that point, 25 kilohertz will come through to us loud and clear, while 24 kilohertz will be silent. And then the predators will become the prey."

Denise raised her hands in the air and crossed her fingers.

Roger smiled. "And how are we getting Paper Clip and its rocket to the weather balloon?"

"Willie and Felix will bring it to the Kennedy Space Center tonight, clandestinely attach it to the weather balloon, and be back by early morning," Denise said.

"Willie, Felix, I'm sure you've checked out their security? What's it like?" Roger asked.

"Remarkably light," Felix said. "It won't be any trouble. It's not an important balloon for them, just part of the National Weather Service update. Security's nothing out of the ordinary, just a couple of sleepy guards."

"Okay," Roger said. "But let's act like we're breaking into Fort Knox, okay, gentlemen?"

"Will do, Chief," Willie said.

"Thank you, Denise and Stephen," Roger said. He looked around the table. "Okay, folks. We have our marching orders. Let's go."

As everyone filed out of the room, Roger telepathically asked Simone to meet him in his office. The two sat down before the tall windows and watched the rain fall.

Simone knew why Roger wanted to speak to her. He wanted to know what progress she was making on freeing Andor from Kleper's grasp. Obviously, he didn't want to share the information with other team members who were not privy to her work. That could mean only one thing: Roger feared the team had been infiltrated by a spy.

"How are things going with the boy?" he asked.

"I'm currently strengthening Lysenko's shield," Simone said. "I hope that by making the layers of his field more dense, we can protect him against Kleper's thoughts and mind control."

Roger asked how she was doing that.

"Through astral projection, I've been with Andor at night while he's asleep. I've been sending the boy lots of life energy through a constant stream of supportive thoughts. In essence, love. It's one of the things that happen when people pray for each other. They send each other thoughts of love, bundles of life energy that enhance their loved one's field and thus their overall life condition.

"Kleper has shaped his thoughts into tentacle-like structures that are embedded in the body's field, especially at the etheric and astral layers. Through those tentacles, he is able to read Lysenko's mind and feed him a constant stream of orders.

"I've been utilizing this life energy to boost the boy's etheric and astral layers, as well as the outer layers of his field. That's creating a kind of energetic container around the boy's body. I hope to remove Kleper's tentacles from Lysenko's etheric and astral layers and install them into a dummy field at the periphery of Lysenko's field. Kleper will think he's still connected to the boy, but Lysenko will be free to experience his own thoughts and feelings."

Roger shook his head. "What's the difference between etheric and astral?"

"As you know, the energy field is made up of multiple layers. The etheric layer is the part of the field that is closest to the physical body and is embedded in the nervous system. Its purpose is to give life energy— what the Chinese call chi, the Greeks called *pneuma*, and the Indians call prana—to every cell in the body. The astral body is the emotional body, which is farther out in the field but is still connected to the etheric and physical bodies. The layers of the field that are even farther out connect us to different dimensions of consciousness, of life, and even different universes. What some Ordinaries refer to as string theory.

"I am attempting to strengthen Lysenko's field at every layer, especially the etheric and astral layers. This will give him a greater sense of self and freedom from Kleper. By strengthening the outer layers, I'm also trying to create a buffer in the boy's field that will protect him against Kleper's thoughts and mind control. The challenge is that I have to keep Kleper from knowing he's disengaging from Lysenko. Hence, the creation of the dummy field, a kind of container around the boy's field—which I hope will make Kleper feel he's still in control of the boy, even when he's not."

"How soon before he experiences some degree of freedom from the Klepers' influence?" Roger asked.

"That should already be happening. But give me two more nights, and he should be feeling much more like himself."

"Has there been any progress breaking into Kleper's communication with the boy?"

"No. Kleper's coded communication is virtually unbreakable. This approach is the only way I can save him from Kleper's control."

"I suppose I don't have to mention to you that all of what you just told me is to be shared with no one else." Roger said.

"Of course", Simone said. "I understand your concerns."

Roger nodded. "I'm sure you do."

Chapter 23

Roxanne Meets with Jason Phillips, And Writes to Roxanne

That morning, Roxanne was out of her house early. The weather was good for a change—the sky a faraway autumn blue, the air cool, the sun a crystalline yellow. She parked her car in the student parking lot and then walked over to the teacher's lot. She sat in a sunny spot on the grass to wait.

She didn't have to wait long. Even before she saw him, Roxanne felt the ping of Dr. Phillips's presence as he pulled up in his silver Acura. She was already walking toward him before he got out of his car. They greeted each other out loud, and Roxanne asked if she could talk to him for a few minutes.

"Yes, of course. Let's go inside. My classroom will be empty for another half hour."

Roxanne kept her shield up to prevent him from knowing her thoughts. For his part, Dr. Phillips seemed relaxed and glad to have an opportunity to talk to her. In his classroom, he closed the door as she sat in a desk at the front of the room. He pulled up his own chair and sat down in front of her.

"You know, I've wanted to talk to you," he said, smiling. "I've heard wonderful things about you from my old boss, Alexander Astrakhan.

Of course, I've known both of your parents for a long time. Alexander thinks the world of you."

"Thank you," Roxanne said. "My parents love and respect him. And I like him too."

"I do have some concerns that I wanted to share with you," Dr. Phillips said, and lapsed into telepathic communication.

"This is a bit sensitive," he communicated, "so please bear with me for a moment. I'm concerned about the persona you maintain at school. Playing dumb requires a lot of courage and character, and I admire you for it. But at the rate you're going, none of your teachers will pass you, and even if you start to do good work, some will doubt you're doing it yourself. They'll believe you're cheating or copying someone else's work. So here's what I recommend: request tutoring from a few of your teachers, especially the ones who have the greatest doubts about you. You know who they are. If they know you're getting help and that you're trying, and then you get good grades, they'll attribute it to your diligence and their teaching ability and none will be the wiser."

"You're right," Roxanne said telepathically. "I feel like I have taken this act a little too far. I've sort of boxed myself in. I'll get some tutoring and pull my grades up."

Dr. Phillips relaxed. "Good. It's hard to be one of us and living in the world of Ordinaries. But don't worry, it gets easier, especially after you're out of high school."

Roxanne smiled. "The truth is, I can't wait to get out of here."

Dr. Phillips laughed. "I understand. Now what did you want to talk to me about?"

"Well, what I have to say is also sensitive, and I wouldn't blame you if you didn't want to answer, but I'm troubled and just felt I had to ask you some questions."

"Of course, anything. What is it?"

"Well, what I need to ask you is, why didn't you use your powers to help us during the raid? We needed you."

A shadow descended over Phillips's face, and Roxanne felt him close off his shield. She sensed a powerful hostility arise within his field. His expression, which had been open and welcoming to Roxanne, became guarded as his mouth tightened and his eyebrows furrowed. As he looked at her with piercing eyes, she immediately put up her shield, preventing him as best she could from knowing her thoughts and sensing her rising fear. No sooner had she raised her shield than she felt Phillips's mind attempt to probe her inner world. The mental act was aggressive and ominous, even assaulting.

"Why do you ask?" he asked, apparently unable to read her thoughts.

Roxanne became afraid and defensive. "Well, we needed your help," she communicated. She could feel her confidence draining from her. She wished she hadn't come at all. "Maybe you were not feeling well, or something, or maybe you weren't even on campus." She was offering him, and herself, an easy way out of the conversation.

Phillips got up from his chair and turned his back to her. Ironically, the gesture added to the sense of menace. Beneath his black sport coat, his back seemed to swell and hunch over, as if he were undergoing some kind of bizarre transformation. Roxanne looked quickly at the door. He'd closed it. Had he locked it? She felt an impulse to run, but before she could get up, Phillips turned.

"Right before the raid," he said, "I experienced a severe headache. I went to my car and laid down, and I fell asleep. I slept through the raid."

"That's so terrible, Dr. Phillips," she said, trying to placate him. "Perhaps you need more rest."

"Yes, that may be what I need."

Even telepathically, his tone was flat and distant. Again, he gave her a hard stare, as if he were looking deeply into her inner world, searching for something.

"Well, Dr. Phillips, thanks for talking to me. I should be getting to class." Again, she looked toward the door and this time saw students out in the hallway. "Oh, look, the hallway is full. I should be going."

She hurried to the door, threw it open, and made her escape.

Just after eleven that night Andor was back in his bedroom in Silver Spring. After Senator Thompson had had lunch in Phoenix with a group of potential donors to his presidential campaign, he and his entourage had flown back to Washington. Andor was home in time for a late dinner. Now, he prepared himself for what he was about to do. In a desk drawer he found a pen and paper. He placed both on the surface of his desk and then walked toward one of the two windows of his room, which was on the second floor of the small house.

He looked out the window onto the street below. It was a working-class neighborhood of mixed ethnicity; people who worked hard every day and watched television at night. Most of them were early to bed and early to rise, which meant that by 11 p.m., a deep quiet had fallen over the neighborhood. The street in front of Andor's house was illuminated by streetlights that cast a hard, gray glow upon parked cars and front yards. He could see some children's toys strewn on the ground in front of a couple of houses across the street. A tricycle sat in the middle of a small patch of grass. A doll lay on her back not far from a ball and a toy fire engine. These were the objects of sunlight and children's laughter, but in the shadowy darkness of night, they seemed possessed by a spectral glow, as if they had become the toys of phantoms.

Spirits were the theme of the night, for in a corner of Andor's room, completely invisible, stood Simone's astral presence, her arms extended, and her hands radiating a river of light. It flowed into Andor's every cell; it surrounded his body like a brilliant halo; it encased him in love.

An adept with an awakened eye could see a portal—or opening to another dimension. From that aperture flowed another river of light, this one viscous. It cascaded onto Simone, who directed it to Andor, imbuing him with the viscous light. The light filled and illuminated his field, surrounding him in golden fibers. Simone sculpted the mass of illuminated fibers, moving them here and there, closing holes in the field, and directing them to individual organs and to various layers of Andor's electromagnetic field. Meanwhile, she removed oddly shaped objects that cast no light at all. Just the opposite, like black holes, they absorbed the light into their own darkness. She worked rapidly, aware that time was short.

She collected more energy from the river of light and wove a dense shell around Andor. The shell was thicker than the light of his field. Now she created layers of light and wove them into the shield, adding thickness and density, giving the shield a brilliance that was nearly visible to the naked eye.

To Simone's awakened sight, she could see Kleper's dark poisonous thoughts reaching into Andor's field, very like tentacles from an evil octopus. She reached into his field and pulled Kleper's tentacles away from Andor's etheric body. She was careful not to free Andor entirely, an act that would immediately alert Kleper to the loss of contact with his pawn. Instead, she attached the tentacles into the thick, illuminated shield. They settled in and began spewing forth their river of inky-dark poison.

The shield of woven light was so bright and so multilayered that Kleper's evil thoughts could not fully penetrate into Andor's inner field. The layers of light were moving like the river, taking Kleper's commands away from Andor's etheric body and nervous system.

Simone could see that Andor was gaining strength from the life force she poured into him. She watched as Andor, as if sensing his newfound independence, closed his eyes and allowed his emotions to rise to the surface and engulf his awareness. His intention was to become engulfed in emotion in order to seal off his inner thoughts from Kleper and give him some time to complete his plan for that night.

Images of his mother and father came to mind. His father was a diabetic who, when he didn't get proper care, quickly became weak and frail. Without adequate insulin, he would die. Andor's mother was loving and caring, but was given to bouts of anxiety and nervous tension. Both were vulnerable in their own ways. And now they were being held in some dank prison cell in Siberia, wasting away. He knew his father was close to death and his mother close to a nervous breakdown. Unless they were freed and given proper medical care, neither would last much longer. He felt completely powerless to help them. His tormented soul reached out to them from the other side of the world.

"Mom, I am so sorry. I love you so much," he said to the night. "Dad, I love you. Take care of each other. Hold on." As a young Genius, though, his powers of telepathy were insufficient to communicate with people on the other side of the world.

He said no more to them, not wanting to alert Kleper to any hint of his plan. Instead, he allowed himself to be engulfed even further by his emotions.

He saw himself as a boy in his village in southern Slavistan. His father was teaching him to ride a bicycle, which he had just purchased for Andor for his birthday. The bicycle was red and had tassels flowing from its handles. He and his father were in the street in front of their house, a street not very different from the one he was now looking out on. His father had one hand on the back of the bicycle seat as Andor, barely five years old, pedaled awkwardly.

"Yes, yes," his father said to him. "Keep pedaling, Andor."

His father ran next to the bike, holding the seat, as Andor pedaled, unaware of anything but this new and strange motion that his legs and feet were learning.

Andor pedaled furiously, the motion becoming more familiar with every rotation of his legs and feet. He was well down the street when he said, "Dad, I'm riding my bicycle! I'm riding, Dad."

He turned to look at his father, but no one was there. The realization that he was riding by himself surprised and frightened him. His arms stiffened and his grip on the handlebars tightened. He turned the wheel to his left, toward a neighbor's grassy front yard.

"Dad!" he called out. "How do I stop?"

The bike lurched onto the grass, listed, and he fell on the soft earth. Andor smiled brightly and looked back at his father, who was standing well down the street. His father shot his hands up into the air in victory and yelled, "You did it! You rode the bicycle, Andor!"

Now, as he stood before his window, Andor couldn't help but smile through his tears at the memory. More, he thought. The emotion had to take him over. It had to engulf him so that Kleper would detect only the raging emotion and not his intention, which lay below the storm of his feelings.

He remembered the day that four of Victor Grozny's goons stormed into his house and took his parents captive. A fifth man, one of Kleper's Genius lieutenants, a man named Kovalev, followed behind Grozny's thugs, clearly enjoying the terror of Andor's parents. Tall and broad, Kovalev had a low brow and a jaw like one end of a brick. He was a former Slavistani boxer and now one of the Klepers' enforcers.

It was dinnertime when the thugs burst into the house. Andor's mother still had her apron on; his father had tucked a napkin into his shirt at the neck, as he prepared for the meal. They had no idea what was happening, why these men had burst into their home.

Andor had felt the ping of Kovalev's presence as he approached the house and had maybe a second's worth of warning before the thugs kicked in the Lysenko front door. As the four men grabbed his parents, Andor flew into a panic. He turned to Kovalev and communicated telepathically to him.

"Karl Kleper told me that if I cooperated, he'd leave them alone," he said to the big man. "He promised me that if I went along with his plan, no harm would come to them."

"Let's just say that these are Kleper's insurance policy, boy," Kovalev said, not a trace of mercy in his voice. "You step out of line and they're both dead. Not a pleasant death, either."

Kovalev hovered over Andor. "I could kill them both right now with a single thought and not bat an eyelash. To me, they are nothing but ants. Got it? You do as Karl Kleper says or I step on a couple of ants."

They pulled Andor's parents out of the house and shoved them into a black van that waited out front. Kovalev followed and got into the passenger seat of the van. He cast one last look at Andor, who stood at the door of his house, shocked, powerless, and terrified. He didn't know what to do.

He could hear screaming inside the van. "Andor, what is this? Why is this happening? Where are they taking us? Please, tell us where are you are taking us."

Andor heard the sound of a slap and realized that one of the thugs had just hit his mother. He heard sobs and some protests from his father as the van sped away.

The memory of that day exploded in Andor's chest like napalm, setting every organ within him on fire. His body was filled with hatred and love and sympathy and rage. His lust for revenge was a hunger he had never known. Using all the discipline in his great mind, he pushed aside Kleper's image but nonetheless welcomed the yearning to kill with his bare hands.

On the other side of the world, Karl Kleper, well aware of Andor's feelings, smiled. He enjoyed the boy's intense hatred of him. He fed on the hatred others felt for him. It reminded him of how powerful he was. But in the end, Andor's feelings were inconsequential to Kleper, and he quickly dismissed them.

Meanwhile, salty tears of rage and sorrow rolled down Andor's cheeks and into his open mouth. He was ready to do what he had to do.

He went to his desk and, while still engulfed in emotional flames, took pen in hand. He had considered texting Roxanne but rejected the idea because he feared that if he sent a message over the airwaves, Kleper could easily intercept it and know his plan. But if he wrote a letter while he had disguised his thoughts in the fire of his emotions, he might be able to get a message to Roxanne without Kleper ever knowing. He took a deep breath and exhaled long and hard. Then he held the image of Roxanne in his mind and began to write.

> Dear beautiful, wonderful, brilliant Roxanne,
>
> I have found my soul. You have helped me find it. You are the light in my heart that has revealed my darkness. I love you with all that I am. I must speak to you. I have to tell you all. I must speak to your father. There is much he has to know. If I do not speak to you both soon, all will be lost. Meet me tomorrow morning.
>
> I am yours, always,
> Andor

He folded up the paper, inserted it into an envelope, sealed the envelope, and wrote Roxanne's name on its front. Then he got out his cell phone and dialed the first of the two people he knew he could trust,

Sarah Doherty. The phone rang several times and then went to voice mail. Andor hung up.

Next he dialed Lyla Bell. The phone rang three times and Lyla answered.

"Lyla, it's Andor. I can't talk long, but you've got to do me a favor."

"Andor, do you know what time it is?"

"I know it's late but I need your help."

"I hope that this doesn't have anything to do with me getting out of bed, Andor."

"I'm afraid it does, Lyla. I've got to give you something and it's got to be tonight."

"Andor, is this some kind of prank? Let me look at my caller ID so I can be sure that this isn't somebody impersonating the fool who treated my friend with so much evil. I don't know what you did to her, but every time I bring up your name, she looks real hurt. Now why should I do anything for you, tell me that?"

"Lyla, I'm sorry. I really am. But that's the reason I'm calling you. I've got to give you a letter that I wrote to Roxanne. And I've got to give it to you tonight. And you've got to give it to her first thing in the morning. It can't wait, Lyla. I know this sounds crazy—"

"It sure does sound crazy. Why should I get out of bed for you, Andor? Huh? Why should I do that?"

"Because you're Roxanne's friend whom she loves and trusts, and she'd want you to get out of bed and receive this letter from me tonight and give it to her in the morning, that's why."

Lyla was silent, and then she said, "You're smarter than you look, you know that, Andor?"

Andor smiled. *And you've got a bigger heart than you know.*

"You don't have to come out," he said. "Just meet me at your door in fifteen minutes. Take the letter and give it to Roxanne in the morning. That's all I am asking."

"Okay, but you better get your butt over here fast, while I'm still feeling well disposed toward you, Andor. Otherwise, you are one out-of-luck white boy, you catch my drift?"

"Thank you, Lyla. I'll be there in less than fifteen minutes."

Chapter 24

Andor and Roxanne Back Together

The next day, Andor paced back and forth in front of the entrance to the school cafeteria. It was just before lunchtime and he was hoping Roxanne would show up as promised. Earlier that day, Lyla had delivered his letter to Roxanne in Dr. Phillips's first-period social studies class.

"That is one strung-out young man, if you ask me," Lyla said after Roxanne read the letter. "I'm sure he wants to see you, today. What are you going to tell him if he asks?"

"He already has," Roxanne replied.

"So?"

Roxanne pulled out her phone and texted Andor that she would meet him outside the cafeteria before lunch. She told Lyla.

"Be prepared for an emotional train wreck," Lyla said. "He's a mess. If you don't show up at English after lunch, I'm going to come looking for you."

Roxanne smiled and put her arm around Lyla's shoulders. "I'll be all right. I'll fill you in after I've seen him."

"You better, girl. I want details, *Inside Edition* stuff. All this mystery has my curiosity boiling."

As he waited anxiously for Roxanne, Andor rehearsed what he would say to her. He knew he had to be careful. Kleper was always listening, or so it seemed. Still, he had to admit that of late he was feeling somewhat free of Kleper's dark shadow. He didn't understand this new freedom, but the feeling, which he trusted, made him bolder and all the more committed to confiding in Roxanne. He knew she was his only way out of the mess he was in.

Andor's reverie was interrupted by a hostile voice that seemed to spear him from behind. "Well, if it isn't the traitor himself."

Andor whirled around and faced Paul Grinsky. "Paul? What are you talking about?" Even as he spoke, Andor knew perfectly well what Paul meant.

"Don't play dumb with me," Paul said. "You're selling out our people, our country. Do you know who you're working for, or are you as stupid and ambitious as you appear to be?"

"I'm trying to keep innocent people from being killed," Andor said lamely.

"You're working for the butcher, Victor Grozny. You're giving him a free hand. The less international pressure on him, the more freedom he has to invade the border countries and kill innocent people on both sides. I've got family in Slavistan near the border. Do you know what they're saying? That those are not Bulgaristanis, or Czeckostanis, or Cossackians coming over the borders and killing our people. They're mercenaries from Somalia, Libya, Serbia, and South Africa. They're hired thugs. Grozny's army knows they've been hired to make it look like Slavistan is being attacked, so the army isn't even killing them. They're firing rubber bullets at them, or shooting over their heads. Our people know this. But word isn't getting out because the international community and the press believe people like Thompson, and his UN lackeys, and his flaks, meaning you."

Andor was trapped. He knew every word Paul said was true, but he wasn't in a position to argue with him.

"What are you, some kind of hero for Slavistan?" he asked Paul.

"No, I'm no hero, because if I was, you'd be unconscious and stuffed in a garbage can with the rest of the trash. But don't think I'm going to let you do your dirty work without a fight."

"What are you going to do, Paul?"

"I'm going find a way to expose the lies that you and Thompson are putting out." Andor was about to reply when he saw Roxanne approaching. "We'll resume this conversation later," he said.

"The next time we talk, it will be over battle lines," Paul said, and turned and left.

"Paul's angry at you," Roxanne said flatly, not a trace of sympathy in her voice. "He's got good reason."

"Yes, he does," Andor said. "I'm going to have to get right with him, and my country. That's part of what I want to talk to you about. Can we talk for a few minutes?"

"I'll speak to you on one condition. I want to meet your parents first."

"Roxanne, we haven't got time for that now."

"Introduce me to your parents tonight or forget about talking."

"Why? What have they got to with anything?"

"Something tells me they've got everything to do with what you want to talk to me about."

Andor let out a long exhalation and felt his shoulders drop. Once again, he marveled at her intuition and judgment. It seemed she was always certain about what she wanted and what was right.

"Okay," he said. "Be at my house at seven tonight. You'll meet them and I'll tell you everything afterwards."

Roxanne nodded and walked into the cafeteria without another word.

That evening, Roxanne arrived at Andor's house precisely at seven. In a steady rain, she ran to the front door, rang the doorbell, and was welcomed into the house by Andor.

She sensed his tension and distance as soon as she stepped into the foyer. To her left was a small living room, to the right, an even smaller dining room. Directly in front of her was a staircase that separated the two rooms. Beyond the staircase was a hallway that led to the kitchen. The furniture in the living and dining rooms looked like bargain-basement utilitarian. The walls, originally white, were dull gray. On each wall was a framed print of a lifeless nature scene. The floors were covered with cheap wall-to-wall carpet, and the air was heavy and stale, smelling of cigarette smoke. Overall, the house was not a home but a bleak stage, the sort of place that turned up in bad dreams, even nightmares.

A man and a woman, both a head shorter than Roxanne, approached via the hallway. The woman said hello but the man was silent. No one offered a hand to shake.

"Roxanne, allow me to introduce Egor and Masha Lysenko," Andor said.

"Pleased to meet you both," Roxanne said.

Roxanne did not let her gaze rest on either of them for more than an instant, but that was all she needed to form an unfavorable opinion. Egor, with dark hair and a swarthy complexion, stood like a boxer, his feet well apart, his arms slightly away from his sides. He seemed prepared to attack. Like Egor, Masha had a low forehead and a thick head of hair. Her skin was mottled, her features cheesy and dense. She tried to appear benign, but she could not hide the scowl that Roxanne guessed was permanent. When she made a half-hearted attempt to smile, she revealed a line of yellowed teeth and one startling gold canine tooth.

Roxanne scanned both of them and saw the terrible violence in their respective pasts. Both were low-ranking former KGB agents. They were assassins, specializing in explosive devices and killing at close range. The two had posed as householders and innkeepers many times in the past.

Egor's eyes were fixed on her and she felt his hunger rising. Beads of sweat appeared on his forehead and temples. Heavy breaths whooshed through his mouth. As a chill raced down her spine, Roxanne wondered if she would have to defend herself.

"Would you like something to drink, dear?" Masha asked in heavily accented English. Charm was as foreign to her as mercy.

"No, thank you," Roxanne said with a light-hearted smile, as if she were meeting a pair of perfectly wonderful people.

"Well, I guess we'll be going," Andor said.

Egor made a rapid move for the door, and even though Roxanne had been monitoring his thoughts, his sudden movement triggered the tension in her body. She raised her shield reflexively, preparing to defend herself, but Egor only opened the door to see them out. Roxanne controlled her desire to turn his brain into scrambled tofu.

"What time will you be back?" Masha said. It was less a question than a command.

"Late," Andor said. "Don't wait up." It was less an answer than an order.

"Remember, you've got school tomorrow," Masha said. It was less a reminder than a form of coercion.

Andor shot her a look that said, *Don't push me.* It was less a demand than a threat.

Masha switched to Slavistani, unaware that Roxanne would understand everything she said. "All I have to do is to tell Karl Kleper that you are not cooperating, boy. Don't forget that."

Roxanne figured Masha was used to having the last word.

They left the house and headed for Andor's car. He started the engine and sped away. The two rode in silence, shielding their thoughts from the other.

Andor drove to Hamilton Street and parked just a few doors down from Roxanne's home. He did this deliberately to allow her to relax. He could feel the tension go out of her body as he pulled up to the curb. He turned off the engine and stared out the windshield. The rain continued to fall.

"They're horrible," she finally said.

"Yes, you're right," was all he could say.

Roxanne looked down at her hands. "It must be pure hell living there. How much do they know about you? Don't they realize that our kind know their thoughts and understand all human languages?"

"They don't know anything about us." Andor was silent for a long moment, and then he said, "My parents are locked up in a prison in Siberia. If I don't complete my mission here, they'll die."

"Are your parents like us?"

"No, they're Ordinaries. My great-grandfather was a Genius. My mother was close to him and loved him very much. Apparently, he was born in a small, remote village in eastern Slavistan. He grew up with all the same abilities that we have, but he didn't know there were others like him. Pretty soon, the villagers became afraid of him and wanted to kill him, so he left. That became a way of life for him, moving from town to town, until he met his wife, my mother's mother. They settled in a village in Ukraine. My great-grandfather hid his abilities, but used them to become a wealthy landowner. He also kept to himself. He and my great-grandmother had three children, two of whom were Ordinaries. One of them, my great-uncle, was like us. My mother told me that when her uncle started to manifest strange abilities, his father took him aside and helped him develop his talents, but also trained him to keep them secret. A kind of folklore developed in my family about my great-grandfather and great-uncle. When I came along, my mother recognized my talents and knew what to do. She supplemented my schoolwork with lots of other books, trips to museums, music lessons, anything she could think of. She also trained me to keep my real abilities hidden from my classmates and teachers.

"Two Geniuses from the Eastern Council found me and brought me to a school in Georgia, where I learned Genius math, biology, physics, and medicine. I also studied gymnastics and played football. One day, Karl Kleper showed up at my school and told me he had an important job for me to do, and that if I didn't go along with him, he'd kill both my parents. I said I would do whatever he asked as long as he didn't hurt my parents. He agreed, but then he sent a bunch of his thugs to my house and arrested my parents. One of them told me that my parents were their insurance policy against me having any second thoughts."

Andor turned to Roxanne. "I can't go through with it. I can't follow Kleper and Grozny anymore, not since meeting you. But if I don't do what they tell me, they'll kill my parents. My parents are very good people, but they're frail. My father's a diabetic. My mother is the nervous type. They won't last much longer in their prison cell.

"Even now, I'm afraid Kleper is monitoring my thoughts and listening in on our conversation. It's strange, though. I felt his presence really strongly during the entire time I've been in the US, but lately I've felt freer of him. It's like I'm being released from his grasp, like he's no longer so close or something. Yesterday I tested my theory by thinking that I was going to quit my assignment; that I wouldn't go through with it, and nothing happened. No threats from Kleper, no coercion, no sudden heart attack." He smiled. "Something's different."

He took a breath and let it out in a long exhalation. "Anyway, even though I feel freer, I know that if I make a wrong move that Kleper can detect, he'll destroy my parents and me. I'm trapped and I don't know what to do, except to turn to you and your parents for help. Can you help me?"

"Yes," she said emphatically. "My parents will help you. My father can get your parents out, I know it. He can get you out of this. Just tell me all you know. We'll go to my father together. What exactly does Kleper want you to do?"

"I'm to bring Senator Stewart Thompson under my control and use all my ability to help him win the presidency of the United States in the next election. That means turning the heads of important people in his favor, getting him his party's nomination, and making decisions for him that will allow him to win. In the meantime, I've been ordered to alter his mind so that he'll become more vulnerable to Karl Kleper. Kleper intends to gain complete control of Thompson when he's well along in the presidential race."

He paused and then said, "There's more. Kleper also told me to await further instructions. He's got other plans for me. That's part of what I need to speak to you and your father about. There's a lot more going on than simply controlling Thompson. There's a collaborator here. One of our kind is working inside the Council of Western Geniuses. I was at their fortress, getting my training, when I overheard Karl talking about the collaborator. He got really angry at his brother Klaus and yelled at him for making a mistake. He said, 'The collaborator will have your head if you step out of line again.' Then he realized that I was in the next room and he closed his shield and went back to telepathic communication.

"That's when I realized something else was going on in the background. I think Kleper, the Eastern Council, and the collaborator are trying to take control of the American institutions of power."

"How would they do that?" Roxanne asked skeptically.

"They have me studying banking and Wall Street, and stocks, bonds, all kinds of financial instruments, the entire financial sector. I think the second part of my mission will involve the US economy. They're either going to cause a catastrophic event that will help Thompson become president, or something terrible will happen once he's in office. Either way, some kind of economic disaster is going to occur that will allow them to take control of the United States and eventually the world. We need to talk to your father immediately so we can stop them."

Roxanne was silent for a moment. "I think I know who the collaborator is," she said finally.

Andor became excited. "Who? Who do you think it is?"

"I'm not sure, but it could be Jason Phillips. He didn't help us in the raid. When I asked him about it, he became so strange that I was suddenly afraid of him. It was like he instantly became evil or something. I couldn't read his internal state. His thoughts and emotions were completely walled off from me. But I could read his face and it wasn't nice."

"We should quickly let your father know of your suspicions about Jason Phillips, and he'll tell us what to do.""

"No. I mean, I know that's what we should do, but my father thinks of all Western Geniuses as his friends, even family. You'll be meeting him for the first time and asking him to believe that a close friend is a traitor. I don't want him to mistrust you. There must be another way."

"So we need to prove to your father that Dr. Phillips is a collaborator. How do we do that?" Andor asked.

"I don't know."

"Wait a minute. I've seen him on his laptop before class and between classes. I'll bet you that everything we need to know is on that computer."

"Yes, you're right, but it will be encrypted."

"We can't steal the computer," Andor said. "He'd know the minute it was gone. And he'd know we were on to him. We've got to find a way to get into that computer without him being aware of it."

They were both silent, and then Roxanne smiled as inspiration struck. "I know how we can do it."

"How?"

"We have to use the Central Computer at Western Council Headquarters."

"Have you ever used it before?"

"No…never. I've only heard stories about it from my parents. They've told me that it contains the entire history of the human race. All the knowledge that our kind has accumulated over the millennia is contained within that computer. All the societal mysteries that we think are unsolved, it holds the answers. There's no computer, no firewall, no security program on earth that can block the Central Computer from entering and reading its data. The Central Computer can read Jason Phillips's files and he would never know his data had been compromised."

"Oh my God, that's the answer," Andor said. "What are we waiting for? Let's go."

She laughed. "Are you kidding, Andor? You don't just stroll into Western Council headquarters and tell Cecil Pasternak that you want to use the computer to break into Jason Phillips's files. And by the way Dr. Pasternak, who did kill JFK? All Pasternak has to do is send a single thought to security and there will be more Genius cops descending on that computer room than both of us have fingers and toes."

Andor was suddenly amused. "Who is Cecil Pasternak?"

Roxanne smiled in return. "Oh, he's this sweet old man who's in charge of the Central Computer, kind of its gatekeeper. I had met him when I was a little girl, and my mother introduced me to him again when we visited Western Council headquarters forty-two days ago."

"We've got to get in there, Roxanne. Think. How can we do it?"

Roxanne paused and recalled in detail her conversation with her mother and Dr. Pasternak while the three of them were in the elevator at the Council headquarters. "My mother mentioned that Dr. Pasternak was old—399 years old. Can you believe it? She asked him how he stayed so youthful and he said that he took a daily nap at 12:45, right after his lunch. He's very exact about his nap, he said. Claims it's some kind of prescription for keeping him youthful.

"We've got to be in that computer room at exactly 12:41. And we'll have to be out by 1:04. You're good with computers, Andor. Do you think you could figure out how to use the Central Computer, download Dr. Phillips's files, and get us out of there before Pasternak wakes up?"

"Yes. You get me into that computer room and I'll have us out of there with Phillips's files in fifteen minutes."

Roxanne communicated her plan telepathically. With every thought he received, Andor became more excited. He knew the plan could work.

"So we'll meet at the snack bar after second period tomorrow," she said. "That will give us enough time to get to the headquarters by 12:41."

"You're a Genius," Andor said, smiling.

Roxanne smiled and started to get out of the car.

"Wait," he said. "Your car is at my house."

"My mother will give me a ride to school tomorrow. I'll get my car after we've got Dr. Phillips's files."

"Okay."

Again, she turned toward the door.

"Wait, Roxanne," Andor said. When she looked back at him, he leaned over and kissed her.

Their lips met, gently at first, aware of the boundaries, careful not to intrude, protective of what was delicate and cautious in the other. Then, in an instant, their respective shields came down. They drew each other closer, their kiss hungry. Their telepathic natures opened and torrents of emotion, longing, and desire for each other flowed unfettered. In that moment, Roxanne became fully aware of the sincerity of Andor's love, his passion and desire for her heart and her body. There was no guile in him, she realized, only a deep love and a great mind. But also so much confusion and fear of what might lie ahead, especially for the parents he cared for so deeply.

Andor knew the ocean of Roxanne's wisdom, compassion, and tenderness, her innate goodness and her longing for him. He knew she loved him and wanted to give herself to him, but an innate sense told her she had to wait until the time was right.

She wanted him, he knew, but not before both of them could relax and open to each other—when he knew he and his parents were safe; when she knew he could give himself fully to her.

Roxanne gradually drew away from him. Looking into his eyes, she placed her hand on his face. "The time will come," she said. "But there is a lot we have to do first."

"I'll see you in the morning," he said.

Roxanne got out of the car. Andor waited until she was inside her house before driving away.

Hours before daylight broke on the east coast of the United States, the day was well underway in London. Roger and Stephen Elliot sat in Roger's office before the window that looked out onto Parliament Square. They were communicating telepathically, but then their thoughts were shielded from the rest of the world. Each of them was keenly aware of the delicate nature of their discussion.

"The weather balloon was shot down at 18:55 GMT, as you suspected it would be," Stephen said. "The balloon exploded twelve minutes after launch. NASA put out a small notice for those who might have seen the balloon go up in flames. They're saying a malfunction of the small directional rockets on board caused the explosion, but they've contacted the FBI in case it was sabotage. As for the rocket that was launched from Edwards Air Force Base in California and the Slavistani spy satellite over Reykjavik, both were destroyed hours later. Neither country has announced the destruction of the two craft, but the presidents have conferred with each other. Their respective intelligence services haven't got a clue who might have destroyed their satellites, or how. They discussed possible Chinese interference, or perhaps atmospheric anomalies, or even a UFO. Both sides are investigating. No doubt, the Klepers' have numerous satellite killers circling the globe, waiting for the moment when they need to take out an American or Slavistani spacecraft."

"And our Paper Clip?" Roger asked. "How did it perform?"

"Fine and operational, as planned. It was on board the Chinese U7T85 rocket that was launched from Beijing at 17:15 GMT, Saturday. It intersected with Archangel over Manila and made its soft landing. It immediately bored into the satellite's fuselage and took control of its internal computer. Archangel is now under your command and will do whatever we tell it to. There's no sign that the Klepers have any knowledge we've taken over their little toy."

"Well done, Stephen," Roger said, but his tone was regretful.

"It's Felix, isn't it, Chief?" Stephen asked.

Roger nodded. "Yes," he said, his sadness evident.

"Why? He's been with us for what, twenty-one years?"

"Felix was always his own agent. No matter what we did, he never became part of the family."

"How do you think the Klepers got to him?"

"They met him in Istanbul on his return from a mission in Greece three years ago."

"What did they offer him?"

"More power, a place on the Eastern Council, freedom to form strategies in a new world order. He saw the wisdom in their plans. He's betting they succeed this time around."

"Willie's presentation at our meeting… that was all a charade for Felix's ears, right? As was Denise's Rube-Goldberg plan to get Paper Clip onboard Archangel."

"Yes. And William and Denise performed their roles masterfully. I'll be calling a meeting for the entire team at four this afternoon. Circulate the word, Stephen. I'll see you later."

After Stephen left, Roger looked out onto Parliament Square pensively. His mind went to Roxanne with sudden concern. Instinctively, he reached out to Rebecca.

She opened to him immediately. "Hi," she said, soft and welcoming. "This is a nice surprise. I wasn't expecting to hear from you for another two hours."

"Just checking in. How's Roxanne?"

"Let's see, I took her to school this morning. She left her car at Andor's last night. Seems she met his parents, or rather the former KGB agents posing as his parents."

"We know all about them. We've been monitoring them for weeks. We also know where his real parents are imprisoned. Willie is working on ways to get them out when the time is right. But what about Roxanne? How's she doing?"

"She was quiet this morning; lost in thought, really. She was closed off from me and I didn't push it. I think she's in love, which, as you know, makes her very difficult to read. It also causes me great concern. How are you progressing with getting Andor free from Kleper's grasp?"

"We're making progress. Simone has managed to extract Kleper's tentacles from the deeper parts of Andor's field without Kleper realizing it. Simone and Denise have been monitoring the boy and it seems he is all but free of Kleper. He's very much on our side. I also think his love for Roxanne is sincere."

"I think so too. If I didn't believe it, I wouldn't be able to sleep at night. But why are you asking about Roxanne now?"

"I think something's up. She and Andor may be planning something. But as you say, being in love makes her difficult to read. Anyway, please check on her when you get the chance."

"I'll do that. How are you?"

"All's well here. The game's afoot, as our old friend Sherlock used to say. The team is going through some challenges, but I think we'll be all right."

"I love you," Rebecca said.

"I love you so much. Let's talk later."

Roger closed the channel and then reached out to Simone and Willie, asking them to come to his office. After they arrived Roger asked them about the plans for rescuing Andor's parents from their prison.

"We've got a clear layout of the prison," Willie said. "We know the personnel, we know the cells where the two are located, and we've got a sound plan for getting them out."

Roger turned to Simone. "Are you satisfied with the plan?"

"Yes," she said. "We need three men, one to pilot our jet, and another two on the ground. The plan should work fine. It's not a high-security prison and there is only one of our kind watching over them. Apparently, he takes a walk every night for about an hour. He stays in telepathic communication with the senior guard, but we can handle things without much dust being stirred up."

"Good," Roger said. "Please finish up your work on the plan and be ready to go on my order within a day or two."

"We'll be ready, Chief," Willie said.

Chapter 25

Roxanne and Andor at Western Council Headquarters, the Oracle of Delphi

A t noon the next day, Andor was driving himself and Roxanne through the streets of Washington on their way to Western Council headquarters. They had gone over their plan and were ready to break into the Central Computer.

At 12:30, they walked through the illusion of the construction site at the entrance to the headquarters and entered the great atrium. Andor stood in awe, marveling at the play of sunlight through the glass, the colors, the flower-bearing trees, and the works of art that were arrayed throughout the atrium.

"Come on," Roxanne said. "No time to gawk."

He followed her to the elevators. While they waited for one, he looked to his left, into the great hall, and glimpsed a couple of holographs in action. He was almost disappointed when the elevator arrived and Roxanne grabbed his hand, pulling him into it.

"Seventeen, please," she said to the computer.

In a moment, they were on the seventeenth floor. They exited the elevator and Roxanne checked her watch. "It's 12:37. We've got four minutes. Let's go."

They walked along the curved hallway with its glass wall to their left. The great American capital lay spread out before them.

"What an amazing view," Andor said.

Roxanne did not reply. When they arrived at Dr. Pasternak's office, she checked her watch again. "Twelve forty-one. It's time."

She opened the door to the outer office and found Dr. Pasternak telling his secretary—a woman who appeared nearly as old as Dr. Pasternak—to enjoy her lunch. Dr. Pasternak's face was lined and yet vital. It communicated a certain peace, even a subtle joy. At the tender age of 399, he was still a handsome man.

"Oh, my goodness," he said when he saw her. "Roxanne. What a surprise."

"Dr. Pasternak, this is my friend Andor. I wanted to introduce him to you and to ask if we could see the Central Computer."

"Oh, dear, yes. I mean, oh, no. Your timing is a little off, dear. I take my nap in a couple of minutes. I cannot give you much of a tour in three minutes."

"We don't need a tour, Dr. Pasternak. We just wanted to see it and be in its presence for a few minutes. If you let us look inside, we'll leave on our own. Just show me how to lock the door and we'll let ourselves out."

Pasternak was momentarily flustered and troubled. He scanned Roxanne's field. Her shield was closed and she was obviously in love, which made it nearly impossible for him to read her. *Teenagers. So impulsive.* He shifted his focus to London and made a quick exchange of information, shielding his thoughts from Roxanne and Andor.

"Dr. Pasternak," Roxanne said, "I promise we won't hurt the computer. And we'll be happy to lock up after ourselves."

"Oh, you can't hurt the computer, dear. That thing is so armored and armed; I worry more about you than it. But I suppose no harm will be done if I let you in to have a look at the thing. You can even run a few equations through it, if you like. Maybe Delphi will show up for you, though I doubt it. She doesn't deign to show up for strangers. She'll probably send one of her minions out to ask you what the computer can do for you."

Roxanne had no idea what Pasternak was talking about—except that he was about to give them permission to enter.

"Thank you, Dr. Pasternak. Thank you. I promise, we'll lock up and leave before you finish your nap."

"Okay, my dear. Follow me."

He led them down a short hallway to a set of tall metal doors painted a dull gray. Roxanne and Andor looked at each other quizzically, and Andor telepathically asked Roxanne if he was taking them to the boiler room. Roxanne shrugged; as if to say, your guess is as good as mine.

Dr. Pasternak grasped a large handle on one of the gray doors, and the handle glowed with a golden light. The door opened to what appeared to be a foyer that was brightly lit in pure white light. The ceiling was perhaps twenty feet high. On the other side of the foyer was a pair of tall white doors.

Dr. Pasternak led them across the expanse and grasped the handle of the white doors. Again, the handle glowed golden. He opened the door and led Andor and Roxanne into a vast room that was bathed entirely in white light. The light was so bright, Roxanne couldn't make out the dimensions of the room, or for that matter see exactly where the walls and ceiling were located. The floor, too, was entirely white.

She looked at Dr. Pasternak and realized that he had been transformed upon entering the room. He was wearing a white suit and his electromagnetic field was illuminated in white light. He literally glowed with a soft yet brilliant aura.

"Dr. Pasternak, you look beautiful," she said in awe.

"Thank you, my dear. As do you. And you're not so bad yourself, Mr. Lysenko."

Roxanne looked at Andor, who was dressed in the soft tunic of a white knight. He had on white leggings, white boots, a white shirt, over which lay a white surcoat. On the surcoat was emblazoned a coat of arms.

She looked down at herself and saw that she wore a long white dress, made of fine linen and elaborately embroidered. Aware of on odd sensation on her head, she lifted her hands and found a crown of flowers in her hair.

"Yes," Andor thought. "The flowers are white, and look great with your golden hair." Then he added, "The crown has your family's Double R on it." "

Roxanne turned to Dr. Pasternak. "How is this possible?"

"No time to explain," he answered. "All I can say is that Delphi approves of both of you."

"But where is the computer?"

"It's everywhere, my dear. The walls, the ceiling, the floor, every atom and molecule in this room hold information, knowledge, and wisdom." He held up his hands and looked around the room. "All of this is the computer. Now, if the two of you walk into the center of that circle, Delphi will answer your questions."

Not far from them, a circle of golden light appeared on the floor.

Roxanne looked at the golden circle and then back at Pasternak. He smiled warmly. She was seeing him as he really was for the first time, she realized, and tears of joy filled her eyes. In this awesome light, Dr. Pasternak was revealed for who he was—a great sage, whose wisdom and powers were hidden from the masses by his self-effacing humility.

"Thank you, Dr. Pasternak," she said.

"It's all right, dear. Just stand over in the circle and Delphi will take it from there. Don't worry about locking up. The computer will do that for you. Just leave through the doors you came through, unless the computer instructs you otherwise."

With that, he turned and left the room.

Andor and Roxanne took each other's hands and walked to the center of the golden circle.

The instant they stepped inside the circle, the room was transformed into a beautiful temple, complete with columns, yellow stone tile at their feet, a radiant blue sky and sunlight above. Gardens surrounded the temple as far as the eye could see. Birds of every hue flew and sang above their heads. Directly in front of them stood an ornate altar; upon which sat a golden chalice. Beyond them was a stone wall into which were engraved two large mandalas. The mandalas contained a multitude of symbols, all densely arrayed in concentric circles with an engraving of the sun, glowing with a golden light, at their centers.

Andor and Roxanne felt as if they had been transported to another dimension.

"From what I understand," Andor said, "mandalas are symbols of the self, our souls. They reveal who we really are. I'll bet that all those symbols represent some kind of maps of what we've experienced, what we're going through now, and what our futures will be."

"Can you read them?" Roxanne asked, also mesmerized by their mysterious power.

"No. The symbols are completely foreign to me."

"They're beautiful."

Suddenly, a man appeared in front of the altar. Like Andor, he was dressed like a knight, though his white tunic was far more ornate than Andor's. The large coat of arms on his surcoat was rendered in gold. Unlike Andor, the knight also wore a long sword at his side.

"I am Sir Percival," he said, "of King Arthur's round table, pure of heart and a seeker and finder of the Holy Grail. I am at your service."

Roxanne and Andor were momentarily speechless. Neither could fathom what they were experiencing. Finally, Andor spoke.

"Computer ... I mean, Percival, can you locate the laptop computer of Dr. Jason Phillips?"

"Of course, Andor. What would you like us to do with it?"

"We need you to open that computer and make certain files available to us. We're looking for a particular set of files that can help us discover what the Eastern Council of Geniuses is trying to do to bring the United States and perhaps the rest of the world under its control."

"And who authorizes you to conduct such a search, young Andor?"

Andor was taken aback. He had no idea where to turn for any kind of authorization. He considered bluffing, but his knowledge of Percival stopped him. Among all of Arthur's knights, only Percival and Galahad were considered holy for their purity.

"Percival, I am Roxanne Reynolds, daughter of Roger Reynolds, the chief of operations for the Western Council of Geniuses."

"We know who you are, Roxanne," Percival said. "You are of our lineage. Your ancestor, Sir Reginald Reynolds, was a valued friend of King Arthur and the Knights of the Round Table. We are at your service. However, the request you and Andor are making requires authorization. Can you provide us with your father's authorization code?"

Roxanne was silent for a moment. "Yes, Percival, I can. The code is as follows: Alpha, bravo, tango, 764658278 echo, sierra, delta, 8816512276, alpha, ranger, zulu."

Andor looked at Roxanne in disbelief. "How did you know that?" he communicated to her telepathically.

She smiled and answered in the same way. "My father mentioned the code to my mother in the living room one day when I was five."

"Authorization code confirmed," Percival said. "The files you requested are appearing in the hologram before you."

A holographic screen appeared before them and presented three file folders. One of them was marked, Stock and Call Acquisitions. Another read, Puts and Short Sales. The third was labeled, Air Strike.

"Let's start with Stock and Call Acquisitions, Percival," Andor said.

"As you wish," Percival said.

Andor and Roxanne read the file quickly, and then Andor asked for the Puts and Short Sales file.

"As you wish," Percival said.

Again, they read quickly.

"Open the folder entitled Air Strike, good knight," Andor said.

"The file is open," Percival said.

Roxanne and Andor read this file in horror. It revealed detailed plans for the hijacking of a US Air Force B-52 bomber on October 31. The bomber would be armed with a bunker buster, the type of bomb designed to penetrate and destroy targets deep in the earth. The bomber would also carry a full payload of conventional ordinance. The hijackers had been instructed to take over the plane and drop the bunker buster on the Ghawar oil field in Saudi Arabia, the largest oil field in the world. The bunker buster would not only destroy the oil field, it would set fire to the enormous reserves of oil and gas held within those lands.

Once the bomb was dropped, the hijackers would proceed to Dubai in the United Arab Emirates and drop the conventional ordinance on the headquarters of Baxion Insurance Group, which provided insurance to most of the world's airlines and multinational corporations.

Andor turned to Roxanne. "Jason Phillips has arranged for various financial institutions to make $180 billion in short sales and to acquire vast numbers of put options, all designed to produce enormous profits for Phillips and his partners in the wake of a terrorist strike. Once that bomb hits the Saudi oil fields on Halloween, and the Baxion headquarters is destroyed, they will have brought about a worldwide economic crisis. When the insurance industry and the banks are thrown into crisis, Jason Phillips and Karl Kleper will be able to buy their assets for a song. They'll also purchase and control a great bulk of the world's most valuable stocks. All of this will make them the most powerful men in the world."

Andor looked back at Percival. "Percival, please send an encrypted e-mail containing these three files immediately to Roger Reynolds."

"It is done," Percival said.

"Percival," Roxanne asked, "can you block anyone from knowing that we've read these files and sent them to my father?"

"Yes, if you order such an action, I will comply. I will keep this history secret, unless someone releases me from your order by utilizing your father's code."

"Very good, Percival," Roxanne said. "Make it so."

At that very moment, Jason Phillips sat alone in the teachers' lounge grading student papers. His leather briefcase was open and lying beside him. His computer was in the briefcase.

He concentrated on one of the student papers, which was on the use of chemical weapons during World War I. Parts of the paper had been plagiarized from Wikipedia, which Phillips knew word for word—at least on the subjects he was interested in and had read. He had already decided to fail the student but was curious about the student's motives. Was he merely trying to pull one over on his teacher, or were there extenuating circumstances? As he considered the student, he was attacked by one of his searing headaches. He reflexively dropped his head, hoping to minimize the pain. That was when he saw his laptop was on. The edges of the computer glowed with a bright white light. He sat bolt upright, instantly understanding.

"The Central Computer," he muttered.

He contacted Lionel Clearwater, the security chief at Western Council Headquarters.

"Clearwater, this is Jason Phillips. I believe someone has broken into the Central Computer and instructed it to open my laptop and read encrypted files. Please go to the Computer Room and apprehend whoever is stealing my documents."

"On my way, Jason," Clearwater replied.

"Get back to me as soon as you know who's tampering with the Computer.

"I will."

Clearwater sounded the alarm and ordered twenty policemen to the Central Computer.

In the computer room, three more beings suddenly appeared next to Percival—a stately, mature, and obviously powerful woman, dressed in a beautiful flowing white dress; a man with a crown on his head, obviously a king; and a younger woman of great beauty.

"I am Delphi," the older woman said. "These are my companions, King Arthur and his wife, Guinevere." The king and queen bowed. "Your cause is just and you both have been found worthy. We will help you in many ways, most of which will be unknown to you. Roxanne, tell your father that when you need help, he is to take you to the Crystal Cavern. He knows the place."

King Arthur said, "Roxanne and Andor, you are both in danger. Security forces are on their way to apprehend you. You will find a doorway to your right. It leads to a secret elevator that will take you to the courtyard, where you can make your escape. Go now. We will keep them at bay."

A white door appeared on the right side of the computer room. Andor grabbed Roxanne's hand and the two ran to the door and flung it open. They found themselves in a foyer similar to the one they had entered. On the other side of the foyer, a small elevator awaited, its door open. They ran into the tiny box, held on to each other, and ordered the computer to send them down to the ground floor.

At that moment, Lionel Clearwater and twenty Western Genius police offers gathered in front of the large gray doors that opened into the Central Computer foyer. Clearwater grabbed the door handle and tried to turn it, but nothing happened. He tried again, but the door was locked to him.

"Where is Pasternak?" he called out. "Find him now!"

Cecil Pasternak was just waking up from his nap. Sitting up on the sofa in his inner office, he rubbed his eyes awake as he heard someone banging on his office door. Lionel Clearwater, he realized. What did he want?

"Pasternak, where are you? Get out here!"

Pasternak got up from the sofa and opened the door. Lionel Clearwater was clearly under great stress..

"The door to the Central Computer is locked, Pasternak," he said.

"The door's locked? That's very odd." He put up his shield and thought, *Delphi is protecting the young ones from someone.* "Okay, okay, let's see what we can do."

As he walked down the short hallway to the gray doors, he sent a telepathic message to Delphi to keep the door locked to him until Roxanne and Andor were safely away.

He tried the handle. It wouldn't budge. "Oh, dear," he said. "Something must be wrong. Let me find my key."

He feigned a limp as he walked slowly back to his inner office. "Where's that key?" he said aloud as he searched his pockets. With great deliberation he went through the drawers to his desk. "No, not here." He walked over to the couch where he lifted and fluffed up its cushions.

"Sometimes things fall from my pockets and get lost under the cushions," he said. "Here, Clearwater, help me look."

Clearwater rolled his eyes. He turned to a young police officer who was standing nearby and said, "Get in there and help him look for those keys."

Pasternak and the young officer threw off the cushions but found nothing.

"Look down into the folds of the couch," Pasternak said to the young officer. "Don't be afraid. Just push your hand down there and see if they fell behind the back cushions."

The young officer did as he was told but found nothing.

Pasternak called to his secretary, "Molly, where is the key to the gray doors?"

"I think I've got an extra one here, Dr. Pasternak."

"Ok, good girl. Let's have it."

Pasternak took the key and walked slowly to the large gray doors. He inserted the key and opened the door. The policemen rushed into the foyer, only to find that the great white doors were locked as well.

Lionel Clearwater nearly had a stroke. "Pasternak, get the key and open this door!"

"Oh, dear," Pasternak said. "Is that door locked too?"

He walked slowly to his outer office. "Molly, have we got a key to the inner doors too?"

"Yes, Dr. Pasternak. Here it is."

"Oh, good girl. Here we are, Lionel. Here's the key."

"Get over here and open the doors."

Pasternak was suddenly very old and shaky. He had great difficulty getting the key into the lock. When he did, he found that it was the wrong key.

"Oh, dear," he said. "Molly," he called to his secretary, "I'm afraid you've given me the wrong key."

"Oh, Dr. Pasternak, I'm sorry." Molly walked down the hall and through the foyer. "Try this one."

"Yes, Molly. Let me give that one a try."

When Cecil Pasternak finally got the doors open, the twenty police officers and Lionel Clearwater burst into the computer room, only to find a standard-looking room, very modern, very clean. A gray carpet covered the floor. Two dozen holographic pedestals were arrayed along the walls of the computer room. A large floor-to-ceiling control panel stood against the far wall some forty feet away. Nothing seemed amiss, nothing out of the ordinary.

"Well, well," Cecil Pasternak said. "Looks like everything is under control in here, wouldn't you say, Lionel?"

"Yes, I guess so," Clearwater said, finally exhaling. He knew of no other way out of the computer room. "But I want to know if anyone has compromised the system."

He looked up at the ceiling. "Computer, has any unauthorized personnel been in this room and utilized this facility?"

"There have been no unauthorized personnel utilizing this computer," the computer answered.

Clearwater was relieved. Still, he wanted to cover every base. He directed his thoughts to Alexander Astrakhan and informed him that Jason Phillips was afraid of a possible breach into the Central Computer.

"I will be down in three minutes," Alexander informed Clearwater.

Alexander strode into the Central Computer room like a great general laying claim to a conquered territory.

"Computer, have there been any unauthorized inquiries?" he asked.

"No, there have been no unauthorized requests, Dr. Astrakhan," the computer replied.

"Has anyone made any extraordinary requests to open sensitive files that were not specifically under the ownership or authorization of the person making that request?"

"No such extraordinary, unauthorized requests have been made, Dr. Astrakhan."

Alexander blew out a long breath. "Computer, who was the last person to authorize any inquiry?"

"Roger Reynolds was the last person to make use of our services, and the request was, by his standards, routine."

"And what, pray tell, did Roger utilize the computer for?" Alexander asked.

"That information is restricted."

"Understood," Alexander said. He had expected that answer.

Both Alexander and Clearwater knew Roger accessed the computer on a daily basis, and that Roger's work was entirely in secret, save for what he shared with Alexander. For example, Alexander was well aware of Roger's secret Paper Clip project and assumed he had used the computer to help him construct the device.

Clearwater, for his part, knew that everyone in Western Council headquarters used the computer every day, and many used it remotely from their stations around the world. That Roger's purposes for using the computer would be protected information was not in any way out of the ordinary. Clearwater himself used the computer every day and all his files were protected by passwords and encryption.

"Thank you, computer," Alexander said, convinced that everything was in order and there had been no breaches of security. He turned to Clearwater. "I think we're done here, Lionel, wouldn't you say?"

"Yes sir, I'm satisfied that no breach has been made," Clearwater replied.

"Good, than let's go back to work, shall we?"

As he left the room, Clearwater contacted Jason Phillips telepathically.

"Everything appears in order here, Jason. No one was in the computer room when we arrived. Both doors were locked. Nothing has been tampered with and there have been no unauthorized uses of the Central Computer. Everything here is secure."

"Are you certain, Lionel?" Phillips asked.

"Absolutely certain, Jason."

Phillips had already checked all of his computer files thoroughly. Nothing had been stolen and there was no evidence that his firewall had been breached. The Central Computer was the only computer on earth that could steal files from his computer and leave no fingerprints behind, but apparently the Central Computer had not invaded his laptop. Jason began to question his own suspicions, indeed, his own mental clarity. The headaches were coming more frequently now, and they were often accompanied by short blackouts. Though it was impossible for a Genius to forget a single moment of his or her day—and thus impossible for him to turn his computer on or off without remembering doing so—he had to admit that the headaches were causing periodic lapses. He might start forgetting small events, so it was possible that during one of these headache-induced lapses, he could have turned his computer on, or left it on when he intended to turn it off, and not remembered. He was not comfortable with that answer, but given the extreme nature of the headaches, many things were possible that in the past he would not have even considered.

Suddenly, Phillips felt taken over by another of his dark interludes, as if he was possessed by an irresistible force. A raging headache arose and flared in intensity. Involuntarily, he found himself considering the hijacking plan that was about to unfold in two days. Should the plan be changed in light of the mystery surrounding the computer? No, he decided. He'd put too much time and attention into the plan. It had to go forward. The anomaly surrounding the computer was the consequence of one of his lapses. The plan would go forward.

He turned his attention back to Lionel Clearwater.

"Okay, Lionel. Thank you for checking. I apologize for the intrusion on your day."

"It's not a problem, Jason. We'll consider it a good training exercise for the younger officers."

With that, the two broke off communication.

Five miles away, Andor and Roxanne were racing out of Washington on their way to Golden Gables, still giddy from their coup. They were back in their street clothes, having undergone another strange transformation in the elevator.

"We did it!" Andor said. "We did it! Now all we have to do is stop them from dropping that bunker buster and keep them from destroying Baxion. If we can do that, we'll break the back of their plan. Can your father stop that B-52 from taking off?"

"Of course," she said. "You know what? I'll bet my mother could do it, too."

Chapter 26
A Mother's Work
Is Never Done

On Friday, October 30, Roger and his team gathered in their conference room. Outside, the rain fell in thick sheets. As the team collected at the round table, everyone knew the news was bad. All they had to do was look at Roger to know he was unhappy. They all took their cues from him, which meant that everyone in the room was just as serious and dark as their leader.

"Yesterday, the weather balloon carrying our Paper Clip was destroyed," he began telepathically. "NASA reported that one of the directional rockets on the balloon exploded while the balloon was in flight. The craft went up in flames and crashed in a dense wooded area in Georgia."

Everyone in the room looked at one another, trying to assess who might have leaked the information about Paper Clip and the weather balloon to the Eastern Council. The entire team knew that they had a mole. No one said a word, however.

"There's no time to create another Paper Clip," Roger continued. "I feel certain that Ubitzov and his team of assassins will seize the opportunity and strike in the next day or two. Therefore, I have decided to scrap Willie's defense plans for us and, instead, go to the mattresses, so to speak. I want us all to relocate to the House, starting tonight."

The House was a manor home, approaching small castle status, in Kent on the southern coast of England, some sixty-five miles south of London. The House was surrounded on three sides by a high wall and could be defended effectively from an attack. At the rear of the house, at the very edge of the property, was a cliff that dropped off some three hundred feet to the shoreline of the English Channel. The House was a stronghold and would afford the team much more protection than their individual homes could possibly provide.

"Please round up your families and prepare for an extended stay in the country until this business with the Klepers and Ubitzov's assassins is finished. We leave tonight. That's all for now."

The team broke up and they all went to their respective offices. Over the decades that they had worked together, the team had faced many crises, and had been forced to relocate to the House several times. But they had never had to abandon Westminster Abbey and seek refuge at the House while knowing they had a traitor in their midst. A family member had betrayed them. They were professionals, who knew their jobs, but each team member was charged with tension and anger, and they were eager for a reckoning.

Roger retreated to his office and recalled the conversation he had had with Rebecca the night before. The two had communicated immediately after Roger had examined the Jason Phillips's files. Rebecca already knew about Roxanne and Andor's adventures at headquarters and the information they had found in Phillips's files. Both were on edge, and neither wanted to discuss the dangers that lay ahead. Roger decided to ease into the harder matters by turning first to happier thoughts, basking in the pride he felt for his daughter.

"She's really something, isn't she?" he said.

"Yes, she's full of heart and courage and brilliance—just like her father," Rebecca said.

"No, she's much more like you. At least the you I have come to know."

"Isn't it amazing that Cecil Pasternak let them use the Central Computer?"

Roger smiled. "Actually, Cecil communicated with me right before he let Roxanne and Andor into the room. His instinct was to let them in, but he reached out to me just in case. And I gave him my permission. I told him that you and I have great faith in our daughter. That sealed it for him and he went ahead."

"Roxanne may complain about you from time to time," Rebecca said, "but she knows how much you love and honor her, and how proud you are of her. And that's what matters most. I'm proud of you too."

They were both silent for a moment, and then Rebecca went on.

"What do you make of the Central Computer's advice to Roxanne: 'Tell your father that when you need help, he is to take you to the Crystal Cavern. He knows the place." "What does that mean, Roger?"

"I don't know yet. The only thing we can do is wait for clarity."

Again the two were silent, until Rebecca asked how he was going to stop the B-52.

"I'm still formulating the plan," he said. "The hijacking and bombing mission is central to their plans. The Klepers are going to send some of their best men. I'm guessing three or four of our kind—one to pilot the plane, another to copilot, a third and possibly a fourth to serve as bombardiers. They'll probably bring along an Ordinary or two to serve as scapegoats, cover their tracks, and provide support and cover fire, if needed."

He paused and then said, "I'm sending Freddy, Ellis, and Max. I need my entire team here, especially Willie and Stephen, to help me defeat Ubitzov's assassination team."

They both knew that the three Western Geniuses would not be enough to take out the Klepers' team, recover the plane, and then fly it to safety. The best they could hope for was that the three would crash the plane into the ocean. In short, Roger was sending them on a suicide mission.

Rebecca spoke from that steely certainty that Roger would never be able to penetrate or dissuade. "Freddy, Ellis, and Max will not be enough. I have to be on that plane. Freddy and Ellis can take out the Klepers' goons. I can fly the plane. We need Max to fly a second plane to bring us home once we land the B-52 safely. Either I go, or Freddy, Ellis, and Max are dead men."

Roger felt the walls suddenly cave in on him. He couldn't bear putting Rebecca at risk, but he knew she was right. Rebecca was a skilled pilot. She had learned to fly when she and Walter were stationed in San Diego, and had flown regularly ever since.

Still he said no. "I can't let you do that. I cannot put you in danger."

"Roger, you have no choice. I know you care deeply for Freddy and Ellis. If I'm on that plane, we'll all make it back. If I'm not, they haven't got a chance."

He wanted to keep fighting her, but he knew it was pointless. After a long pause, he finally said, "You're right. I suppose I knew you had to be on that plane the whole time. I just didn't want to face it."

"Don't worry, Roger. We'll make it."

Roger heard an intimation in the words "We'll make it", and feared she had something up her sleeve.

"What do you mean, 'We'll make it'?"

"I'm going to bring along Roxanne and Andor to deal with the Ordinaries. They've already insisted on it and I agreed. We need them. Freddy and Ellis can handle the four Eastern Geniuses, but we can't have the Ordinaries get in the way, or even worse, get off a shot."

"Were the three of you up all night discussing this?" Roger asked ruefully.

"Just half the night," she said with a smile in her voice.

"If I lose the two of you, I've lost everything. I hope you know that."

"You're not going to lose us. We know we can handle this."

"Okay," Roger said, realizing that this was how it had to be done. "We have a couple of big advantages. They're not expecting you. They don't know that we've seen the Phillips files, which means they believe the mission is merely taking control of a crew of Ordinaries. A walk in the park for them. Our other big advantage is that we now control the Archangel satellite. Stephen will order the satellite to silence the ping the Eastern Geniuses hear when near us right before you drive onto the base, so the Klepers' men won't have any warning when you get on that plane.

NEIL W. FLANZRAICH

They'll think you're a secondary crew of Ordinaries participating in the training exercise. But be careful when Freddy and Ellis are dealing with the bad guys. Anything can happen in the middle of that fight."

"We know what to do, Roger," Rebecca said. "Don't worry. I'll have that plane back on the ground tomorrow afternoon and Freddy and Ellis will be in London by evening."

Roger sent an enormous stream of energy that enveloped Rebecca in love. His life force embraced her, filling her with vitality and power.

"I love you," he said. "Kiss Roxanne for me. Take care of each other. I will be monitoring your every thought."

"I love you too," Rebecca said.

Andrews Air Force Base, located in Prince George County, Maryland, is famous for being the home of Air Force One, the personal jet for the president of the United States. It is also the arrival point for most of the world's leaders who come to Washington. In fact, Andrews is a small military city, with 18,000 residents, most of them members of the air force, navy, army, marines, or national guard. The base also plays host to hundreds of thousands of visitors each year, and from all outward appearances the five people who drove up to the base's entry gate in the late model Volvo were no different from any other military guests.

They were dressed in Air Force fatigues—a female lieutenant colonel behind the wheel, a male major beside her, another male major in the backseat, along with two young airmen—well, an airman and an airwoman—seated next to the major.

The gate at Andrews is a series of glass-enclosed booths. Within each booth is a military police officer, who checks every visitor's credentials and determines whether or not he or she can enter the base.

The lieutenant colonel pulled up to one of the booths and handed her military ID to the MP, along with the military IDs for the four other people in her car. The young MP looked carefully at the four IDs and then peered into the car, matching each ID with a face in the car. He then handed the IDs back to Rebecca, saluted her, and waved her onto the base. It was 9:05 and on this cold autumn day, the sun was shining brilliantly—an anomaly, given the weather of late.

Rebecca drove along the winding roads of the military installation. Her fatigues were gray camouflage, and above the right breast pocket of her uniform was her alias, Roberts. Seated next to her was Major Edward Davidson (aka Ellis Davies), who was similarly dressed. Directly behind Major Davidson was Major Francis Daniels (aka Freddy Davies), also in combat fatigues. Beside Major Daniels were Airmen First Class Regina Roland (Roxanne) and Anthony Sokolov (Andor). They were dressed in combat fatigues, as well.

They arrived at the air field and approached a row of enormous hangers. Beyond the hangers, Rebecca could see the huge B-52 waiting on the tarmac for the remainder of its crew. A staircase descended from the bottom of the plane, near the cockpit. The wings of the jet stretched out from its upper shoulders, each one equipped with two sets of double engines, a total of eight giant engines in all. She could already hear the sound of the engines as she parked the car.

They all got out and Rebecca opened the trunk. Each pulled out a duffle bag. From the duffels they extracted a gun belt that carried a Glock and additional cartridges. After strapping the gun belts on, they walked onto the tarmac toward the great jet. Rebecca felt like an ant in comparison.

The massive B-52 could carry up to 70,000 pounds of munitions, which could include nuclear weapons. It could fly at an altitude as high as 50,000 feet, and sustain speeds of 650 miles per hour, or just below the speed of sound. Its range was 8,800 miles. The Klepers' planned route—from DC to Saudi Arabia, to Dubai, and then over to Tehran—was less than 7,500 miles, well within its range.

Rebecca and her team ascended the staircase and entered the belly of the beast. Once inside, they felt four pings sound inside their nervous systems, indicating the presence of four Eastern Geniuses. When there was no reaction to their presence, Rebecca knew Stephen had done his sleight of hand with Archangel.

Traveling with the Eastern Geniuses was a single Ordinary, a young marine.

The B-52 was on a training session. The mission was to head out over the Atlantic and engage in maneuvers and practice bombing runs over the Bahamas and Bermuda. The crew was also instructed to perform a midair refueling, although they were starting out with full fuel tanks.

The crew of a B-52 normally occupied two levels of the cockpit. The pilot, copilot, and navigator sat in the upper level, while two bombardiers occupied the lower level. Because this was a training run, there was no gunner on board. He would be stationed in the tail of the airplane.

The B-52 had been modified over the decades, and this one had a cabin that had been expanded and widened to allow additional flight crews to train on the plane. Both Rebecca's and the Klepers' team sat in the cabin on the upper level, directly behind the cockpit. The narrow doorway between the cabin and the cockpit was open. Anyone sitting in the cabin could see the pilot, copilot, and navigator in their respective seats.

Rebecca and her team casually looked over the four Eastern Geniuses, all of whom were dark, tough-looking men, obviously experienced and combat hardened. The single Ordinary saluted Rebecca, Ellis, and Freddy.

Even though the cabin had been widened to accommodate two training crews, they still had to sit one next to the other along each side of the plane. The Western Geniuses sat on the port side wall of the jet. The Eastern Geniuses sat directly across from them on the starboard side.

On a rack behind their heads were earphones with attached microphones that allowed the passengers to speak to each other over the screaming of the B-52's engines.

One of the four Geniuses, whom Rebecca instantly recognized as the leader, asked her if she and her soldiers were part of the crew. He was broad shouldered and heavily muscled. His sleeves were rolled up high, revealing large, well-defined biceps. The lapels on his fatigue shirt showed two bars, indicating a captain's rank.

Rebecca reinforced her shield and then covered over her inner world with a barrage of thoughts that she wanted the man to hear.

Who is this junior officer daring to ask a lieutenant colonel whether or not she's part of a training exercise?

"Yes, we're the brains of the exercise, soldier," she said aloud.

The man nodded and looked away, satisfied with both her answer and her inner thoughts. Since he wasn't bothering to shield his thoughts, she read them clearly. *Just another Ordinary with an attitude. We'll see what happens to that attitude when things get hot.*

Rebecca wasn't the only one with her shield up. Freddy, Ellis, Roxanne, and Andor had theirs up as well. In London, Roger had Simone reinforce Andor and Roxanne's shields, thus protecting them from any attempts by the Klepers' men to read their thoughts.

Without looking up, Freddy communicated to Ellis, "I'll take Hercules," meaning the muscular leader of the group, "and the goon sitting next to him."

"No, I'll take Hercules and the goon," Ellis replied.

"How about I take Hercules and the goon and you take the other two?"

"Okay, bro, but don't play around with those two. Hercules is Anton Popovich and he's a nasty one. He carries a knife in his right boot and another one in his belt at his back and he's good with them. I've seen him before, a lot of years ago, from a distance. He took out a couple of old friends of ours, Gerry Falkoff and Benny Talon—Berlin, '47, just after the war."

"Oh yeah, I heard tell," Freddy said. "All the more reason to enjoy this. Who are the other three?"

"Next to Popovich is Anatoly Kushnir, tough as a tree trunk. To his left is Peter Ovseeko and next to him is Anatoly Babich. Both are veterans of the massacres in Ukraine. Love to kill at close range, hand to hand. They show up when the killing has to be brutal to make a point. They put down insurrections fast."

"Got it," Freddy said. "Okay, you have Ovseeko and Babich, and I'll take Popovich and Kushnir. Agreed?"

"Okay."

The whine of the jet engines dramatically increased in volume—the sound would have been deafening were it not for the earphones—and the B-52 rose out of its torpor and taxied to the runway. When it reached the foot of the runway, the engines screamed with all their might and, like the dragon that it was, the great beast hurried down the rubber-stained highway until it finally lifted off the ground and roared toward the sky.

The climb toward altitude was like driving a car over a long series of deep potholes. The thing bumped and shook and dropped and lifted until, by sheer relentless force of will, the enormous machine overcame gravity and leveled off well above 45,000 feet.

The B-52 was now over the Atlantic and headed northeast on the first part of its training run.

"Okay, kids, are we ready?" Ellis communicated to the other four.

"Ready," Rebecca said.

"Ready," Andor repeated.

"Ready," Roxanne came back.

"Ready and able," Freddy said.

"Then let's go," Ellis said. "Now!"

They all took off their earphones. Rebecca stood up and turned to the cockpit, but Anatoly Kushnir rose quickly and blocked her way.

One of Freddy's gifts was that he had lightning fast reflexes and could move at speeds that were too fast for the Ordinary human eye to follow. The sheer density of his peripheral nervous system, coupled with an athletic musculature, gave him blinding speed and enormous physical power.

When Kushnir got up, his shield was up, protecting him from Freddy's electrical blast. But even with his shield intact, Kushnir was no match for Freddy.

In a flash, Freddy was between Kushnir and Rebecca and drove his fist into Kushnir's solar plexus, a blow that blew the wind out of his lungs. As Kushnir flew backward across the tiny cabin, Freddy whirled and drove his right boot into Kushnir's jaw, breaking it. As his circular motion continued, Freddy brought his foot around and cut Kushnir's legs out from under him, throwing him to the floor. Kushnir was barely conscious and his shield was down. In an instant, Freddy had his knee on Kushnir's stomach and his hand over his chest. He sent a lightning bolt into Kushnir's heart that killed him instantly.

Popovich, eyes wide as sunny-side-up eggs, was in shock. He couldn't believe anyone could move that fast and take out Kushnir so efficiently. Shaking off his shock, he lunged at Freddy, but before the Slavistani could land a blow, Freddy raised his right arm and in a sweeping motion drove Popovich to the floor. Reaching for Popovich's neck, Freddy was about to send a high-energy beam into the Slavistani's throat, but Popovich was alert and hit Freddy's arm with a left cross that freed him from Freddy's grasp.

In an instant, Freddy was on his feet and about to strike again. Popovich crouched and prepared to send an electrical blast at Freddy, but suddenly the pilot banked to his right, sending everyone to the starboard side of the jet. Popovich's electrical blast went awry. Instead of hitting Freddy, the bolt of electricity flew into the cockpit and hit the navigator, killing him. He slumped forward and fell on his controls.

The two pilots turned in horror. The ship's captain yelled into his communications mask, "Mayday, mayday! We have a hijacking in progress. In need of immediate assistance. Repeat. Mayday, mayday! Hijacking in progress!"

In the midst of Freddy's battle Rebecca had lost her balance, but when the plane tacked to starboard, she regained her footing and darted into the cockpit. She placed her hand on the back of the copilot's neck and instantly rendered him unconscious.

In the narrow cabin, the fighting was at close range. As soon as Popovich had engaged Freddy, Ovseeko and Babich were out of their seats and heading toward the cockpit door. Ellis jumped up and swung his left leg in front of Ovseeko, knocking him to the floor. Andor, who had been seated at the far right, leaped on top of Babich, grabbing him around his neck. He tried to send a blast of energy into Babich, but was too slow. The Slavistani whirled and tried to throw Andor into Ellis, but Ellis ducked and Andor managed to kick Ovseeko in the forehead as he held on to Babich. The Ordinary marine was aghast. As he got up to join the battle, Roxanne blasted him with a series of powerful thoughts that knocked him out.

Popovich hadn't found his footing and could not marshal another blast of energy at Freddy. Instead, he reached behind him, grasped his knife, and threw it at Freddy. Freddy's shield was up, and the knife's path was diverted into the cockpit where it embedded itself into the pilot's back. The pilot fell forward onto the yoke. Instantly, the plane went into a steep nose dive. The jet seemed to pick up speed as it hurtled toward the ocean more than eight miles below.

As the plane turned down, the copilot's body fell forward and collapsed on the control column as well. Everyone in the cabin was thrown forward.

Popovich flew toward Freddy, and Freddy was ready. Braced by the wall separating the cabin from the cockpit, Freddy was the only one with sure footing. He thrust his right fist forward in a powerful arc that found Popovich's neck. The impact of the deadly blow snapped Popovich's trachea. As Popovich gasped for air, Freddy blasted him with a bolt of electricity, killing him.

As the plane fell, Ovseeko and Babich landed on top of Ellis, but then they slid forward over Ellis and toward the cockpit. As soon as his assailants slid off him, Ellis got up and jumped on top of both of them, placing his hands at the backs of their necks. He sent two enormous surges of electricity into their nervous systems. Their bodies jumped; both were dead.

Rebecca frantically tried to lift the pilot out of his seat. The cockpit of a B-52 is relatively tiny and there was little space to put the pilot's body. With all her strength, she pulled the pilot back off the controls and angled his body into the entryway of the cockpit. She then hauled the copilot's body away from the controls, leaving him slumped in his seat. She jumped into the pilot's seat and with all of her might pulled back on the joystick. She calculated that there was plenty of altitude to pull the great dragon out of its free fall, if she could find the strength to get the beast to climb again.

All the bodies rolled toward the cockpit and bunched up at the door. Andor reached out for Roxanne, who lay near him, and pulled her toward him. He held her head close to his chest and telepathically told her that they were going to make it. "I love you," he told her. "And we're going to get through this alive."

Physical strength alone was not going to be enough to pull the yoke back and right the aircraft, Rebecca realized. She stopped pulling instead relaxed her entire body, allowing her mind to become one with the machine. Like a flow of golden light, her mind reached into every inch of the craft, caressing every molecule and moving into the spaces between them. In the process, she and the B-52 bomber became a single integrated unit, a solid state being.

Freddy scrambled to get into the copilot's chair. He placed his left foot against the control panel, which was now nearly horizontal, and used what leverage he had to yank the copilot's body out of his chair.

Rebecca turned her concentration to the wings of the plane, focusing on the flaps. With an irresistible force of will, she turned the wing flaps upward, causing the free-falling jet to slow its descent and angle itself toward its parabolic trough. The yoke was now moving toward Rebecca of its own accord.

Freddy managed to get into the copilot's seat and frantically grabbed hold of the yoke, only to find it moving back toward him without his effort. He looked over at Rebecca, who was in some kind of trance.

"Rebecca?" he yelled telepathically.

Without opening her eyes or looking at Freddy, Rebecca held up one finger and said, "I'll be with you in a minute, Fred."

Freddy took his hands off the handlebars and watched as the plane continued to hurtle toward the ocean at unimaginable speed. He could see the ocean in terrifying detail now. It looked like rippled death.

The plane began to angle out of its vertical descent, turning its nose away from the water. In becoming one with the ship, something of Rebecca's life force and consciousness had been conveyed to the jet, bringing to life the many years of engineering intention and brilliance that gave the ship its singular purpose, which was to fly. The great beast howled with its determination to survive. It turned its nose upward and let out a scream of victory. The dragon had found its wings and was headed toward the sky.

Rebecca came out of her trance and physically took control of the yoke.

The dead bodies and the unconscious marine rolled toward the back of the plane as Ellis, Rebecca, and Andor got to their feet, holding on in order to sustain their balance.

Roxanne cheered. "Mom, you're amazing! You did it. You saved us."

Ellis leaned against the doorway to the cockpit and smiled in exhaustion. He was the first to start applauding, and then Freddy, Roxanne, and Andor all joined in. Andor let out a "Whoopee," and everyone laughed in relief.

"Now, what are we going to do with this thing," Freddy, "as well as with the two guys downstairs, who must be shitting in their pants?"

Rebecca spoke into the communications mask. "Pilot to bombardiers, we have regained control of the ship and are returning to base. You are safe."

She turned to Ellis and Freddy. "I need you guys to disarm the bunker buster so that it's in no danger of going off after we ditch this thing."

Ellis examined the bomb with his mind, found its trigger, and rendered the bunker buster inert and harmless. As for the remaining ordinance, they would present no danger as long as Rebecca landed the plane safely.

She examined the controls, made her calculations, and realized they were over the Atlantic on a latitude with Boston. She banked to her left and informed Logan Airport's air traffic control of her intention to double back toward Andrews.

"We have been informed there's been a hijacking attempt of your aircraft," said the air traffic controller in the Boston tower. "Please inform us of your status."

"The situation has been averted, Boston," Rebecca replied. "Repeat, the crisis has been averted. We are returning to Andrews."

Such a statement would not have been enough to put off a full-scale alert, but she had already taken hold of the air traffic controller's mind and made him believe that the situation had been restored to normal. He informed his superiors that all was under control.

Meanwhile, Andor, who had been trained in medicine, attended to the pilot, who had been stabbed by Popovich's knife.

He reported to Rebecca that he'd stopped the bleeding and was doing what he could to heal the wound, but the pilot would need medical attention once they landed.

"Very good," she said. "Please wipe away any memory our friend might have of us or how he came by that wound. Can you do that?"

"Yes ma'am."

Ellis reached out to Max Louri.

"Are you with us, Max?"

"I'm on your port side, guys and girls," Max came back. "You're looking good."

Everyone in the B-52 turned to their left and waved to Max Louri, who was flying a triangular-shaped ship that did not seem to have engines. It looked like a giant silver arrow's head. No windows could be seen from the outside, though Max could see everything clearly.

"We're going to put down at Atlantic City Airport, Max," Rebecca said. "Follow us in. We'll get out quickly and jump into your ride."

"Understood," Max said. "I'll put the coffee on."

Rebecca reached out to Roger, whom she could feel pressing on her consciousness. "We're all fine, Roger."

"You just gave me the biggest scare of my life," he said. "Are you and Roxanne all right?"

"Yes. We had some trouble for a few minutes and I thought we might have to abandon ship, but we came through fine, Roger."

"Max has been keeping me informed and I've been monitoring all of you, but it's been hard to watch, let me tell you. What are your plans? You can't go back to Andrews."

"No, we'll put down in Atlantic City. Max will get us out."

"Okay," Roger said. "I can't tell you how much I love you."

"I'll contact you as soon as we've landed safely."

Rebecca informed the tower at Atlantic City, a military and civilian airport, that they were coming in and would need emergency medical attention for three members of the crew.

"We've never had a B-52 land on our runway," the Atlantic City air traffic controller told Rebecca. "The runway may not be long enough for you to make a safe landing."

"Have no fear, Atlantic City Approach," Rebecca said. "We can do it." She turned to Freddy. I'll need you to dump the bodies of our Eastern friends over the ocean once we get to a lower altitude."

"Already on it, Rebecca."

Freddy moved to the back of the jet, positioned the bodies over the bomb bay doors, and opened the doors just enough to let the bodies fall into the ocean. "See ya, fellas," he said as he waved good-bye.

Rebecca then told Ellis that once they land, he needed to selectively erase any memory of them in the minds of the air traffic controllers. He assured her he could do that.

Rebecca performed the shortest landing of a B-52 ever achieved. The plane literally came down on the ground and rolled to a stop within the length of a football field. The air traffic controllers in the tower watched the landing with their mouths agape. They shook their heads, and one of them said, "How did she ever do that?"

Rebecca taxied the jet to an unused runway and turned off its engines. Max made a soft landing to the starboard side of the plane, out of sight of the airport terminal and air traffic control. The aircraft Max piloted was invisible to Ordinary radar. As soon as the B-52 came to a stop, Rebecca, Ellis, Freddy, Roxanne, and Andor jumped out of the giant beast and scrambled to Max's waiting bird. Once they were on the jet, it lifted off the ground silently and sped away.

As all five settled into their seats, Ellis said, "Good to see you, Max."

"Yes, Max, it's been awhile," Rebecca said, smiling. "And it's very good to see you."

"Roger has been informed every step of the way," Max replied. "My orders are to bring Rebecca, Roxanne, and Andor home to Washington, and then bring Ellis and Freddy to Kent. Any objections?" Before anyone replied, Max gave a sly smile and said, "Not that they'll matter."

Everyone laughed.

"No objections, Max," Freddy said. "Let's go."

Once he knew that Rebecca, Roxanne, and the rest of the team were safe, Roger sat back in his chair and let his body go limp. He was exhausted. It had been tougher to witness Rebecca and Roxanne in danger than to be in danger himself. Now as he relaxed, he said a silent prayer of thanks and let his mind go blank.

In that instant, out of the blue, he received a piercing and ominous cry of rage and revenge. The intensity of the energy cut through him like a knife. Roger could not make out the identity of the source, but he knew the message came from the Collaborator.

In a fit of hysterical rage and hatred, the Collaborator roared at the top of his lungs, **"Nooo! Nooo! Five hundred billion dollars are lost! All that was mine is gone!"**

Roger could feel the pause as the Collaborator calculated his next move. "I promise you, Reynolds," the Collaborator communicated. "You are a dead man. I will have my revenge."

A chill swept down Roger's spine. He tried to ascertain the Collaborator's identity, but the Collaborator's power blocked him. Nonetheless, Roger's resolve hardened. He returned the Collaborator's threat with a message of his own.

"I'll be waiting for you."

Chapter 27
Ubitzov's Assassins
and Andor's Parents

The White Cliffs of Dover extend for about ten miles along the southeastern coast of England and abut the English Channel. The cliffs are named for the abundance of white chalk in the soil, which gives them their most defining feature. They are very tall, about 360 feet in many places, and make a sheer vertical drop to a narrow strip of rocky beach. When viewed from the English Channel, the cliffs are stunning and unmistakably heroic, a great white wall that has come to symbolize the majesty and enduring courage of England.

Roger stood on a grassy field at the edge of the cliff, the rain whipping his face and black overcoat. The red brick Tudor mansion that he referred to as the House stood tall, wide, and illuminated behind him. It was nearly midnight and rain fell in black sheets along the English coast.

Roger didn't care about the rain. In truth, he was grateful for it. The rain soaked his face and hid his emotions. On the rocky beach, far below Roger's feet, lay the broken body of Felix Novak, Roger's protégé and teammate for the previous twenty-one years. Though he had known for months that he had lost Felix, Roger still mourned the terrible loss of his former friend. Death had been the order of the day that day. Indeed, the previous twenty-four hours had been filled with killing. But there was more: a single revelation had emerged, a dark clue to a mystery that had been tormenting Roger for days—ever since Simone had extracted an unexpected nugget from the troubled mind of Vladimir Ubitzov.

Simone had been searching Ubitzov's mind for any information that might reveal how he planned to kill the members of Roger's team. Today, as it turned out, was the day of reckoning, the day Roger and Ubitzov finally met.

Ubitzov's strategy for assassinating the London team seemed both simple and foolproof. Three teams of Eastern Council commandoes, a total of twenty-five assassins, were to launch an attack on Roger and his coworkers at the House at midnight on November 2. The commandoes would arrive in three separate aircraft. Each aircraft would hover above the house and fire a series of rockets directly into the building. Once the initial bombardment had ceased, the aircraft would take low positions just above the house. Commandoes would repel from the hovering craft and enter the house, killing anyone who remained alive—except for Roger, who was to be spared if he survived the rocket attack. As part of Ubitzov's plan, Felix would volunteer for guard duty at 11:00 p.m. and then sneak out of the house. He would thus be absent when the rocket barrage began.

Ubitzov's team was to gather on November 1 in Berlin, Germany. The twenty-five commandoes, ten of them Eastern Council Geniuses, fifteen hardened mercenaries from Eastern Europe, Somalia, and the Sudan, were to meet on the evening of November 2 at an industrial park owned by the Eastern Council. The park, which appeared to Ordinary eyes to have been abandoned years ago, was well outside the city, isolated, and all but forgotten by city officials. Three Genius-designed aircraft would be sitting on the rooftops of three large warehouses in the park. The jets were capable of making a silent, vertical ascent and, once airborne, could reach supersonic speeds in thirty seconds. The trip from Berlin to Kent, which was for Ordinaries a three-hour flight, would take just under thirty minutes.

Ubitzov initially believed his assassins would have to take out Roger's team on the streets of London, which would prove challenging but doable. He had come up with a plan that he felt sure would work.

There would be casualties, but most of them innocent bystanders, which meant nothing to Ubitzov. But when Roger decided to move his team to Kent, Ubitzov was both surprised and gratified—like a card player who was suddenly dealt a series of cards that were exactly the ones he needed. In fact, Roger's move made Ubitzov's work almost too easy. That alone should have sent up a red flag, but Ubitzov, despite being a Genius, was a blunt instrument. Too many years of killing had left him inured to the subtlety of the chess match. Why concern yourself with subtlety when you've got the equivalent of three howitzers aimed directly at your target? Ubitzov would have argued.

The initial part of his plan did not change when Roger's plan did. Ubitzov's team would still meet in Berlin on November 1, as earlier decided, but the attack would take place on the grounds of the Kent estate. At least there collateral damage would be minimized, except of course for the house, which would be obliterated.

It could be argued that Ubitzov himself was the weak link, since Simone could penetrate his shield and find out what he was planning. But as Roger had predicted, Ubitzov was under immense pressure from Karl Kleper, which made him vulnerable to the point of distraction. His hatred of Kleper, and his overwhelming need for revenge, weakened him considerably. So did the alcohol. Every so often, Ubitzov would indulge in an extended fantasy, made even more manic by an excess of vodka, of how he might kill Kleper. He knew he would have to be extremely cautious. Kleper was the most powerful man he had ever encountered, and the thought of failure terrified him. But the memory of what Kleper had done to him made revenge an absolute necessity. And if life had taught Ubitzov anything, it was that anyone could be killed. All it took was enough planning and a skilled assassin. Indeed, nothing gave him more satisfaction than the thought of killing Kleper. He would sometimes spend an hour or more thinking of how he could render Kleper powerless, perhaps even paralyzed, so that he could strangle the fat walrus with his bare hands. What great joy that would be to see Kleper's eyes bulge in desperate terror, knowing he was about to die at

Ubitzov's hand. Such sweet victory for all the abuse and humiliation Kleper had heaped on him.

Ubitzov's fantasies were dangerous, because plotting to kill Kleper distracted him from the job of killing the Reynolds team. They were, however, a great value to Simone. When Ubitzov was indulging in one of his drunken reveries, she could read his thoughts like an open book. True, she had to navigate the storms of his emotions and dodge the lightning bolts of his rage. Eventually she would get past his fulminating insanity and reach the rational part of his mind, where she found the plan for the assassination of the Reynolds team.

Simone was able to extract most of the details of Ubitzov's attack plan that Roger needed, but she also got one potentially explosive bit of information that neither she nor Roger had expected. She stumbled upon a single reference in Ubitzov's mind to *the Collaborator*. When she found those words, Simone was instantly on the alert. She subtly inserted a question into Ubitzov's unconscious: "Who is the Collaborator?" She received no answer.

Simone and Roger communicated regularly to debrief, and when she passed this new information on to him, Roger thanked her and then withdrew into his own thoughts.

Roger easily found a flaw in Ubitzov's plan, and that flaw originated with one of Ubitzov's character traits: he was a control freak. He also lacked respect for his fellow professionals. Thus, he demanded that the team assemble in Berlin on November 1, to check in with him, and then to meet again at 8 p.m. on November 2 to receive further instructions. They would leave for England several hours later. That left the team exposed for more than twenty-four hours, depending on when each member arrived in Berlin. And that single day was enough for Roger's team—which was composed of the Davies brothers, Max Louri, Simone Laurent, Willie Mayfield, and Roger himself—to take out every one of Ubitzov's assassins.

As for Felix, Roger wasn't taking any chances. He drove Felix from London to Kent himself, and when the two arrived, Roger incapacitated him with a jolt of electromagnetic energy. Felix would remain unconscious for twelve hours. Roger left Stephen and Denise to babysit Felix. Before the team left Kent, Roger had Stephen send a signal to Archangel, programming the satellite to silence the Western Geniuses' warning pings. Ubitzov's assassins never saw them coming.

It was, in Max Louri's words, like shooting fish in a barrel. Six of Ubitzov's Ordinaries stayed at the Berlin Sheraton, two per room, and upon arrival all six ordered room service. Simone and Willie arrived at their doors posing as waiters. As she handed over the check for a signature, Simone gave her victim an irresistible come-hither look, which disarmed the man completely. As he took the check from her, she grabbed his hand and sent an overwhelming barrage of energy and information into his nervous system and brain. Implicit within the cascade of electromagnetic force were the experiences of people who had been victims of violence and injustice. The assassin experienced in his very cells what it was like to be attacked, tortured, and falsely imprisoned. The shock of the experience would change the man forever and render him powerless to engage in such acts again. Of course, the flood of electromagnetic energy also knocked him out. In each case, his partner responded to the attack, but before he could do anything, Willie put him down in precisely the same way. Simone and Willie worked all three rooms, quickly incapacitating the six Ordinaries in rapid succession. In the hours ahead, all of Ubitzov's Ordinaries were dealt with in the same fashion.

The Eastern Geniuses were another matter. In general, one Genius could not reprogram another; their nervous systems were too strong. Also, as long as their shields were up and intact, Geniuses could protect themselves from attacks by other Geniuses. Geniuses also had tremendous recuperative powers, thanks to the enormous amount of energy in their bodies. All of which meant, of course, that battles between Geniuses were usually waged to the death. When it came to killing the assassins, however, Roger and his team accepted the necessity. And because the warning signal had been silenced, all the Eastern Geniuses would be caught off guard, with their shields down.

Seven of the Eastern Geniuses who arrived in Berlin on November 1 had decided to sample one of the city's better brothels. Sex lowered a

Genius's shield, thus making him or her vulnerable to attack, which was exactly what happened at the brothel. Freddy, Ellis, and Max sneaked into the brothel, and while each Eastern assassin was otherwise occupied, finished them off by sending a lethal shock wave through their nervous systems. In one room, Freddy found an assassin enjoying the attentions of two women.

"*Entschuldigen Sie*," Freddy said matter-of-factly to the women. The Eastern Genius, in a state of utter confusion and dismay, looked up at Freddy and said, "Uh …" It was his last thought before Freddy microwaved his brain. Before the women had a chance to scream, Freddy pointed at them, putting both of them to sleep and erasing any memory of what had taken place.

Max and the Ellis carried out variations of the same maneuver until the seven Eastern Geniuses were disposed of. When the work was done, Ellis and Freddy met in the upstairs hallway of the brothel.

"Where's, Max?" Ellis asked.

"I thought he was with you," Freddy said. Suddenly, he knew where Max was. Rolling his eyes, he said, "I'll get him."

Max had always had a weakness for the ladies and had decided to dawdle a bit in the brothel. Freddy found him in a room, sitting on a bed as he kissed a tall, Rubenesque brunette.

Freddy cleared his throat. "Max, it's time."

Max broke off the kiss and looked at the brunette. "I'm sorry, but it's time for Max to go, sweetheart," he said in German.

"Who's going to pay me for the hour, Max?" the woman asked, her mouth turning down in an exaggerated pout. She looked at the dead man lying on the floor. "He doesn't look like he's in any shape to pick up where he left off." She ran her finger over the buttons of Max's shirt and then pressed it to his lips. "Besides, you don't want me to remember what you look like, do you, Max?"

"I see your point," Max said. "Tell you what. You're going to suddenly feel very sleepy. When you wake up, you'll find some cash under your pillow, and the only memory you'll have is that the tooth fairy came by and left you a present."

Max placed two fingers on the woman's forehead and sent her a series of thoughts that put her to sleep for the night. After slipping several bills under her pillow, he turned to Freddy and said with mock annoyance, "You guys don't know how to enjoy yourselves, that's your problem. You've got to stop and smell the roses from time to time."

"I don't think those were roses you were trying to smell, Max."

For the other Geniuses, they knew their names and their room numbers at the hotel. Without the warning ping, Ubitzov's assassins were sitting ducks, whether it was in the hotel elevators or hallways. A couple of them made it out of the hotel, but they were followed and disposed of on a quiet street or alleyway. The many cadavers would be yet another unsolved mystery in the annals of Berlin's crime files.

By 7:30 p.m. on November 2, Ubitzov's entire team had been eliminated. Roger ordered Freddy, Simone, and Willie to fly to Siberia and rescue Andor's parents.

At 8 p.m. Ubitzov waited for his team in a conference room in a warehouse in an industrial park. The room had a utilitarian décor and was illuminated by harsh fluorescent lighting. Ubitzov was seated at the far end of the room in order to see the members of his team as they entered. His was the power seat, he had decided.

The door opened and three men and a woman entered, all dressed in black pants and black leather jackets, and with black hoods over their heads. Roger had insisted they wear hoods so that anyone standing guard at the warehouse would assume they were members of Ubitzov's team. As Ubitzov stared at the four, one of them sat at the table, opposite Ubitzov. Another man took up a position directly in front of the door. The seated man took off his hood, and although Ubitzov had never met the man before, he instantly recognized him—Roger Reynolds. The other three took off their hoods, as well. Ubitzov saw Simone Laurent and Max Louri, the latter man a particularly bitter sight for Ubitzov. He then looked at the man guarding the door and recognized Ellis Davies.

Instantly, Ubitzov realized that the Klepers' satellite had failed him and his entire team. He felt his life force collapse within his chest. He knew his life was over.

"It's like déjà vu all over again, eh, Vladimir?" Max said with a smile.

"It's up to you how things go from here," Roger said to Ubitzov. "We're prepared to make you an offer."

Ubitzov regained his composure and his nerve. He was prepared to die with dignity. "I'm listening," he said.

"We need to know who the Collaborator is. Who is the traitor in the Western Council Headquarters?"

Ubitzov had heard stories about Roger Reynolds, legendary accounts of the powers of his mind. Roger supposedly had highly advanced telekinesis skills; he could lift objects with his mind and hurl them considerable distances. Such stories might have been apocryphal, Ubitzov didn't know. One thing he did know, however: Roger Reynolds was one of only two men whom both Kleper brothers truly respected, and perhaps even feared. The other, of course, was Alexander Astrakhan.

Ubitzov had seen it in Eastern Council board meetings. When Roger's name came up, Karl became quiet at first, even withdrawn, until he found some insignificant event, an excuse really, to fly into a rage. He'd then attack a board member until he had humiliated the person, broken him or her down, and reasserted his dominance. People knew better than to mention Roger's name—unless they wanted to anger Karl, which everyone knew was a dangerous move.

Ubitzov wasn't going to take any chances with Roger. He didn't know what the man was capable of and he was not going to find out. Besides, he had already made his decision.

"There is a collaborator," he said aloud, "but his identity has never been divulged to me. I cannot help you. If you are half as powerful as they say you are, you know that I am telling you the truth."

Ubitzov paused before he spoke again. "I have heard that you are a man of honor, Roger Reynolds, someone who lives according to his own code. Whatever you may believe about me, I too have lived by my own terms. Men who understand these things know that each of us has the right to die with dignity. My time is over. I am asking you not to interfere with my decision."

With that, Ubitzov placed both his hands over his chest and sent a fatal pulse directly into his heart. He slumped forward, his head hitting the table with a loud thud.

No one said a word.

Finally, after a long silence, Max said, "Well, it looks like our work here is done."

Well outside the city of Novosibirsk on the Siberian plain, a small military installation glowed in the snowy night. According to Simone's reconnaissance, 123 military personnel were stationed on site, about seventy of whom were soldiers who guarded the compound. The rest were officers as well as medical, supply, and commissary staff, along with the technical support personnel who operated the radar systems, satellite communications, and the computer spying and eavesdropping equipment. The installation had evolved over the decades. During the Cold War, it was a gulag for political prisoners. When the Cold War ended and the Soviet Union collapsed, the installation went from being strictly a prison to a base for gathering intelligence. It still housed about one hundred prisoners, most of them dissidents, white-collar criminals, or social misfits.

Freddy, Simone, and Willie flew to Novosibirsk in one of the Western Council's multipurpose jets—meaning a jet that was capable of flying silently at supersonic speeds and, once on the ground, converted to what looked like a high-tech recreational vehicle.

The four landed on a nearby farm, converted the jet to an RV, and drove to the Novosibirsk installation. The base was roughly a rectangle, surrounded by a tall electrified fence that was crowned with razor wire. At every corner of the installation, a guard post stood high atop the fence with an armed guard in each watch tower. At the compound's entrance was a booth that housed two sentries. Inside the fence, guards with dogs roamed the periphery of the compound. The base was surrounded for miles by open fields and forest, which themselves were laced with sensors and cameras.

Simone, Willie, and Freddy pulled up in their impressive-looking RV and stopped at the guard booth at the main entrance. All four were dressed in Slavistani military uniforms, all with officers' ranks. The two young guards manning the entrance were immediately on high alert. One looked over the RV with a country-boy's awe and then saluted the officers inside. Simone informed the guard they had orders to transfer two prisoners.

"Could I see some ID, Comrade?" the guard asked Simone.

She handed the soldier a laminated photo ID indicating that she was Major Helena Tischenko. The guard said that he would have to call his superiors for confirmation, but once he reentered the guard booth, he and his partner collapsed on the floor. Willie had put them both to sleep.

He then ordered the fence doors to open, and Simone drove the SUV onto the base and headed for the main headquarters.

The challenge was to get into the prison section of the compound and escape with the Lysenkos without bringing the entire military arm of the base down on them. Complicating the problem was the presence of the two Eastern Geniuses who ran the base. If they discovered that Roger's team had arrived, they would instantly kill the Lysenkos. They would then order a full-scale assault on the Western Geniuses, which would likely kill them all.

Simone and Willie had surveyed the base carefully and come up with a plan, starting with a way to deal with the two Eastern Geniuses. The first big advantage, of course, was that the Eastern Genius's internal warning signal had been silenced. The younger of the two Eastern adepts was Gregory Drubich, twenty-one years old, thin, inexperienced, and introverted. He loved to read and play chess, and he hated being in the army. The other was Ivan Pugach, thirty-five years old, six foot six inches tall and 260 pounds of muscle and girth. Among his many claims to fame were his enormous strength and his capacity to drink and eat quantities of alcohol and food that matched the appetite of large bear. He had been posted to the base by Klaus Kleper and one did not disobey an order that came from either of the Klepers. Still, Pugach had been there for six months and was bored beyond measure. Out of his boredom came a string of fantasies, the latest of which was the ambition to become a great actor or director. Indeed, he loved to sing, especially when he was drunk, but his singing often led to barroom brawls and conflicts with the police. Of late, his boredom and rapacious appetite for vodka had become a problem, and that was especially the case that night. Pugach had passed out on his bed, thoroughly intoxicated.

His condition might have been due to the open case of fine vodka in his room, an anonymous gift from a "secret admirer." Willie had chuckled over that when he packed up the crate and sent it to Pugach. Most of the bottles were empty and strewn all over the floor. Thanks to Simone, every one of those vodka bottles contained an herb that would have put a small elephant to sleep. A large, open tin of caviar was on his desk, along with the remains of a loaf of dark bread. The caviar had been similarly spiked. Pugach was out cold and done for the night.

That left Drubich as the single duty officer at the prison.

Once past the guard post and the gate, Simone drove the RV to the main double doors of the installation. The doors were made of heavy steel and each had a small wire-reinforced window embedded within it. Two guards stood before the doors. Simone parked the RV, and remained in the driver's seat, as Willie and Freddy got out. Simone turned inward focusing intently for a few moments. Suddenly there appeared in the seat next to her an exact double of herself. Both Simone and her newly created double got out of the RV. The double walked around the vehicle, nodding at Simone as she passed her. Using the door which Simone had left open, the double got into the driver's seat. Simone at the same time caught up with Willie and Freddy as they marched toward the two guards. Simone handed her ID to one of the guards, and as he looked down at it, she took command of the minds of both guards.

"Both of you, follow us inside," she ordered.

Both guards, who were heavily armed, each with an automatic rifle and a hand gun holstered at their sides, obeyed.

All five went through the main doors of the compound and entered a foyer. At the end of the foyer was a gray wall. In the center of the wall was a window, six feet wide and four feet tall, which opened onto a large room. The window was thick reinforced glass. One long panel of the glass could slide open to allow papers or other items to pass between the military receptionist on the other side and any visitors.

Inside the room were rows of chairs and desks, each one with a computer screen sitting atop it. About half the desks, perhaps twenty-five of them, were occupied with people staring intently at their computer terminals.

To the right of the window was a large steel door with an electronic key pad. Beyond the door was a hallway that ended in a set of steel doors. These were also accessible only through an electronic key pad. Looking at those double doors, Simone knew they were the entrance to the prison.

With Simone leading the way, the three Western Geniuses and the two Slavistani guards approached the window and were met by a tough-looking sergeant in his late 50s. The sergeant on the other side of the window, Gregorovich, a lean and grizzled veteran of the Afghanistan war, stood and demanded their ID. As Simone handed him her card he asked what their business was.

"I want you to arrest Commander Drubich," Simone said.

"What? What the hell are you talking about?"

Simone looked directly into the sergeant's eyes and held them in her gaze. "Take these two guards standing behind me and eight other soldiers, enter Commander Drubich's office, and arrest him. You are to tell your men that you are acting on orders from Commander Pugach. Do you understand me?"

"Yes, Comrade, I understand you," the sergeant said.

"You, Sergeant, are to shoot Commander Drubich in the left leg, at the outer part of his thigh, in order to disable him. You are not to inflict a fatal wound. Instruct the two guards behind me to shoot Commander Drubich in the thigh if you become incapacitated during your attempt to arrest the commander. Once you shoot Commander Drubich, you are to place him in handcuffs. Do you understand me, Sergeant?"

"Yes, Comrade, I understand."

"Good," Simone continued. "Once you have him in custody and handcuffed, you are to bring him to the infirmary, under guard, where his wound will be treated. He must remain there under arrest until he can be transferred to a prison cell. Do I make myself clear, Sergeant?"

"Yes, Comrade."

"Now give me back my ID, open the door to these two men, and do what you have been ordered to do."

Gregorovich handed her ID back to Simone and then buzzed open the door to the big room behind him. The two guards entered the main room and followed the sergeant to the other side of the room, where Drubich's office was located.

Gregorovich immediately ordered eight men to get their weapons from the armory, which was a glass-enclosed closet attached to the back wall of the room. "Get off your arses, get your weapons, and follow me to Commander Drubich's office," he commanded. The soldiers scrambled for their weapons and followed Gregorovich to the commander's door.

"I am going to shoot Comrade Drubich in the left thigh," the sergeant told the soldiers. "If I fail to hit him or if I am shot myself, you are to shoot Commander Drubich in the thigh and then arrest him. You are then to bring him to the infirmary. Understood?"

"Understood," the men said in desultory accord.

Gregorovich cocked his firearm and burst into Drubich's office, with the ten men remaining in the doorway, blocking it.

Drubich was young and inexperienced and not particularly powerful. He had never received much training, and like Andor and Roxanne, he had not yet come into his full powers.

Still, the instant he saw Gregorovich, he knew exactly what the sergeant was up to. Before Gregorovich could get off a shot, Drubich flattened him with a burst of energy. Gregorovich fell to the floor, unconsciousness.

Drubich got up from his desk, but before he could stop them, two guards fired at him. Drubich's shield was up. One shot missed him by a hair, but the other grazed his leg. The shallow but painful wound weakened Drubich and he lowered his shield. One of the guards fired again, this time hitting him directly in the left thigh.

Gregorovich, meanwhile, regained consciousness and came up shooting, hitting Drubich again in the thigh. Drubich fell to the floor in agony.

"Are you crazy?" he screamed.

"Commander Drubich, you are under arrest by order of Commander Pugach," Gregorovich said. He turned to the soldiers behind him. "You men, pick up Commander Drubich and carry him to the infirmary."

Drubich's voice rang in Pugach's mind as if from far away. It was a voice in a dream. Pugach tried with all of his strength to rouse himself. He opened his eyes, but the room rolled to the portside. Pugach moaned and fell back on his bed, instantly asleep again.

Drubich continued to scream telepathically to Pugach, but his calls fell on deaf ears.

As Simone, Freddy, and Willie ran toward the cell where the Lysenkos were held, they could hear gunshots going off inside the compound. Simone smiled and looked at the two men. "Gregorovich is a man who follows orders," she said telepathically.

The prison was on three floors. The Lysenkos were located on the first floor at the end of a long corridor. Both sides of the corridor were lined with heavy steel cell doors, behind which were thirty-five prisoners. In front of the Lysenkos' cell were two powerfully built guards, who had been ordered to stop anyone from approaching.

"Stop!" one of the guards commanded as Freddy, William and Simone approached.

The three kept coming.

The guard brought his weapon to his shoulder. "Stop or I will shoot!"

Willie pulled out what looked like a toy ray gun. The guard was about to shoot, but before he did, Willie fired.

A blast of light illuminated the corridor, and the two guards were thrown back some twenty feet. Both lay unconscious as Simone, Freddy, and Willie arrived at the cell door of Mikael and Arianna Lysenko.

Willie placed his hand on the door and the lock flew open with a loud clank. The three hurried into the cell.

On one side of the cell Mikael lay on a thin cot, dying of diabetic shock from lack of insulin. Arianna sat next to him, deep in grief. The Klepers had made it clear to the prison staff that they had no long-term interest in the Lysenkos and that minimal care should be given to them. If they died in prison, well, it was an efficient way to deal with a problem. Consequently, the infirmary staff administered only occasional doses of insulin, and even then the doses were usually inadequate. Mikael had hung on for months, but he was clearly near his end.

When the three Western Geniuses entered the cell, Arianna placed her hands over her heart and cried, "Leave us alone, please leave us alone!"

"We're here to help you, ma'am," Willie said in Slavistani. "We're going to get you out."

Simone kneeled beside Mikael's cot. She took a small black case out of her coat pocket, removed a syringe, and then administered a Genius medicine for diabetes to Mikael. Next she took a vial with a clear liquid from the case and poured the elixir into Mikael's mouth.

Within seconds of receiving the two medicines, Mikael opened his eyes. Arianna fell down on the side of his bed and kissed her husband on the cheek.

"Mikael, Mikael, Mikael, I thought you had left me."

As though awakening from a long sleep, Mikael raised his hand and stroked his wife's head. Tears flowed from Arianna's eyes.

Willie looked deeply into the weakened woman and radiated waves of healing energy into her, filling every cell of her body and invigorating her with new life.

"We have to go," Freddy said. "Mrs. Lysenko, can you hurry?"

"Yes," she replied. Indeed, she suddenly looked healthy enough to run back to her home. "But my husband is weak."

"We can take him," Freddy said.

Willie helped Mikael from his bed and lifted the emaciated man onto Freddy's back. From the hallway they could hear the other prisoners chanting, "Let us out! Let us out!" Simone sent a telepathic message to her double, waiting in the RV, that they were on their way. Simone took

Arianna's hand and the three ran out into the hallway, running away from the prison door through which they had come.

Slavistani soldiers were swarming through that door. A spray of bullets peppered the hallway, all of them missing their intended targets. Willie looked back and fired his ray gun, flattening the first line of guards.

"Willie, the doors!" Freddy yelled telepathically.

Willie placed his right hand on one of the locked cell doors, closed his eyes, and sent a shockwave of energy into the door. In an instant, all the cell doors in the building were flung open. Prisoners rushed into the hallways and immediately began attacking the guards.

Simone's double transformed the RV into a jet again. Wings unfolded from the sides; landing gear rose from below as a tail assembly emerged from the rear of the vehicle. The windshield angled downward, giving the craft a sleek fuselage. Simone's double threw a series of switches on the jet's controls, and great gusts of wind sprang from below. The jet lifted straight up from the parking lot. Guards shouted "Stop!" as alarms rang out in the night.

Simone's double flew the jet slowly over the compound to the roof of the prison, projecting thoughts of confusion to the guards. Bullets flew in all directions, but none hit the jet.

Inside the prison, the Geniuses and the Lysenkos had made it to the end of the hallway and a metal door that opened to a staircase. Willie flung open the door and they ran up the stairs. On the third floor, a ladder led to a door in the roof. The roof door was bolted and locked shut. A single shot from Willie's ray gun blasted open the door, revealing the snowy night above. With Mikael Lysenko on his back, Freddy climbed the ladder and made it to the roof. Arianna, still inspired by her newfound energy, easily climbed the ladder. Simone and Willie followed.

Simone's double landed the jet on the rooftop, opening a door in the side of the craft. Freddy carried Mikael Lysenko inside and strapped him into a seat. The three others jumped in as Simone's double disappeared, and Simone replaced her in the pilot's seat. Shots were fired at the jet but bounced off in sparks, harmlessly. Simone closed the door, gunned the jets, and instantly the craft was gone.

By 10:30 that night all of Roger's team was back at the House. Roger was at the back of the property, standing at the edge of the cliff and looking out into the darkness. "Everything is proceeding", he thought, *but the day wasn't over.*

Stephen joined him. "Are you all right, Chief?"

"Yes, Stephen.. Please wake Felix and bring him to me in the library. And ask Simone and Willie to join me there as well."

The room was a classical English library, complete with an eighteen-foot ceiling, dark wood paneling, and a floor-to-ceiling bookcase. The beauty of the room pulled a visitor's eye in all directions—to the Oriental rug on the floor and the magisterial oak desk; to the sitting area, which looked out onto a veranda through floor-to ceiling windows; to the large fireplace with its array of Queen Anne chairs and a small sofa; to the French doors that opened to the back of the property. Someone had made a fire that burned brightly in the hearth. The room was softly lit by small ensconced lamps, as well as a couple floor lamps. The large crystal chandelier that hung from the ceiling was turned off. Roger chose to conduct his meeting with Felix in front of the fireplace, sitting in a chair to the left of the fireplace.

The door to the library opened and Felix walked in, followed by Simone and Willie. Roger gestured for Felix to sit opposite. Willie stayed by the door while Simone sat in a large leather chair near the French doors.

Felix looked as if he had just awakened after a hard night of drinking. His blond hair was disheveled, the collar of his shirt was open, and his mottled face looked much older than it had ever appeared to anyone who knew him. He also looked especially nervous.

"What time is it?" he asked Roger as he sat down.

"Ten thirty-five," Roger replied.

Felix looked visibly concerned and Roger knew why. He had an hour and a half before the cannons started firing.

"Are you concerned about the time, Felix?"

"No. Not at all."

"They're not coming, Felix."

Felix acted baffled. "What are you talking about?"

"Ubitzov and his assassins. They're not coming. They were all put down earlier today. Ubitzov ended up taking his own life."

Felix let go of the charade and permitted himself a bitter smile. "I thought they'd finally found a way to beat you. I should have known that you'd figure things out. You always do."

"How did they get Jason Phillips to come over to their side?" Roger asked.

"I don't know."

"What could they offer him?" Roger asked. "He had all the wealth he needed. He was immune to greed or any lust for power. What could they give him that would have turned him?"

Felix indulged in a rueful smile. "I don't know. They got me, didn't they?"

Roger delved deeper. Jason Phillips was one of a rare breed whose loyalty was to a set of principles and higher truths. That alone made him one of the most trustworthy men Roger had ever met. "Speculate for me, Felix, knowing Kleper and his cohort as you do. What could they have offered Jason that would have turned him?"

Felix realized that Roger's only concern was for Jason Phillips. He had no interest in talking about Felix or what might have motivated him. The air went out of his lungs and his shoulders sagged. He had failed his mentor so completely that Roger was letting him go. All he wanted was a bit of information, a clue or two, that would move him to the next step in his relentless sense of purpose. In that moment, Felix felt the depth of his betrayal. Despair engulfed him. He wanted to throw himself at Roger's knee and beg forgiveness.

"I'll tell you what I think," he said, "but please do one thing for me."

"What do you want?" Roger asked.

"Take a walk with me out back."

"The weather is bad, Felix. It's not a night for a walk."

"Indulge me, Roger. I promise, I'll tell you what I think. I just want a moment with you in private."

Roger looked over at Simone and nodded to her. She got up and stood by the French doors. Willie got Roger's coat and handed it to him. He then took off his own jacket and offered it to Felix. Felix smiled but refused the coat. He placed his hand on Willie's shoulder and gave him a look of deep affection. "I'm sorry, Willie," he said.

"Me too, mate."

Roger threw on his overcoat and the two men stepped out of the house and into the misty rain. Roger turned up his collar, but Felix appeared oblivious to the weather. The two men walked toward the cliff, stopping partway there.

Felix turned to Roger. "You know, you were the only father figure I ever had," he said. "I grew up hating my father for abandoning my mother and me. I suppose my father ruined my relationship with you. As much as I admired and even loved you, I was always angry at you. Maybe it was partly your fault too. You're always so remote, so mission oriented. I wanted your attention, your fatherly love. I needed you to see me as more important than the mission...not all the time, but once in a while. People are more important than the job, Roger. And you hold a position in our lives that makes you more than our boss." He looked at Roger and gave a small, bitter smile. "Our Chief."

"What about Jason?" Roger asked. "What drove him to the other side?"

Felix wanted to kill Roger right then and there. "Always in character, Chief. Always in character."

Felix looked out into the bleak night, the rain suddenly getting heavier. It soaked his face and clothing. He walked farther away from the house. When he was about ten yards from the cliff, he stopped and looked at Roger.

"Someone is running him," he said verbally, his voice loud to be heard over the rain. "Someone has taken over his mind. I've always liked Jason, and I couldn't believe it when they told me that he was with us. He was always the straight-arrow type. After he gave the presentation to the bankers, I contacted him and congratulated him on what he had done. He didn't know what I was talking about. He was utterly confused. I covered my tracks and he let it go. But that's when I realized that someone had gained control of him."

Roger was stunned. He nearly fell over from the impact of Felix's words. What could have blinded him to so obvious a truth?

"Yes, your focus on mission has kept you from seeing the obvious," Felix said. "You can see the steps, but not the people who make them."

Roger was looking down at the ground. The implications of what Felix had said rolled over him like a tidal wave. He felt dizzy and for a moment thought he might throw up. For a moment, he became disengaged and forgot Felix's presence.

"Good-bye, Roger," Felix said, and suddenly he bolted for the darkness at the edge of the cliff.

"Felix, no!"

But Felix had already reached the cliff's edge. He jumped into the abyss and was gone, swallowed by the darkness.

Chapter 28
Andor Goes off Script, Andor and Roxanne in Love

They could hardly bear the intensity of their desire for each other. For two weeks after the B-52 mission, Roxanne and Andor were possessed by a fever that grew more intense with every passing day. Their hunger for each other, and the emotions that their yearning generated, illuminated every part of their lives. All of life was different now, because every moment, even the most boring parts of their day, were imbued with love. Roxanne was at the center of Andor's world. Social studies, mathematics, gym, even the few minutes he spent at home with the goons posing as his parents were colored by her presence, infused by her light. She was everywhere in his life. Yet she was beyond his reach, his longing for her unfulfilled.

For Roxanne, all that had mattered in the past was now irrelevant, trivial, even meaningless in comparison to her love for Andor. She would sit in class and wonder what he was doing. She couldn't bear the distance that separated them. From the other side of the Laurel, she would interrupt his thoughts with her own entreaties.

"Are you feeling what I'm feeling?" she would ask him telepathically as she sat in social studies class while he was in math.

"All I can think about is you," he communicated back to her. "If there was somewhere safe for us to go, I would walk out of this worthless class right now and take you there this very instant."

"Tell me more," she asked, teasing him.

As her teacher prattled on about some irrelevant point concerning the Civil War, and as his teacher presented some elementary algebraic steps, they continued mentally exchanging thoughts of love and teasing each other.

Their worlds were joined in a dream of love. Their telepathic abilities acted as a feedback loop, each one knowing the other's thoughts, and thus heightening their mutual yearning. At lunch, they sneaked away to the pond and embraced and kissed. They stopped off at the coffee shop after school and tucked themselves into a booth, locking eyes and holding each other with looks of longing. Every little touch was electric. Andor could barely graze her hand with his own without feeling an electric charge through his body.

At night, he would pick her up at home and take her to the movies, or to the coffee shop, and later they would park on a deserted street and kiss and caress each other until frustration exhausted them. They discussed making love in the backseat, but Roxanne rejected the idea. Too small, too cramped, she told him. She didn't want it to be that way.

"This is my first time," she told him. "I want it to be right."

"You're so beautiful and I love you so much. I want it to be right too. But I cannot stand waiting."

Both realized the waiting was a painful ecstasy all its own.

She smiled, amused by her power over him. "Maybe I'll just keep you waiting. That way you'll always be my slave."

"I'm already your slave, your fool, your Romeo." he said. And then quoting the Bard, Andor said, "I would I were thy bird."

Roxanne, not missing a beat, picked up Juliet's next line.

"Sweet, so would I.
Yet I should kill thee with much cherishing.
Good night, good night! Parting is such sweet sorrow
That I shall say good night till it be morrow."

"Leave it to Shakespeare to ruin the moment," Andor said ruefully.

"No moment with you is ruined," Roxanne told him. "Not for me." She pulled him close and kissed him.

They held each other in silence. Both knew that the only right place was Roxanne's bedroom, but her mother was home at night, and Roxanne didn't know when she might go out with friends.

"Sooner or later she is bound to go out," Roxanne said. "If she doesn't, I'll just confess it all to her and tell her that we want to be together."

"You'd tell your mother?" Andor asked, amazed yet again by Roxanne's remarkable honesty.

"Yes. I would. But I think my mother would understand. I love you, and she always told me that love is what makes the first time right."

Little did Roxanne know that she wouldn't have to tell her mother. Rebecca already knew. She and Roger were well aware of what was going on—or at least, aware enough to know the intensity of their daughter's feelings. That night after Roxanne got home, Rebecca discussed the situation with Roger.

"What should we do?" he asked.

"The only thing we can do," she said. "Let nature take its course."

"You trust him?"

"Yes. His feelings are genuine. I'm convinced he loves her and would die before he did anything to hurt her. I'm fine with him. And I know she loves him. And you know our daughter. When she wants something badly enough, she'll find a way to get it. Besides, she just had her eighteenth birthday and she's of age."

Roger laughed. "You're right. But you realize what you've got to do?"

Rebecca sighed. "Yes, I suppose it's time I spent a night out with Elizabeth."

Elizabeth Rawley was a Genius librarian who worked at the headquarters of the Western Council. She was married to another Genius, Hank Rawley, who worked as a plumber and electrician in Washington. The two Geniuses had five children and were immensely happy. Elizabeth was a lovely woman, but she loved to cook and bake and to make great feasts for Hank and her children, so all of whom were a little on the plump side. Rebecca had long ago realized that Elizabeth wanted to be soft and round. It was who she was in her heart and soul. She loved to hug people, to enfold them in her oversized bosom and mother them. Cooking delicious meals and making people feel safe and at home was how she gave her love.

"I'll contact Elizabeth and ask if we can get together soon," Rebecca said to Roger. "She'll want to know what's going on and I need some mothering myself."

"Seems like you've already thought this through."

She sighed again. "Do you think we're doing the right thing?"

"Yes, I do. He's a good young man, and he's made an incredible transformation. With grooming, he may work with me some day. I trust him too."

Three days later, on a Thursday evening, Rebecca told Roxanne that she would be going out with Elizabeth Rawley on Saturday night. They'd probably see a movie and then sit in a café and talk for a few hours. She'd be out late.

Before she went to bed that night, Roxanne reached out to Andor and told him the good news. "Saturday night. We'll be together. Come prepared."

"Prepared?" he repeated. "This condom I've been carrying around for the past three weeks is getting worn out from fantasy."

Andor was about to add something when another set of thoughts invaded his consciousness. Roxanne felt his sudden shift in mood.

"What's wrong?" she asked.

"Nothing, I suppose I just got nervous about the speech I have to give tomorrow. I hope it goes all right."

"Andor, don't worry. You're going to be great. You are going to help so many people tomorrow. Did you text Paul?"

"Yes, but I didn't get anything back."

"He'll be there. I know him. He will not run from a fight."

"Neither will I."

"That's one of the many reasons why I love you."

The following day, Andor stood under a large black umbrella on the steps of the Lincoln Memorial, along with a cadre of dignitaries that included the mayor of Washington, DC, two congressmen from Maryland, and Thompson's senatorial staff, which included Martin Chipulsky and Molly Handwringer. In front of the group, with his back to Andor, was Senator Thompson, who faced about five hundred people at the foot of the steps leading up to the memorial. At the front of the crowd were about a half dozen television cameras. TV and print journalists held their digital recorders aloft. Thompson stood at a podium that was crowded with microphones, most of them from the television stations. At his feet, heavy cable wires ran like a snake pit of boa constrictors.

The event was ostensibly to rally public opinion against any US involvement in the war in Slavistan, but in fact it was yet another thinly veiled presidential campaign appearance by Thompson. A heavy rain had fallen earlier that morning, but the sky, though gray and heavy, rested for the moment. Still, umbrellas remained open throughout the crowd and among the dignitaries in anticipation of a sudden downpour.

Andor had arrived at 10:30 a.m., as requested by Thompson's staff, and had met briefly with the senator in the large tent the senator's staff had erected on the grassy ellipse behind the Memorial.

"Damn this rain, dammit all to hell," the senator was saying to his speechwriter, Martin Chipulsky, as Andor approached. "We've got to have a good turnout today, Chipulsky. We've got the major networks coming this morning and all the big newspapers and magazines. You promised me a crowd, Chipulsky, and you better deliver."

Chipulsky and fellow staff members had been working on the event for weeks, and they had managed to bring in a handful of local dignitaries and the actor Chuck Norris. "The people will show up, Senator," Chipulsky said. "We're busing in people from five senior citizens homes and a local VFW. Everyone is excited to meet Chuck. He said he would hang around to take pictures with people and sign autographs."

Thompson seemed momentarily reassured, and then he brightened when he spotted Andor walking toward him.

"Andor, my boy, wonderful to see you. We've got a big day in front of us, son, a very big day." Thompson threw his heavy right arm around Andor's shoulders and pulled the young man toward him. As he held onto Andor, Thompson snapped his fingers at Chipulsky and opened his hand in a signal for Chipulsky to give him something. Chipulsky reached into his briefcase, removed a sheaf of papers, and handed them to Thompson.

"Andor, Martin's written a fine speech that I want you to deliver to this great American crowd that will be showing up for this event today." Thompson handed the speech to Andor. "Do you think you can sit down over there"—he nodded to a corner of the tent—"and memorize this speech? You've got a couple of hours."

Andor looked at the speech, which was ten pages long. "Yes, I think I could memorize this in the next couple of hours."

"That's my boy," Thompson replied, all smiles. "You're a smart young man. I know you can memorize this in two hours. Piece of cake for you, right, son? Piece of cake."

Andor noted that Thompson reeked of men's cologne, probably to cover the smell of alcohol that would be discharging from his pores.

Thompson was talking again. "I'm sure you've heard about the Lincoln Memorial. Do you know that this is the place where Martin Luther King gave his 'I Have a Dream' speech? Are you aware of that, Andor? This is a place where history is made, and today you and I are going to make history. I want you to put your heart and soul into this great speech that my staff has written for you." Thompson waved his hand over the horizon as if he was seeing Martin Luther King giving his great oration. "Make Dr. King proud today, Andor, Make him proud."

Andor looked directly into Thompson's eyes and said, "I plan to, Senator."

"That's my boy."

Now, three hours later, Senator Thompson walked to the podium on the steps of the memorial and prepared to address the crowd. The event would unfold according to the usual plan. Thompson would begin with a short, rousing speech. He would then introduce Andor, who would address the crowd in his role as envoy for the youth of Slavistan and the future alliance between the young people of Slavistan and America. He would speak for about twenty minutes, after which Chuck Norris would bellow a few platitudes about US debt and the need for independence from the United Nations. Thompson would then follow with another rousing speech meant to bring the crowd to a frenzy. Members of Thompson's staff, along with a dozen hired hands from the local unemployment office, had been placed throughout the audience carrying signs that said, Thompson for President, Thompson for America, and President Thompson for a Peaceful World. These plants would also chant "Thompson for President" whenever the crowd was whipped up.

From the podium, Thompson looked over the audience and began his remarks.

"Ladies and gentlemen, esteemed members of the press, honored guests who stand with me on the steps of this sublime monument to our greatest president, I thank you for braving the weather today to show your support for a more peaceful and just world."

As Thompson spoke, Andor searched the crowd frantically, hoping to find the one person he needed in order to accomplish his mission. Finally he spotted him. A few rows back behind the press was Paul Grinsky, his arms folded, his brow furrowed, looking every bit like a man ready for a fight. Andor couldn't help but smile. The previous night, Andor had texted Paul a simple yet provocative message: *if u wnt 2 mk a diffrnc, b @ Lncln Mem tmrrw at 1 and b redy 2 spk.*

And Roxanne had been right—Paul had come.

Andor shifted his gaze to the many members of the press who were all bunched up in front of the crowd. Network labels abounded—CNN, Fox News, CBS, NBC, ABC, and MSNBC all were accounted for. Andor recognized journalists from the *Washington Post* and the *New York Times*, who had interviewed him after the attack at Laurel Glen. Photographers peered through their lenses and snapped a continuous stream of pictures.

Good. They're all here, Andor thought. *Now, let's hope we get it right.*

He turned his attention back to Thompson, who was winding down the initial part of his talk.

"Slavistan and its neighbors have to be allowed to work out their disagreements on their own. They don't need us, and they surely don't need the UN messing around in their internal affairs."

The crowd let out a half-hearted set of cheers. Someone yelled, "Thompson for President," but those who heard the man merely turned around and looked at him as if he were a fool. Thompson continued.

"Now, folks, I've got a couple of very special guest speakers for you, starting with a young man, Andor Lysenko, who just arrived here in the United States from Slavistan. Andor, as you all know, saved the lives of hundreds of people at Laurel Glen High School just a month ago. He's a bona fide hero, folks, and he's going to give you a firsthand account of what's going on in Slavistan and why we need to give the young people of that great nation the time to work out their problems on their own. It's their future, and they've got to be the ones to shape it. Andor Lysenko, why don't you come up here and address this great American crowd? Folks, let's give a big, warm American welcome to this wonderful young man, a real life hero from Slavistan, Andor Lysenko!"

People cheered as Andor walked to the podium and shook Thompson's hand. Thompson hurried to the back of the group of dignitaries who were gathered behind the podium to consult with Chipulsky on his speech, which Thompson felt was not being met with the kind of enthusiasm he was looking for.

"Thank you, Senator Thompson," Andor began. "Americans should ask themselves: Do we have any moral responsibility for protecting unarmed peasants, shopkeepers, and farmers against heavily armed mercenaries and soldiers who are trying to steal the land of a free and peaceful people? The people of Slavistan, Bulgaristan, Cossackia, and Czeckostan are being murdered, mutilated, and raped as they try to defend their homelands against Slavistani soldiers and hired thugs who are posing as ordinary citizens. Those same thugs are crossing back into Slavistan and killing innocent Slavistanis in order to make it look like the people of Bulgaristan, Cossackia, and Czeckostan are engaged in hostile acts of aggression against Slavistan. It's all a made-up war. And why? Because Victor Grozny, the president of Slavistan, is attempting to take over and annex those three small countries, and he will murder anyone who stands in his way. He's trying to restore a kind of Soviet empire, and he's starting by taking over three powerless nations.

"Meanwhile, men like Senator Thompson are doing Grozny's dirty work by keeping Americans in the dark and blocking the US government from demanding that the United Nations investigate the atrocities taking place along the border between Slavistan and its neighbors. The people of Slavistan do not want this war, nor do the people of Bulgaristan, Cossackia, and Czeckostan. The only people who benefit from the fighting are Grozny, his corrupt regime, and men like Senator Thompson, who want to use the war in order to advance their political ambitions. In Thompson's case, he wants to be president of the United States and he'll allow innocent people to be murdered in order to reach his ambition."

Chipulsky was the first to realize that Andor had gone off script. Dumbfounded and shocked, he said to Thompson, "What is he saying? Are you hearing what he's saying? He can't say that. You've got to get up there and stop him!"

But Thompson had fallen into some kind of trance. Chipulsky took one look at Thompson and realized he was either falling asleep—which made absolutely no sense—or he was fainting, due perhaps to the shock of Andor's words or the onset of some disorder. "Are you all right, Senator? What's going on?"

"Nothin', nothin'," Thompson said, slurring his words. He struggled to lift his arm, as if to wave Chipulsky off, but clearly he was too weak to complete the gesture.

Chipulsky was on the verge of panic. He thought about running up to Andor and tackling him, but realized that that would be the end of his political career. He'd be known forever as the guy who tackled the whistleblower on the steps of the Lincoln Memorial. Terrified, he searched the group of staffers around him for help, but the aides merely shook their heads and raised their shoulders as if to say, I'm not going to ruin my career for Thompson, either. Chipulsky looked over at Molly Handwringer, but the poor girl was far too busy filing her nails to notice that her Hollywood ambitions were, at that very moment, sinking like the Titanic. A sudden inspiration hit Chipulsky: he would get Chuck Norris to push Andor off the stage. Have Chuck be the hero and get them back on message. He searched the dignitaries on the steps for Norris, but apparently he had fled the scene. Suddenly, Thompson swooned toward Chipulsky and passed out. The speechwriter caught the senator and leaned him back toward his chair, whereupon the senator fell onto the concrete floor of the memorial, landing with a thud.

Meanwhile, Andor had continued his speech. He held up his hand and waved a thick sheaf of papers.

"I'm holding more than fifty e-mails from relatives and friends in Slavistan that document the horrific atrocities taking place along the Slavistani border. In addition, right here in this crowd is an American-Slavistani who wants to speak to you about the tragic events in our country. His name is Paul Grinsky, and he's a classmate of mine at Laurel Glen High School. Paul, why don't you come up and tell the people what's happening in Slavistan?"

The television cameras and photographers turned and found Paul Grinsky in their lenses. Without hesitation, Paul bounded across the grassy mall and ran up the steps to the podium where Andor stood. Andor yielded the microphones to Paul.

"Hello, everyone," Paul began. "My name is Paul Grinsky and I'm an American citizen who was born in Slavistan and still has family living there. In fact, my relatives are living right on the border with one of the three countries that are being invaded by Grozny's goons every day. My grandparents, who are in their eighties, had to flee their village on the Slavistani border in order to keep from being killed by mercenaries. Innocent people on both sides of the border are being killed and having their homes stolen every day. Everything that Andor says is true. Victor Grozny is staging a war in order to steal the land of innocent, law-abiding citizens. We need the United States government to insist that the international community, especially the United Nations, stop this tyrant. We as Americans have to stand with those who are fighting to keep their homes and their homelands. Let's stand with the people of Slavistan and against the criminal, murderous, imperialistic regime of Victor Grozny!"

Paul and Andor grasped each other's hands and lifted them into the air in a gesture of solidarity.

The crowd went crazy. Raucous applause rang out, and the VFW members seemed to be applauding the loudest. Television cameras panned from Andor and Paul to the hundreds of people who clapped and shouted their approval. Photographers, their cameras hungry for the moment, consumed every word and gesture. Print media and television journalists called questions out to the two young speakers. And then the heavens exploded and rain fell in heavy sheets. The dignitaries on the Lincoln Memorial steps scattered. Andor and Paul ran from the podium for cover, a flock of journalists, photographers, and television cameramen hurrying after them. In seconds, the Lincoln Memorial and grounds had been abandoned by all but two men—Senator Stewart Thompson, who was still in deep slumber, and Martin Chipulsky, who was waiting for medical help to arrive.

Saturday night, Rebecca put on her coat and fished through her purse for her car keys. She walked to the bottom of the stairs and called up to Roxanne that she was leaving. Roxanne hurried down the stairs and embraced her mother.

"Thanks, Mom," she said with genuine warmth and gratitude. She didn't for a second think her mother was unaware of what was going on.

"Thanks for what?" Rebecca asked, feigning innocence.

Roxanne hesitated and smiled. "Thanks for ... being you."

Rebecca continued to fish through her purse, seemingly oblivious to her daughter. Finally she found her keys and looked at Roxanne. She pretended not to notice the perfume that Roxanne was wearing, or the fact that her white button-down blouse was open low on her chest and hung over a tight denim miniskirt. She wore no shoes or socks.

"I'll be late," she said, "figure around midnight. We're seeing a film and then we'll go out and catch up. Elizabeth wants to know all about our adventure with the B-52. Apparently the word got out at HQ and they all want details. As librarian, Elizabeth will record the history of the event. Anyway, you know how Elizabeth is. She loves a good story."

"You have fun," Roxanne said, suddenly feeling maternal toward her mother. "And let her love you up. You deserve it."

Rebecca hugged her daughter and kissed her on the cheek.

"Love you too," she said, and left.

Andor was parked on the other side of the block and he nearly raced to the open parking spot in front of Roxanne's house after she informed him that all was clear. He entered the house with an air of stealth.

"You needn't be secretive," Roxanne said. "Both my parents know." She kissed him. "We have their blessing."

Now that they were together and free to fulfill their fantasy, both were nervous. Neither wanted anything to go wrong, and both felt the pressure to make the experience live up to their hopes and expectations.

"Would you like something to eat or drink?" Roxanne asked.

"No," Andor said, looking deeply into Roxanne's blue eyes. She was the most beautiful girl he had ever seen. She was an angel, a goddess. "I only want you."

She took his hand and led him upstairs to her bedroom.

Only one light shone in her room, a small lamp at the far corner glowing soft and warm. Andor closed the door behind them and put his arms around her, kissing her softly on the lips. Their minds reached out, and they communicated their love and desire for each other. Andor felt Roxanne's vulnerability and tenderness; and Roxanne felt Andor's decency and love for her.. Both knew to go slowly at first, each aware psychically that the other's defenses were still up but desperate to fall away.

He unbuttoned her blouse slowly, concerned that he might appear to be all thumbs. Her expression of amusement calmed his fears. She was happy and eager and enjoying the moment immensely. Looking at him with innocence and desire, she unbuttoned his shirt.

Yes and yes, he thought, answering the questions Roxanne was wondering how to ask … even though she already knew the answers.

"I love you, Roxanne. I will always love you. There is no me without you." Then he answered her second question by taking a condom from his pocket and tossing it on the bed. He caressed her golden hair, and they embraced in a long and passionate kiss … each opening and allowing the other to enter more deeply into their inner worlds.

Their defenses were falling, their fears receding. Roxanne fell backward onto the bed, and Andor followed. They lay next to each other, more and more excited by their closeness. They tenderly embraced and kissed.

Now their defenses were completely down. They explored each other's bodies and minds, sharing their intense mental and physical sensations. Each one's pleasure was greatly amplified by sharing the other's as their excitement continued growing. For an instant they were gone from this earth and this life, partners on a journey into the heavenly realms. And then they were back. They looked at each other with love and gratitude and joy.

She smiled at him, raising her hand to his head and pushing a lock of hair away from his forehead. "I love you," she said out loud.

"I love you so much," he replied, also aloud, his hand caressing her face. He was overcome with a joy he had never known.

Roxanne's head fell back suddenly, as if all her strength had left her. Her body went limp in his arms. She was unconscious and gone.

Shocked and confused, Andor called her name. "Roxanne. Roxanne!"

He got up on his knees and took her by the shoulders. "Roxanne!" He put his ear to her chest and listened. Yes, her heart was still beating, though faintly. He pressed his fingers against her carotid artery to make sure that what he had heard was true. Like her heartbeat, her pulse was faint but present.

He placed a hand on her heart and another on her abdomen, sending waves of life force into her body, hoping to jolt it back to consciousness. Nothing. No response.

He knew he needed help.

Roger Reynolds bolted awake. He sat up in his bed and searched the ether for his daughter. Whatever link that joined them had informed him that something terrible had happened. He could not feel her life force as he usually did. She was faint, far away, as if she had been taken into another dimension.

He reached out to Rebecca.

"I'm on my way," she told him. She was already in her car and speeding home.

Roger contacted Max Louri. "Max, I need you to fire up the jet and get me home in the next two hours."

"I'm on it, Chief."

"Meet me at the rendezvous point in Hyde Park in twenty minutes."

"I'll be there."

Rebecca burst into her house and ran up the stairs to Roxanne's room. Andor was dressing her.

"What happened?" Rebecca screamed. "What did you do?"

The instant she spoke those words, she knew Andor had not done anything wrong. Something else had happened, someone had taken control of her daughter.

"I don't know!" Andor said. "I swear it. I love her. She was so happy, and then she collapsed." He was beside himself, on the verge of hysteria.

Rebecca placed her hands on her daughter's body and sent pulsations of energy into her. Roxanne's pulse strengthened slightly, but she did not rise from her coma.

"Roger," she called out. "We need you."

"I'm on my way. Get her ready to travel. We have to take her to the Crystal Cavern, like Delphi said."

Chapter 29
Challenges on the Way to the Crystal Cavern

With Max at the helm, the jet was hovering over Golden Gables in two hours. Throughout the trip, Roger had struggled to make contact with his daughter's mind and free it from the terrible force that had taken control of her. Every effort failed. Roxanne's mind was dark and her life force had been sent fleeing into the deep woods of her unconscious. She was alive, but barely. Clearly, whoever had taken possession of her mind meant to kill her, but slowly. Roger understood that the killer wanted Roger and Rebecca to watch their daughter waste away; he wanted them to suffer excruciating pain before they lost Roxanne forever.

Roger could feel his daughter struggling to stay alive. Her awareness had found a place to hide deep inside her. If he did not rescue her soon, she would let go of this mortal life and flee into the great beyond. He had to find a way to defeat the Genius who had taken control of his daughter. He had a plan, but it was tenuous at best. In the meantime, he infused his daughter with a constant stream of life force that would help her remain alive and give her limited protection, which he hoped would buy him enough time to save her.

Among the first things to enter Roger's mind was to ask Alexander for help. But the weight of Felix's statements and his natural caution stopped him. He didn't know who the Collaborator was, and it might be someone with access to his communications with Alexander. He wasn't willing to risk any action that might make Roxanne, or even Rebecca, more vulnerable.

As Roger had instructed, Max landed the jet in the Reynolds' backyard, although he inadvertently put it down on top of three outdoor chairs that were instantly crushed under the weight of the jet as if they were made of papier-mâché. Max cut off its engines and activated the cloaking technology as Roger sprinted to his house. Rebecca and Andor were waiting in Roxanne's room. She was dressed but still comatose, lying on her bed.

"I didn't do anything to hurt her," Andor said, speaking out loud. "I don't know what happened. She just collapsed. I don't know why." He dropped his head and confessed, "I love her, Mr. Reynolds. I would never hurt her."

"I know, Andor," Roger said, well aware of Andor's overwhelming emotions. "It's not your fault. You didn't do anything wrong."

He sat down beside Roxanne and looked at his wife. "Any improvement?"

"No real change," she said, her voice full of fear. "What could have happened? Who could have done this to her?"

"I don't know," he said, as if from far away. He was searching for answers, but was not ready to speculate.

He looked deeply into his daughter's face, once again attempting to penetrate the powerful force that had taken control of her mind. "Andor, I'm going to ask you to step outside for a few minutes."

Andor nodded and left the room.

Roger was adept at all the Genius healing arts, and now attempted to restore his daughter as much as he could. With utmost care, he applied the most sensitive touch to specific points on her body. He called forth his daughter's life force to the surface of her body in the hope that she would be able to take back some of her simple motor skills. Meanwhile, he sent Roxanne a series of messages.

"Your mother and I are here, Roxanne.

"We have a plan and you're going to be all right. We are with you! I am here for you! Your mother and I will protect you! We love you so much and our love will protect and make you safe!! You are going to be all right!!!

"I know you can hear me, Roxanne. Send me a signal if you understand."

A strong ping sounded in Roger and Rebecca's minds. Rebecca's eyes filled with tears, though she smiled with hope.

"That's my girl," Roger said, proud of his strong and courageous daughter.

Stay safe where you are. But we need you to take control of your motor cortex as much as you can. We need you to walk. Your mother and I will guide your every step with our minds, but we need you to take sufficient command of your nervous system so that you can travel. Another strong ping sounded in Roger and Rebecca's minds, and they knew she understood.

Roger lifted Roxanne into his arms and then placed her feet on the floor. He held her upright and spoke to her telepathically again. "We need you to walk a short distance, Roxanne, to a jet in the backyard. Once we're inside the jet, you can lie down and rest."

Andor was visibly confused when he saw Roxanne walking downstairs. "Is she coming around, Mr. Reynolds?" he asked, his voice full of hope and bewilderment.

"Not yet, Andor. She's still in a coma. We're going to get her some help. I need you to guard your thoughts very carefully for the next seventy-two hours. Keep your shield up. That's how you can help Roxanne. Understood?"

"Yes." After a pause, Andor added, "When she is awake again, please tell her I love her."

"I will, Andor." Then he added, "Andor, we will save Roxanne. Everything will be all right. We have to go now."

Roger sent a telepathic message to Simone to reinforce Andor's shield to make certain that nothing he thought would be communicated to the enemy.

Andor ran to the back door and opened it. Max lowered the ship's cloaking in order to open its door for the three Reynolds. Roger and Rebecca helped Roxanne into the jet.

"Where to?" Max asked as they all settled into seats, Rebecca with her arms around Roxanne.

"Lima, Peru, Max, and don't take your foot off the accelerator."

Roger unfolded a large ancient map that he studied for several minutes. Once he was satisfied with his calculations, he gave Max the coordinates for their destination. He then reached over to Rebecca, putting his arms around her. Sitting back, he considered the great beings whose help he so desperately needed.

According to legend, the Enkefalons were disembodied beings, living consciousnesses whose only connection with physical existence was the continued life of their brains. The legend explained that many millennia ago, Geniuses found a way to preserve the brains and minds of particularly powerful members of their kind. Even after their bodies were long dead and gone, it was believed that the pure thought and life forces of these beings—even something of their personalities—remained alive and accessible to living humans. Indeed, the Enkefalons were thought to be still deeply engaged in the affairs of Geniuses and Ordinaries, though no one knew exactly how or to what extent.

Roger needed the Enkefalons to free his daughter from the grip of the powerful Genius that had taken her and restore her to health. He would, he knew, have to make an extremely effective case to convince the Enkefalons to save Roxanne. There were other requests he would make of them, including the answer to the most obvious and haunting question of all: Who did this to my daughter?

As the jet flew south, Roger knew he was getting ahead of himself. Just getting an audience with the Enkefalons would be quite a feat. Their home was miles below ground, and it was protected by traps and challenges that were legendary in Genius circles. There were no reliable reports of anyone surviving a journey to the land of the Enkefalons. There were a few ancient stories of actual encounters with them, more myth than fact. The risks associated with attempting to reach them were so great, Roger had never even considered contacting them, even during the darkest days of World War II. Still, he had no other choice. His daughter's life was at stake.

In three hours, the jet had reached Cordillera Blanca, a mountain range of the Andes. Max gingerly set the jet down on a large ledge, the place that was thought to be the secret entrance to the legendary Crystal Cavern. The peaks of the mountains were covered in glacier ice, but at the lower elevations, the mountains were tree and brush covered.

Roger and Rebecca helped their daughter out of the craft. The three were dressed in warm spelunking gear, complete with helmets that had thought-controlled lights that could provide 360 degrees of illumination. Rebecca and Roger also carried full backpacks. They were ready for their journey to the lair of the Enkefalons, deep beneath the roots of the Andes Mountains.

Roger turned to Max. "We'll need you to wait for us. I don't know how long we will be gone. It could be days. I'll be in touch when I can."

Max's eyes were soulful. "Don't worry, Chief. If it takes a year, I'll be here. Godspeed."

With Roxanne standing in a comatose state between them, Roger and Rebecca faced the mountain and the place where they believed the entrance to the Crystal Cavern was. Roger pulled out his map again and examined it carefully. *Yes, this must be the entrance,* he told himself. He was as sure as he could be.

But no entrance to a cave could be seen. He saw nothing but vines, trees, and rock face. Still, he knew the entrance had to be there. He could feel emanations of powerful mental activity.

He turned to Rebecca. "They covered the entrance with a persuasive illusion of overgrowth." He sent a stream of clarifying thoughts toward the cliff face, and the illusion was dispelled. The opening to the cave suddenly appeared before them.

"Let's see if there are any surprises," Roger said. He picked up a long, thick branch and probed the cavern's entrance. The branch was snapped in two by a falling stone that had been honed to a razor's edge. Roger looked at Rebecca. "Someone doesn't want visitors."

He picked up another branch and again pushed it through the entrance. Nothing happened. He then threw the branch into the cave, but nothing stirred.

Powerful laser flashlights in hand, Roger and Rebecca entered the cave, keeping Roxanne between them. They kept in constant contact with Roxanne, directing her every footstep and turn, as they followed the multiple beams of light emanating from their laser lights and helmets. Initially, the ceiling was low and all three had to bend down.

After thirty minutes, they came to a crossroads. To the right, the path was narrow and rocky and would require them to walk in single file up a gradual incline. To the left, the path was flat and covered with soft moss. Roger allowed his mind to travel down the moss-covered path and intuitively felt increasing danger. With every step, the path grew darker and more threatening. He did the same with the path to the right, allowing his spirit to walk along it and feel what dangers might be lurking. There were obstacles, he felt, but the path was the safer one.

"This way," he said to Rebecca, pointing to the path to the right.

The three held hands as Roger led the way up the rocky path. They walked slowly, feeling their way. When the path turned right again, a trap door opened beneath them and sent them falling into a pitch black subterranean world. They fell for perhaps fifty feet before soft netting caught them. The netting acted like long springs, breaking their fall and then lowered them to the ground.

Roger and Rebecca had lost their laser lights during the fall, but their headgear lanterns were still functioning. Roger reached into the darkness and located the laser lights. Using telekinesis, he brought the laser lights back to them.

"Are you all right?" he asked Rebecca.

"Yes, I'm fine," she said, getting to her feet.

Both parents scanned their daughter and found her physically intact. Roger searched through his backpack and came up with a telescopic long-burning torch. He activated it, and the torch instantly illuminated a huge cathedral-like cavern, easily ten stories high. Long cone-like stalactites hung from the ceiling, reaching for the stalagmites that emerged from the cavern floor.

Roger examined the long rock face from which they had fallen. Apparently, the opening to this cavern was only partway up, for the ceiling was high above the place where they had fallen. Had it not been for the nets, they would surely have fallen to their deaths. Roger considered the other path they could have chosen, and out of curiosity ventured along the wall to his left. Far above he saw the other choice, the path that had been covered with moss. He held the torch higher and saw, high above him, that the path ended in a trap door, just like the path they had chosen, but the sheer drop did not lead to the life-saving netting. A shudder went through him and he returned to Roxanne and Rebecca.

This cavern offered several possible paths. He felt a strong intuition toward a single opening in the eastern wall and pointed at it, telling Rebecca that he sensed the Enkefalons wanted them to go that way. They took Roxanne's hands and made their way deeper into the darkened recesses of the earth. The temperature was much colder at this depth, and the air was moist and heavy. As they walked, they felt a thousand eyes watching them.

"Bats," Roger said to Rebecca. "They're escorting us along the way."

"Yes," she said. "Some of the largest I have ever seen. They give me the creeps."

He smiled at her. "How long has it been since we took a family walk, all of us holding hands like this?"

She looked taken aback, simultaneously surprised and amused by her husband. "Since when do you enjoy family walks?"

"I'm changing, haven't you noticed? But anytime I'm with you and our daughter, I'm happy." He added, almost to himself, "I guess I've been too distracted to know what was really important."

"Well, better late than never," Rebecca said, but she was smiling.

The three descended deeper into the cave. Soon, their path came to a dead end. A tall stone wall stood before them, blocking their progress. Roger moved the torch close to the wall. Words were carved on it in the language of the ancient Incas, which both Roger and Rebecca could decipher.

"Death awaits the proud and the self-righteous," the message read. "Only those who can answer this question may enter."

The crucial question followed, but a word, or perhaps more than one word, was indecipherable. *Why does the [illegible] not fear the beast?* Had the missing word or words been worn away by erosion and the passage of time? Or had they been deliberately omitted? Even if they solved the riddle, how would they communicate the answer, and to whom?

Both Roger and Rebecca realized that time was likely a factor. They had to come up with the answer quickly or face fatal consequences. Roger swung the torch around and saw several human skeletons lying to the left and right of the path.

"'Death awaits the proud and the self-righteous,'" he said telepathically to Rebecca. "That's the clue." And then it hit him. In a loud voice, and in the language of the Incas, he called out, "Why does the enlightened warrior not fear the beast?" He paused and then answered the riddle. "Because he has tamed the beast within himself."

His words echoed throughout the cavernous halls. When finally the repeating calls of his voice fell silent, an ear-splitting, grinding sound emerged from the wall as a great stone doorway slid open.

Rebecca looked at her husband. "How did you know?"

"The enlightened warrior has only one relationship, which is with truth. He discovers and conquers the beasts within. The self-righteous never see the beast within themselves. It's always in someone else."

He examined the opening carefully. There were no obvious traps, so he stepped inside the room. Suddenly, a terrifying roar sounded. He reflexively jumped back, attempting to shield Rebecca and Roxanne from the monster he had just seen. Again a blood-curdling roar echoed from the room. Regaining his composure, Roger held the torch aloft and leaned into the room as much as he dared. At first he saw nothing, and then he heard the shuffling of feet and the clanging of iron chains. He turned to his right and saw a beast, perhaps ten feet tall, standing on two large feet. It was covered in long, tangled brown hair. His long, heavily muscled arms hung loosely at his sides, both hands curled into great fists. His face was almost human, dominated by an animal nature but clearly self-aware. He was ready for battle, but when he saw Roger, he stepped away until his back was against the wall. He became quiet, almost wary.

Roger entered the room while Rebecca stayed in the doorway, holding Roxanne close to her side.

"Who are you?" Roger asked the monster.

The beast roared again, this time with enormous rage. "At last we meet face to face, Roger Reynolds," it said.

"Do I know you?" Roger asked.

"Don't you recognize the monster inside yourself? Have a good look at your own inner demon."

Roger's face became contorted with grief, for he knew it was true. "How is it possible?" he asked the beast.

With a rattling of chains, the beast approached Roger, only to be held back by the limits of his bonds. "Do you still think this is just a mountain you have entered? Don't be a fool. This is as much a journey into your own mind and heart."

Roger paused at the implications of such insight. Somehow, the journey into the cave of the Enkefalons had become a mirror into his own soul. This beast was the manifestation of all the dark emotions, fears, and denied beliefs he had repressed in his life.

"How can I help you?" he asked.

The beast laughed at him and then roared again with rage. "That's not the question you really want to ask," it said. "What you really want to know is how I, this chained beast, can help you."

"Yes," Roger confessed. "You're right. I need your help."

"In more ways than you know." It pointed to the far wall, where three different pathways could be seen.

"There are three paths before you. Along one path fire, violence, and death await you. Another leads to passivity, confusion and death. On the third lies safe passage to your next challenge." The beast roared. "You must choose now."

The three openings to the three paths were identical, tall and cavernous. So if the openings were the same, Roger thought, then it was the placement that mattered, along with the clues the beast had given him. Violence and passivity were opposites, like dark and light, like yang and yin. The beast itself represented parts of Roger that he had not yet integrated. The path he chose must be the path that represented harmony and unity within him.

"I choose the middle path," Roger said, "the way of balance and integration." The beast roared, shook its chains, and then fell silent. "You have chosen wisely. Now go."

"Thank you," Roger said. "But now that I have what I need, please answer my question: How can I help you?"

"You control me with discipline," the beast said, holding up its chains to reveal their true meaning. "But only your heart can set us free and make us one."

"Haven't I found my heart?" Roger asked incredulously.

"Don't ask me that question, you fool, ask her."

The beast raised its arm and pointed to Rebecca. Roger looked into Rebecca's eyes and saw the naked truth written on her pale face. He had his answer, but it left him reeling. His gaze fell to the cave's floor.

Finally, he looked back at the beast. "Thank you again, my friend. I will free us both in this life, I promise."

"Go," the beast said, uncertain perhaps of how their shared destiny would unfold, "before it's too late."

Roger went back to Rebecca, took her hand, and led his wife and daughter through the room, to the middle opening and the next pathway.

The three had gone a dozen steps when the floor gave way and became a long, winding slide that hurtled them deeper into the cavern. As they slid, their bodies accelerated, until Roger estimated they were traveling at perhaps forty miles an hour. He dropped the torch and tried desperately to grab the walls, but they were too slick for him to grasp anything, and nothing he did slowed their momentum. They were now sliding even faster. Their helmets flew off, throwing them into total darkness. Roger held onto Rebecca and Roxanne and created an energetic bubble around them, hoping the shield would protect them from impact with a stone wall. Suddenly, their bodies were launched from the slide. They flew blindly into the unknown, but rather than hitting a wall, they were plunged into a deep and icy pool of water.

Their senses were turned upside down. They didn't know which direction was up. Roger told Rebecca telepathically to relax her body and hold onto Roxanne. They would float to the surface. Meantime, he reached into his pocket and found his laser light. He switched it on and turned the light in all directions until he saw the surface. He grabbed Rebecca, who still held Roxanne, and kicked hard to the surface. Rebecca and Roger gasped for air once they broke out of the water, but Roxanne was inert. Roger used the laser light to find the shoreline, only about fifteen feet away. They pulled Roxanne from the water and Roger immediately gave her mouth to mouth resuscitation. When Roxanne gagged, he turned her onto her side. She coughed and heaved water from her lungs and stomach. Soon she was breathing normally again.

Rebecca held her tightly, trying to keep her warm. Roger, water dripping off him, stood and held the torch up, turning all the way around as he tried to find a way out. He did not see a single opening. There was no exit. He lowered the torch and concentrated on the water. Watching it carefully, he realized that although the flow was barely discernible, the water was moving in a specific direction. There must be an underground aquifer from which fresh water entered the pool. And since the pool was not flooding, it could only mean the water flowed out as well. He followed the direction of the flow and saw it—a thin slip of darkness where the water left the cavern. It was no more than a foot wide and only inches above the water line. He walked over to Rebecca and handed her the torch.

"I'll only be a minute," he communicated telepathically to her.

She was stunned. "You're leaving us?"

"I'll be right back."

He removed his backpack, took off his shoes and socks, and waded into the pool. Holding his laser light, he then swam to the far wall where the water exited the chamber. When he was near the wall, he took a deep breath and dove.

The water was clear, though his movements stirred up some silt from the bottom of the pool, which was perhaps fifteen feet deep. The laser light illuminated the water and silt with an eerie yellow glow. He could see that the water flowed into a tunnel that was perhaps four feet wide. He entered the tunnel and swam along, searching with the laser light for an opening to another chamber. But the tunnel was longer than he had hoped and no such chamber was visible. The width of the tunnel varied, narrowing to three feet at one point and opening to eight feet at another.

As he swam, he realized the current was getting stronger. Probably other openings to the aquifer fed into the tunnel and strengthened the current. Roger realized that if he continued swimming, he could be swept along by the current and might have difficulty getting back to the pool and the chamber where Rebecca and Roxanne waited for him.

He turned around and swam back. Surfacing, he gasped for air. Rebecca held the torch aloft and watched him intently. He could see the fear on her face.

He strode out of the water and walked immediately to his backpack, pulling out three Genius-designed oxygen tanks. Eight inches long and with tiny mouthpieces, they would allow them to stay submerged for perhaps thirty minutes, depending on their exertion levels and the amount of oxygen they used.

He sat down next to Rebecca and took a few breaths to center himself. He knew he had to communicate gently to her. He didn't want to frighten her further. Putting his hand on her shoulder, he sent her waves of love and support.

"There's an opening to a tunnel in that wall over there," he communicated, nodding in the direction of the opening. "It's our way out of here."

"How far will we have to swim?" she asked.

"I don't know. I couldn't swim far enough into the tunnel in order to find the next chamber." He gave her a reassuring smile. "I'm sure it's not too far. Once we're in the next chamber, we'll dry off and rest."

She nodded. "Okay."

"I'll take Roxanne," he said. "The tunnel is narrow in places, so you'll have to swim ahead of us. When it widens, we'll swim side by side."

After putting his shoes and socks into his backpack, Roger tore a strip of fabric from the bottom of his cotton shirt. He ripped it into two pieces and rolled both into small balls. He inserted both into Roxanne's nostrils. Immediately, Roxanne began breathing from her mouth. He placed the mouthpiece of an oxygen tube into her mouth and communicated to her that he needed her to breathe from the tube in her mouth. They were going underwater and swim for a little while.

He inserted his laser light into an elastic strap on the right shoulder harness of his backpack. The light shone directly upward, toward his head. Rebecca had already put in her backpack the larger light tube, along with her own shoes and socks. She held her laser light in her hand.

"Ready?" he asked her.

She nodded and inserted the mouthpiece of her oxygen tube. After she looked deeply into her daughter's eyes, she waded into the water, with Roger and Roxanne close behind. Soon all three were underwater and entering the tunnel, their lights casting yellow beams in the darkened waters.

Roger held Roxanne close to him with his right arm while swimming with his left. His laser light shone directly in front of him. Rebecca held her light in one hand and swam with the other. She remained just ahead of Roger and Roxanne.

There was no way to determine how deep in the earth they were, but Roger estimated they were perhaps a mile below the surface. The water was icy cold, somewhere in the low fifties Fahrenheit. The current strengthened, moving them along rapidly.

They swam steadily, breathing as rhythmically as they could. Both Roger and Rebecca knew that every bit of oxygen in the tubes had to be used sparingly, since they didn't know how long the tunnel was or how long they would be underwater.

Occasionally, Rebecca would shine her light downward to see what kind of terrain they were swimming over. The floor below was highly irregular. In places, it ran very deep, too deep to actually see the bottom; in other places, it rose in various kinds of rock formations, similar to stalagmites.

After a time Roger realized with growing concern that the tunnel was much longer than he had anticipated, and that they had gone too far to return. They were exhausted and almost out of oxygen. But he had not come this far to let his beloved wife and daughter drown in a water-filled subterranean chamber. Roger searched his mind and his vast memory to find a solution, a way out. The only thought he came up with (and he knew its chance of working was little better than infinitesimal) was to use a trick Simone had taught him almost a century ago. Could it work? Could he possibly use his mind and the forces of nature to disassemble the atoms in the bodies of his family and instantaneously project and reassemble them safely at the end of this tunnel?

Using all his mental energy and his last ounce of strength, he tried. Suddenly everything went black. Later, was it seconds or years, Rebecca broke through the surface of the water, with Roger and Roxanne emerging a moment later. Roger and Rebecca took out their oxygen tubes and Roxanne's, and gasped for air. Exhausted, they slowly swam to the beachhead and walked out of the water, as Roger held Roxanne in his arms. He gently placed Roxanne down on the ground, and then he and Rebecca collapsed on either side of Roxanne, coughing and heaving for air.

Once Rebecca caught her breath, she telepathically told Roger, "Thank you, Darling. I won't even ask how you did it. You're wonderful."

Rather than reply, Roger hugged Rebecca. He gently asked her to take off her and Roxanne's wet clothes, and then he quickly searched through his backpack until he found a torch. When he turned it on, it illuminated the cavern. He searched the backpack again and found a water-tight plastic bag that contained a blanket. Though thin as paper and folded into a square foot, when he unfolded it, it was an eight-foot-long rectangle. Made from a Genius-designed cloth, the blanket was both soft and shiny. In cold temperatures, the cloth attracted heat; in hot temperatures, it cooled. He threw the blanket around Roxanne and Rebecca, both of whom were stripped to their underwear. From the plastic bag he pulled out a box of matches and a small can that contained a wax-like substance. He opened the can and lit the waxy fuel within it. Instantly, a fire came alive. He placed the small furnace between Roxanne and Rebecca.

"That'll burn for hours," he said, trying to be cheerful. He knew they could not go any further. Stripping off his clothes, he took all of their clothing to the pool, where he squeezed out as much water as he could.

As he wrung out the water, he raised his light to scan the cave. In the endless crevices of its walls he saw multitudes of bats. They were all focused on him, as if they were a silent yet thoughtful audience. It was time, he realized, to have a chat with the bats.

He directed his thoughts to the thousands of winged creatures gazing at him. "I apologize for invading your home like this," he said in the language of the bats. "We mean you no harm, nor disrespect." He explained to the bats why the three of them had come to the caverns, and how important their mission was. "My daughter needs the help of very special beings who live in this mountain. I think you know who I mean. As soon as we accomplish our mission, we will leave this mountain and these caves. I hope you will help us on our journey, should the need arise."

The bats were impassive; no message was returned to him. He lowered his laser light and went back to wringing out the clothes.

After draping the clothes on a row of rocks, he opened Rebecca's backpack and found a small array of food rations. He handed them to Rebecca.

"We need to eat something. The food will revitalize us and generate some body heat. Once we've got our strength back, we'll concentrate some of our energies on our clothing. That will dry them quickly enough."

He smiled at her and kissed her forehead. "But first, we have a picnic."

Rebecca's smile was filled with love and gratitude for his care and protection. "How did I ever find you?" she asked.

"How did you put up with me for so long?" he replied. "Besides, I was the one who found you, remember?"

Before she ate anything, Rebecca spooned small portions of food into Roxanne's mouth. Roger took the food and spoon from Rebecca. "Here, let me do that. You eat."

As he fed his daughter, he wondered how long had it been since he had done this. He remembered when she was a little golden-haired angel sitting in her high chair, waving her arms and banging her spoon against the tray. Inevitably, food would be all over her face and bib. She was so beautiful, so innocent, so eager for life. Now, deep in a coma, her life hanging by a thread, she was immensely vulnerable. He gave her another mouthful and guided her to chew. A small portion of food fell out of her mouth. He scooped it up and then wiped her mouth with his fingertips. He touched her cheek. So many years had passed, so much of her life he had missed. He looked back at Rebecca, who was eating her small meal and still shivering. These were the two most important people in his life. How could he have been so blind to that colossal truth for so long?

He put the spoon down for a moment and embraced his wife and kissed her forehead. She held him and kissed him, and then returned to her meal.

An hour later, they were dressed and dry. From where they rested alongside of the pool, they had seen a corridor that led farther into the caverns. It was the only opening in the cave, so they took it. The corridor was narrow for about a hundred yards, but then it opened onto a long, wide staircase that descended into the darkened abyss. On the left side of the stairs was a wall; on the right side, a sheer drop into endless darkness. There was no way to determine how far down the chasm went, but it seemed to drop into the depths of hell. They couldn't even see where the stairs ended. With all of them holding hands and Roxanne in the middle, the three began their descent single file. It was Rebecca's turn to guide Roxanne's steps.

The stairs, wet, hard, and slippery, seemed to go on forever. They had to concentrate on every one of them in order to keep from falling into the abyss on their right. As they descended, the air grew colder and thicker, the darkness ever more dense. An hour passed, and then two, but they didn't seem to be making any progress. The stairs went on and on. A third hour was gone, and now a fourth. Still no sign of the bottom. The challenges were clearly wearing them down. They were physically and emotionally exhausted, and the journey seemed hopeless. Yet by pure will they continued downward, ever deeper into a darkness from which they knew they might never return.

Roger sensed that a group of powerful minds was attacking their will, sapping their energy, imposing the belief that their journey was pointless and futile, that they would never reach the bottom of these stairs, much less their goal.

Suddenly, a gigantic fireball exploded in front of them. The light from the fire illuminated an enormous dragon flying directly at them. The thing opened its mouth, revealing its razor teeth, and then the winged menace sent another ball of fire hurtling toward them. Rebecca jumped back in terror.

"It's only an illusion," Roger called out.

But Rebecca lost her footing and her connection with Roxanne. Roxanne took a misstep, fell, and then tumbled over the edge of the staircase and into the darkness. In utter horror, Rebecca saw Roxanne fall head first into the abyss. She was about to jump after her but Roger blocked her. In the same movement he rose several feet into the air. Using the power of his mind, he caught Roxanne after she had fallen about fifty feet.

For a moment she was suspended in midair, and then Roger pulled her back toward him, as if reeling her in from the blackened depths of death. Like the sudden apparition of a lost loved one, Roxanne emerged from the darkness and floated over the staircase. Rebecca grabbed her and pulled her toward the stone wall for safety. She sat Roxanne down on the step and desperately held her close, placing her daughter's head on her shoulder.

She looked up at Roger, floating back to the steps and then alighting next to his wife. He was dazed, as if coming out of a trance.

"How?" she asked, her voice trembling with terror and awe. "How did you do that?"

"I have no idea," he said, still faint from the experience. "All I knew was that I had to save our daughter."

Rebecca hugged Roxanne and then pulled Roger close to her. Rocking back and forth, she burst into tears. The three of them huddled on the stairs, unable to move. They remained there for about a half hour. Roger knew Roxanne and Rebecca could go no farther, so he began sorting through the two backpacks. He pulled out a length of nylon rope and tied it to the clamps on the backs of both backpacks. He then took another length of nylon cord and tied it to his waist, and then to the waists of Rebecca and Roxanne.

"What are you doing?" Rebecca asked.

"I've called for help," he said. "And fortunately, help is on the way. Strap on your backpack and make it tight. Hold onto Roxanne."

No sooner had his thoughts entered her mind when they heard the screeching of bats and the flapping of wings. Hordes and hordes of the black creatures—vampire bats, many of them enormous—stormed toward them and then gathered around them in a great and ominous cloud.

Rebecca stared, momentarily terrified.

"Don't be afraid," Roger said to her. He turned his thoughts to the bats. "Gently, gently, my winged friends. Thank you for coming to our assistance."

The bats grabbed the nylon cords that were bound to their backpacks and waists. With utmost care, they lifted the three of them off the steps, and carried them over the edge of the stairs and into the abyss. Roger held the torch aloft, but all they could see were walls along the side and a deep black void before and beneath them. Down, down they went, flying for more than thirty minutes before they reached the bottom of the chasm. Finally, their feet found solid ground and the bats released them.

Swarming as one, the bats circled over the family, as if expressing their solidarity with them, and then flew into the darkness and were gone. Both Roger and Rebecca sent a stream of gratitude to the bats as they left.

Roger estimated they were perhaps ten miles underground. He retrieved the blanket from his backpack. They huddled beneath it, and in an instant they were all asleep.

How long they slept, they did not know, but they were shocked awake by the blasting of musical instruments that combined to play a deafening cacophony. The sound was alarming, sending a kind of electric shock through their bodies that instantly awakened Roger and Rebecca.

As soon as the blaring music stopped, a deep, loud, and resonant voice boomed an ominous command. "Name the musical pieces and hum or sing the next series of notes, or your journey ends here."

Rebecca and Roger looked at each other in disbelief.

"What?" Roger said. "What does he mean?"

Rebecca replayed the sound in her mind, pausing to analyze what she had heard. "It wasn't a single chaotic sound, Roger, but five musical pieces all played very loudly and at once."

Roger replayed the sound in his head and understood. "Yes, you're right, Rebecca. I can start to make them out, too." His wife had a gifted musical ear, which he had always admired. "What do you hear?" he asked.

"There are five pieces," she said. She paused, apparently sorting through the notes in her mind, and then looked up at Roger and laughed. "The first piece was Haydn's Symphony no. 94, the second movement."

"Why is that funny?"

"Haydn called it his 'surprise' symphony because he hated people sleeping through his concerts. He played a series of low tones and then followed them with loud instrumentals to wake up those who were snoozing."

"How appropriate," Roger said. "Apparently, our tormenters have a sense of humor, in addition to knowledge of music."

"The second piece was Beethoven's Fifth Symphony," she continued. "I use it to get myself energized when I clean the house."

Again, she smiled at Roger. The thought of music was lifting her spirits, he realized, taking her mind away from all they had been through.

"I see that you fit right in down here," he said, encouraging her enjoyment. "Maybe the Enkefalons will hire you to come up with more musical tortures."

Rebecca was already lost in thought. "The third piece was Mozart's Symphony no. 40, considered by many to be the greatest symphony ever composed. The fourth was George Gershwin's 'Rhapsody in Blue.'"

"Which I consider to be one the greatest musical pieces ever written," Roger said, knowing full well that his musical appreciation was limited.

"Now we're getting into music I can relate to. By the way, I heard that one, I want you to know."

"Yes, I love it too," Rebecca said, smiling at him. "As for the fifth one …"

"I got the fifth one," Roger said. "'Let It Be' by the Beatles. Even my tone-deaf ear could hear McCartney's sweet falsetto in that mélange."

"Yes, you're right, 'Let It Be' ". Rebecca said.

She turned and spoke to the disembodied voice that had announced the challenge. She named all five pieces, the artists who wrote them, and sang the succeeding notes in a beautiful soprano voice. Roger marveled at her and, even under these conditions, felt his body respond with desire for her.

Suddenly, the earth shook and an entire wall opened up to reveal a new passageway. When the wall finished moving, the same ominous voice spoke. "You have one more challenge. If you answer correctly, you will be granted the audience you seek. If you fail, you will all be lost in these caverns and perish."

Rebecca and Roger held Roxanne's hands again as they walked through the entrance to the passageway. They traveled along the corridor for perhaps a half mile, and both Roger and Rebecca noticed that the walls of the caverns had changed. They seemed to radiate a powerful energy. Indeed, everything around them seemed imbued with awareness, as if the great minds they sought had filled these caverns with consciousness. They knew they were close to their goal now.

Finally, the corridor opened to a new chamber, this one large and glowing with a light of its own. As they entered the chamber, they saw a mathematical formula written on the wall to their left. Roger read the message aloud.

"Use $a^n + b^n = c^n$ to find the correct door to the opening you seek."

A booming voice emanated from the walls. "Solve the mathematical challenge and use the answer to choose a door inside one of the four rooms. Enter the room and accept your fate."

Rebecca turned to Roger. "That's Fermat's Last Theorem, the most difficult mathematical problem that's been solved in the last 350 years."

Roger gave a small smile. "Yes, Pierre de Fermat was one of us. He came up with the theorem in 1637 to give Ordinaries a challenge that would advance their mathematical skills. And it worked. It spawned more mathematical advances among Ordinaries than any single math challenge ever constructed. And it wasn't until 1994 that Oxford University professor Andrew Wiles actually proved Fermat's Last Theorem."

"Roger, it took Wiles nearly a decade, using advanced supercomputers, to prove Fermat. And he based his proof on the work done by other twentieth-century mathematicians. What have we got, twenty minutes?"

"If we're lucky."

Rebecca guided Roxanne to some soft earth and made her lie down, and then covered her with the blanket. Roger held up his torch and surveyed the cavern. It was odd, to say the least. Unlike the other chambers, this expanse had undergone a significant amount of work. The walls had been carefully reconstructed to form four recessed niches, or rooms, that were set back into the walls themselves. Roger quickly surveyed the four rooms. Each was shaped in a different geometric design. The room carved into the north wall was a large right triangle. The room in the east wall was, in fact, four rooms—three perfectly shaped cubes surrounding a right triangle. The western room was an isosceles triangle, with the two sides equal in length. The room in the south wall appeared to be a tunnel.

Roger pondered the problem for a minute and then said, as if to himself, "There is something in Wiles's proof that tells us which room has the door that opens to the Enkefalons."

Deciding to inspect the rooms more closely, he walked to the north wall and entered the right-triangle room. As with the rest of the cavern, the room glowed with its own light. Roger marveled at the precision with which the room had been hewn from the rock walls. The left wall was perpendicular to the ground, forming a perfect angle with the floor. The wall to Roger's right was at a forty-five-degree angle—a perfect Pythagorean hypotenuse.

At the back of the room was a large stone door and above the door were the words: I choose to enter this doorway and accept my fate.

What the room might have to do with Fermat was immediately apparent to Roger. Fermat had based his last challenge on the Pythagorean Theorem, which stated that in a right triangle—the very shape of this room—the square of the hypotenuse was equal to the sum of the squares of the other two sides. Pythagoras wrote out his theorem as $a^2 + b^2 = c^2$.

Fermat stated that if any other number was substituted for the exponent two, the Pythagorean Theorem would not work. You could go from three to infinity, and no other number would make $a^n + b^n = c^n$ correct. For 350 years, the world's greatest mathematicians attempted to prove, or disprove, Fermat's Last Theorem, but none could come up with a mathematical proof for the great Genius's challenge. Fermat tantalized the mathematical world by stating that he had come up with the most elegant proof for his theorem, but he never revealed it.

Suddenly, Roger understood. He ran to the four square rooms in the eastern wall and realized they were a physical representation of the Pythagorean Theorem. To verify that, he quickly gauged the floor area of the three rooms in square feet, and determined that the area of the large room was equal to the sum of the areas of the two smaller rooms. The larger room's area represented c^2, or the sum of $a^2 + b^2$.

In the back of the largest of the four rooms was a door that was identical to the one in the north room, with the same words written above it: I choose to enter this doorway and accept my fate.

Roger ran out of the eastern room. Looking back at the room to the north, he realized he was seeing a progression of Pythagorean thinking, from the original geometric form of a right triangle to the genius of the Pythagorean Theorem, which was physically represented by the four rooms in the eastern wall.

The answer to the challenge lay in either of these rooms.

He walked to the south wall and inspected that room, which appeared to be a tunnel. Once he entered the room, he realized that the room was shaped like a donut. Within the circular passageway, the walls were made of individual panels. Rather than being uniformly rounded, like the inside of a tire, the walls and floor were composed of hundreds of panels that together formed the rounded donut shape, much like a geodesic dome can create a rounded igloo shape. It was a modular room, or a modular donut.

One of the panels in the back was clearly a doorway. The same words were inscribed above it.

Finally, Roger went to the fourth niche, the room shaped like an isosceles triangle. This room also had a tall stone doorway with the same words. Roger looked over the room, ran through some of the math for isosceles triangles, and decided that this room was the least relevant of the four. Time was important now, he realized, and his intuition told him this room was a red herring.

He walked back to Rebecca. "Let's go through Wiles's proof together."

"As I recall, Andrew Wiles' proof was more than a hundred pages long."

Roger smiled. "We'll hurry."

Roger and Rebecca began to run through the calculations of Andrew Wiles's proof of Fermat. Their minds raced in unison, passing formulas back and forth as if they were sharing exotic plates of food. The calculations became electric for them. In rapid fire, they presented equations to each other, and answered each other's questions faster than an ordinary computer could.

As they worked through Wiles' proof, Roger felt his logic leading him toward the room in the eastern wall, the niche composed of four rooms, but he was also mysteriously drawn to the southern room, the geodesic tunnel room, though he couldn't determine why.

Their work was abruptly interrupted by the ominous voice that had challenged them before.

"It's time to make your decision. You have three minutes to choose a doorway or die."

Roger and Rebecca shifted into another gear, frantic now for an insight that would identify the right doorway.

"Andrew Wiles realized that in order to prove Fermat," Roger said, "he would have to prove the Taniyama-Shimura conjecture."

"Yes," Rebecca said. "And Taniyama-Shimura maintained that all elliptical curves are modular."

Roger was momentarily stunned. "What did you just say?"

"Taniyama-Shimura asserted that all elliptical curves are modular. Wiles proved Taniyama-Shimura, which was the key to proving Fermat."

Roger was suddenly beside himself with excitement and enthusiasm. He grabbed Rebecca and kissed her. "You're a genius! Elliptical curves are shaped like donuts. And because they're modular, they're composed of vast numbers of symmetrical panels. They're paneled donuts."

He looked at the south wall. "The modular donut is what ultimately proved Fermat. And the north, east, and south walls represent a progression from Pythagoras to Fermat. The south wall, Rebecca! That's the modular room and the door that has our answer!"

They both raced back to get Roxanne and then together the three hurried to the south wall and the door in the back of the modular room.

Roger read the inscription aloud. "I choose to enter this doorway and accept my fate."

A horrific grinding sound assaulted them as two enormous stone walls began to part. Roger and Rebecca were momentarily deafened by the power of the pings that seemed to explode around them, and blinded by the immense light created by all the energy stored in the room. Their senses overwhelmed, they took hold of Roxanne, who stood between them, and reached across their daughter to take each other's hands. The light intensified and they were forced to look away, awed and terrified.

Chapter 30
The Crystal Cavern, the Enkefalons, the Double R Prophecy

"T his is one of the reasons the Enkefalons survived for so many thousands of years," Roger said. "Energy! The place is exploding with it."

The energy was so great, he wasn't sure he, Rebecca, and Roxanne could bear it. He and Rebecca shielded their eyes and protected Roxanne from the light, which was like staring at the sun.

The beings must have read his mind, because the light dimmed sufficiently for the three of them to lower their arms.

"Enter," the same booming voice said.

The three stepped forward and entered an enormous cavern the size of a cathedral. Roger estimated that the ceiling, what he could see of it, was three hundred feet above, and the cavern's width was probably half a mile. Like the previous cave, this enormous cavern was alive with energy and light. The place was bathed in luminous earth tones, along with flashes of orange and gold.

Before the three had a chance to walk deeper into the cavern, they were lifted up and transported to its center. The light was especially bright there, almost white. In front of them, perhaps fifty feet away, a row of low stalagmites formed a semicircle. Roger's gaze drifted upward, and he was shocked by what he saw. Approximately thirty feet above their heads were two dozen floating brains, each far larger than the size of an ordinary brain. All but three of the twenty-four brains were engulfed by an illuminated golden mist. The three exceptions were held within a darkened cloud. They seemed lifeless, inert.

Roger was still examining the brains when an enormous stalactite hurtled at the three of them like a missile.

"Roger!" Rebecca shouted, and he leaped in front of Rebecca and Roxanne. Just before the missile hit the three of them, it exploded into particles of dust. Their shields up, Roger and Rebecca blocked any of the particles from hitting Roxanne.

Roger wheeled around and looked for the source of the attack. Instead of confronting an assailant, he faced twenty-one regal-looking men and women who had materialized in the same place where the stalagmites had been. Each of them sat in a throne-like chair. Most of them appeared to be middle-aged, late forties to fifties, with a few in their sixties. All of them projected an unmistakable sense of power and ease. They were dressed in long flowing robes of different hues, some white, others red, or yellow, or deep blue.

Directly behind the Reynolds, three high-backed chairs appeared. Rebecca led Roxanne to the middle chair and sat her down, and then sat to her left. Holding her daughter's hand, she looked at the council.

Roger remained standing, his fists clenched, ready for battle.

"We apologize for that most unkind welcome, Roger, Rebecca, and Roxanne."

The telepathic communication came from the figure at the center of the semi-circle, a man whom Roger took to be the leader of the council. He appeared to be among the oldest, though his age only increased the gravitas that emanated from him. He was bald, save for small amounts of hair on the sides of his head. His face was lined but strong, his eyes blue, clear, and penetrating. Whatever his age, he gave off an aura of immense power and wisdom.

"There will be no more attempts on your life, I assure you," he said telepathically. "We welcome the three of you to the home of the

Enkefalon Council. I am Gentaurus, council leader. On behalf of the council, I congratulate you on your brilliant victories over every obstacle we put before you. Over the millennia, many have tried to enter our domain but few have succeeded. You have earned this audience."

Considering he and his family had just been put through a series of life and death trials, Roger had run out of patience.

"Who or what are you?" he asked, his strained voice indicating his awe and anger. "And what are those brains hovering above us?"

"We are twenty-one individual consciousnesses that are rooted and preserved in the brains floating above you. Thousands of years ago, ancient Geniuses discovered methods for achieving extraordinary longevity. You have read in your great books about long-living humans, Noah and Methuselah, for example. Ancient Inca Geniuses also discovered ways to preserve the life essence of human beings in this physical realm. They did it by sustaining a person's consciousness—his memory, wisdom, judgment, and temperament—and preserving his brain in the energetic and chemical field that appears before you as a golden mist.

"Our consciousnesses remain rooted in our individual brains. What you see when you look at me is an image I project in order to make a more comfortable communication. The men and women you see seated in these chairs are projecting their own images in the same way."

Roger was impressed. "I see that the mist around three of your brethren has darkened. Are these council members dead, and if so, are you all dying?"

"Yes. Like all material existence, we are decaying and dying As the millennia pass, we experience some of the sufferings of old age, including dementia. The stalactite was thrown at you by a very old council member whose dementia had progressed beyond his ability to control himself. He had murderous thoughts toward you and your family, so we intervened. Alas, we had to mercifully release him from this realm. He will not cause you any more trouble. But more to the point, all of us are very old, and although new members join us from time to time, all of those you see here will eventually depart this world. But not for some considerable time, and we are now ready to hear and act on your petition."

"What keeps you here?" Roger asked.

"We have volunteered, so to speak, to endure this less than fully satisfying form of existence in order to serve humankind. For as long as such existence continues, we remain present in the physical world and thus can have a significant influence on this material dimension and on human affairs. We intercede, you might say, between higher and more powerful forces above us and less advanced beings below. We fulfill an important place as guides in a larger plan that the Universe is unfolding."

Roger was speechless. He felt small and insignificant.

"We understand your feelings, Roger. Even your great mind is but a small awareness before the limitlessness of the Infinite.

"Now," the counsel leader said, "tell us why we should help you."

Roger realized the Enkefalons knew very well why he and his family had come, and his presentation was the final test.

He began by explaining the life and death struggle taking place between Western and Eastern Geniuses. One of the cardinal principles of Western Geniuses was that they would not use their abilities to interfere in the lives of Ordinaries, except under limited circumstances that involved preserving order and life, especially on a large scale. Some Eastern Geniuses felt that leaving Ordinaries to their own devices would result in chaos and perhaps global destruction. However, they were using that argument to justify world domination. Their latest attempt at achieving this end was being played out on several fronts.

Some Eastern Geniuses had attempted to gain control of the world's economy via a strategy that included stock market manipulations and a terrorist act that, if their plans had not been thwarted, would have given them enormous political and economic power over the entire world.

They had attempted to run a candidate for the US presidency whose mind they controlled.

They succeeded in creating a technology that enabled them to silence the warning signal Western Geniuses experience in the presence of Eastern Geniuses. They did this in order to assassinate Western Geniuses who opposed their efforts at worldwide domination.

This same group of Eastern Geniuses had taken control of the government of Slavistan and was attempting to annex three of its smaller neighbors. They were engaging in surreptitious acts of war in order to justify an invasion and take control of those bordering nations. Their larger plans were to reestablish a kind of new Soviet Union that would be a launching point to an even greater empire and world domination.

"In order to cover their own identities," Roger continued, "they have taken control of a good man, a Western Genius by the name of Jason Phillips, a longtime colleague of mine, whose mind is still under direct influence by an unknown Genius. This Genius has forced Dr. Phillips to participate in their plan for economic hegemony.

"And finally, and most important to my wife and me personally, they have taken control of my daughter Roxanne, who is now in a coma and is slowly dying."

"So far," Gentaurus said, "you haven't told us anything we didn't already know. Tell us what you want and why we should help you."

Still confident of having the moral high ground, Roger continued. "I come here with four requests. First, give my daughter back her life. Restore her health, vigor, and consciousness and free her from the grip of the Genius who has taken control of her mind.

"I realize that saving the life of a teenage girl might not seem important to you, but the culture we Western Geniuses have created places great value on every human life, especially the lives of innocent children and young people. We also value love of family as the foundation of an orderly and healthy society. We see caring for and loving children as among the greatest and most noble of human characteristics.

"Roxanne has not yet had a chance to live and love. It would be an unbearable cruelty if a traitor is allowed to destroy this innocent child's brilliant mind and life. She would never know the joy and love that she is just beginning to experience. Nor would she be able to fulfill her life's purpose, which could have enormous consequences for the entire world."

Roger paused to regain control of his emotions. "Second, I ask that you reveal to me the identity of the Collaborator, the Western Genius who is aiding the Eastern Council's efforts to achieve world domination.

"Third, I ask that you tell me who so cruelly attacked my child's mind and took her captive.

"Fourth, I ask you to free Jason Phillips from the evil grip that has enslaved him.

"I have no idea what you can do to help establish balance between our kind in the West and East, but whatever you do in that regard will be for the good of the world. That is all I have to say."

"Thank you, Roger," Gentaurus said.

A strange stillness fell over the entire council. Their eyes appeared closed as they sat motionless. Roger speculated they were meditating or communicating with forces greater than themselves. After a short period of silence, the Enkefalons began their deliberations. They were obviously communicating with one another because they kept turning to face different members, occasionally nodding ascent. Their communications were shielded and Roger could not ascertain what they might be saying.

Among themselves, the Enkefalons communicated with the speed of thought. Rapidly they weighed various factors in deciding whether or not to help Roxanne Reynolds and her family. They were well into their discussion when one of the senior Enkefalons asked whether they should take into account the so-called Double *R* Prophecy. Most of the Enkefalons had at least heard of the legend concerning the golden-haired Reynolds family of Geniuses, all of whose first names also began with the letter *R*.

A younger Enkefalon immediately stated he was against even considering the legend, because legends and prophecies were notoriously unreliable. For the benefit of those Enkefalons who did not know the legend and prophecy, Gentaurus explained them. He added that full knowledge of the prophecy had been passed down for over 1,500 years but only to a very few Geniuses. He was one.

He explained that as Sir Reginald Reynolds, knight of the Round Table, lay dying, he beseeched his friend Merlin to peer into the future and tell him whether his murder and that of his dearly loved wife and young daughter would be avenged and what would happen to his line.

Gentaurus noted that even among Geniuses, Merlin had extraordinary powers of precognition. He told the other Enkefalons all he knew of the prophecy, including the parts that had already come to pass. After he concluded his explanation, the Enkefalons continued their deliberations.

Roger and Rebecca held their breath as they waited for the council's decision. Less than a minute passed before Gentaurus broke the silence.

"We have decided to help you," he communicated. "I must warn you, however, that your daughter is in a far more vulnerable and dangerous state than either of you realizes. The tentacles of the enemy are deep within her. They have already caused considerable damage to her nervous system and physical body. In our efforts to free her from her assailant, we may cause further injury and we could fail in our attempt to fully restore her to health. She could be left permanently impaired or she could die. Knowing this, if you still wish us to try, we need your permission to take control of her mind and body. Do we have that permission?"

Roger looked at Rebecca. She silently communicated her permission, and Roger expressed their agreement. Instantly Roxanne's body was lifted from her chair and raised high into the air until she was suspended, horizontally, some thirty feet above the cavern floor. Her golden hair shone with special brilliance, reflecting the light emanating from the brains of the Enkefalons. The images of the council members in their chairs disappeared and the Enkefalon brains encircled Roxanne's body. The golden mist that surrounded the brains brightened and the brains began to vibrate.

Rebecca walked over to Roger and took his arm. He put his arms around her and held her close to him.

Beams of light emanated from the golden mists and flowed into Roxanne's body. Roger and Rebecca could see the rivulets and cauliflower-like contours of the individual brains vibrate as the light grew more intense. Clearly, the Enkefalons were working hard. Thirty minutes passed; the beams of energy continuously became stronger. The light of the golden mist became so brilliant; Roger and Rebecca had to shield their eyes. But then they stared in shock as Roxanne's body vibrated violently and then rotated at blinding speed. She was literally a blur far above the floor.

Rebecca turned away and buried her face in Roger's chest. She prayed with a fervor she had never known. He did the same.

Another thirty minutes passed. Just as Roger and Rebecca felt they could bear the tension no longer, the beams of light softened, gradually disappearing. Roxanne was lowered toward the floor. Roger scooped her up and placed her on the chair. Rebecca sat beside her again and held Roxanne, stroking her head.

The council members reappeared in their chairs.

"Your daughter is indeed a strong and determined human being," Gentaurus said. "She has a great heart, an enormous commitment to her life and her purpose, and a deep love for both of you—and for a young man, Andor Lysenko. She has been restored to health, though she will need time and rest before she has fully recovered."

The fear that Rebecca had held within her body dissipated, leaving her drained and limp. She couldn't hold back tears of gratitude.

"Thank you," Roger communicated. He turned from the council members to her and Roxanne, and then back to the council. "Thank you."

"Yes, thank you all so much," Rebecca communicated. "We are eternally grateful."

Then she watched in puzzlement as Gentaurus apparently communicated privately with Roger for several minutes. She was locked out. At one point, Roger seemed to go into a state of shock. His body buckled and he clearly struggled to keep himself upright, as if he'd just been given some new and terrible knowledge. Without looking up, he then nodded several times to the council leader. Their dialogue continued for another minute, and then Gentaurus included her again.

"The ramifications for the world will be far-reaching, Roger Reynolds," he said. "Make no mistake. If you fail, the Collaborator and his cohort will succeed and the earth will be shrouded in darkness for many centuries to come. All that we have done for you and your family will be lost."

Roger drew a deep breath. "I will not fail."

"You will now be returned to the surface," Gentaurus said. "Your ship and pilot are waiting for you."

"Thank you," Roger said. "Thank you for everything."

In the blink of an eye, Roger, Rebecca, and Roxanne were standing on the mountain ledge, looking at the jet's open door. Max Louri grinned at them as he started the jet's engines and waved them to the craft.

Chapter 31
The Final Battle above the London Eye

The message was short and to the point. "I've got Rebecca and Roxanne. Meet me at the Eye at 6 tonight. Come alone."

Roger had been waiting and hoping for that communication for much of the day.

Just nine hours earlier, Max had flown the Reynolds family to London and landed the ship in a hidden part of Hyde Park. It was 7:30 in the morning and the sun was just coming up.

Max drove the jet to a large garage and parked inside. A standard-looking black London taxi was waiting for them. Roger and Rebecca helped Roxanne into the taxi's spacious backseat; Rebecca got in with her. Roger sat beside Max, who was driving.

They went to Roger's townhouse, located on a quiet side street in the Kensington section of London. Max parked across the street, on the left-hand side of the road. "I'll go unlock the door while you see to Roxanne," Max said to Roger as he got out.

Roger got out of the car and was about to open the door for Roxanne when a terrible realization hit him like a lightning bolt. Instinctively, he put up his shield and telepathically yelled, "Max! No, wait!"

He was too late. Max had already put the key in the lock. In a flash, Max was no more.

The explosion blew away the entire front of Roger's house and ripped Max into a million pieces. The blast hurled Roger back some twenty meters, flinging his body through the front windows of the house behind him. The blast impacted that house as well, and Roger was buried beneath rubble, unconscious.

Rebecca had experienced the warning just as Roger called out to Max, and she managed to put up her shield as well. She pulled Roxanne to the floor of the taxi, sparing them both the direct impact of the blast and the shards of glass and brick that blew in all directions.

Within fifteen minutes, Stephen, Willie, Simone, Ellis, and Freddy were on the scene, where they uncovered Roger, who miraculously had suffered only some bad bruises and a mild concussion. Rebecca and Roxanne, however, were nowhere to be found.

And now, eight hours later, the message arrived. I've got Rebecca and Roxanne. Come to the Eye at 6 tonight. Come alone.

Of course, Roger knew the source of the telepathic communication. The Enkefalons had revealed the identity of the Collaborator, the powerful Genius who had taken control of Roxanne's consciousness and who, with the help of the Klepers, had engineered the latest assault on the West.

At this moment, however, nothing of that geopolitical drama mattered. What mattered was that the Collaborator and the Klepers had Rebecca and Roxanne, and that Rebecca had been badly injured in a fight with the Collaborator after Roger's house blew up. Roger knew all of this because Rebecca had managed to get off a short communication to him a few hours earlier. Apparently, Rebecca had fought hard while trying to protect Roxanne and keep the two of them from being kidnapped by the Klepers and the Collaborator. The Collaborator had hit her with a blast of electromagnetic energy that not only wounded her left shoulder, but damaged her heart. She had been weak and barely holding onto consciousness when she managed to contact him.

Roger had no doubt the Collaborator had wanted her to contact him. The Collaborator wanted Roger to know that any failure to follow his instructions to the letter would mean death to both Rebecca and Roxanne.

That evening at 5:45, Freddy drove him the short distance from his office in Westminster Abbey to the south bank of the Thames. The evening was clear and cool. They sat silently as Freddy drove the car across Westminster Bridge. Roger felt his every cell quicken as his mind raced. He was on the way to the most important battle of his life. Would he be able to defeat the Klepers and the Collaborator... his mind against theirs, and save Rebecca and Roxanne? Was there anything he could do to improve his chances? In the minutes remaining before the battle, he turned, as always, to his mind, and he thought:

"Since my parents were brutally murdered, I have been emotionally detached. This has been painful for my wife and daughter. I have been so guarded that I have not been emotionally there for them. I've long understood the problem, but have not been able to overcome it."

"But all this began to change when my darling daughter Roxanne was attacked and was close to death. When in the caverns I met the beast within me, I learned how painful my emotional distance has been for Rebecca and Roxanne. And I also found out that I would never achieve my full potential as a person until I become one with my feelings. The cocoon I had created and within which my heart has been encased has at last begun to crack. Now that the lives of Rebecca and Roxanne are in the murderous hands of the most powerful evil Geniuses, will my heart finally be freed from that cocoon, and will I truly become one with my feelings and with the beast within? If that does happen, will I perhaps become more powerful? Will I be able to defeat the Klepers and the Collaborator, and save my family? I pray to God that I will."

Freddy turned the car left toward Jubilee Gardens, and Roger caught sight of his destination.

The London Eye, the giant Ferris wheel that dominated the London skyline, was lit against the twilight sky. Four hundred and forty two feet tall and nearly four hundred feet wide, the Eye was a magnificent bicycle wheel suspended over the great river. Or rather, it was two bicycle wheels, aligned side by side and joined by steel struts that formed the foundations for the thirty-two glass pods the passengers rode in. Because of the angle of the Ferris wheel's frame, the passengers literally rode over the river.

Roger had always liked the Eye. To him it was a reminder of playful innocence and eagerness for life. But all such feelings were gone now. The Eye was no longer a place of innocence and youth, but the end of things—the point of no return.

Freddy dropped him off at the entrance ramp of the Eye, which Roger ascended with his characteristically long-legged stride. He was dressed for the business of killing: leather jacket, a thick sweatshirt, jeans, running shoes, and gloves, all the color of midnight. As he approached the Ferris wheel, he felt the single ping of his adversary, as well as four other pings. Rebecca and Roxanne were close by, but a powerful shielding force prevented him from knowing exactly where they were. He quickened his pace.

Each glass capsule on the Ferris wheel held up to twenty-five people. As a capsule reached the base of the Ferris wheel, the glass door opened automatically and an attendant ushered passengers on. Roger reached the landing as the capsule meant for him was arriving. The door opened and the usher signaled him into the capsule. Roger entered and sat down on a wooden bench in the center of the glass bubble next to its only other occupant, Alexander Astrakhan.

"Where are Rebecca and Roxanne?" he asked, his telepathic voice low and full of loathing.

Astrakhan remained silent as the capsule began to climb into the London sky. He looked south over the London skyline as a breathtaking view of Big Ben and the Houses of Parliament appeared, but his expression gave nothing away. He seemed unimpressed, even disinterested in the external world.

Roger studied his former mentor. He was dressed in an expensive camel-colored coat. On his head sat a black fedora. His hands were cupped over the top of a thick hardwood walking stick. Switching his attention to Astrakhan's face, he saw that Alexander's avuncular countenance, with its usual expression of joyful wisdom that Roger had long assumed was the light of an inner love, was gone. In its place was a hard, closed mask, a killer's face. The eyes were narrowed and mean, and the turned down mouth blatantly malicious, framed by a now satanic-looking Van Dyke. Astrakhan was out of patience, Roger realized. He had played his last bluff. He was showing his cards now, and he didn't give a damn who saw them.

Finally, he spoke telepathically to Roger. "Patience. You'll see them in just a few minutes."

A chill raced down Roger's spine at the icy confidence with which Astrakhan spoke. He had Roger right where he wanted him. He was holding all the aces.

Astrakhan went on. "You have caused me quite a lot of trouble these past few months, Roger."

"Don't worry," Roger replied. "You won't be feeling any pain once we finish our business tonight."

Astrakhan turned and looked at Roger with surprise. "You were always confident, Roger, I'll give you that." His voice remained calm, resolved. He was certain of the outcome of this confrontation.

Roger knew he had to play along in order to find out where Rebecca and Roxanne were. The Eye made a complete revolution in approximately thirty minutes. Astrakhan would make his move, and perhaps give some clue as to Rebecca's and Roxanne's whereabouts, before the Eye made one complete revolution. Roger had to keep him talking.

"Why did you do it?" he asked. "How many times did we have this discussion, that the grab for ultimate power is the act of madmen like Hitler or fools like Icarus? Which one did you become?"

"One tailors his words to suit his audience," Astrakhan replied. "You were always a boy scout. Why disabuse you prematurely?"

"Why attack my family? You could have killed me many times. You didn't have to save my life in Vietnam when you used your mind to push me away from that trap."

"I didn't save you in Vietnam, you saved yourself," Astrakhan said with just a trace of bitterness. "You tapped into your innate telekinetic powers in order to shift the trajectory of your flight. Your own ridiculous modesty kept you from seeing the obvious—just one of many such occasions when your pitiful smallness blinded you to the bigger picture, Roger."

"What do you mean?" Roger asked.

"Roger, you're a fool."

Astrakhan's words struck him like a slap in the face. He turned and faced Roger, his expression a mixture of dark menace and self-satisfaction.

"One hundred and sixty years ago, I rode onto your parents' farm with a team of black men. Your parents welcomed me and those men with open arms. You'd think I was Abe Lincoln himself and those men were a band of slaves fresh off the plantation. They dropped the plough and welcomed us into their house. Your mother made us a meal. She was an excellent cook. She set out all the food they had and, of course, in our presence they dropped their shields. Such trusting fools."

Astrakhan's expression was that of a sociopath—completely devoid of emotion, yet chilling in its hatred.

"I stabbed her to death with the knife she put in front of me. You should have seen the expression on both their faces as I drove the knife into her chest. Total incomprehension, Roger. It was as if they had just landed on Saturn. Too much trust and too little creativity, if you ask me. Before your father could react, I shot him. I could have killed him with an energy blast, but that would have raised questions among the locals. Besides, I've always liked the gun."

Aghast with horror but fully shielded, Roger needed every ounce of discipline to restrain himself from attacking Astrakhan right then and there. But that would surely seal Rebecca's and Roxanne's fate. He had to wait. He had to make sure that when he finished off Astrakhan, he would be in a position to save Rebecca and Roxanne. Somewhere in the back of his mind he wondered if he had missed some signal, some hint of the evil in this monster....

He said the only word that could be spoken: "Why?"

"Your father opposed my plan to unify the Western and Eastern Councils of Geniuses. He wanted to maintain the principles of the Western Council. He argued that if the Councils unified, Geniuses would be even more likely to try to take over the entire world. That was, of course, exactly what I wanted. But when he was dead, the other Western Council members took up his cause and I knew I had to bide my time. During the twentieth century, West and East became polarized, and the chance of unification of our kind was obviously impossible."

"Why didn't you kill me when I was young?" Roger asked. His anger toward this man was so powerful; he was barely able to contain himself.

"I saw you as a potential pawn in my ultimate plan," Astrakhan said. "You demonstrated rather unique abilities early in life. You could lift small objects with your mind and you had a strong influence on people. You were a born leader. But you also had a fatal flaw, which I saw quickly. You were loyal and idealistic, a family failure. I knew I could control you and play you against the Eastern Council. As you became more powerful, I put you in places of leadership and then used you as a bargaining chip in my negotiations with the Eastern Council. If they gave me what I wanted, I would dispose of you. They were forced to play ball, as the Ordinaries say. The Eastern Geniuses were losing every battle they engaged with you, so they had no choice but to give me what I wanted. Control of the US government and the world's banking system in exchange for what? A new Slavistani empire and your head. Really, quite little to pay for what I wanted. So, Roger, you were my strongest card when it came to dealing with the East while your loyalty to me blinded you to my plans and actions."

"Then why attack Rebecca and Roxanne?" Roger asked again.

"Oh, I'll admit it bothered me when the Western Council heaped praise and honors on you. All of that was rightfully mine. But that was all eclipsed when—" He grimaced and his eyes blazed with insane rage. "When you dared to oppose and frustrate my financial plans," he yelled, suddenly losing control of his calm demeanor. "I am the world's rightful leader!" he shouted, shaking his stick. "I am the only one alive who can bring order to the chaos that life has become." He brought his face closer to Roger's and spoke in a stage whisper. "And tonight I settle accounts with you and clear the path to what is rightfully mine."

They were high above the Thames now, the Ferris wheel still ascending toward its apex. Darkness had fallen. At the horizon, a giant

385

full moon was rising. Directly below, Roger could see the lights from the commercial and tourist boats that skimmed along the Thames, whitewater creases in their wake. The great buildings of London were lighted and glorious—the Houses of Parliament, Big Ben, St. James Cathedral, the London Egg, and Windsor Castle. They seemed like tiny golden Lego toys from where Roger and Astrakhan sat.

Astrakhan rose from the wooden bench and went to the edge of the capsule. His left hand held onto the steel railing at the periphery of the glass bubble, his right hand still holding his walking stick. His back was to Roger as he spoke. "The Reynolds line is over," he said flatly. With shocking speed, he whirled around and faced Roger, his walking stick pointing at Roger's heart. Astrakhan fired five shots in rapid succession, all of them hitting Roger in the chest, tearing the leather jacket apart and sending its insulation flying.

Roger fell over the back of the bench and lay on the capsule's floor, inert. Astrakhan lowered his walking stick, as the elation over his long-anticipated victory began building. He walked around the bench and stood over Roger's body, but before he could assess Roger's state—before he realized that Roger was wearing bullet-proof armor—the younger man leapt to his feet and in a single motion kicked Astrakhan in the side of the head, hurling him against the door on the other side of the capsule. The impact of Astrakhan's body threw the door open. Wind whipped through the capsule, blowing both men against its walls. Astrakhan's fedora flew off into the night. Roger crouched down and sent a burst of energy at Astrakhan. His powerful shield was up, though. Roger's blast illuminated the sphere of energy that surrounded Astrakhan; within that protective circle, Astrakhan was surprised, but untouched. The same could not be said for the glass wall directly behind him, however. The blast blew a gaping hole in it, and another great gust of wind blew through the capsule. Astrakhan aimed his walking stick and fired several more rounds at Roger, but this time Roger was able to change the trajectory of the bullets telekinetically, just enough to keep from being hit. Bullets whizzed by him and shattered the glass behind him.

Astrakhan threw his stick aside. Extending both of his hands, he fired an enormous burst of energy at Roger. Roger's shield was illuminated, and like Astrakhan, he too was protected. But the blast threw him back against the glass wall that had already been punctured by the bullets. The glass immediately gave way as he hit it, and for an instant he was suspended four hundred feet above the earth. Somehow Roger controlled the flight of his body enough to grab hold of the wheel's outer rim. He hung from the steel circle as it slowly reached its zenith.

Astrakhan quickly climbed outside the capsule to stand on top of the narrow rim. He crouched low, hanging on with his left hand to one of the metal supports upon which a glass capsule sat. He was just three feet from where Roger hung on for his life. Roger could sense him readying to blast him with a fusillade of electromagnetic energy, and he reached out to his feathered friends for help. Just as Astrakhan was about to release his barrage, a flock of birds flew directly into him, pecking his face and throwing him off balance. Astrakhan fell back and landed on top of the capsule just below where Roger hung.

Roger swung his feet upward, toward the base that supported one of the capsules. He climbed between the two steel rims and then got on top of the capsule directly above the one Astrakhan stood upon.

Against the backdrop of the full moon and an ink-black sky, Astrakhan and Roger fired blasts of energy, each burst electrifying their shields and illuminating the night. The two were like a pair of Greek gods, hurling lightning at each other.

Every capsule on the Ferris wheel was filled with passengers. Hundreds of people in the capsules and on the ground watched in terror and fascination as Roger and Astrakhan flung beams of light at each other. Parents on the ground clutched their children and hurried away while others froze in horror, unable to run or even look away.

The capsules the men balanced on had passed their apex and were rolling downward now, but both men were still more than 350 feet in the air. They struggled to keep their footing atop the slippery glass bubbles as the wind whipped violently at them.

When Roger felt four more pings in the immediate vicinity, he realized that Rebecca, Roxanne and their captors were nearby, very likely on the Eye. He reached out to Rebecca and tried to penetrate the shield that had been thrown up around them.

"Rebecca, I can feel your presence. Where are you?"

"We're getting on the Eye, Roger," she answered.

"I'm coming for you. Hang on."

Astrakhan looked inside the capsule he was standing on. A family of four stared up at him in horror. Pointing a finger at the capsule, he released a beam of energy that shattered the glass bubble. All that remained was the glass floor. Astrakhan controlled the scattering of the glass enough so that he landed directly on the capsule floor. Before anyone could react, he grabbed the father and threw him over the edge of the capsule. The man hurtled in a kind of swimming motion toward the Thames. The woman grabbed her youngest child and screamed in terror. Astrakhan pushed them overboard, and then grabbed the small boy and threw him over as well.

A chorus of screams rose from below.

Roger reached out with both hands and caught the four family members in flight, creating a web of energy that took control of their fall and drew them together.

The instant Roger caught them, his mind was flooded with information about each family member. Virtually all of it, he dismissed instantly, but the father had to be dealt with. John Holder, a welder from Manchester, had brought his family to London. As he hurtled toward the Thames and certain death, he was about to experience a fatal heart attack. If Roger did not open his arteries instantly, Holder's heart would explode. He'd be dead before he hit the river, safely or otherwise.

Holding the four family members in his web, Roger connected his mind to John Holder's nervous system. He ordered it to produce more prostaglandins, a group of hormones that would open Holder's coronary arteries wider and allow more blood to flow to his heart. The welder's arteries instantly began opening, but before the four landed safely, Astrakhan shattered Roger's capsule.

Roger was thrown into a free fall toward the Thames. He searched desperately for something to grab hold of while sustaining his concentration on the plunging family.

Summoning all of his powers, he directed his fall to one of the long spokes that gave the great wheel its support. He clung to it as the wind tore at his body and the darkness reached into his soul. His mind never let go of the family, however, and he brought them to a soft landing. The four Holders collapsed on the ground and immediately gathered into one another's arms. John Holder kissed his wife and children, happy and amazed that they were all alive.

Astrakhan levitated into the air and flew toward Roger, landing on the steel rim directly above where Roger hung. He looked down at Roger and laughed a hard, evil laugh.

Roger continued to cling to the spoke of the giant Ferris wheel, his arms aching and tired. He had faced death many times, and had come to accept its inevitability. He did not fear it. Now, Roger calmly assessed his chances of survival, and they were slim indeed. For a second, he wondered whether his impact with the river would be very painful...perhaps the pain would be heightened by his powerful nervous system ....before death would bring him peace? His last thought would be of Rebecca and Roxanne...how much he would miss them!

As Alexander Astrakhan stood over his dangling body, Roger began to accept that his own great intelligence and mental powers would not be enough to overcome the mind of his older and more powerful mentor, who was about to kill him.

Alexander shook Roger out of his sepulchral thoughts, by shouting: "You fool. You're no match for me. My ancestors have been killing Reynoldses since the time of King Arthur. But tonight, all the fun ends." He pointed toward the lower part of the Eye. "Look, Reynolds, look below."

Roger looked down toward the lower capsules on the Eye. In horror, he saw Rebecca and Roxanne standing on top of one of them. Their hands were tied behind their backs and a hangman's noose was wrapped around their necks. The ropes were tethered to the rim of the Eye. If they fell or were pushed, they would be killed instantly. Both women were barefoot and struggled to maintain their balance as the capsule rose high above the Thames. Roger remembered how badly injured Rebecca's heart was. She was weak and couldn't stand much longer.

Roger lowered his gaze and saw Karl and Klaus Kleper sneering at him from within the capsule Rebecca and Roxanne were standing on. Both sent him a barrage of telepathic hatred, in which they announced their pleasure in killing the two most important people in Roger's life.

In his overconfident communication, Klaus Kleper opened his shield just enough for Roger to read his thoughts. Once Astrakhan killed Roger, the brothers intended to shoot Astrakhan with a shield-penetrating Genius-designed weapon. It was a big night for the Kleper twins, and the two were already overjoyed with what lay ahead.

Astrakhan again shouted at Roger. "You and all of these Ordinaries are in for some old-fashioned entertainment tonight, Reynolds: the hanging and electrocution of a pair of witches. On my command, the Klepers will blow off the roof of that capsule. We'll see if those two bitches of yours can fly. And while they're hanging, I am going to burn those witches, personally electrocute them until their flesh turns black right in front of your eyes. And then I'm going to kill you."

Alexander's words tore at Roger's heart. What would the world be like without his beloved wife and daughter? His conclusion was swift: for him there was no life, no world without Rebecca and Roxanne. His fatigue and pain evaporated, and he was overwhelmed by emotion. His heart, not his mind, was now in control. In an instant Roger was overcome by what he would later describe as the joining of three rivers—one of pure rage, another of pure power, and a third of pure love. A storm was raging within him and was bringing about a tsunami of change and transformation. As he hung from the steel spoke, Roger began evolving at an accelerated pace. His DNA was being supercharged with new energy. Genes that were common in the human genome but rarely utilized came to life. And rare genetic sequences and patterns suddenly fired within him. The image of the beast in the cave appeared in his mind, roaring with awesome power.

"Now is the time we become one, Roger Reynolds," the beast within him cried.

Roger felt the chains that had long constrained the beast shatter into tiny pieces. His voice roared with the power of the beast as he shouted out to the universe. And at the peak of his call, something happened that Roger could not have predicted: he disappeared.

And then he let go of the spoke to which he clung and flew directly at Rebecca and Roxanne.

Astrakhan stood in the wind, bewildered beyond anything he had ever experienced. Both Klepers gaped. But Astrakhan was fast on his feet and instantly told the Klepers to kill Rebecca and Roxanne. "Kill them both now!"

Astrakhan conjured up a fireball the size of a bathtub and flung it at Rebecca and Roxanne. Before it hit them, Roger was there. He swooped down upon the women, severed their nooses, and gathered them up into his arms. In a flash, they too were gone.

Astrakhan's fireball hit the capsule like a bomb hitting a glass house. The resulting explosion deafened everyone within a half-mile radius and threw the Klepers a hundred yards into the Thames.

Roger carried Rebecca and Roxanne to a waiting van on the bank of the Thames, where Simone was ready to attend to both women. Roger set them down and like a rocket flew directly back at Astrakhan.

Astrakhan, still perched on the rim of the Eye, never saw Roger coming. With all the momentum of his flight, he hit the older man in the face with the force of a sledgehammer, shattering his jaw. Astrakhan's shield dropped instantly and he started to fall. Roger grabbed Astrakhan by the throat with his left hand, cutting off his air supply, and with his right hand took hold of his coat. Roger lifted him and flew high above the Eye. Powerless in Roger's grasp, Astrakhan saw the moon and the night sky expand before his eyes, as if it were an enormous blanket that was about to take him into its embrace. Roger turned downward toward the Thames, holding Astrakhan's body as if he were a sack of straw.

Far below, a forty-foot sailboat floated on a soft wind up the Thames, its mast a tall finger pointing skyward. From Roger's point of view, the mast was the spike of justice that had divine coincidence written all over it. Astrakhan, for his part, felt the inevitability of the moment fall on him. There was no turning back. He was about to die, and in that instant his mind was flooded with a thousand images, all of them crucial moments when his decisions had been driven by greed, a lust for power, and an obscenely inflated picture of himself. In his moment of surrender, he felt great pain and terror.

Roger slammed Astrakhan's body into the spike-like mast. The spike was thick and blunt, and when it broke through Astrakhan's back and out his sternum, it brought with it most of Astrakhan's internal organs. Astrakhan's expression was blank, his eyes and mouth open, his body run through and lifeless.

Roger hovered above his old mentor's body for a moment, gazing directly into his death mask. Then he turned his attention away and headed upriver for the Klepers.

The malevolent brothers, both injured badly and still stunned by the blast, floated on the surface of the Thames. Two fishing boats drew near to them. Before they realized what was happening, they were caught in a pair of fishing nets that curled above and beneath them. The brothers fought frantically to free themselves, but the nets were Genius designed and virtually indestructible. The Klepers cursed wildly and screamed death threats to anyone who could hear.

Then they heard a voice that was all too familiar, at once jocular and deadly.

"Got 'em, bro," Freddy called out to Ellis. "Just netted the fat boy and he's none too happy."

Karl struggled ferociously, releasing bursts of energy in all directions. The water rippled all around him and dead fish floated to the surface. Roger sent an enormous flow of his own energy to his team members, reinforcing their protective shields against any attack by the Klepers. Klaus, trapped in the second net, fought as best he could, but nothing could free either of them and soon they were sinking.

From the helm of one of the fishing boats, Ellis coordinated the fishing expedition. "Freddy's got the fat fish in his net. Stephen, Willie, how're you doing?"

Stephen was at the helm of the second fishing boat. He turned to Willie and asked him the status of his catch.

"Got the little fish," Willie said. "My, my, he does have a rather foul vocabulary."

Ellis turned to his brother. "Fred, we're ready when you are. Toss anchor."

"Tossing anchor."

Freddy threw a lever at the anchor winch, releasing an enormous anchor that was joined to the net that held Karl Kleper. A thick steel cord unwound swiftly from a wide spool. With irresistible force, the anchor pulled the net and the fat man down into the black river.

Ellis communicated to the second boat. "Willie, whenever you're ready, drop anchor."

Willie pulled a lever and the winch spun as the steel cord unspooled into the Thames, chasing the anchor that pulled Klaus Kleper to the bottom of the river.

Roger, floating above the scene, reached down into the water with his mind and found the Kleper twins, weakened but still struggling. He drained the last remaining power from their bodies.

The Klepers sank to the bottom of the river, where they were surprised to see so many skeletons littering the floor of the Thames. The skeletons were everywhere, hideous and permanent smiles on their skulls. Were these skeletons real or just images created by their guilty consciences to torment them? Klaus now understood that he was dying and that, as he had long suspected, he was an evil, worthless thing, coming to the bad end he deserved.

Karl, on the other hand, fought wildly with a terror he had never known. He had brought death to countless men and women, but he was woefully unprepared for his own end. The illusion of his power dissolved in those waters. Now all his powers were gone, and with his last breath came the realization of what he really was….an angry, cowardly, pathetic, inhuman monster.

At the surface of the river, bubbles rose and popped and dead fish floated in the swells, but eventually the waters calmed. The Klepers were no more.

Roger flew to the back of the van, where Simone was working to rescue Rebecca. Once he touched down, Roger emerged from his cloaked field and jumped inside the van.

Rebecca lay on a cot to his right; Roxanne sat on a cot to his left. He opened his arms to Roxanne and she fairly leapt into his embrace. He held her tight for an instant and then turned and knelt down next to Rebecca. Immediately, he realized how perilous her condition was.

"We've done all we can for her," Simone communicated to him alone. "I've given her every form of medicine and treatment I can. Astrakhan's blast injured the electrical fibers embedded in her heart. Her heart has been thrown into arrhythmia and I can't stop it. She's about to go into heart failure, and if we don't restore normal sinus rhythm, she'll have a fatal heart attack in minutes."

Roger nodded. He looked into Rebecca's eyes with a love so great, his own heart nearly burst. "I need you to close your eyes, Rebecca, and open your mind and your heart to me. I need you to be completely open, no holding back. Can you do that for me?"

Rebecca was getting weaker by the instant, but she nodded.

"I'm going to lift you just enough to get my left hand under your back, right behind your heart." He did so, placing his left hand on her back. "Now I'm going to place my right hand over your heart." He did that as well. "Now the hard part, Rebecca. You're going to let go and open your heart entirely to me."

Rebecca was terrified of surrendering, because she knew that the moment she let go, she would be dead.

"You're going to have to trust me, my love," Roger said. "That's all there is to it. You're going to make it. *We're* going to make it."

She looked deeply into his eyes; her expression told him everything. Still, her mind gave him one last message: "Thank you, Roger. I love you so much. Take care of Roxanne."

Roger fought back his fears and concentrated on his heart. The power of its enormous electromagnetic forces filled his chest like a growing river of golden light. The light ran down his arms and into his hands. The energy flowed into Rebecca's chest cavity, filling it with golden light, and then directed itself into her heart.

In that moment Rebecca closed her eyes, let go, and immediately suffered a fatal heart attack. Her body jumped involuntarily and then collapsed. Her heart stopped. She let out a long exhalation. She was dead.

Roxanne screamed, "Mom, no! No, Mom, you can't leave! Come back, do you hear me? Come back!"

She lunged toward her mother, but Simone held her. "Wait," Simone said.

Roger continued to direct the life forces from his heart to Rebecca's. His breathing became deeper, more powerful, as if he were reaching with his breath for powers greater than his own. His mind was completely open now, his body a pure channel for a love that exists in higher realms. He let his consciousness dissolve into that love as he searched for the Source of Life on higher planes of existence. Like a torrent from a limitless waterfall, a great flow of energy poured into Roger and then into Rebecca. It coursed directly into her heart and took it over.

Roger's love was part of that flow, and his heart became hers. They were one heart in two bodies, animated by a life force that would not be denied. And then Roger felt it, a sudden movement within Rebecca's heart, as if a struggling engine had caught a spark and fired on its own.

Rebecca's heart started to beat again, at first furtively and then with commitment. As if returning from another dimension, Rebecca opened her eyes and inhaled with a force that was both terrifying in its hunger and exhilarating in its determination. She was alive again.

For an instant, everyone in that truck stared in awe. The incomprehensibility of life blew away their rational faculties. And then Roxanne fell at her mother's side and cried.

"Mom, you're back. Thank God, you're back." She lifted her head and looked at her mother, and said, "Don't ever do that again!"

Roger laughed and smiled.

"I knew you wouldn't leave us," Roger said. "We're all helpless without you."

Simone reached over and embraced both Rebecca and Roxanne. She couldn't say another word....she was overcome with joy and relief.

After a few minutes, exhausted from her ordeal, Rebecca held Roxanne with one arm and placed her other hand on Roger's face. Her eyes held his. "Thank you," she said again, this time from the land of the living.

Simone checked Rebecca's heart and shoulder. All had been healed. "That must be some kind of record."

When Simone was done, Rebecca lifted both arms and wrapped them around Roger's neck. He kissed her on her lips and cheeks, feeling her tears soak his face.

Roxanne returned to her mother's side. Roger looked at Roxanne and asked if she was okay.

"Yes, I'm fine," she said. "But I hope all three of those men are dead."

He nodded. "It's all over."

"Good." She hugged her father again, harder and closer.

Simone got into the driver's seat of the van. "Hold on, everyone. We're out of here."

As the van rumbled down the road, Roger received Ellis's communication.

"Everyone all right, Chief?" Ellis asked.

"Yes, Ellis, we're all fine. Thank you."

"Only too happy to help out. See you soon."

In the illuminated Crystal Cavern deep in the earth, the Enkefalons observed the events with satisfaction.

"Eighty generations after the betrayal of Reginald Reynolds at the hands of Salanous Astrakhan," Gentaurus said, "Alexander Astrakhan's ancient ancestor, the Reynolds line has finally found justice." His fellow Enkefalons expressed their approval. "The Reynolds' line has been vindicated and can finally find a deeper peace. And Astrakhan has no heir. An evil line has come to its end."

The council members signaled their agreement, again satisfied with all that had transpired.

"And what of the whole Double R Prophecy?" asked Constanople, a member of the council. "The first phase of the prophecy has now been realized: the Reynolds line has been vindicated. Reginald Reynolds smiles upon us and his progeny in peace. Roger Reynolds will ascend to lead the Council of Western Geniuses and for a brief time, there will be equilibrium between the Councils of West and East. There will be peace, but only for a short time. Then the second phase of the prophecy begins, with all of its dangers and unanswered questions."

Gentaurus was silent for a long moment, as were the other council members. Each consulted his or her inner knowing for the possible outcome of the second phase of the prophecy. But there was no Merlin among them, and they could not clearly see the future.

The sun was bright and clear on Thanksgiving Day at the Reynolds house. The traditional feast had been placed on the table—a great browned turkey with all the trimmings, a bounty of vegetables, potatoes, cranberry sauce, and salads.

At one end of the table sat Rebecca, joyful at having her family all together and healthy. At the other end was Roger, every bit the proud patriarch. On Roger's left sat Andor's father, Mikael Lysenko, looking fit and dignified in his tweed jacket. To Mikael's left was his wife, Arianna, aglow with joy. To Roger's right sat Andor, and next to him, resplendent and beaming, Roxanne.

Over the weekend, Roger's entire London team, the Davies brothers, and Jason Phillips – who had fully recovered in the wake of Astrakhan's death - would join the family for another celebration. But today was just for the Reynolds and Lysenko families. It was a day for being together, for getting to know each other better, and to celebrate their happiness. .

Before the food was served, Roger bowed his head and led the whole family in prayer, giving thanks for all that they had miraculously come through. In a shielded communication, Roger prayed for Max Louri's soul and hoped that somehow he would know that Roger and his team would always remember him as a dear and loyal friend.

"Thank you all," Roger finally said aloud. "Let's enjoy the meal."

As the food was passed around, people made small jokes and conversation, and then they all settled down to their meals.

"It's good to see the sun again," Roxanne said. She glanced at her father. "I assume you neutralized the Klepers' satellite."

"Yes, Roxanne. Once we concluded our business with the Klepers, we ordered Paper Clip to shut down Archangel." He winked at her. "But the satellite is still under our control."

"That's good, Dad. You never know when that thing will come in handy."

The conversation naturally went to the future.

"I'm so looking forward to joining you in London, Mr. Reynolds," Andor said to Roger. "I'm honored to be part of your team."

"You're going to like Oxford too, Andor. Some of the greatest Western Geniuses are there teaching young people and preparing them for life. Between studying and working with us, you'll have a full plate, let me assure you."

Andor turned to Roxanne. "I'll be happiest when you're visiting me."

Roxanne smiled and then turned coquettish. "Oh, but I'll be so busy with my senior year of high school. You know, all that studying, all those books to read, papers to write, tests to take."

"Well, I guess I'll just have to come to you," he said.

A joyful, mischievous smile crossed Roxanne's face. "You'd better," she said.

Mikael Lysenko raised his glass and proposed a toast.

"Roger, Rebecca, and Roxanne, our family is eternally in your debt," he said. "We thank you with all our hearts."

They drank their toast, and then Roger said, "A lot of good came from your son, Mikael. Thanks to Andor, Senator Thompson's duplicity and the truth of what's been happening in Slavistan has become public knowledge. The UN has brought about a ceasefire and the atrocities have stopped. Without the Klepers, Victor Grozny will have to govern in an entirely new way or be swept aside by the people who put him in power. It's a new day in Slavistan. You did well, Andor, and you, Mikael and Arianna, have a lot to be proud of."

The meal proceeded in joy and celebration, and when it was over, they cleaned-up together. Roger and Rebecca were the last two out of the kitchen. Instead of joining the others in the living room, they sneaked out the back door for a little air on the patio. Roger took Rebecca in his arms and kissed her passionately.

"I love you so much," he said.

"You're happy and you're concerned," she said. "Why the concern?"

He hesitated, wondering whether or not to share his worries with her. In the past, he had refused to share any burden with Rebecca, always believing he had to protect her from his problems. He was different now. His love for her made him want to share his inner world with her—just as he wanted her to share her inner life with him.

"It's probably nothing," he said. "But I think the Enkefalons sent me a message this morning. A warning."

"What was it?"

"Something's coming, they told me."

Rebecca pulled him closer to her. "Don't worry. You can handle anything that comes your way. And I will be there at your side to help you any way I can."

Roger kissed her with all his heart, and then the two looked into each other's eyes and minds, sharing their love.

About the Author

Mr. Flanzraich was born in Brownsville, Brooklyn, New York City. His parents were European immigrants. On a scholarship, he graduated from Harvard College, magna cum laude and Phi Beta Kappa, and from Harvard Law School, magna cum laude.

He has been in the pharmaceutical industry for over thirty years and is currently the chairman and CEO of a biotech company. He is a member of the boards of directors of two public companies. He and his wife, Dr. Kira Flanzraich, live in Coral Gables, Florida. They have two sons, Derek and Jordan, who live in New York City.

Mr. Flanzraich wrote fairy tales for his sons when they were little. His sons later introduced him to the Harry Potter books, which eventually led to his writing this book.

About the Book

Roxanne Reynolds is just beginning her third year at a Maryland high school. She is one of a very small number of people with IQs of over 1,000 who call themselves "Geniuses". They secretly live among us while concealing their extraordinary intelligence and mental powers.

The Geniuses living in the Western Hemisphere protect ordinary people from Eastern Geniuses who use their abilities to try to control ordinary people and dominate the world. Over thousands of years this has resulted in numerous confrontations between Western and Eastern Geniuses.

Andor Lysenko, a young Eastern European Genius, has just transferred into Roxanne's school. What does Andor's arrival mean for Roxanne … and what does it mean for the safety of the world?

Acknowledgement

This book would have never happened without the inspiration, assistance, love and support of my family. My sons Derek and Jordan years earlier introduced me to the Harry Potter novels, which I greatly enjoyed and frequently discussed with my sons. I consider my sons extraordinarily intelligent young men, and so the word "geniuses" often comes to my mind when I think of them. My sons definitely influenced the book's idea and its development, with numerous comments and suggested changes. I also began sharing drafts with my wife, Kira, who – although born in Russia – is the best English editor I have ever worked with. So, I gratefully acknowledge my family's major contribution to this book.

Additionally, my editor, Tom Monte, did extraordinary work in making this book a reality. I will be forever grateful and in his debt for all his extensive and creative editing and assistance. And I also gratefully acknowledge the excellent editorial assistance provided by the AuthorHouse Editorial Division.

I also gratefully acknowledge the excellent and creative work of the AuthorHouse illustrator, Joshua Allen, on the front cover illustration.